ROME'S SACRED FLAME

Robert Fabbri read Drama and Theatre at London University and has worked in film and TV for twenty-five years as an assistant director. He has worked on productions such as *Hornblower, Hellraiser, Patriot Games* and *Billy Elliot*. His lifelong passion for ancient history inspired him to write the Vespasian series. He lives in London and Berlin.

ROME'S SACRED FLAME

ROBERT FABBRI

CORVUS

First published in hardback in Great Britain in 2018 by Corvus,
an imprint of Atlantic Books Ltd.

Copyright © Robert Fabbri, 2018

The moral right of Robert Fabbri to be identified as the author of this
work has been asserted by him in accordance with the Copyright,
Designs and Patents Act of 1988.

Map copyright © Jeff Edwards

10 9 8 7 6 5 4 3 2

A CIP catalogue record for this book is available from the British Library.

Hardback ISBN: 978 178 239 7045
Trade paperback ISBN: 978 178 239 7052
E-book ISBN: 978 178 239 7076

Printed in Italy by Grafica Veneta S.p.A.

For Ian Drury, Gaia Banks, Nicolas Cheetham, Sara O'Keeffe, Toby Mundy and Will Atkinson, with gratitude for the parts you all played in publishing the Vespasian series.

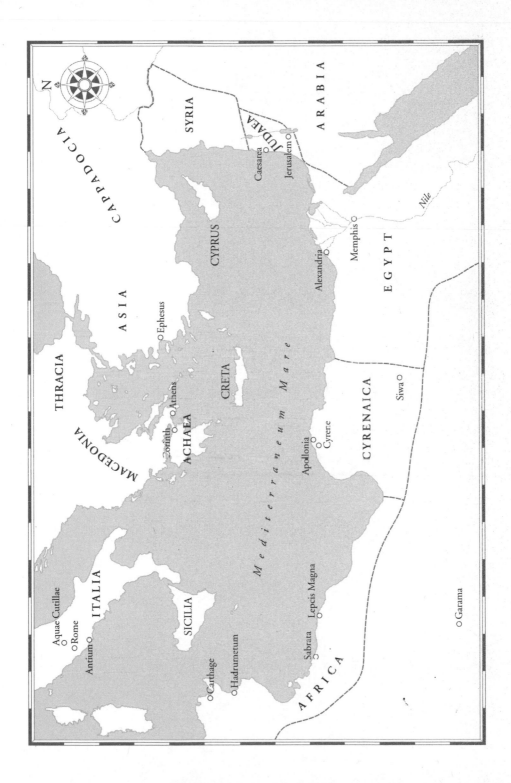

PROLOGUE

ROME, NOVEMBER AD 63

THE CHILD DID live no more than a hundred days; now she was being immortalised in the heavens. Born in January to great rejoicing throughout the Empire, Claudia Augusta, the daughter of the Emperor Nero and his Empress, Poppaea Sabina, had succumbed to a childhood ailment soon after the spring equinox. Divine honours for the late infant had been voted by the Senate to help ease the pain of the mourning father who was as immoderate in his grief at his daughter's death as he had been in his joy at her birth. And it was with tears streaming down his pale-fleshed cheeks and catching in the golden beard growing beneath his chin that Nero, resplendent in a gold-edged purple toga, took a taper and plunged it into the flame brought from the Temple of Vesta by her six priestesses.

With folds of their togas draped over their heads, in deference to the latest deity to join Rome's Pantheon, the assembled senior senators – all former praetors or consuls – watched, with an air of suitable solemnity, as the Emperor touched the burning taper to the kindling piled upon the altar. The fire caught; wisps of smoke spiralled to the roof of the new temple, next to that of Apollo, on the Palatine Hill. Constructed by slaves working day and night in the seven months since the child's death, and with no expense spared, Nero had personally overseen every lavish detail of the building, devoting most of his time to the project whilst completely neglecting the business of Rome.

In the front row of the congregation Titus Flavius Sabinus struggled to suppress a fast-rising urge to laugh at the ludicrousness of the ceremony unfolding before him. He had witnessed deifications before and had always found it rather unsettling to think that with a form of words and a fire kindled from Rome's Sacred Flame, housed in the Temple of Vesta, a dead human being could be resurrected as a god. That was not how gods were made, Sabinus knew: they were born of rock in a cave, as was his Lord Mithras. The idea that a babe who had done little more than suck on its wet-nurse's teats could be a divine inspiration and required worship was beyond belief and, as the sacrificial ram, bedecked in ribbons, was led forward to the altar to the sonorous imprecations of the two priests of the new cult, Sabinus almost lost the battle with his mirth. 'The next thing, I suppose, is we'll have a public holiday in the Divine Claudia Augusta's honour,' he whispered under the prayers to his neighbours, Lucius Caesennius Paetus, his son-in-law, and his uncle, Gaius Vespasius Pollo, a magnificently portly man in his seventies with many chins and bellies.

'Hmm? What, dear boy?' Gaius said, his expression a mask of religious awe.

Sabinus repeated his assertion.

'In which case I'll be seated in the most prominent position at the games, having made a more than generous sacrifice to the divine babe, so that the Emperor can witness my piety. Perhaps he'll be less inclined to invite me to open my veins, having, firstly, made a will in his favour, the next time he has urgent need of funds; and, judging by the quality of the marble and the amount of gold in this temple, that time will come very soon.' He flicked a carefully tonged dyed-black ringlet of hair away from a kohled, porcine eye and, with exaggerated reverence, watched one priest stun the ram with a mallet an instant before the second slit its throat in a spray of blood that cascaded down into a bronze basin. Disoriented from the blow, the juddering beast slowly gave its life for the sake of an infant goddess who would have had no concept of what sort of creature it was.

More prayers were intoned as two acolytes rolled the carcass over; with slow precision, the knife was drawn up the belly, skin and ribs pulled back and heart and liver exposed. The Emperor looked on, kneeling, his arms outstretched, tears welling, a picture of grief in the classic mode as depicted by many a famous actor.

Between them, the priests removed both heart and liver; the former was set sizzling on the growing flames whilst the latter was placed on the altar next to the fire. All watching held their collective breath. Proceeding slowly, so as to build the tension, the priests wiped the blood from their hands and forearms before patting the liver dry and then returning the cloths to the acolytes.

Now was the moment all had been waiting for; now the time had come to examine the liver. Nero shuddered, his body wracked with sobs as he looked to the sky, grey and brooding, through a window high in the back wall of the temple; he lifted his right arm and slowly clenched his fingers as if trying to grab a hidden thing from out of the air.

Veneration grew on the countenances of the two priests as they turned the liver over, examining it minutely.

Nero began to whimper with tension.

Having scrutinised both sides twice, the priests looked to one another, nodded and then turned to the Emperor.

'Divine Claudia Augusta has been accepted by the gods above and now sits in their midst,' the elder of the two announced, his voice weighted with reverence.

With a gasp, Nero fainted – his arms carefully ensuring that he did no damage to his face as it hit the marble floor. The assembled senators broke into cheers of rapture and called on the new goddess to hold her hands over them.

'We should be very grateful to the gods for accepting their latest little colleague,' Gaius observed without a trace of irony whilst wholeheartedly joining in with the applause. 'Perhaps now Nero will have his mind free to concentrate on the business of government.'

Sabinus slipped the fold of his toga from his head as the religious part of the ceremony was now concluded. 'I hope so. He hasn't heard one appeal or taken a petition since construction of this temple began; I've at least a hundred convicted or accused citizens from all over the Empire, awaiting their chance to appeal to the Emperor, scattered around the city. It shouldn't be the business of the prefect of Rome to be acting as a gaoler to common criminals, even if they are citizens.'

Paetus frowned as he too uncovered his head. 'Prisoners have always been the prefect's responsibility.'

'Yes, with the help of one of the praetors, but never so many at once; normally no more than two or three at any one time if the Emperor hears the appeals on a regular basis. I've had that odious little Paulus of Tarsus causing no end of trouble, writing his filth in letters to all sorts of people; my agents intercept and destroy most of them but some slip through. When I challenge him about it he says that until Caesar has passed his judgement upon him he has the right to write to anyone he likes even if it's seditious and attacking the very laws that he's hiding behind – our laws. But with Nero back I'll soon have the runt off my hands, and, well …' Sabinus glanced with regret at his son-in-law. 'It also means you'll have to face him.'

'I was hoping he hadn't noticed that I was back from Armenia,' Paetus confided, scowling; his boyish face had been weather-beaten from campaigning in the East, making his pronounced front teeth seem even whiter.

More thoughts on the subject were cut off as Nero raised both arms, asking for silence that was soon apparent. The emotion of the occasion was too much for him and for a while he stood there breathing deeply and giving his best expressions of relief. 'My friends,' he said at last, gathering himself. 'What a thing we have witnessed here in this place: I, the son of a god and the great-grandson of a god, have now become the father of a goddess. I, your Emperor, have divine seed.' He turned to his freedman, Epaphroditus, and held out a hand. 'My *cythia*.' From behind the altar the freedman produced the seven-stringed lyre that the Emperor had been studying for five years now. 'In honour of the day and in praise of my divine daughter sprung from my loins I have composed a paean of thanksgiving.' He plucked a chord and attempted to sing a note of similar pitch without noticeable success; his voice, husky and weak, struggled to fill the chamber.

Sabinus grimaced and braced himself. Gaius looked around anxiously for a seat; there were none.

With two more chords that had no business being played in conjunction, Nero launched into a dirge of disharmony, erratic scanning and stretched rhyme.

On he went, verse after verse, as the senators stood, listening with the intense looks of those who consider themselves to be in the presence of genius and are unable to believe the good fortune that had brought them to that place.

But in this they were all experienced: for the past couple of years, Nero had been shamefully performing to small audiences of senators in private, as if he were a slave or a freedman rather than the Emperor of Rome. Since the death of his mother, Agrippina, murdered on his orders, and the sidelining of his tutor, Seneca, who had attempted to keep the young Princeps on a dignified and sober path, Nero had come to realise that there was nothing that he could not do. He had murdered his mother because she annoyed him, his brother because he was a threat to him and, most recently, his wife, Claudia Octavia, so that Poppaea Sabina could take her place – Poppaea's wedding present had been her predecessor's head. No one had censured him for these deeds for no one dared. All in the élite of Rome's society knew that Nero could not bear anyone to think badly of him; he wished only to be universally loved and those who made it obvious that they did not share that view had no business in Nero's city.

For Rome now, more than ever, was Nero's city.

Gone was the pretence that the Emperor could not take anything he wanted that had been the sleight of hand with which Augustus had cloaked the actuality of his absolute power. Even the brash young Emperor Gaius – known as Caligula, the nickname of his youth – had paid some attention to law in that if he wanted a man's property he had had the decency to have an ambitious informer trump up a charge of treason against the individual. Now, however, everyone knew the stark reality: everything, ultimately, was the property of the Emperor. For who could argue with a man who had almost ten thousand Praetorian Guardsmen to secure him in power? And who would wish to curb his desires? And if he desired to sing a paean in praise of the goddess sprung from his divine loins then so be it; none of those present gave the slightest sign that what they were listening to was anything other than the greatest composition ever set down, being performed by the most loved man ever to exist.

So, almost half an hour later, as the paean ground to a grisly end, as unheroic as it was uninspiring, the senators vied with one another to be the first and loudest to congratulate and applaud their virtuoso Emperor who, naturally, was overwhelmed and taken totally by surprise by the enthusiasm of the reception and found it impossible to refuse entreaties of a reprise.

'My friends,' Nero croaked as the applause died down after the second rendition; his voice raw from much usage. 'Now I have set my daughter in her rightful place in the heavens and provided her with suitable accommodation here in Rome, my thoughts turn to my own comfort and that of my wife, the Augusta, Poppaea Sabina.' Raising the back of his hand to his forehead and gazing up to the smoke swirling high above, beneath the ceiling of painted panels set between cedar-wood beams, he let go a melodramatic sigh. 'But that shall have to wait, dear friends, as I am well aware that my presence is required in the Senate; I shall come immediately. Corbulo's despatch on the conduct of the renewed war with Parthia in Armenia must be read and our policy and the course of the struggle there be considered, seeing as I was obliged to reinstate him in his eastern command after Lucius Caesennius Paetus' humiliating defeat by the Parthian king, Vologases.' He paused for cries of 'shame' and 'disgrace'.

Paetus stood, stiff-backed, as the insults were hurled at him.

Sabinus shifted uneasily. 'I should never have lobbied for that command for him after he stood down from the consulship,' he muttered to his uncle so that Paetus did not hear. Nero, through jealousy and fear, had removed Corbulo, the greatest general of the age, from overall command of Rome's forces in Armenia after a series of despatches from which it had been evident that he had done far too good and efficient a job in removing Vologases' brother, Tiridates, from the Armenian throne and replacing him with Rome's client, Tigranes. An emperor loves a victory but not necessarily the man who provided it for him and Nero's lack of thanks had been deafening. Hostilities had flared up again when Vologases had, in turn, removed Tigranes and replaced him with Tiridates. Sabinus had used his influence as prefect of Rome to

15

get Paetus appointed Governor of Cappadocia and to be given two legions in order to bring Armenia back under direct Roman rule; something he had conspicuously failed to do. Corbulo had eventually been authorised to come to his assistance.

Gaius' jowls wobbled with indignation. 'Dear boy, you two brothers are not doing too well with sons-in-law, it has to be said. Vespasian's lost his whole legion in the Britannic revolt and now your son-in-law takes the gloss off his consulship by surrendering his two legions to the Parthians who then force them to pass under the yoke before allowing them to withdraw from Armenia without their weapons or armour.'

Nero signalled for quiet and then looked directly at Sabinus even though Paetus was standing right next to him. 'Now that your son-in-law is recently returned to Rome you can tell him that in honour of my daughter's deification I will pardon him immediately so that he won't die of chronic worry as he awaits my verdict, seeing as he is evidently a man prone to panic.'

The assembly burst into bellows of laughter; Paetus coloured with impotent rage.

Sabinus blanched. 'Indeed, Princeps.'

Nero gave a smile that more than hinted at the cruelty lurking within him. 'And then, of course, after the Senate has risen, I shall hear appeals; have all those wishing the benefit of my judgement waiting in the forum, prefect.'

'I shall make the arrangements, Princeps.'

'Good. I will work my fingers to the bone in the service of Rome to the extent that my own comfort will be secondary.'

This drew mighty cheers from his audience, this time born out of greater sincerity, as, for the first time since the death of his daughter, Nero would be coming to the Senate to tell them how to think.

'It was Corbulo refusing to come to my aid, Father,' Paetus insisted as he, Sabinus and Gaius, along with the rest of the senators, descended the Palatine.

'But that's not the version that the Emperor heard,' Gaius reminded him. 'We all sat there in the Senate listening to

Vologases' crowing letter about how he *magnanimously* let you go when he could have crushed you and destroyed both of your legions. Unfortunately that letter arrived well before yours.'

'As did Corbulo's report,' Sabinus added, 'in which he made it abundantly clear that you got yourself into a mess but were too proud to admit it or ask for help; and now the Emperor accuses you, in public, of panicking, and makes you a laughing stock.'

'For which I'll never forgive him!'

Gaius winced and looked around in alarm at the other senatorial groups as they turned left, onto the Sacred Way, and headed to the forum. 'Not so loud, dear boy; that's the sort of remark that has a habit of coming back on you.'

Paetus scowled. 'Well, don't think I shan't be avenged for the insult in some way.'

Sabinus grabbed his son-in-law's arm and pulled him close. 'Now listen, Paetus; for the sake of my daughter, you will do nothing stupid, nothing that endangers you. Put all thoughts of vengeance from your mind and concentrate on working your way back into Nero's favour because, like it or not, he has complete control over every aspect of our lives and is a terrifying creature of whim. Understand?'

Paetus snatched his arm away. 'It's intolerable; we're not even allowed our honour any more.'

'Our honour faded with the death of the Republic and now that is no more than a distant memory. Nero holds all power in his hands so, of course, we have no honour; but we do have life.'

'And what is life without honour?'

Gaius had no doubts. 'Far more pleasant than death without honour, dear boy.'

'And furthermore, when the Parthian puppet-king, Tiridates, sent emissaries to discuss peace, I did not rebuff them,' Lucius Verginius Rufus, the junior consul, declaimed, reading from a scroll containing Corbulo's despatch, 'as news had come to me of a rebellion in the east of the Parthian kingdom and I realised that Vologases would not wish to prosecute two wars at once; consequently, the Great King agreed to a truce. However, as the discussions continued, I executed or drove into exile all the Armenian nobles who had sworn allegiance to us and then switched sides after Paetus' debacle, thus ensuring the loyalty of those who remain.' Verginius paused as a growl went through the ranks of senators seated in rows on stools to either side of the Senate House.

Sabinus put his hand on Paetus' wrist, keeping him in his seat.

'And then I razed all their fortifications to the ground so that they could not be used against us again. Tiridates asked for a parley face-to-face and chose the very place where Paetus had been cornered. I did not shy away from this as I thought that coming in strength to the scene of their earlier victory would emphasise the contrast between the two situations.'

Again a rumble went through the meeting and Sabinus felt many pairs of eyes turn to his son-in-law; seated next to Verginius on a curule chair, Nero tutted demonstratively.

'I was not going to let Paetus' disgrace distress me so I sent his son, who is serving on my staff as a military tribune, in advance with some units to wipe away all trace of that unfortunate encounter. He went willingly, anxious to help expunge the memory of his father's folly.'

This was almost too much for Paetus who had to be physically restrained by all those around him. Nero sneered at the sight.

'I arrived with an escort of twenty cavalry at the same time as did Tiridates with his entourage of a similar number. I am pleased to report that he did me the honour of dismounting first; I did not hesitate and went to him and, clasping both his hands, praised the young man for rejecting war and coming to seek terms with Rome. We have come to an honourable compromise: he for his part declared that he shall place his crown at the feet of our Emperor's statue and then come to Rome so that he can take it back only from Nero's hand. I have agreed to this in principle, subject to imperial approval, and the meeting ended with a kiss.'

All eyes turned to Nero, conscious of his reaction the last time one of Corbulo's despatches had proclaimed a swift settlement in Armenia: the Senate had broken out into cheers only to be silenced by an outburst by Nero declaring that Corbulo had only done what anyone present in the chamber could have achieved. This time they wanted to be told how to think before they reacted and they did not have to wait long.

'What a spectacle that will be!' Nero declared, rising from his seat, raising an arm and gazing into the future. 'Imagine: a king from the Arsacid dynasty, brother of the Great King of Parthia, no less, coming to Rome as a supplicant. Coming to me! Not going to his brother, but to me for I am the most powerful. In acknowledging me as the ultimate giver of the Armenian crown, he acknowledges my dominion over Armenia. I have won!'

Nero opened his arms to encompass the whole House as they rose, almost as one, and hailed their Emperor, the master of Armenia.

'Get up!' Sabinus growled, hauling Paetus to his feet to join in the praise, 'and look pleased.'

Paetus added grudging applause.

'Corbulo seems to have learnt the art of flattering the Emperor,' Gaius observed, sweating profusely from the exertion of lauding Nero. 'That should keep him alive for a little while longer.'

On they went, clapping, shouting, waving folds of their togas and holding their hands out towards the Emperor as he basked in the glory. Eventually even the most hardy of the Senate had begun to tire and Nero, sensing the volume begin to trail off, brought the applause to a close and sat back down.

'Is there any more?' he asked Verginius, once all were again seated.

'Just a couple of lines, Princeps.'

'Well, read them before I go to hear the appeals.'

'Given that it has always been accepted that the Governor of Syria has authority over Judaea and given that I have already taxed Syria hard to pay for this war, I have ordered the procurator, Porcius Festus, to substantially increase the taxation due in that province and will ensure that his replacement, Gessius Florus, continues that policy when he arrives in the new year; it's nothing that they can't afford, the Jews being notoriously wealthy as one look at their temple complex will confirm. The extra revenue will go a long way to re-equipping the two legions that Paetus so carelessly lost and which I have since brought back to Syria under my command.'

The last word echoed around the chamber and then there was silence.

Nero sat, shaking with fury as he grasped the arms of his chair before composing himself, abruptly standing and then storming from the Senate House in a swirl of purple and gold.

'Oh dear, dear boys,' Gaius muttered as uproar broke out after Nero's departure. 'By being seen to amass legions, I rather think that Corbulo has just undone any good he did himself by making Nero the ultimate dispenser of crowns.'

'And just when I thought that nothing good was going to come from this,' Paetus said, his face fixed in an unpleasant leer.

'Plea dismissed!' Nero screamed; yet another convicted citizen, an eques who had been originally found guilty of murdering his business partner, fell victim to the Emperor's foul temper. 'What was the original sentence?'

Epaphroditus briefly consulted the scroll on the table before him. 'Execution by decapitation, Princeps.'

'Strip him of his citizenship and damn him to the beasts for wasting my time.'

The large crowd of mainly common people, surrounding the outdoor court, cheered appreciatively, always pleased to see one of their betters condemned and caring not unduly about the fairness of the hearing.

The doomed man fell to the ground, pleading for mercy, only to be dragged away by his ankles as his fingers tried to grip the gaps between the paving stones covering the forum.

Sabinus looked back at the twenty or more other supplicants who had witnessed nothing but dismissed appeals in the two hours of Nero sitting in judgement; none looked confident. None? No, one man caught his eye; short, balding and with bandy legs, Paulus of Tarsus wore an expression of serenity that could, almost, be construed as the vacant stare of the bewildered, considering the danger he was in.

'An interesting reaction, wouldn't you say? Most, er … what's the best word for it? Most composed, yes, that's it, composed, considering he's going before an emperor whose worry about a potential rival in the East seems to have removed every last vestige of justice that remained in him.'

Sabinus turned to look into the bloated face of Lucius Annaeus Seneca. 'Who are you talking about, Seneca?'

'Paulus of Tarsus, obviously; I couldn't help noticing that you were studying him so intensely.'

Sabinus' curiosity was piqued. 'You know him?'

Seneca beamed in his avuncular fashion and placed a chubby arm around Sabinus' shoulders. 'He's been pestering me, since he came to Rome to appeal to the Emperor, to use my influence with Nero to have the accusation against him of sedition quashed.'

'You don't have any influence over Nero any more.'

Seneca patted Sabinus' shoulder. 'Now that's not necessarily true, and you know it. I still have access to him, it's just that he no longer takes my advice on principle; he likes to humiliate me by doing the exact opposite to what I recommend, and Epaphroditus encourages him in order to emphasise to me that he is now the power behind the Emperor. It's, er … what would you say? It's galling, yes, galling – at least it was.'

Sabinus understood immediately. 'Until you started to advise him to do the exact opposite of what you wanted?'

'Ah, my friend, how well you understand our Nero. And having read some of that disgusting atheism that Paulus espouses and the way he urges his followers not to acknowledge the Emperor as the ultimate power on earth and yet, hypocritically, he's quite happy to appeal to him, I decided that I would grant his wish and have urged Nero to leniency in his case.'

Sabinus nodded in approval. 'Good. I had to nail up quite a few of his followers whilst I was Governor of Thracia and Macedonia; they deny the gods, refuse to sacrifice to the Emperor – or even on his behalf as the Jews do – and believe in an afterlife that is better than this world and therefore seem to have very little fear of death, which, apparently, is imminent, as

21

what he calls the End of Days will be upon us very soon. It's dangerous, irrational and bigoted as well as being contrary to everything our ancestors have believed for generations.'

'I agree; although he has got one thing right.'

'What's that?'

'I saw a copy of one of his letters to some Greek follower in which he says that women should be silent; if only Poppaea Sabina would take that advice.' Seneca chuckled at his own observation. 'As, I'm sure, your brother, Vespasian, would now agree,' he added as Paulus was brought forward to stand before the Emperor.

Epaphroditus consulted a scroll. 'Gaius Julius Paulus; accused by Porcius Festus, the outgoing procurator of Judaea, of stirring up anti-Roman and anti-Jewish feeling and causing a riot. He refused trial in Jerusalem and decided instead to appeal to you directly, Princeps.' He handed the scroll to the Emperor. 'Seneca recommended leniency in this case,' he added, giving Seneca a sly look.

Nero eyed Paulus as if he were scrutinising an unpleasant skin disease. 'Well?'

Paulus smiled at the Emperor with exaggerated benignity and opened his arms to him. 'Princeps, may the peace of the Lord soothe you and—'

'Just get on with it!' Nero was in no mood to be soothed.

Paulus stepped back at the vehemence of the order. 'I, er … I'm sorry, Princeps.' Rubbing his hands together, Paulus hunched his shoulders and smiled with an ingratiating demeanour that made Sabinus feel queasy. 'Princeps, I was misunderstood. I had come to Jerusalem to bring money that had been collected for the poor. The priests in the temple refused to let me distribute it as they thought that it should be their duty, which would have meant that they would have kept it all. When I protested, the High Priest had me arrested by the Temple Guards and handed to the Procurator. That's when the riot broke out.'

Nero had had enough. 'So there was a riot and you did disobey your priests who do make sacrifices on my behalf.

What's more, you were wanting to distribute money to the poor in person as if *you* were the font of all bounty and not *me*, your Emperor?'

Paulus looked unsure. 'Well, yes, and then no. I—'

'Take him away,' Nero ordered, 'and execute him.' He turned towards Seneca. 'Leniency?' He shook his head in disgust.

Even Sabinus was startled at the arbitrary nature of Nero's justice that day. 'I'm very pleased to see the last of Paulus but I'm relieved that he pardoned my son-in-law before he heard Corbulo's report.'

'Very fortunate,' Seneca agreed, smiling, as Paulus was manacled and made no attempt to struggle. 'And a very gratifying verdict.'

'Do you think there's any chance of wiping the stain Paetus has left from my family's record?'

'That entirely depends upon two things: how your brother, Vespasian, acquits himself in Africa; and also upon your decision as to that suggestion I made to you.'

'I told you, Seneca; I won't make a decision until I've spoken to my brother upon his return next spring.'

'By next spring we may all be dead.' Seneca smiled without mirth and walked away as a change seemed to come over Paulus: his ingratiating manner evaporated as the finality of his sentence sank in; he glanced down at the manacles and then stood erect looking Nero in the eye. 'Your sentence means nothing to me. This world is not for long; I will just be leaving it sooner than you, but not by much for judgement is in sight. Until then I shall be with my Lord, Yeshua bar Yosef, the Christus.'

'Wait!' Nero raised a hand. 'What did he say? Christus?'

'I believe so, Princeps,' Epaphroditus confirmed.

Nero peered at Paulus. 'A follower of that new cult with the crucified god, are you?'

'I believe the Christus died for our sins,' Paulus stated with certainty, 'and will come again very soon at the End of Days, which is fast approaching. The rise of the Dog Star will herald it in and it will start here.'

Nero's pleasure was obvious. 'Will it, now? Will it indeed?' He turned to Sabinus. 'Keep him safely locked away in the Tullianum, prefect; I may well have a use for his death.'

PART I

GARAMA, 400 MILES SOUTH OF THE
ROMAN PROVINCE OF AFRICA,
DECEMBER AD 63

CHAPTER I

IT WAS NOT the city of Garama itself that impressed Vespasian most but, rather, the environment in which it was set. Fields of wheat and barley interspersed with orchards of fig trees and grazing pastures were not an uncommon sight in most parts of the Empire; but here, four hundred miles across scrag and desert, beyond Rome's frontier to the south of Leptis Magna in the province of Africa, it was surely a work of the gods.

Just over an hour after dawn the previous day, shortly before the caravan had made camp to sleep away the hours of burning sun, following its night-march, the line of distant hills could be discerned as being verdant. Now, as the sun rose a day later and the caravan was forty miles further south, the full beauty of this unlikely oasis could be enjoyed. For at least ten miles to either side of a high-towered city, not more than a couple of miles away, perched on a hill three hundred feet above the desert floor, was nothing but arable land; and within that sea of green, gangs of tiny figures laboured.

'That's a sight that's about as unlikely as seeing a Vestal doing the splits naked.'

Vespasian looked at the originator of the remark, a battered man in his early seventies with the cauliflower ears and broken nose of an ex-boxer, sitting on a horse next to him and sporting, as did Vespasian, a floppy, wide-brimmed straw hat. 'And what makes you so sure, Magnus, that Vestals don't go in for nude gymnastics?'

Magnus turned to Vespasian, one eye squinting against the rising sun, the other just reflecting its glow, for it was but a glass replica – and not a very good one at that, Vespasian had always found himself thinking. 'Well, I ain't saying that they don't cavort naked and do all sorts of interesting stretches, leaps, acrobatics and the like; all I'm saying is that I'm unlikely to see them do it, if you take my meaning?'

'I'm sure I do and you're probably right: even if they did allow spectators you look far too unsavoury to be allowed in.' Vespasian grinned, his dry lips cracked, causing a stab of pain; he winced and put his hand to his mouth.

'There; that serves you right for your constant mockery, sir.' Magnus gave a satisfied nod and leant forward to address the man on the other side of Vespasian. 'Does he ever accuse you of unsavouriness, Hormus? Or is he politer to his freedman than he is to his oldest friend?'

Hormus scratched his wispy beard that part concealed an undershot lower jaw and then gave a shy grin. 'Seeing as I have no wish to see females naked, Vestal Virgins or not, it would make no difference to me whether the master thinks me un-savoury or not.'

'That didn't answer my question.'

'I know.'

Magnus grunted and then returned his attention to the wonder before them. 'So, under those hills is a sea?'

Vespasian sucked a drop of blood from his finger. Sweat trickled down from under his hat, catching in the heavy growth on his chin and cheeks, causing it to itch; his eyes squinted against the sun making the strained expression that he constantly wore on his rounded face seem even more tense. 'A sea or a big lake; who knows? But what is certain is that they have hundreds of wells that feed an irrigation system that runs through buried pipes and so that water must come from somewhere.'

'Well, I wish it didn't and then we wouldn't be here.'

'And I thought you liked visiting new places.'

'Bollocks I do.' Magnus rubbed his back and groaned. 'At my age the only new thing I like to see is a new day.'

Vespasian, for the sake of his lips, refrained from smiling at the joke made by his friend of nigh on thirty-eight years; instead he kicked his horse forward towards the road that snaked its way up to the city, wishing, too, that he was not there.

But the sad truth was that he had no choice but to be there; he was, once again, the victim of political manoeuvring in Rome but this time he had no one to blame but himself in that he had been guilty of advancing his position through manipulation. However, that was the only way to get any preferment in Nero's Rome. When a document implicating Epaphroditus in a business that would not have pleased Nero had fallen into the hands of Vespasian's mistress, Caenis, herself a palace insider, it had seemed only natural for her, if Vespasian were to become the Governor of Africa, to inform the powerful freedman of its existence. Epaphroditus had no alternative other than to use his influence over Nero to have Vespasian granted the position in return for the document. He had not been at all content as he could normally have expected to have received a substantial bribe for such a prestigious governorship. But it was not just the enmity of Epaphroditus that had earned Vespasian this trip to the extremity of the known world; it had been a force far more potent: the Empress, Poppaea Sabina. Quite why she had behaved so spitefully towards him, Vespasian did not know but he knew enough about imperial politics to understand that often there was no reason for maliciousness other than the thrill of exerting power over those weaker than you.

So, as vengeance for forcing him to forego a substantial bribe, Epaphroditus had suggested to Nero that whilst Vespasian was serving as Governor of Africa he should be responsible for securing the release of the scores, if not hundreds, of Roman citizens enslaved on the farms in the Kingdom of the Garamantes. Poppaea Sabina had enthusiastically supported the idea, saying that it would be a great coup for Nero achieving something that previous emperors had tried but failed to do before. Nero had therefore charged him to send a mission to Nayram, the king of the Garamantes, with the power to negotiate on the Emperor's behalf. It had been with a cold smile and darkened eyes that Poppaea had suggested to her husband that it would be much better if Vespasian went himself, and that if he did not succeed then it would be much better if he did not return. After due consideration of one heartbeat's duration, Nero had concurred.

Vespasian had inwardly cursed but could not blame Epaphroditus for doing what he knew anyone would do to repay a bad debt; however, Poppaea's sudden malevolence had perplexed him. He had had no choice but to comply and saw the positive side of the deal in that he would be out of Poppaea's reach for over a year whilst his elder brother, Sabinus, back in Rome would, perhaps, be able to find the cause of the Empress's malice. And so, at the age of sixty-three, he had departed for Africa, soon after the marriage of his elder son, Titus, to Arrecina Tertulla, Sabinus' niece, for what should have been a year of luxury and ease but instead had been quite the opposite.

Thus, here he was at the head of a caravan made up of merchants, who plied the desert route, and a half ala of Numidian auxiliary cavalry on their stocky little ponies that seemed to be able to go all day on as much water as their riders, such was their habitude to the desert. Also with him were his eleven lictors, mounted for the purposes of the journey with the fasces strapped over their horses' backs.

Vespasian kicked his own mount again to get it to put some effort into the ascent as he wished to be in the city away from the sun before it reached much higher in the clear, desert sky. The city's towers loomed overhead and horns boomed out from watchmen within, warning of the approaching, much enlarged, caravan.

For fifteen days – or, rather, nights – they had been travelling from Leptis Magna via a series of wells, oases and water dumps along the caravan route that connected the Kingdom of the Garamantes with the Empire. However, the journey had taken far longer in its planning than in its execution as the water supplies en route were sufficient only for a small caravan of twenty to thirty merchants and Vespasian needed to take many more people and then bring hundreds more back.

Immediately upon his arrival in the province, back in April, he had given orders that the water dumps be greatly enlarged, sending thousands of amphorae south to be buried along the way; it had taken six months to achieve once the Suphetes, the two leading magistrates in Leptis Magna, the closest city to

Garama, had been threatened into complying with his will. He had set sail from Carthage, the capital of Africa, in November once the work had been completed. Hugging the coast, he had stopped off at Hadrumetum, the province's second city, to hear appeals, only to find that the backlog was considerable as his predecessor, Servius Salvidienus Orfitus, had neglected to leave Carthage for the entire duration of his tenure. Anxious to be pressing on, Vespasian had left the city after only one day, before even a tenth of the appeals had been heard, and, consequently, despite the presence of his eleven lictors, received a barrage of turnips from disgruntled appellants as he re-boarded his ship. Cursing Orfitus for his negligence and vowing some sort of retribution for the insult to his person, he continued on to the port of Leptis Magna; this city was as close to Carthage as it was to distant Cyrene in the neighbouring province of Cyrenaica where he had served as a quaestor twenty-five years previously.

The port-city's remoteness was the reason for the Suphetes' reluctance to obey him as, up until the beginning of the year, Leptis Magna had been a free city over which the Governor had minimal control. Nero's constant quest for cash had changed that and, in return for Latin Rights, he had made the city a *municipium*, something the locals had resented but, as with the new taxes imposed, could do nothing about. The Suphetes' truculence had been the result; unused to receiving orders, they had automatically reacted against him and one of his early messengers, an optio with an eight-man escort, had failed to return, causing Vespasian to demonstrate his resolve with a serious threat. This obstinacy had much amused Vespasian as Leptis Magna had been the birth-city of his wife, Flavia Domitilla, whom he had met when serving in Cyrene.

Vespasian smiled to himself as he finally reached the summit and Garama's gates came into view; his wife's wilfulness, which had dogged him all their marriage, could, perhaps, be explained by the independent-minded ethos of the city she had grown up in.

'What's so amusing?' Magnus asked, taking off his floppy hat and wiping his brow for the hundredth time that day.

'What?' Vespasian pulled himself out of his reverie.

'Were you thinking about your being pelted by turnips? Because I was and I still find it hard not to burst out laughing every time I look at you.'

'Yes, very funny; just about as funny as Orfitus will find it having a turnip rammed up his arse when I see him back in Rome. If you must know, I was just thinking that the Suphetes' attitude to authority goes a long way to explaining Flavia's demeanour, seeing as she spent the first twenty years or so of her life in Leptis Magna.'

Magnus grunted in a non-committal way. 'Perhaps; but you ain't got the same power over her as you have over them.'

'How do you mean?'

'Well, it stands to reason, don't it? They soon came into line after you wrote to them saying that if they didn't want to help expand the water dumps, that was fine by you so long as they came along on the expedition to show you where to find the extra water you'll need. The difference is, with them you would have done it, but would you ever try and get Flavia to bend to your will by threatening to take her with you and have her endlessly complaining?'

Vespasian shuddered at the thought.

'Whereas you'd have loved to see those two fat bastards sitting, sweating on a horse two hundred miles from the nearest bath house and boy-brothel, but you'd rather go eye to eye, as it were, with Medusa's arsehole than have Flavia here.'

Vespasian could only agree. 'But at least I'd know that she wasn't spending all my money like she tried to do the last time I was away for any length of time.'

'True; and I'm sure that she'll be calculating that you'll make a fortune out of your position here and has therefore already doubled or tripled her expenditure.'

Vespasian shuddered again at that thought.

'So my advice is start using your power to make a lot of money before the sailing season opens up in March and your replacement arrives, because my bet is that you'll find yourself going home to a wife who now has four slaves each to bathe her and then do her hair, make-up and then dress her. Of course, that doesn't even include the ones selecting her jewellery or her shoes or just hanging around on the off-chance that she might feel like nibbling on something sweet or getting absolutely Bacchurlitic on the very finest Falernian, bought, at no expense spared, from the most fashionable of wine-merchants in the forum, frequented by the Emperor's steward himself because why would the wife of a governor want anything less?'

Vespasian frowned at his friend as he caught his breath after his tirade. 'Have you quite finished?'

Magnus grunted again. 'I'm just saying, that's all.'

'Well, thank you; you must be exhausted after that.'

'Well, don't forget that I was right about her when you brought her back from Cyrene: I said she'd want more than two hairdressers and you had a massive argument with her when you sold the third one that she'd bought, behind your back, stupidly thinking that someone as tight with money as you are would never notice.'

'I thought you'd said you'd finished.'

'I have now.'

'Good. Then perhaps I can get on with negotiating the release of all Roman citizens enslaved here?'

'Just make some money on the deal,' Hormus said, almost under his breath.

Vespasian looked at his freedman in shock; he had never been so outspoken before. 'You too, Hormus?'

Hormus nodded. 'Magnus is right: Flavia will spend it before you have it so make sure you get it.'

Vespasian tried to dismiss the remark but in his heart he knew that Magnus had a point; a very good point. He pulled his horse up as the gates of Garama opened and an excessively fat man in a litter was carried out by straining bearers, surrounded by half a dozen slaves all wafting him, energetically, with huge palm-frond fans so that his robe rippled in the breeze and his long beard swayed, rather disconcertingly, from side to side.

A chain of office hung about his neck and fitted snuggly into the crevice between his breasts. 'I am Izebboudjen, chamberlain to His Most Exalted Majesty, Nayram of the Garamantes, The Lord of the Thousand Wells. His Most Exalted Majesty demands to know who approaches his capital.' He spoke in Greek with the accent of a highly educated man.

Vespasian studied the chamberlain for a few moments and found it remarkable how little sign of sweat there was on either his clothes or his exposed brown skin; the slaves fanning him must have been doing an extremely good job and, judging by the streams of fluid dripping from their bodies, as well as those carrying his bulk, they were certainly making up for their master's lack of perspiration. 'My name is Titus Flavius Vespasianus, the Governor of the Roman province of Africa, come to speak with your master, Nayram.'

'You mean, of course, Governor, His Most Exalted Majesty, Nayram of the Garamantes, The Lord of the Thousand Wells.'

Vespasian dipped his head with his best impression of solemnity. 'Indeed I do, Izebboudjen.' Believing in the innate superiority of his race he was not about to kowtow to some petty potentate, no matter how many wells he was lord of.

Recognising that it was probably best not to force the issue of getting the Roman to acknowledge his master's full title, Izebboudjen bowed as deeply as he could for a man of his girth seated in a litter. 'Welcome, Governor. Your troops must make camp outside the walls along with the merchants in the caravan; they shall be given food and drink – whatever they desire, we will not have anyone wish to accuse The Lord of the Thousand Wells of ungenerosity. You, however, may enter with a small escort; rooms will be prepared for you in the palace. How many will you be?'

'I will be bringing my eleven lictors and two companions.'

'Very good. Follow me and I shall arrange an audience for you with The Lord of the Thousand Wells.'

Garama was old, very old; that much was certain from the wide thoroughfare that opened out on passing through the gate. The buildings, mainly two storeyed and constructed of sun-baked mud-bricks with small, shuttered windows, to either side of the street had many differing layers of repair and paint as succeeding generations had seen to their upkeep; none of them were shabby but, equally, none of them were in pristine condition. But it was the road itself that gave away the extreme age of the place: deeply worn stone from the passing of many wheels, hoofs and feet gave testament to centuries of usage; smooth and undulating, it dimly reflected the burning sun in many different directions. But what was so intriguing was just how clean it was. Nowhere was there any sign of the normal detritus one would expect to find in a public street, whether it be rotting vegetables or fruit, or human and animal waste or just, even, lumps of indeterminate refuse. There was nothing, not even a nutshell, and it was not even as if the street were empty. There were many people, all male and all rather corpulent, either walking with friends or frequenting the open-fronted shops or sitting playing some sort of game with counters on a strangely marked board whilst eating from Roman-import tableware or drinking from cups of the same provenance.

Delivery carts, too, made themselves busy and it was through them that Vespasian saw how the place was kept so tidy when a mule eased itself copiously in the middle of the road. The driver did nothing about the resulting steaming mess and drove off; as he left, two slaves ran out from wherever they had been waiting, one with a shovel and sack and one with an amphora and cloth. The pile of nuggets was soon in the bag and the stain washed down with water and rubbed clean with the cloth. 'Did you see that?' he asked in surprise.

Magnus nodded. 'Never seen the like of it. Does that happen with every bit of rubbish?'

'If so, who pays for the slaves?' Hormus wondered.

As they progressed up the hill, the lictors drawing curious looks, it became apparent that it happened everywhere: two more piles of fresh excrement, a dog that had expired in the heat and a few mouldy cabbages, rejected by a costermonger and thrown to the ground, also ended up in the street-cleaners' sacks. Any time a piece of rubbish fell to the street another scuttling slave appeared from somewhere to retrieve it.

'Do you keep all your streets so clean, Izebboudjen,' Vespasian asked the chamberlain, 'or is it just this main thoroughfare?'

Izebboudjen strained to turn his head; his expression was of amusement. 'Clean? We don't do that to keep the city clean; cleanliness is just a by-product of collecting every scrap of waste that we can to fertilise our fields with.' He gestured to the desert below, stretching as far as could be seen. 'We're surrounded by wasteland so here nothing must be wasted. The only things we burn are our corpses; those of freeborn citizens, that is. Slaves and freedmen are consigned to the fields.'

'Freedmen?'

'Yes. There are very few of them and it is part of the deal that guarantees their manumission. They are always willing to make that small sacrifice in return for their freedom.'

'Master!' a voice called out in Latin from behind Vespasian. 'I'm a Roman citizen!'

Vespasian turned around to see a slave pelting up the road towards him. Pedestrians scampered to either side of the street to get clear of his path as he closed on Vespasian's party, shouting and waving his arms.

Vespasian twisted his horse round.

'Be careful, Governor!' Izebboudjen shouted.

The moment Vespasian kicked his mount forward, back towards the slave, the man gave a sharp cry and flung his hands in the air; he pitched forward, back arched, and crumpled to the ground, sliding a few feet over the smooth stone of the street before coming to a stop, his eyes wide and glazed. Blood trickled down from behind his ear and dripped into a slowly increasing pool. Down the hill, two huge, muscled men, shaven-headed and dressed only in leather kilts, strolled towards the body swinging slings in their right hands.

'You were lucky, Governor,' Izebboudjen said. 'The slave-keepers don't often miss but it's always advisable to move away from a rogue slave as everyone else in the street was doing.'

Vespasian looked around: the street was full again with pedestrians carrying on about their business as if nothing were amiss. One of the slave-keepers hefted up the limp body and slung it over his shoulder to bear it away to whatever process it went through before it enriched the soil.

Vespasian turned back to the chamberlain, outraged. 'He was a Roman citizen!'

Izebboudjen shrugged. 'What he was before he became a slave is neither here nor there; here he was just a slave bought and owned, as are all the slaves in the kingdom, by The Lord of the Thousand Wells himself. He tolerates no insubordination from them.' He indicated to his bearers and wafters, ordering them to move on. 'There are far more of them than there are of us. That's why we free a few of them, the strongest, to act as the slave-keepers. If for one moment we let our grip slip then imagine what would happen. I believe that it is much the same situation back in your Rome, but perhaps not quite as acute as it is here.'

Vespasian could see Izebboudjen's point – an idea to make slaves in Rome all wear a distinctive mark had been scrapped for the very reason that if they were to realise just by how much they outnumbered free and freed, the consequences could be devastating. 'Yes, but this man was a Roman citizen; he shouldn't have been a slave.'

'Why not?'

'Because … because he's a citizen of Rome.' Vespasian could think of no logical reason and knew perfectly well that there was no law against citizens being enslaved. He had met Flavia after her then lover, Statilius Capella, had been captured by the Marmarides, a tribe of slavers east of Cyrene. Had Vespasian not rescued the man he would have made the hazardous journey across the desert to this kingdom and would now be still toiling in the fields, or, more likely, be a part of them. 'It's wrong to enslave freeborn Romans.'

'Why? How many Garamantes have you got enslaved in your empire? Or Parthians for that matter; Nubians, Scythians, Germans. Shall I go on?'

'Yes, but they're all … well, none of them are Roman citizens.'

Izebboudjen chuckled. 'I think that it would be best if we discontinued this argument before one of us embarrasses himself.'

Vespasian bit back a stinging retort that he knew would just sound like empty bluster and was painfully aware of who of the two of them was in danger of embarrassing himself. Besides, he had no wish to aggravate Izebboudjen as he did not know whether he would be of help when negotiating with his master, he of the many wells.

Nayram was, quite possibly, the fattest man in existence; he was certainly the fattest that Vespasian had ever seen. 'Don't say a word,' he hissed out of the corner of his mouth to Magnus as his friend stifled a gasp. Vespasian adjusted his toga so that it fell to his satisfaction, feeling refreshed from the bath and shave that he had enjoyed upon arrival in his quarters at the palace. His eleven lictors, resplendent in their pure white togas, added dignity to his appearance, standing behind him and to either side, their fasces held upright before them.

All in the cavernous audience chamber were on their feet as more than a dozen very burly slaves carried in His Most Exalted Majesty, Nayram of the Garamantes, The Lord of the Thousand Wells, reclining on a bed of immense proportions that Vespasian imagined he rarely strayed far from. His exact girth was impossible to tell as he was festooned in voluminous robes that blended with the bedding and echoed the deep blue, pale green and soft red hues of the glossy ceramic tiles decorating the floor, walls and domed ceiling of the chamber. All that could be ascertained was that there was much blubber beneath, as the contents of the bed seemed to be in constant motion, gently wobbling. His head was covered with an enormous, ill-fitting red wig that tumbled over his shoulders, partly concealing the rolls of fat that constituted his neck.

Izebboudjen led the bowing as Nayram was paraded before the company. The chamberlain seemed positively svelte in comparison to his master; indeed, the assembled courtiers, Vespasian thought, were the plumpest collection of individuals he had ever been in the presence of – which was quite a claim considering the physiques of many of the top echelons of Roman society.

With much care and straining, the slaves managed to lower Nayram's bed so that it settled on the floor without disturbing its occupant who seemed to be mid-nap. From the shadows a swarm of wafters appeared with their fans and set to work keeping the mountain of flesh cool.

Izebboudjen then turned to the assembly and declaimed Nayram's titles, which were far more numerous than Vespasian had been led to believe. When he had finished he turned to his king. 'Most Exalted Majesty, before you stands Titus Flavius Vespasianus, Governor of the Roman province of Africa.' With that he sat down, cross-legged on the floor; the rest of the courtiers followed his lead, leaving Vespasian, Magnus and Hormus, along with the lictors, still standing.

For a while there was absolute silence.

Nayram gave no indication of being awake, or, for that matter, alive. Vespasian stood, not wanting to break protocol and speak before his host had addressed him. Manners, he felt, would be an ally to him and after his conversation with Izebboudjen he knew he needed all the help he could get, especially as Roman honour dictated that he would not be using the king's titles.

Another fifty heartbeats went by before Nayram opened one, bloodshot, eye. It perused Vespasian for a few moments before the other opened. 'Titus Flavius Vespasianus, you are welcome in my kingdom.'

'King Nayram, it is with great pleasure that I come on this embassy from the Emperor, Nero Claudius Caesar Augustus Germanicus, and in token of his friendship he sends you this gift.' He nodded to Hormus who stepped forward and handed a heavy, gem-studded silver casket to Izebboudjen. With some difficulty, the chamberlain heaved himself to his feet and presented the casket to Nayram who smiled with greed and adjusted himself on his bed so that he could open his gift, suffering a resounding, but totally ignored, bout of flatulence as he did so.

Pulling aside some loose tresses of hair, he unfastened the clasp and opened the lid; delight lit up his face as he looked at the contents and ran his fingers over them. 'Hmmmm,' he purred, the sound rumbling in his throat. 'You may tell my brother, the Emperor Nero, that his gift pleases me.' He plucked a black pearl, almost a quarter of the size of Magnus' glass eye, from the casket and examined it, purring again at its lustre as he revolved it around the palm of his hand. Dropping it, he then scooped out a handful of the precious objects, each of similar proportions, and let them clatter back, one by one. 'It pleases me greatly; it is a gift worthy of one equal to another. What would my brother have in return?'

Putting aside the rather fanciful notion that being lord of a thousand wells was the equivalent of ruling all the lands around the inner sea and many beyond, Vespasian graced Nayram with his most solemn countenance. 'The Emperor Nero asks only this of you, King Nayram: your beneficence. In that box are five hundred pearls; each one's value is greatly increased being so far from the sea. Nero would ask that you equate each pearl with the freedom of a Roman held in bondage in your great kingdom; should there be fewer than five hundred then he would have you keep the balance.'

Nayram fingered his gift again, rumbling as he ruminated upon Vespasian's words. 'And what if there are more than five hundred? Hmmmm? What then?'

'Then we negotiate.'

'Negotiate? The Lord of the Thousand Wells does not negotiate; he does his pleasure, for who is there to tell him otherwise?' Nayram closed the lid and stared Vespasian in the eye. 'Look around you, Vespasian; see where you are. There is nothing beyond my fields for hundreds of miles in all directions. It is the water from my wells that makes this fertile oasis in the midst of a wasted land. The desert keeps us safe, for what army could cross it and still be in a fit state to assail us? Thus we need no troops of our own, apart from the slave-keepers, so that the citizens of my realm are free to enjoy a life of leisure. That same desert that protects us also acts as a cage for the slaves who till our fields; where can they run to? How long would they survive away from my wells? So, you see, Governor, I have no need to negotiate with anyone. I can just take this gift and give nothing in return, if it pleases me; and what would my brother Nero do then? Hmmmm?'

Vespasian bit back his fury at the blubberous petty potentate who dared to consider himself in such an exalted position that he could threaten to dictate terms to Rome. 'The Emperor knows that you would not do that, King Nayram, because he knows that you, like himself, are a man of honour.'

Nayram seemed to consider this, on all levels, blatant untruth to be a fair and just observation. He reopened the lid and gazed once again at the pearls. 'Nero is right: we share the same sense of honour. Very well, Vespasian, you may purchase back your citizens.' He signalled to Izebboudjen. 'Summon the Keeper of the Records.'

Izebboudjen once again struggled to his feet and bowed. 'Most Exalted Majesty, Nayram, The Lord of the Thousand Wells, he awaits your pleasure.' With a nod to the steward of the doors they were swung open to reveal a portly figure with a skewed lower jaw and a flattened, unsymmetrical nose.

Vespasian caught his breath, his throat contracting; he knew that visage well for he had been the cause of its violent restructuring. He checked himself as he looked in shock at the man whose actions had led to the deaths of eighty thousand Roman citizens and as many natives in the province of Britannia; the man who had ordered the flogging of Boudicca and the rape of her daughters as he stole her money and left Vespasian to her mercy. The man who had fled the province, as it erupted in revolt in direct consequence of his actions, and then had disappeared without trace.

Now Vespasian knew what had happened to the former procurator of Britannia as he looked into the hated face of Catus Decianus.

CHAPTER II

'I SHOULD KILL YOU now!' Vespasian hissed in Latin; he felt Magnus grab his arm, restraining him.

Decianus smirked, his mouth lopsided from the shattered jaw that Vespasian had dealt him two years previously in Britannia. 'It would be a fatal mistake even to attempt to, Vespasian; I'm a man of great importance here.'

'What are you saying?' Nayram demanded in Greek.

'Most Exalted Majesty,' Decianus crooned, switching to the same language, 'I was advising Vespasian of the foolishness of trying to kill me as he just threatened to do.'

'Kill you? Why would he want to do that when I'm about to order you to aid him? Hmmm? Why?' The bloodshot eyes turned to Vespasian.

Vespasian shook off Magnus' grip and pointed an accusatory finger at his enemy whilst addressing the king. 'Because that man left me to die at the hands of a queen he had robbed and violated.'

'And yet you're still here? Hmmm?'

'Thanks to the queen's honour being in inverse proportion to that snake's! She let me and my companions go despite what she and her daughters had suffered in Rome's name at his hands.'

The king looked unimpressed. 'Then there's no harm done.'

'You tell that to the eighty thousand Roman citizens killed in Boudicca's revolt.'

'If she killed that many then I think that Decianus was right to rob and violate her. Hmmmm?'

Magnus put a hand on Vespasian's shoulder. 'It won't do any good arguing, sir,' he whispered, 'no one here gives a fuck what happened so far to the north.'

Vespasian felt himself tensing but knew Magnus to be right: of what interest was it to Nayram what his Keeper of the Records had done in Britannia? The fact was that somehow the ex-procurator had found himself a secure bolthole outside the Empire and had quite evidently wormed his way into the king's favour. He drew breath and forced himself to relax, unclenching his fists.

From deep within Nayram came a gurgling sound that seemed to be an expression of mirth. 'That's better, Governor; diplomatic missions are rarely enhanced by displays of emotion or letting personal feelings interfere with the objectives of your superiors.'

Vespasian was forced to take the patronising putdown, well aware, out of the corner of his eye, of the pleasure it gave Decianus. 'I agree.'

'And addressing me with such a lack of courtesy is also counterproductive, I would suggest.'

Vespasian swallowed his pride and puckered his lips. 'I agree, King Nayram.'

The king waved a dismissive hand. 'I suppose that's the best I can expect from an arrogant Roman. You should take a lesson from Decianus, Vespasian: he feels no qualms about using my titles. Do you, Decianus?'

Decianus bowed his head. 'No, Most Exalted Majesty, The Lord of the Thousand Wells; it is only natural to address so glorious a ruler as such.'

Nayram indicated to the casket of pearls. 'Take these and tally them against every Roman citizen that you find. I trust you to do a full accounting.'

'I am honoured, Most Exalted Majesty.'

Suppressing the shock that Decianus should be trusted with such a sum, Vespasian thought it unwise to point out that the ex-procurator had no honour and, instead, steered the subject back to his original purpose. 'I'm grateful, King Nayram, for the assistance that you have offered in this matter and I would like to assure you that I will be only too pleased to take whatever advice the Keeper of the Records gives me in locating all those Roman citizens enslaved in your kingdom.'

'I'm pleased to hear it, Governor; I suggest you go with him before I change my mind. And if I hear of any harm done to him or any insult given then I shall consider it an affront to my person, and your status as an ambassador will be forfeit. Do I make myself clear? Hmmmm?'

Vespasian inclined his head a fraction. 'Admirably so, King Nayram; and I would ask that Decianus shows the same restraint in his dealings with me.'

'You are in no position to make any demands, Governor; you are a guest in this kingdom and Decianus is a trusted minister. You may go.'

Finding himself summarily dismissed, Vespasian had no choice but to comply with the monarch's wishes however much it went against his *dignitas* as a Roman governor. He flicked a terse gesture to his lictors to turn about and precede him out and followed at a dignified pace, head held high and simmering with rage.

'That went well,' Magnus observed as the doors were closed behind them.

'If I want your opinion, I'll ask for it.'

'No, you'll get it whether you want it or not. And it's this: now that you've shown the arbiter of life and death in this gods-forsaken place, miles from anyone who would lift a finger to help us, that you would like nothing more than to rip his Keeper of the Records' balls off for him and then choke him on them, I think it's pretty much a certainty that said Keeper will manufacture some incident that will result in us all being used to enrich the soil in time to be an intrinsic part of next year's harvest.'

'I know! And I acted pathetically.'

'Like a petulant slave with a trivial grudge against one of his fellows trying to get an unsympathetic master to take his side in the matter.'

'Trivial?'

'Yes, trivial.'

'He left us to die!'

'And, as the king rightly pointed out, we didn't. And now that you've gone and told all the great and the good in this kingdom what you intend to do at the first opportunity, how are we going to take our rightful vengeance on the slippery shit and then be allowed to travel back to the Empire across four hundred miles of desert without someone coming and asking us to explain ourselves to that fat shit in a red wig?'

A shout from behind prevented Vespasian from blustering an answer.

'Governor!'

Vespasian looked round to see a palace functionary scurrying after them. He stopped and faced the man. 'What is it?'

The man bowed deeply. 'The Keeper of the Records has asked that you meet him in the agora at the west gates tomorrow at the second hour of the day to begin a tour of the kingdom.'

'And leave your lictors behind, Vespasian,' Decianus ordered.

Vespasian, astride his horse, cocked his head, frowning, as if he had not heard correctly. Spray from the many fountains that dominated the agora cooled the air in the face of the sun burning already, despite the earliness of the hour. Bored-looking citizens milled around the market stalls, idly examining goods, mostly pottery imported from the Empire, without much enthusiasm; again, there were no women to be seen.

'Leave them,' Decianus repeated, 'they'll only slow us down.'

'Slow us down!' Vespasian gestured to the cumbersome, four-mule carriage in which Decianus lounged, shaded by an awning and surrounded by wafters. 'That thing will struggle to go any faster than the slaves fanning you.'

Decianus spread his hands and shrugged. 'My slaves will jog if necessary and still perform their function, whereas lictors process at the stately speed of an imperial magistrate; to go any faster lacks dignity. I know, I've had lictors.'

'You've already told me to get rid of my cavalry escort; am I to be totally unprotected?'

'You're protected by your status as an ambassador.' Decianus gestured to Magnus and Hormus waiting on their mounts behind Vespasian. 'And you have your freedman and, er ...' He made a show of trying to recall a name but failing to. 'Him; whoever and whatever he is.'

Magnus smiled with exaggerated pleasantness at the ex-proc-urator. 'He does have "him", Decianus; and "him" may only have one eye, but "him" knows well where to focus it.' He turned to Vespasian. 'Just leave it, sir; he's going to insist upon having his own way however much you argue.'

Decianus signalled his driver to move on through the crowd of citizens, each one well fed and rotund, who had migrated from the market stalls to watch their departure for want of anything else of interest to do. 'Of course I'll have my own way; I'm in charge.'

'How very lovely for you,' Vespasian said under his breath as he turned his mount to follow the carriage through the south gates, dismissing his lictors with a wave.

The track was blown sand on red-brown stone and bordered on both left and right by irrigation conduits, filled with running water; every few hundred paces they branched off to feed the fields beyond. Gangs of slaves were being herded along, overseen by the slave-keepers who were free with the use of their whips. In the first half an hour of the journey they passed three such groups comprising male and female, young and old alike, almost all naked, dark and wrinkled from exposure to the sun, stomachs betraying malnutrition and all exuding an air of misery and hope-lessness. It was a marked difference from the slaves in the city that Vespasian had seen collecting the waste, who had seemed relatively healthy. The gangs were whipped into fields in various stages of cultivation and set to work with brutality with no consideration for their age or fitness.

At first there seemed to Vespasian to be no agricultural system, for some of the fields were verdant, others golden and then others filled with reapers or receiving the attention of the plough; still more were being sown or just lying fallow. But soon, Vespasian, with his agricultural eye and expertise from his estates, began to understand the reason. 'They do continuous rotation,' he informed Magnus.

'Eh?'

'Continuous rotation; the farming.'

'Continuous what?'

'Rotation. They have the fields in different stages of cultivation because it doesn't make any difference when they plough, sow or harvest because they don't have seasons up here.'

Magnus looked ahead, beyond the cultivated line of hills to the desert that shimmered into a burning distance. 'What? You mean it's always as hot as Vulcan's arsehole?'

'Exactly; they have constant water from the wells which they feed into the fields all year round. The sun is always burning down so it makes no difference what month you sow a field, the crop will always be ready a few months later provided you have enough water, which they do.'

'Ahh, I see. So if you time it that you've always got fields ripening then you have a constant supply of food all year round.'

'Exactly.'

'It's a clever system,' Decianus put in, his eyes closed, surprising Vespasian who thought he had fallen asleep. 'It means that we are not reliant on one harvest, maybe two if the gods are favourable, each year. So, unlike Rome, we can guarantee to be able to feed our people all year round without fear of shortages. Which keeps them docile—'

'And you secure in your position,' Vespasian cut in.

'It has that fortunate side effect, I'll grant you that.'

'And just what is your position?'

'Very comfortable, thank you.' Decianus opened one eye and looked at Vespasian, smiling, before closing it again.

Vespasian decided against enquiring further so as not to flatter Decianus with his curiosity; and, besides, he knew that it would become apparent in the course of the day.

The sun continued on its relentless rise, burning down with increasing ferocity until it was almost directly overhead and Vespasian felt as if he had been forced into a baker's oven. But Decianus made no move to stop and seek shade, being amply supplied of that commodity and cooled by the fan-work of his slaves. On they went at the lumbering pace of Decianus' mules, pausing only to allow the beasts and slaves to drink together regularly at one of the many troughs along the route that ran, almost straight, to the west. Here and there protrusions of orange-brown rock jutted from the ground, soaring high, providing a focus for the countless swifts wheeling about the deep-blue sky as brown-necked ravens cawed from their nests in the crevices high above the fields that supplied them with the locusts and small snakes they favoured. Higher still circled birds of prey, majestic in the air, as they surveyed their kingdom below so full of bounty.

Shortly after noon Decianus stirred from his slumber as they approached what seemed, from a distance, to be a small town; but as they drew nearer Vespasian could see that it was not a town in the normal sense of the word but, rather, a collection of long, single-storey barrack blocks.

'Now you will see exactly how important I am in this kingdom,' Decianus said as a reception committee of half a dozen brown-skinned men in long black robes and wide-brimmed sun hats, from beneath which protruded frizzy black hair, walked from the buildings to meet them.

'We are most honoured by the presence of one so favoured by The Lord of the Thousand Wells,' the leader of the group announced, bowing low, so that he had to prevent his hat from falling off. His brethren had equal difficulty paying their respects, the frizziness of their hair making it hard for the hats to sit firmly upon their heads.

'You are indeed, Anaruz,' Decianus replied with no trace of irony. 'I wish to be away from here as soon as possible so you will provide me with your inventory and a cool place in which to study it.'

'There is nothing that would give me greater pleasure, Lord.'

Decianus seemed to take the lie at face value or, perhaps, Vespasian considered, even believed it, as the group turned and escorted the carriage back towards the buildings. Vespasian, Magnus and Hormus followed, ignored by the reception committee, none of whom had even glanced their way such was the awe with which they had received Decianus.

And Decianus revelled in the attention as he was helped down from his carriage by Anaruz's underlings at the foot of the steps of what was evidently, judging by its portico, the administrative building. He cuffed away a hand that supported his elbow with too much vigour, dismissing its owner from his presence for the rest of the visit; he slapped the slave who rushed to hold a parasol over his head for allowing the sun's rays to touch his skin for an instant; he rebuked Anaruz for the sloppiness of the slave and insisted that the miscreant be returned to field-work; he then rejected, for no apparent reason, each of the three slaves brought forward to replace the man before accepting the services of a fourth as the original was hauled off, screaming, to a slow death through overwork and malnutrition. Having mocked Anaruz's cringing apologies for the incident, humiliating him in front of his underlings, and then issuing an ear-splitting tirade into their faces, berating them for their inability to support Anaruz in the heavy duties of his position, he then selected one at random and ejected him from the compound with orders to walk back to Garama and to report to him for punishment upon his return from his tour. Once confusion had been well and truly sown so that everything was to Decianus' satisfaction and he judged that those around him were in sufficient fear of his power, he turned into the affable master, placing an arm around the visibly bewildered Anaruz and asking after his family as they made their way into the only building in the complex that was not just designed for functionality.

'I'd say that Decianus is confusing importance with fear,' Vespasian observed as he and his companions dismounted.

'One thing's for sure,' Magnus mused, watching the confused Anaruz try to cope with his superior's abrupt change of mood, 'if Decianus were to spontaneously burst into flames you wouldn't see Anaruz rushing to the nearest well with an empty bucket, if you take my meaning?'

'I do, Magnus; I most certainly do.'

'And in this heat there's always hope.'

Leaving their horses with the carriage driver, they followed Decianus up the steps, into the shade of the portico and then on, through a tall set of doors, into a spacious hall, high-ceilinged and lit by north-facing windows that were never subjected to the direct force of the sun. Here, in this cooler atmosphere, desks were set out at which functionaries sat scratching with styli at wax tablets. A barked order from Anaruz sent them all scurrying away to disappear in the shadowed far end of the room.

'Your excellency would care for some refreshment?' Anaruz asked in a voice that betrayed anxiety as to what the consequences would be if this was the wrong subject to bring up.

But his worry was unfounded as Decianus slapped him on the back. 'An excellent suggestion, my dear Anaruz.' Then he noticed Vespasian for the first time since their arrival. 'You may serve Governor Vespasian and myself as I go through the inventory with him.'

The inventory was not at all what Vespasian expected and he began to understand exactly how Decianus had made himself so useful to the king in so short a time. Seated on a large divan and surrounded by his slaves, fans in constant motion, Decianus scanned wax tablet after wax tablet containing one long list of all the slaves housed in the complex; each had a number but no name and each had a purchase date that represented the day that the slave had arrived in the kingdom. That in itself was an impressive piece of bookkeeping but it was the final symbol next to each slave that amazed Vespasian.

'"L",' Decianus said to Anaruz. 'Note down slave ninety-four from the calends of July purchase of two years ago as "Latin Rights".' He carried on down the list as Anaruz scratched the note onto a fresh tablet. '"L"; slave one hundred and twelve from the same purchase.' Decianus looked over to Vespasian seated opposite and sipping a beaker of coconut water. 'It's my system; I had to do something to get noticed by the king when I arrived here so I suggested that I use the organisational skills I'd found that I had a talent for whilst serving as a procurator collecting tax from uncooperative barbarians.' He looked smug and continued consulting the list. '"R"; slave thirty-two from the December purchase of the same year is a "recognised citizen".'

Anaruz noted this number down on a different tablet as Decianus, with remarkable speed, continued going through the inventory.

Vespasian put his beaker down, unable to contain his curiosity any longer. 'Tell me, Decianus; what is your system?'

Decianus made no attempt to conceal his delight. 'Ahh! So you're interested. How gratifying!' He paused to collect himself, his pride in his achievement visible. 'I suggested it to the king when I arrived here with enough money to see me set up in comfort but not in the sort of luxury that I prefer to enjoy. It seemed to me that a kingdom that relies so much on slave labour, to the extent that its subjects have no need to work because all they require is grown on huge farms, like this, and given to them freely and so consequently they lead an idle life, is in grave danger. Apart from the slave-keepers and some of the younger men who, for want of any other excitement, hunt wild beasts for the circuses in the Empire, who is there to protect it should the slaves realise just how vulnerable the kingdom is to a revolt? It would be no Spartacus, let me assure you; the Garamantes kingdom would disappear in a matter of days with just a few hundred slave-keepers and hunters to suppress an uprising. As the king told you, there is no army because there is no one to defend the kingdom against. But Nayram doesn't see the full horror of the threat from within; nobody here does because they're complacent and think their way of life is secure.' He looked at Anaruz. 'Don't you, Anaruz?'

'Not now you have shown me the threat, Lord.'

'The threat. Yes, Anaruz understands the threat and the threat is very real. I decided that if I was going to make Garama my home then I needed to do something about that threat and so I suggested to the king that I make a full inventory of every slave.' He paused for Vespasian to make a comment as to the magnitude of the task but was disappointed; Vespasian had no intention of flattering the ex-procurator. 'As all the slaves are publicly owned – in other words the king pays for them – there are records of all the expenditure going back decades. Slaves

come here from four sources: first from the Empire; mainly
beast-masters bringing in stock in return for the wild beasts
caught by the hunters, for the circuses. These slaves are generally quite low quality for agricultural labour as the strongest in
the Empire generally end up in the gladiator schools or the farms
or mines, but nevertheless we do get some good specimens from
that route, especially in the wake of the rebellion in Britannia.'
He paused, waiting, Vespasian assumed, for him to make some
comment on Boudicca's revolt; when it became apparent that
he would not, Decianus pressed on. 'Then there are the caravans that come across the desert from the south. They bring
outlandish-looking slaves dressed in animal skins and blacker
than Nubians, and strong and healthy, even the women, perfect
for all sorts of things. From the west come a steady stream of
slaves of reasonable quality; but since Claudius incorporated
Mauritania into the Empire, twenty years ago, most of the
traders take their goods to the imperial slave markets up on the
coast. And then there's the eastern route ...'

'The Marmarides.'

Decianus was impressed. 'You know them.'

'I served as quaestor in Cyrenaica. I was obliged to go after an
idiot who had managed to get himself captured by the tribe and
was in danger of ending his life down here.'

'Well, you know all about them then. Suffice it to say that a
goodly percentage of the slaves that come to Garama by the
eastern route are citizens. Now, that in itself was not what I was
interested in, but a record of all the Roman citizens in bondage
here was the by-product of my inventory. You see, there are
twelve centres like this, spread throughout the realm, where the
slaves are housed and each has its own records of what slaves it
receives when a new batch arrives in the kingdom. So I suggested
to the king that I should go around each of the centres and
cross-check who had what slaves because what I was concerned
about was the concentration of too many slaves from the same
ethnicity in the same area. Far better, I think you'll agree, to
have as many different races and languages as possible so that
there is less likelihood of them uniting in a common purpose.

The king understood the scheme perfectly and agreed to recompense me for the work, lavishly I may add.'

There was another pause for a look of complete self-satisfaction. 'And so I began a tour of all twelve centres and went through every slave and cross-checked where he or she had come from and when; it took me over six months as there are over a thousand slaves in each area – two thousand in a couple of them. I had to do it myself as no one locally could understand my methods and, besides, I wouldn't want anyone else to understand the system. But still, I got it done and once the work was complete I began to organise the breaking up of large groups of the same peoples, spreading them thinly over many centres so now there isn't one dangerously large concentration of any sort anywhere in Garama.'

'And that's how you know who is a Roman citizen?'

'Of course; and that way it won't take long to find the four hundred and sixty.'

'I brought five hundred pearls.'

'Did you? I tallied forty fewer.'

Vespasian knew it was futile to argue. 'I'm surprised you only helped yourself to that number.'

'No, I only helped myself to twenty.' Decianus looked pointedly at Vespasian.

Vespasian kept his face neutral. 'But, as I said, we'll negotiate if there are more and I'm sure that you can be of great service in seeing the deal through.'

Decianus understood, smelling profit as Vespasian had intended. 'I'm always happy to be of service to Rome.'

'And yet you did nothing to help her citizens here?'

'What business is it of mine if someone is foolish enough to get themself enslaved?'

Vespasian conceded that Decianus had a point: he had used a similar argument with his wife Flavia, years ago, when she insisted that he should rescue her then lover from the same fate. In the end he had rescued Statilius Capella, not so much because he was a Roman citizen but more to impress Flavia; however, he was not about to let Decianus feel completely justified in his actions. 'Not only did you do nothing about their predicament, you also split them up and potentially made it worse.'

'Naturally; where my safety is concerned no precaution is too great.'

'I noticed that in Britannia.'

'Oh, do stop harking back to that, otherwise I might start remembering the flattened nose and shattered jaw.'

'Are you threatening me?'

'Vespasian, please try to understand that I don't need to threaten you as you are already completely in my power; I can have you killed any time I like.'

'That's a lie, Decianus, and you know it. Your fat master wouldn't be at all pleased if you did because he's well aware that Nero is not going to take the disappearance of one of his governors on a diplomatic mission very kindly. For Nayram it's vital that he keeps on good terms with Rome; why else do you think he agreed to Nero's request in releasing all the citizens here? Now, enough of this; get back to your lists and leave me to marvel at your importance.'

It was mid-afternoon by the time they were back on their way, heading to what Decianus had assured Vespasian was the farming complex furthest to the west of the kingdom; after this they would head south and then east before returning to Garama having completed a full circle of Nayram's domain. Anaruz had been left with a list containing fifty-three numbers and orders to have those slaves mustered at Garama seven days hence.

Reaching their destination – which was very similar in design and layout to the first – before nightfall, Decianus went through the inventory, having terrorised the officials running the farm complex in much the same way as he had done earlier. This list produced a total of thirty-six slaves that Decianus insisted were paraded before him and Vespasian upon their return from their labour at dusk.

It was a weary and bedraggled group of slaves, both male and female, that Vespasian found himself looking at in the flicker of torchlight on the parade ground outside the administrative building that evening. The slave-keepers tried to whip some order into the ragged lines but most were too exhausted and too immune to the lick of leather to care.

'That's enough!' Vespasian shouted as a young woman fell to her knees under repeated lashes.

The slave-keeper looked around to see that Vespasian was addressing him and desisted with a show of reluctance.

Vespasian approached the group, stopping in front of an older man staring at the ground. He lifted the man's chin and looked into his eyes; they were almost vacant and refused to meet his own. 'Where are you from?' he asked in Latin.

The slave said nothing, barely registering that he had been addressed.

Vespasian repeated the question.

This time the slave shook his head a fraction as if trying to clear it; he raised his eyes and looked quizzical. 'What did you say?' His voice croaked; it had not been used for a while.

'I asked where you are from.'

'Why?'

'Just answer me.'

The slave thought for a few moments. 'Apollonia.'

'The port in Cyrenaica?'

'Yes.'

'And you are a Roman citizen?'

'I was.' He made a grim attempt at an ironic grin that convinced Vespasian of the veracity of the claim.

'How did you end up here?'

'I had a fishing boat.'

Vespasian did not need to hear any more having heard a similar tale, many years before, from Yosef, the Jewish tin-trader he had freed from the Marmarides along with Statilius Capella. 'And you pulled in for water along the coast between Cyrenaica and Egypt and were captured by Marmarides slavers?'

The slave looked astonished. 'Yes, three years ago; how did you know?'

'Never mind.' He moved on down the line to satisfy himself

that each slave had a genuine claim to citizenship or Latin Rights; each one was in a pitiful condition and each one had a tale of woe.

It was therefore with some surprise that Vespasian stood before a well-built man in his mid-twenties, standing straight and meeting his eye. 'Marcus Urbicus,' the man said, snapping to attention. 'Optio of the third century, sixth cohort of the Third Augusta, sir.'

Vespasian stared at Urbicus in total surprise. 'How long have you been here, Urbicus?'

'Just over six months, sir. Since the Suphetes of Leptis Magna took me when I came with your message to them to co-operate in the matter of the water dumps.'

'They did what?'

'They took me and my men, sir, and sold us to the Garamantes. Nothing we could do about it, sir!'

Vespasian looked in horror at the optio and then turned to Decianus. 'Did you know about this?'

The ex-procurator shrugged with an air of indifference. 'I can't recall.'

Vespasian looked back at Urbicus. 'Where are the rest of your men?'

'I don't know, sir; there were eight of them before we were separated.'

Vespasian rounded on Decianus. 'You did know about this! You had them separated, you fat—' Vespasian checked himself.

'Careful what you say, Governor; we don't want any unpleasantness. They were slaves in the Kingdom of the Garamantes; I just carried out the policy.'

'And I suppose that it was no business of yours if they managed to get themselves enslaved, eh?'

'Exactly.'

'Well, Decianus, unfortunately for you, it was *my* business! This man was carrying my message and was treacherously taken and then illegally sold into bondage by the Suphetes of Leptis Magna, and the King of the Garamantes was complicit in that crime in that he purchased them.'

'It happens all the time.'

'With legionaries? I don't think so, Decianus. That is a direct attack against the authority of the Governor and therefore an attack on the Emperor himself and you are involved, Decianus, just as much as your mountainous king. And Rome will hear of this if I choose to let it. If you ever had any thoughts about one day being able to buy your way back into favour, you can forget them right now unless you guarantee me your fullest co-operation in the rest of this business, rather than just trying to impress upon me what an important man you are when actually I couldn't care less.'

Decianus' stare was cold. 'And what makes you think that you'll survive the journey back to the Empire?'

'Do you really want to bet against it, Decianus?' He indicated to Magnus and Hormus, standing behind him. 'They may not look much to you but between us we can hold our own, especially as we now have Urbicus with us. Urbicus, go and join them.'

The optio saluted and marched over to join Magnus and Hormus.

'Now, have these people fed and separated from the rest of the slaves. Tomorrow I'm taking them back to Garama and there I shall wait, camped with my Numidian cavalry outside the city walls, whilst you round up the rest of the Roman citizens in this kingdom and send them to me and not to Nayram.'

'But you're meant to be coming with me.'

'Why? All I do is watch you. You can do the job perfectly well on your own. Besides, I don't feel as secure in your company as perhaps I should; I prefer the company of my Numidians. As you said: where my safety is concerned no precaution is too great.'

'But the king—'

'Fuck your king and fuck you. Think about it, Decianus: do you really want to live the rest of your life here, in this shithole, or do you want to have the smallest chance of returning to Rome?'

Decianus' silence was eloquent.

'Then do as I say!'

CHAPTER III

I T WAS WITH great relief that Vespasian watched the eleventh ragged little column of citizen-slaves stumble past the caravan merchants' encampment and on through the gates of the military camp that the Numidian cavalry had constructed a quarter of a mile from Garama's north gate. He reckoned them to be about forty in number and such was their condition that there were only two slave-keepers escorting them.

'The last lot should arrive tomorrow and then we can be on our way,' Vespasian said to Magnus and Hormus as they shared a bowl of dates, watching the arrival from beneath the shade of an awning rigged between three palm trees, which they had called home for the past five days.

Magnus spat out a date stone. 'I can't say that I'll be upset to start a four hundred mile slog across the desert; it'll be far more preferable to being stuck in this camel's arsehole. Not that they have camels here, mind you. Come to think of it, why don't they?'

Vespasian nodded. 'I wondered that when we first arrived in Africa: why are there no camels west of Cyrenaica? It's perfect country for them.'

'Well, someone would make a fortune importing and breeding them, and seeing as you don't seem to be taking Hormus' and my advice and making a considerable profit on this deal then why don't you?'

Vespasian smiled and popped another date into his mouth. 'I might well do – or at least set up a proxy to do it. I've been thinking about it as we've been waiting. Hormus, what would you say to staying behind in Africa for a few months and setting up the business?'

Hormus tried to look enthusiastic but it did not convince Vespasian. 'If you require it of me, master.'

'Well, as a senator, I can't set up a business as you know; and what are freedmen for, after all? Who knows, I might even invest some of the small fortune that I will make from this mission.'

Magnus and Hormus both looked at him astounded.

'How are you going to make any money, master?' Hormus asked, being the first to recover from the surprise.

'Ah! Well, let me put it this way: meeting Decianus here wasn't all bad; in fact, it's rather a good piece of luck. It occurred to me on the way back here.'

But further enlightenment was precluded by the approach of the senior decurion of the auxiliary cavalry together with a slave-keeper.

'Governor,' the decurion said, coming to attention before Vespasian.

'What is it, Bolanus?'

'This man claims Roman citizenship.'

Vespasian looked at the slave-keeper with interest. 'What's your name?'

'Juncus Nepos, sir, from Cumae.'

'And you want to come with us?'

Nepos wrung his hands on his whip. 'If I could, sir.' He was in his mid-twenties, burned by the sun, wearing only a leather kilt and sandals; his hair and beard were long and two sea-grey eyes stared back at Vespasian with all the animation of the dead.

'What's to stop you? You're a freedman after all.'

'Technically, yes; but when they free you here it's to do a job and you have to swear your loyalty to the king. What happens is that instead of dying here as a slave you get to live longer and die as a freedman. Either way you don't get a decent burial and, instead, end up in bits on the fields.'

'Barbaric.'

Nepos shrugged. 'It's their way and if you're unlucky enough to end up here it's all you can expect. Perhaps I would have stayed; after all, what is there for me to go back to in the Empire? I've been here for five years now, three of them as a slave, and I'd have nothing back home any more.'

'So why not stay here?'

Nepos pointed to the citizen slaves who he had just brought in. 'There were only two of us guarding them; normally there would have been five or six keepers for that amount but that wasn't necessary, was it? No, because they knew that they were going to their freedom before Decianus had even got to our farm. The rumour has got about very quickly and most of the slaves know that the Roman citizens are being released.'

'Leaving the vast majority that remain even more resentful of their situation than they were before.'

'If that were possible, sir, yes; and I can tell you that as I marched this lot away from the farm complex this morning my fellow keepers were having a lot of trouble whipping the rest of the slaves back to work. I saw them execute at least two.'

Magnus grunted and picked another date from the bowl. 'A merciful release for them I should think, seeing as being a slave here is a fate worse than death.'

'That's exactly it, and I should know,' Nepos agreed. 'I think that now they're aware that some of them have been saved, the ones that remain have finally really understood that their gods have forsaken them.'

Vespasian nodded. 'That last shred of hope has disappeared and they now have literally nothing to lose.'

'I know the feeling well, master,' Hormus said. 'Before you bought me, I clung to the very small hope that maybe, just maybe, there was a god looking out for me and that someday all would be well. Without that, I would have had nothing to lose by killing my then master even as he buggered me. But I didn't and the gods saw fit to reward me by becoming your slave. But these people? Well, if they've lost that last shred of hope then they, all together, will become a fearsome force.'

'I think you may be right, Hormus,' Vespasian said, a smile slowly spreading across his face. 'Despite all Decianus' efforts to split up the ethnicities to ensure that the slaves don't find common cause, we have just unwittingly given them one. He's just as guilty as the king and all of his subjects of the complacency that he was accusing them of. Had he been wary he would have seen the danger and been far more secretive about what was going on. But no, he had the citizen-slaves parade publicly before us in the middle of the farm complex. The others would have seen what was going on and found out.'

'And the slave-keepers talked,' Nepos added, 'you can be sure of that. They would have taunted the slaves with it. I know, because I did.'

Vespasian shook his head in slow thought. 'That doesn't bode well for Garama.'

'I'd say that it was time we were leaving,' Magnus observed.

Vespasian looked up at Nepos. 'Do you know when the column from the twelfth farm is due to arrive?'

'We passed the farm soon after midday; Decianus was already there so it wouldn't surprise me if they are only a couple of hours behind us.'

'And then he's got to get the citizens from the city itself; that could take all tomorrow.'

'Do we have time to wait?' Magnus asked, getting to his feet and rubbing some blood back into his buttocks.

'We have to.'

'Why?' Magnus gestured to all the ex-slaves sitting around in groups. 'Look; there must be four or five hundred there.'

'Five hundred and eleven, plus what Nepos brought in.'

'Forty-three, sir.'

'So, five hundred and fifty-four all in all,' Magnus calculated, 'that's got to be enough. Let's just go now, before it gets even hotter around here, if you take my meaning?'

Vespasian was reluctant. 'We have to wait for the rest; and, besides, what danger would we be in? We're not the ones who've been working them to death on our farms. They'll attack the city.'

Magnus pointed to the nearby north gate. 'Which is right there; and as they arrive to do that they'll see us still waiting and realise that we have the key to getting across the desert. It's one thing taking five hundred or so back but five thousand or even more? We'd all die.'

'He's right, sir,' Nepos agreed; he looked at the hundreds of citizens sitting around in groups. 'It's going to be virtually impossible to get across the desert with all these people anyway.'

'Everyone has a bag containing some twice-baked bread and dried meat and there are more provisions loaded on the caravan. As for water, we've got dumps and wells on the route.'

Nepos looked dubious. 'Even so; every extra person puts the whole group in more jeopardy.'

Vespasian stared out over the desert to the north, beyond which lay the Empire. 'Very well; not all of us will wait. Bolanus, start moving the citizens out now, all of them, and send a *turma* of your men with them as guides and to make sure that they don't empty all the water dumps – actually, you'd better make that two turmae; you go with them, Nepos. They should march all night to get as much of a head start as possible. Tell the caravan that they must be ready to leave with us in the morning by which time I hope to have collected all our slaves. We'll then follow as fast as we can. Being mounted we should catch up with the column in a day and a night.'

'But the slaves we're waiting for won't be mounted,' Magnus pointed out. 'How will they keep up with us?'

Vespasian shrugged. 'What can I do? My best hope is to get them out. They will just have to follow at their own pace and trust to their gods. But at least my conscience is clear and I've given them a chance.'

Magnus looked at him, frowning. 'There's more to this, isn't there?'

Vespasian said nothing as he watched Bolanus rouse the citizen-slaves, ready for the journey.

The brief southern dusk had just given way to night as a half-dozen flickering points of light in the east came into view through the gates.

'Looks like they're here,' Magnus said, nudging Vespasian to rouse him from a pleasant doze in the cooling air. 'Perhaps we can get going soon.'

Vespasian grunted in a non-committal manner, rising stiffly to his feet and making for the gates.

'Everything is packed, master,' Hormus assured him, following, 'and Bolanus tells me that the horses are fed and watered.'

The torches grew nearer and soon the bulk of Decianus' carriage could be discerned in their midst; behind was a long shadow, darker than the night, that gradually resolved itself into the individual figures of freed slaves.

'I have been good to my word, Governor,' Decianus announced as the carriage approached the gates, his voice, ingratiating, betraying a marked change of attitude. 'I trust that you'll bear that in mind when you consider my request.'

Vespasian played innocent; knowing full well what was to come, he moved close to Decianus so that they could not be overheard. 'What request?'

Decianus gave a brief glance over his shoulder, which told Vespasian more about the situation in the east of the kingdom than Decianus could have imagined. 'I should like to come with you; I think I should resolve any misunderstandings still current back in Rome.'

'You want me to help you now? It's one thing not killing you out of hand in justifiable revenge but actually helping you save your miserable skin? You have to be delusional.'

'I'll pay you well when we get back to Rome.'

'And just remind me why you didn't go straight to Rome after you fled Britannia in such a cowardly fashion.'

'That had been my original plan until I heard that Suetonius Paulinus had defeated Boudicca and that he, you and your brother had all survived. I judged that, even though I was only looking after the Emperor's interests, I would not get a fair hearing if you three brought charges against me and persuaded Seneca to back you.'

'The Emperor's interests? You took the money that Boudicca had gathered to pay off Seneca's loan; it had nothing to do with the Emperor.'

'I was reclaiming the original loan that Claudius had given Prasutagus, her husband, to raise him to senatorial rank after he had sworn allegiance to him.'

'And so you then gave the money to the Cloelius Brothers to transport back to Rome and keep it in their bank in the forum. It was in your name; the Cloelius Brothers admitted it to Seneca.'

'Of course it's in my name; and I had planned, when the time became right, in that Seneca would be dead and I could eventually get back to Rome, to hand it over to the Emperor.' He gave another nervous look into the darkness behind him. 'But circumstances are changing and I believe that now may be a reasonable time for me to risk returning. I think I could make my money smooth the way for me.'

'It's too late for that, Decianus.'

The ex-procurator frowned and again glanced over his shoulder. 'What makes you say that?'

Vespasian felt a warm glow growing inside as he supplied Decianus with the answer. 'Because Seneca made the Cloelius Brothers hand that money over to him.'

'But they can't do that; it goes against all the rules of banking!'

'I'm sure they felt the same way; but Seneca pointed out that the rules of banking don't apply to the deceased and you had disappeared and were therefore assumed to be dead with no sign of having written a will and that the money that you had entrusted them with was, in fact, his. It was something that my brother, Caenis and I were all happily able to confirm. Wisely, in my opinion, the Cloelius Brothers returned it to its true owner and the suggestion that it might be a good idea to review the taxation on banks, in view of Nero's current financial difficulties due to being unable to withdraw from Britannia because of the revolt, suddenly went away.'

Decianus' battered face was a study in despair. 'But that was my money!'

'I thought you said it was the Emperor's.'

The ex-procurator stared in outrage at Vespasian, unable to formulate a defence.

'Well, it's irrelevant now as Seneca has been forced to give the Emperor a few substantial loans which Nero has no intention of paying back, so the money has ended up exactly where you meant it to.'

'But what am I to do? You must take me along with you.'

Vespasian nodded towards the east. 'Why, Decianus? What's happening out there that you're so afraid of, eh? Are things getting a bit out of hand despite the brilliance of your system?'

Decianus swallowed. 'They're coming; they'll be here soon.'

As if to confirm the truth of this statement a distant glow rose in the east.

'Then you had better hurry and get the Roman citizens out of the city itself because we're not leaving without them.'

'If I do that then I can come. I'll find the money to pay you when we get back; I promise you.'

'No, Decianus; you'll pay me now; we both know you can afford it. Do that and I won't stop you following us. That's my best offer.'

'Very well. I'll have all the citizen-slaves here before dawn.'

'Then we'll leave at first light.' Vespasian turned away, feeling torn between relief at securing a substantial bribe and disgust that it was to save the life of the man who had tried to have him killed; but Decianus' co-operation was now crucial if he was to succeed in his mission and extract all the citizens.

Speed was all important now that the burning had begun.

'But you must stay. His Most Exalted Majesty, Nayram of the Garamantes, The Lord of the Thousand Wells, has commanded that you, Titus Flavius Vespasianus, stay to help defend the city with your cavalry,' Izebboudjen the chamberlain stated again with more desperation, his eyes drawn to the growing glow in the east. His litter-bearers' breath was laboured as they tried to keep up with Vespasian's quick pace.

'Does he now? And why would he think that I should be interested in doing that?' Vespasian increased his pace in an attempt to get away from the insistent chamberlain who seemed incapable of taking no for an answer.

'Because he knows that his brother, the Emperor Nero, would command you thus.'

Vespasian rounded on Izebboudjen, forcing the bearers to come to an abrupt stop. 'Let's just drop Nayram's pretence that he is equal to Nero, shall we? You know as well as I that Nero wouldn't lift a finger to save your kingdom or your fat king. I'm leaving as soon as Decianus arrives with the rest of the Roman citizens and you can either try following our column or stay here and attempt to explain to ten thousand very angry slaves just why they should spare your life.'

'But they'll never do that.'

'No, I don't suppose they will.'

'But I've sent messages to the hunters to come; with them, your cavalry and the slave-keepers we'll be able to defeat the rebels; they're no more than a rabble.'

'A rabble that has nothing to lose other than lives not worth living, which makes them the most dangerous of rabbles. Face it, Izebboudjen, it was unsustainable and you should have seen this coming and trained your people to defend themselves rather than allowing them to sit around in a heap all day doing nothing. It took a few crack legions to stop the Spartacus rebellion and what have you got? An overweight population who have everything found for them. Well, my friend, if there was ever a chance for them to show their quality then I would say that it'll be tomorrow.'

Izebboudjen's face registered just what he thought the chances of the citizens of Garama showing any quality were. 'I beg you, Governor, please.'

'No!'

A vengeful glint appeared in the chamberlain's eye. 'Very well.' In response to his terse order his litter-bearers turned about and headed back towards the gates of the city, illumined by two torches flaring to either side.

An hour before dawn the eastern sky was glowing as if the sun were only just below the horizon; in the west it seemed as if it had recently set, such were the fires that now burned. Already, small groups of refugees, silhouettes running in the night, hurried towards the city gates, banging on them for admittance and then slipping through as their pleas were answered.

Vespasian paced about the entrance to the camp, glancing at the gates every time they were opened in the hope that he would see people exit but each time he was disappointed; the knot in his stomach grew. 'Come on, Decianus,' he said under his breath as the gates opened again for a group of a dozen or so fleeing the oncoming rage.

'I'll bet you never thought that you would be anxious to see Decianus,' Magnus observed as Bolanus led his Numidian auxiliaries, filled water-skins over their mounts' rumps, out of the camp to form up between it and the caravan that was now moving off down the winding track leading into the desert far below.

'It's a novel feeling,' Vespasian confessed, thinking as much about the pearls as the citizens, as his lictors joined the Numidians in preparation to move out.

As the gates began to close, the refugees safely within, angry shouting came from the other side, followed by a couple of screams, one long and drawn out that faded into a gurgle.

Vespasian glanced at Magnus. 'Was that what I thought it was?'

'Yes, and why would someone get killed just as they entered the gates looking for some sort of safety? Unless, of course, they were trying to get out.'

'That's what I was wondering. I've a nasty feeling that we may have a treacherous chamberlain to deal with. Bolanus!'

The decurion turned in his saddle. 'Yes, Governor.'

'Have two dozen men dismounted and ready for action immediately, swords and shields only.'

It was with believable urgency that the Numidian trooper thumped on the city gates, calling out in the local language to be admitted. His comrades, armed with their straight cavalry *spathae* and small round, hide-covered shields, then joined in the chorus, howling for ingress as if they had been chased through the night by the Furies themselves.

Vespasian and Magnus waited, swords drawn, at the centre of the gates, with Bolanus just behind them.

The Numidians continued the clamour for admittance, their shouts increasing in volume until finally they were rewarded with the sound of the bar on the other side being removed. The left-hand gate began to swing back.

'Now!' Vespasian shouted, leaping through the gap with Magnus barrelling after him. Through they went, followed by

Bolanus and his men, crashing into the gatekeepers as they heaved on the ancient wood, bowling them to the ground. Looking up the street, Vespasian saw a tangle of figures in the torchlight and accelerated towards it. Kilted figures, brandishing whips and daggers, at least a score in all, were struggling to hold back a large group of men and women; a few were prone on the ground, some completely still.

'Vespasian! The slave-keepers won't let us through!'

The voice was that of Decianus; the outline of his carriage could be discerned within the scrimmage.

The shout alerted the slave-keepers to the threat behind them; they turned to face it. But men used to dealing out punishment to the downtrodden and receiving little or no resistance in return were at a loss when faced with a concerted charge of professional soldiery and they could not run as they were penned by their potential victims.

Up the hill Vespasian charged, his chest burning with the exertion, Magnus in his wake, he too gasping for breath, as Bolanus and his younger, fitter, dismounted cavalrymen outpaced them. On they ran towards the visibly wavering slave-keepers; the sight of armed assistance put heart into the slaves they had been attempting to hold back. Tooth and nail ripped into the slave-keepers' backs, hands clenched on throats, crushing with slow relish, as arms were flung about their chests, restraining them so that, as the first slashes and stabs of the Numidians' swords tore at their bodies, the slave-keepers were helpless. Down they went in a whirl of brutality dealt to them from fore and aft as blade sliced open flesh and bloodied fingers tore at the gashes, ripping them still further.

Vespasian punched his sword forward, groin height, into a man desperately trying to shake off a slave clamped to his back with his teeth embedded in his neck; his wrist jerked as his blade's tip ground against the pelvis but his grip remained firm. The scream that issued from the slave-keeper's mouth rang in Vespasian's ears, momentarily blocking out all other sound; he pressed the honed iron on into shredding guts as the slave wrenched his jaws away in an explosion of blood, ripping out a huge hunk of neck, his eyes maniacally wide with killing-joy. Pulling his arm up with all his strength, Vespasian cut through abdominal muscle, rending open the belly and releasing the stench of viscera. Next to him, Magnus ducked under a blurred swipe of a dagger, catching the wrist as it passed above his head to twist it down and back with sudden violence, ripping the elbow from its socket the instant before his forehead crunched into the owner's face, punching the head back, open-mouthed and shattered-toothed.

Down the slave-keepers fell, slashed and torn; their erstwhile charges giving vent to the years of torment endured under their whips. Eyes gouged, hair ripped, flesh chewed, they succumbed to the wave of fury unleashed by the dispossessed regaining a modicum of control over their lives and avenging themselves on the cause of their deprivation, so that the swift death dealt by a thrusting blade was a mercy gratefully accepted.

'Pull your men back, Bolanus!' Vespasian yelled as spathae slashed into the slaves exposed by the demise of their keepers. 'And make for the camp. We leave immediately.'

A repeated barked order cut above the mayhem and the Numidians pulled back, none of their number fallen. They turned and with haste headed back down the hill.

'Follow them,' Vespasian urged the released citizens in Latin, 'fast as you can!'

The citizens did not need a second invitation and pelted after the Numidians, revealing Decianus' carriage and the ex-procurator looking shaken but otherwise unharmed.

'Izebboudjen has gone to fetch more slave-keepers,' Decianus said as his driver whipped the mules on down the hill. 'They won't be long.'

Vespasian nodded, unwilling to thank Decianus for the information or, for that matter, even acknowledge that it was of use. He turned and, along with Magnus, ran back down the hill. The gates stood open and were deserted by the living. Only the dead remained, slumped, their limbs at strange angles; a group of refugees hurried into the town, their relief at seeking shelter shattered by the sight of death at its entrance. Vespasian and Magnus

passed through the gates with Decianus' carriage in close attend-
ance. Before following the Numidians and citizens to the camp,
Vespasian glanced back up the hill: a mass of handheld torches
was less than two hundred paces away and travelling fast; in their
midst was the silhouette of Izebboudjen's litter. Vespasian
turned and ran.

The Numidians were mounted by the time Vespasian had
traversed the four hundred paces to the camp; Hormus, already
in the saddle next to the lictors, held Vespasian and Magnus'
mounts by their halters. They scrambled up as the rear of the
merchant caravan disappeared into the darkness with the newly
released citizens following.

To the east and to the west the fires had grown and now the
glow was accompanied by the distant roar of thousands of voices
shouting and cheering as more groups of refugees pelted in from
the gloom, their comfortable world having been turned upside
down.

'Move out, Bolanus!' Vespasian shouted as he steadied himself
in the saddle.

Decianus' carriage rumbled past, the driver whipping the four
mules furiously, overtaking the Numidians. Vespasian, Magnus,
Hormus and the lictors turned their horses and kicked them
towards the head of the track that was the only north-facing
route down from the ridge of hills.

'I can't say that any of us will be displeased to leave this
shithole,' Magnus opined, urging his mount onwards, with a
nervous look over his shoulder; torches streamed through the
gate, heading towards them. The slave-keepers were in pursuit.

'They'd be mad to attack us,' Hormus said. 'They should bolt
their gates and man the walls, not come out here; the main force
of the rebellion can't be more than a mile away, judging from the
noise. They'll be caught in the open.'

'At least the slave-keepers will be between us and the rebels,'
Vespasian observed. 'All we need to do is outpace them, which
should be easy seeing as we're mounted.'

'*We* may be,' Magnus pointed out, 'but the citizens that we
just got out of the city ain't and neither are the ones that we sent

on yesterday evening. And if I remember rightly, from my time under the Eagles, a column marches at the speed of its slowest component, not the fastest.'

Vespasian grimaced as dawn began to break, embellished by the handiwork of thousands of rampaging slaves. 'I think you've recalled that quite accurately, Magnus. We've got a long day ahead of us and I—' But his sentence was cut short by a thwack and his horse bucking, kicking out its back legs. As he struggled to control the beast he was aware of a couple of unseen objects fizzing past them. He turned his head, looking back in the direction of the slave-keepers: many of them were whirring their arms around their heads; he ducked involuntarily as another object passed close by. 'Slings! Even at this range they can do damage.'

Magnus glanced back as he kicked his horse into a gallop. 'Then it's time to put some distance between us and them.'

But even as he spoke the sun crested the eastern horizon to reveal, in the distance, backlit, a swell of humanity.

The slave revolt had arrived at the city of Garama.

CHAPTER IIII

FELL WAS THE howl that greeted the dawn; for just as the rising of the sun had revealed the rebel host so had it illumined the object of its deepest hatred: the slave-keepers, distinctive, even in the pale light, in their leather kilts, stood before them in the open; almost two hundred of them.

Too late did they see the danger, intent as they were on carrying out Izebboudjen's will and preventing the escape of Vespasian and his auxiliary cavalry and thereby compelling them to join with Garama's small forces. Indecision split their ranks for there were two options, apart from standing to fight and thereby being ripped limb from limb: there was a rushed return to the gates that were, as yet, still open; or there was flight into the desert in the Romans' footsteps. And as Vespasian looked back over his shoulder, past his mounted lictors, he saw the decision dividing them as those closest to the city turned and ran back whilst those nearest the fleeing Romans sprinted after them, all thoughts of bringing them down with slingshot now forgotten. So the rebel host also divided and the last image Vespasian had of Garama was of a portly chamberlain being run down by a baying mob as the slaves who once bore his litter blocked his escape towards the closing gates.

Vespasian, Magnus, Hormus and the lictors slowed their mounts, fearful of them losing their footing on the stony ground, and cantered away down the hill, easily outpacing the slave-keepers following. Before long they had caught up with the fleeing Roman citizens, bunching together as the track narrowed to no more than four paces across – its average width, Vespasian knew from the ascent, all the way down to the desert floor. Slowing their horses to a trot they attempted the passage through the terrified group who, by now, were well aware of the slave-keepers descending behind them. Hands grabbed at bridles, legs and saddles in attempts either to unhorse the riders or climb up behind them.

'Piss off!' Magnus shouted, drawing his sword and kicking a snarling man in the teeth who pulled at his tunic.

Vespasian and Hormus followed his example and slashed with the flats of their weapons at the desperate people around them, knocking a couple senseless in order to discourage the rest; the lictors were less sensitive and blood was spilt. Slowly they waded through the huddle, their passage pushing a few off the track to slide down the scree of the steepening drop, their cries unnoticed in the growing panic. Onwards Vespasian pushed, until his mount broke free of the citizens and he could see the rear ranks of the Numidians, half a mile along the winding track and two hundred paces below them, snaking to and fro down the steep hillside.

With care they urged their horses on as fast as they dared, while, from above, there came cries of anguish as the slave-keepers crashed into the rear of the citizens, their pursuit by the rebel slaves adding haste to their descent. With thoughts only of their own safety the keepers barged their way into the formation but, unlike Vespasian and his companions who had gone in single file, they occupied the full width of the track. Many of the citizens went down under the feet of their former tormentors, but they were the lucky ones as clouds of dust rising from the loose scree on the hillside marked the swift passage of those barged off the track. Down they tumbled, uncontrolled, their skin grating and their bones cracking on embedded rocks that threw them in the air to crunch down to yet more agony.

'Shit!' Magnus exclaimed as the body of a young woman, either dead or unconscious, her flesh raw, crashed down onto the track just next to him, almost thumping into his horse's front legs. Pulling on the reins, he just managed to control the spooked beast before another, a youth, hurtled down in a flurry of gravel that hit as hard as hailstones, further unsettling the horses.

'Quick!' Vespasian shouted, kicking the flanks of his mount and looking up to the struggle; smoke from the fires above hazed the morning air. 'We need to get out from under them.' On he went, along the track, at a speed he would not have employed unless it were to get clear of danger.

Magnus, Hormus and the lictors followed after him as two more bodies rained down from above in a clatter of falling rock. With another turn back on itself the track began to descend even more steeply so that the horses were forced to slow to a walk as they struggled on the uneven surface, snorting freely with growing anxiety. But Vespasian did not let his control of his beast slacken and steadily it made its way down as shouts and screams still continued to emanate from the heights above, their intensity rising despite the fact that Vespasian and his companions were more distant.

'The rebels have caught up with the slave-keepers,' Magnus said, risking a quick glance above him. 'That should slow them all.'

Vespasian did not look up as his horse negotiated another sharp twist in the track. 'How many of the rebels are there?'

'I don't know; they seem to stretch all the way back up the hillside.'

Vespasian looked up to the rear of the Numidians, now only a couple of hundred paces ahead and just about to disappear around another bend; the third to last before they reached the desert floor. 'If we can keep going we'll outpace them as soon as we're on level ground.'

The gradient lessened gradually, speed was acquired and very soon they caught up with the Numidians who were in turn held up by the lumbering caravan. Above, a battle raged but what its direction was none could guess as dust rising from pounding feet and the many bodies tumbling over the steep inclines screened most of the action. Some fugitives, former slaves, appeared from within the cloud, pelting down the track and often losing their footing in their haste; but of any leather-kilted slave-keepers there was no sign.

Vespasian moved through the ordered ranks of the Numidians with ease and drew up next to Bolanus at the front of the formation, now pressed up against the rearmost mounts of the merchants' caravan. 'As soon as we're down we'll move through the caravan and push on as fast as possible to catch up with the main body; I want to be sure that they're leaving enough water for us at the dumps.'

Bolanus nodded and pointed over his shoulder with his thumb. 'Do you think that the rebel slaves are going to be happy staying here?'

'I don't think they'll have much choice in the matter. Most won't have anything to return home to even if they knew where that home was and how to get to it. And why risk leaving? They've got a good piece of land here and almost everything they need.'

'But who will do the work?' Magnus asked.

'Ah! Thereby will lie the problem. I imagine that the first thing they'll do is put any surviving Garamantes out into the fields but that won't be nearly enough labour.'

'So they'll just go back to the old system, except there'll be different people sitting around doing bugger all but it will still be known as the Kingdom of the Garamantes.'

Vespasian shrugged. 'What do I care? We're out and I've brought most of the Roman citizens with me.'

But Magnus did not respond to this assertion. Vespasian glanced at him and then looked to where he was staring, down at the desert floor in the lee of the cliff now made visible as they rounded the final bend. 'Medusa's unsponged arse!'

Magnus sucked the air through his teeth. 'Did you just say that we were out?'

They looked down to where a unit of two to three hundred horsemen had formed up, four ranks deep, blocking the exit from the descent.

The hunters had come to prevent their leaving.

The caravan halted as the merchants registered the danger, completely blocking the path.

'Move them out of the way, Bolanus!' Vespasian ordered. 'Get your cavalry through; we need to take those bastards head on and hard. They're hunters not soldiers; charge straight into them.'

'They're still armed, though,' Magnus muttered as Bolanus waded into the caravan, shouting and swearing at the merchants to move aside and let his men pass.

'It's pointless moaning about it seeing as, unless we go back up the hill and join in the chaos there, we've got to break through them.' Vespasian looked back to where the battle still raged in the dust and then on up to the pall of smoke that now hung over Garama. 'No choice, I'd say.'

Magnus grunted unwilling agreement as the Numidians began to filter through the caravan. A battle cry, long and fierce, rose from the hunters; the Numidians' horses became skittish as they sensed the threat felt by their riders. Vespasian, Magnus and Hormus followed the tail of the Numidians; they cleared the caravan, passing Decianus in his carriage, and began to pick up speed as they descended the last few hundred paces along the track. At the head of the column, Bolanus rose in his saddle, javelin in fist, shaking it in the air and calling back to his men to follow him; the horn-blower gave a series of shrill blasts on his *lituus*. The Numidians responded with ululating cries; they followed their senior decurion's lead and accelerated their mounts down the track to where the hunters awaited. But the hunters could do no more than wait, as to try to counter-charge would force them into the narrow confines of the track where their superior numbers would be of little account; so they could but watch as the professional soldiers hurtled towards them, gaining advantage from the incline. With nervous looks to one another the hunters hefted their javelins and, on an order from their leader, hurled them forward. But hurling a javelin uphill from a stationary horse is no easy affair and the velocity reached by the sleek missiles was nothing compared to that of the Numidians' as they released their weapons. Down they rained upon the hunters, punching them from their saddles as they sat motionless, waiting for the inevitable rushing inexorably towards them along the narrow track that they thought they had sealed off.

A second storm of piercing hail fell amongst them an instant before contact was made. Slicing into man and beast alike, a swathe was cleared in the hunters' ranks as men went down and horses bucked or bolted in terror or agony. As Bolanus' mount almost shied at contact, the horse facing it, its nerves shattered, turned away, creating a gap into which the Numidians swarmed with little loss of momentum. And as they entered the hunters' static formation so they expanded, left and right, into the chaos created in the wake of the two javelin volleys, ripping their cavalry spathae from their sheaths and bellowing rage at the tops of their voices. Down, across and up they slashed their blades, cleaving a passage through the heart of the enemy's ranks as the hunters tried to wheel their horses away or defend themselves with parries and blocks. But these were men trained in the art of hunting and trapping, not war; these men had not spent day after day hacking at a wooden post, honing muscles and technique as had the Numidians. Through, the professional cavalry swept, in a frenzy of cuts, swipes and thrusts that pierced, dismembered and split open the panicking hunters. Blood exploded from deep rends and freshly carved stumps, spraying and slopping, its metallic tang registering in the senses of those splattered with it and adding to their battle-joy.

Shouting at his lictors to follow him, Vespasian, sword gripped in white-knuckled hand, swerved his mount left so that he did not follow the main bulk of auxiliaries into the hunters but, rather, raced along the fast-disintegrating front rank, slashing at the heads of horse and rider, opening them with arm-jarring cuts, leaving screeching beasts and howling men behind him for Magnus, Hormus and the others following to finish off.

Confusion now was rampant in the hunters' ranks as they attempted to fight off or run from the enemy within their formation and then, at the same time, realising that they were being enveloped. Now what they had considered to be, because of their numbers, a foregone conclusion had become a massacre due to their military ineptitude, and they looked to escape; but to where? From the dust cloud up the hill the rebel slaves were emerging, victorious from their battle with the hated slave-keepers; death certainly lay in that route for the hunters as sure as it did in the opposite direction, the empty miles to the Empire's border with the auxiliaries now reaping their lives, chasing them all the way to Leptis Magna. But frightened men want just to escape the cause of their fear and rather than try to go east or west, along the rough edges of the hill-range where shelter might have been found in caves or gorges, they fled directly away from the blades of their tormentors, out into the desert. And the Numidians followed, hacking at the haunches of the horses or hurling javelins in pursuit, bringing many more down in leg-thrashing agony as they too fled north to escape the rebel slaves swarming down the hill towards the stationary caravan.

Too late did the merchants notice the threat closing on them from above, transfixed as they were by the spectacle of the hunters' defeat still playing out before them. With worried cries they tried to get their mounts and pack-animals up to speed, but they were still in the narrow confines of the track; horse blocked horse and the caravan did no more than lumber forward. Only Decianus, his driver frantically whipping all those around him, managed to get his four-mule carriage going as he had been positioned at the front of the caravan; on he went, down the hill as, to cries of despair, the rest of the caravan was enveloped by escaped slaves with an unsated love of vengeance. The merchants disappeared in a frenzy of hate and with them went the provisions that Vespasian had relied on for the journey.

Cursing at the loss, Vespasian slashed his sword at the neck of a fleeing hunter, almost severing the head; he urged his mount on, through the disintegrating enemy formation, out into the desert, away from the chaos of Garama. All around him the Numidians were dealing out bloody massacre as they surged through the hunters whose cries to their gods rose to the heavens, unacknowledged by the deities who this day had abandoned their people to a hideous fate in a kingdom turned upside down.

'Vespasian! Vespasian! Don't leave me!' The voice was desperate and insistent.

Vespasian turned in the saddle to see Decianus a hundred paces behind, his mules struggling to pull the carriage over rough ground, no matter how much the driver whipped them. But, despite the payment for his passage being still outstanding, Vespasian was not about to go to the ex-procurator's aid even though the rebel slaves had overwhelmed the caravan and were now swarming out onto the desert floor. As Vespasian turned away, Decianus punched a dagger into his driver's ribs, threw him from the vehicle and took up the reins himself. The carriage, lighter now, became less of a burden to the unfortunate beasts hauling it and they sped up, sweat frothing from them, enough to outpace the rebel slaves behind.

'That's a shame,' Magnus observed, kicking his horse on after Vespasian. 'I'd have enjoyed watching Decianus make the acquaintance of the objects of his system.'

Vespasian squinted against the copious amounts of dust kicked up by the cavalry ahead of him. 'And I'm sure they would have been equally as thrilled, but that's not to be.' Hiding his relief at the ex-procurator's survival thus far, he gave another glance over his shoulder; with no chance of catching any more victims to tear apart, the rebel slaves halted, unwilling to venture further into the desert now that they had a kingdom of their own.

The surviving hunters turned left and right, realising, finally, that their best chance of survival was not to run, like frightened rabbits, straight before the pursuer, but rather to try to avoid him. Thus did the Numidians lose contact with them as they steered their course north, towards the first of the water dumps that Vespasian prayed still contained amphorae filled with that precious liquid.

But it was not water that caused Vespasian and the Numidians to halt just an hour later as the sun began to burn in earnest; it was blood. Above the heat haze, vultures circled, descending in languid spirals as more flew in, drawn by the scent of death, from their high places in rocky outcrops.

'I think I can guess what's attracting them,' Vespasian muttered, squinting as shapes began to materialise out of the shimmer that veiled the distance.

'The question is: how many?' Magnus said as the first shape resolved into a slumped body.

And there were many: at least a couple of hundred, Vespasian reckoned, lying dead on stony ground; a banquet of carrion.

'Most of them seem to have been struck down from behind,' Bolanus observed as, leading their horses, they passed the first dozen or so corpses.

Hormus placed a toe underneath a young boy's shoulder and heaved him onto his back; sightless eyes gazed up at the scavenging birds that would soon feast on them. 'The citizens who left last night?'

Vespasian shrugged. 'Who else could it be?' He looked around in all directions; it was as if the column had scattered. 'But not all of them were killed; only about a half, I'd say; there can't be more than two hundred or so bodies.'

'Well, it'll help with the water issue,' Magnus pointed out as they moved on through the sea of corpses.

'That's one way of looking at it, I suppose; but it hasn't helped with the problem of supplies: they've all had their provision bags taken. The real question is who did this?'

'The hunters?'

'They could have but, as we've seen, they're not the best of fighters.'

'But all they had to do was run down unarmed people on foot.'

'Unarmed people who were protected by two turmae of Bolanus' cavalry. Look at the bodies and what do you notice?'

It was Hormus who noticed it first. 'There are only freed slaves, master.' He pointed over Vespasian's shoulder. 'And a couple of Numidians.'

'Exactly. Where are the bodies of the hunters, because some of them must have died and I don't imagine that the survivors took their dead comrades back with them? And, besides, these people left last night; this is about three hours from their starting point. This happened in the dark; if it was the hunters, then why did they wait until they were out in the open desert, where people can run off into the night, as many evidently did, before attacking? Surely it would have been better to have taken them where they tried to take us just now? No, I don't think that it was the hunters.'

'Then who was it?' Bolanus asked, although his look and tone betrayed the fact that he suspected he knew the answer.

'I think what you suspect may well be true, Bolanus, as there are a couple of your men lying out here.'

'But they had two decurions with them; Roman citizens. Trustworthy men. They wouldn't massacre their own.'

Vespasian spread his hands. 'Then you explain what happened, because I can't.'

Magnus heaved himself back onto his horse, groaning with the effort. 'Well, whatever happened, standing around in this heat, chatting about it ain't going to help matters. We better get going because if the Numidian auxiliaries ain't behaving themselves then I'd say that the chances of them leaving enough water for us at the first dump are negligible and we're not carrying enough to get us all to the second dump. We'd better get after them and show them exactly how we feel about that.'

Vespasian could but agree. 'And we can only do that by keeping going day and night.' He remounted, looking about with a growing sense of unease, his eyes eventually falling on Decianus, still driving his carriage, and realised that pearls were of no use to a man dying of thirst in the desert. 'I shouldn't have waited for Decianus to get the citizens from the city.'

It was Magnus' turn to agree. 'In that they're all dead now anyway? Of course you shouldn't have, and besides it would have given you the chance of leaving without that slippery shit; because I can guarantee you that it'll be a lot worse than any thanks that you get for saving his miserable hide, if you take my meaning?'

Looking at the ex-procurator who had just happily murdered his driver to save his own life, Vespasian muttered: 'I do, Magnus, I do; perhaps we should try and lose him along the way.'

'Not before he's paid you what he promised, though; and I hope it's a decent amount.'

Vespasian tried but failed to conceal his surprise.

'It was obvious: why else would you have let him come along?'

The way back was far more arduous than the outward journey; even though it was the exact same route and completely flat. It was the haste that they needed to maintain in order to run down the very real threat to all their lives travelling ahead of them. On the outward journey they had been able to travel at a leisurely pace and so conserve water but this time they drove their mounts hard and were forced to give the best part of the water they carried to the animals. It was with parched throats that they welcomed the setting of the sun.

'We keep the north star directly ahead of us,' Bolanus explained as the swift desert dusk matured into night. 'That's how the caravans do it. There'll be an almost full moon rising later so we should be able to keep up a good speed. With luck we'll reach the first dump soon after dawn.'

'If it's still there,' Magnus said, his tone more than stating his pessimism in the matter.

'If it's not still there,' Vespasian said, trying to hide his irritation at his friend's gloom, 'then we'll just have to make it to the next one.'

'If that's still there.'

'Magnus!'

Magnus made a bold attempt to look contrite. 'Yes, I'm sorry, sir; not good for morale and that sort of thing. I'll spend the rest of the night-march praying to all the gods that the dump is still there; if they're still there, that is.'

But either Magnus' prayers were ignored by the gods or they really were not still there; either way it was a depressing sight that greeted them at the second hour of the day as they arrived at the first dump. It was not just the hundreds of amphorae that had been filled with water but were now in shards, nor the bodies, strewn around the dump, that caused the most anxiety; it was the two headless corpses that had evidently been executed rather than killed in a melee.

'They were good men,' Bolanus said as he looked at the severed heads of his two former decurions.

Vespasian shook his head, puzzled. 'Why did they wait until they got here to kill them? Their men must have overpowered them back at the original massacre; why not murder them there?'

'I don't know; but what I do know is that I'll castrate whoever was responsible.' Bolanus turned to his men who were muttering to one another about the grim sight. 'Get them buried and do it decently.'

As the graves were being dug with swords, Vespasian knelt amongst the broken earthenware; he scooped up a handful of sand, rubbing it through his fingers. Frowning, he looked up at Magnus. 'It's moist.'

Magnus spat. 'The bastards! They destroyed what they couldn't take.'

'It looks that way.'

'Why would they do that?'

'To ensure that they get back, whatever happens, and that no one can come after them with nasty tales of murdering Roman citizens, I assume.'

'But there was no need to kill anyone; we had enough water to get back.'

The strain on Vespasian's countenance became even greater. 'It would have been very tight; some wouldn't have made it.'

'Governor!'

The shout made Vespasian turn, looking east. From behind an outcrop of rock two figures emerged.

'Governor, it's me, Marcus Urbicus, optio in the Third Augusta.'

'Urbicus,' Vespasian muttered to himself, recalling the slave that he had met on one of the farm complexes.

'We were waiting for you, Governor,' Urbicus said as the two men neared. 'Although we didn't think that you would be this close behind.'

'What happened here, Urbicus?'

'It was that fucking slave-keeper.'

'Nepos?'

Urbicus tried to spit but his mouth was dry. 'Yes, that bastard.'

'How did it start?'

'Well, as we were going down the hill, me and my mates – I found four of the lads that I'd been sold into slavery with up at Garama.' He pointed to his companion, not yet out of his teens but hard and muscular with expressionless dark eyes; the eyes of one who has endured. 'This is Lupus.'

Vespasian nodded at the man, thinking him well named.

'Anyway,' Urbicus continued, 'me and my mates were at the front of the column seeing as we were amongst the fittest, so that we were right behind the escort cavalry, and we saw Nepos walking next to them, talking to them all in turn. Well, I didn't think much of it and I didn't hold it against him that he had been a slave-keeper, I mean, who wouldn't if they were given the chance? Any of us certainly would; better to inflict suffering on others than to have it inflicted on yourself, I think you'd agree?'

Vespasian could not fault the argument, especially when the suffering inflicted in the Kingdom of the Garamantes was so severe. 'Quite.'

'Anyhow, Nepos stayed with them all the way down to the desert floor and then on as we followed the north star. And then suddenly they weren't there any more.'

'Who wasn't there?'

'The Numidian cavalry; they just rode off. All of them, except their two decurions who seemed as puzzled as us and could do nothing to stop them. Nepos was still there but he said he didn't know what they were doing. Well, it didn't take long before we found out where they had gone as from the end of the column came shrieks; we were under attack. I thought it was the hunters at first but then it became apparent that it was our own escort.'

'Why?'

'I reckon it was to make sure that they had enough water. Me and my mates managed to pull a couple of them from their horses and showed them what we thought of their treachery, but it was useless and so we scarpered into the night like everyone else that had the energy.'

'What about the decurions?' Bolanus asked.

'They must have realised that hanging around was suicide as, after such an act of mutiny, their men would never allow them to live, so they fucked off north as fast as their horses could carry them; well, it wasn't fast enough, was it? Anyway, once they had massacred as many of us as they could they rode after the decurions.' He nodded to where the bodies were being buried. 'And they caught them here.'

Vespasian frowned, shaking his head in confusion. 'It doesn't make sense. Why go to the trouble of killing all those people when they could just as easily have killed their two decurions and then ridden off into the night?'

'Ah, well, that became clear the following day. The survivors all decided that the only thing to do was press on north as no one wanted to go back to Garama, naturally. We got here a couple of hours before dawn this morning and there they were, the Numidians now being led by Nepos on one of the horses of the men we'd killed. They had the two decurions kneeling on the ground. Nepos came forward and said that now the weak had been weeded out and there were not too many of us so that we would have plenty of water each, we could come with them – on one condition.'

'Which was?'

'Which was that we each had to carry three amphorae of water, one for ourselves, one for the Numidians and one for their horses, and anyone who didn't would suffer the same fate as the decurions. With that he indicated the men guarding the prisoners and with two flashes of a blade both their heads were in the sand. Well, most people agreed to this slavery, but me and my mates plus a few others were buggered if we were going to carry water for those fuzzy-haired bastards who had just killed their citizen officers so we had a bit of a scrap, which, obviously, we lost and a couple of the lads got theirs. Me and Lupus here managed to run off into the night and decided that the best thing to do would be to wait here for you in order to fill you in on what happened.'

'You were right to do so, Urbicus. Tell me, how long ago did they leave?'

'Pretty much straight away; a couple of hours before dawn.'

'Did they now? That means they can't be more than five hours ahead of us and they'll be travelling at the speed of their weighed-down new slaves. We're all mounted, we can catch them in half a day; well before they reach the second dump.'

Urbicus' face betrayed concern. 'Are you going to leave me and Lupus here, Governor, because we ain't got horses?'

Vespasian smiled and looked over at Decianus, sweating in his carriage. 'No, you haven't; but I can get you a mule each.'

CHAPTER V

VESPASIAN'S MOUTH HAD long since ceased to be moist; his nostrils, eyes and ears all felt as if they contained a substantial portion of the desert despite the cloth tied over his face and the wide-brimmed hat pulled low over his head. The misery of real thirst assailed him and the threat of a dehydrated death in the broiling sun was growing with every mile they proceeded without catching sight of the dust cloud that would surely be raised by their quarry. Beneath him he could feel his mount weakening; indeed, all the horses and mules were beginning to show signs of distress and their pace had lessened considerably in the past hour. Even Magnus, riding next to him, had lost the will to moan; he slouched in his saddle with his eyes closed, enduring the heat and thirst in uncharacteristic silence.

Discarded amphorae, lying broken on the sand, attested to the fact that they were on the right trail but also emphasised that the Numidian mutineers had a far better supply of water and would therefore be able to keep going for longer and at a faster pace.

With the skins hanging across the rumps of each horse now almost empty, Vespasian had ordered that water should be given only to the horses and mules for, whilst they lived so did the humans hold out some hope of survival. All had seen the wisdom of this move except Decianus, whose ability to put up with extreme discomfort was being sorely tested, quite literally, by having to ride astride a mule, with nothing but a cloth bag that he had rescued from his carriage slung across the beast to cushion his behind. It had been the one consolation to Vespasian in his present condition that his requisition of two of the ex-procurator's mules for Urbicus and Lupus and then a third one to lighten the loads of the other beasts, thereby necessitating the abandonment of the carriage, had caused Decianus so much obvious distress and outrage; almost as much as Vespasian insisting that he hand over the agreed price of his passage immediately, unless he would rather his remaining mule were not a part of the water distribution. But those small victories were starting to seem insignificant compared to the very real danger that was growing with every step forward. They were well past the point of no return, even if they had wished to go back to the Kingdom of the Garamantes, now well into the distance due south of them, swathed in wisps of smoke and a place now, no doubt, of unspeakable horror. There was no alternative other than to catch up with Nepos and his mutinous Numidians or die and become food for the carrion birds that followed them in hope.

'Governor!'

Bolanus' shout brought Vespasian out of his morbid reverie; he raised his head. 'What is it, decurion?'

Bolanus pointed to a collection of rocks about half a mile distant. 'Straight ahead.' He signalled for the column to halt.

Vespasian squinted, his eyes burning in the glare. There were shapes in the shimmer that cloaked the horizon and some of them could not be rocks as there were signs of movement. And yet there was no dust cloud above them. Straining hard to make out the detail he gradually made sense of what he saw. 'They've stopped; they must be resting. Those are awnings flapping that we can see; your men must have rigged their cloaks up against the sun.'

'They're not my men any more. Nor will they be men for much longer if I get them in my grasp.'

'I think that you may have that opportunity. They must have gambled that we would stop and try to keep out of the sun to preserve our water. That was very foolish.'

'They've got no officers leading them to make decent decisions.'

'We'll approach slowly; with luck the Numidians are asleep and the slaves will realise that we're here to help them, not kill them, and refrain from raising the alarm.'

Bolanus evidently did not share Vespasian's optimism; indeed, Vespasian himself did not believe for one moment that they would be able to get much closer without their presence being noticed and the mutinous cavalry fleeing north to get ever closer to the second water dump. But that did not concern him so much as there was a bigger prize at stake now and, as the camp sprang to life when their approach was finally noted, Vespasian did not feel the same disappointment as Bolanus' series of curses suggested he did. He kicked his exhausted mount onwards as Nepos and his mutineers hurriedly jumped into their saddles and galloped away.

'Stay where you are!' Vespasian shouted at the confused and frightened citizen-slaves who knew not whether they had cause to attempt to defend themselves. 'We won't harm you.' He reined in his mount as he entered the encampment and to his great relief he saw what he had hoped he would: amphorae, scores of them. He finally believed that they had a chance, albeit a small one, of making it back to the province of Africa alive.

And then there would be an accounting.

'We will not leave you behind!' The words rasped in Vespasian's dry throat as he repeated them for at least the fourth time. 'But if we don't go now and take enough water to ensure that we can overhaul the mutineers before they get to the next water dump and destroy it then whether we're leaving you behind or not will be irrelevant. Once we've secured the dump we'll wait for you there.'

'Yes, but how can we trust you?' Again, it was the same man asking the question, shouting above the hubbub; clutching two amphorae to his leathery-skinned torso, with a rotten-toothed leer and desperation in his eyes, he showed absolutely no concern for anyone but himself.

'Because, as I have said, I was the one that had you freed. Why would I do that only to leave you to die on the way home?'

'To make quite sure that you get home.'

Vespasian took a deep breath. 'That may be how you would think in my situation but I promise you that I have a vested interest in getting as many of you back to Africa as possible. In order to do that I need you to give my men some of your water, otherwise I will have them seize it; you can keep one amphora each for the journey.'

The crowd of citizens, over two hundred of them, were surrounding Vespasian's horse and, already vocal, began arguing amongst themselves; his patience finally snapped. 'Bolanus! Do what you have to; we can't lose any more time in this futile debate.' Drawing his sword he drove his horse through the crowd, forcing a passage, slapping some with the flat of his blade and kicking others to the ground.

Fists flew and tempers rose as Bolanus' men waded into the mass, snatching and pulling at the earthenware jars that had now become the price of all their lives. Men and women, wretched from servitude and desert travel, struggled to resist the Numidians, whose strength far out-measured theirs and whose sympathy to their plight – if there ever had been any – had now disappeared, having witnessed their foolish intransigence.

'Try not to hurt them,' Vespasian shouted, more for his own conscience than in a serious effort to stop any violence that was now unavoidable. A goodly number had decided to be sensible and voluntarily brought their spare water over to where the lictors stood guard over the stockpile; but at least three-quarters of the crowd could not bring themselves to trust once again, having lived for so long without that ability. Vespasian watched, impotent, cursing under his breath, as the first wound was carved and the first amphora shattered; blood and water soaked into the parched ground, the former liquid now being far less precious than the latter.

'They don't realise that the water is more important than their lives, master,' Hormus said, walking up beside him. 'It's not your fault.'

'I know; but the fewer I bring back the more it will look like I've failed and therefore the bigger target I make myself for Poppaea's spite.'

'As long as you bring some back.'

Vespasian thought for a moment, his expression hardened. 'To guarantee that, I'm going to have to demonstrate who's in charge. Go around to the far side of the crowd.'

Hormus obeyed as two more men went down, screaming, their amphorae dropped so that they could hold in the grey-blue cords of intestines bulging from vicious gashes in their bellies. This was enough for the others to realise that if it was a choice between life with one container of water or death, the first was the better option, and the disturbance dwindled into bad-natured muttering and the groans of the seriously wounded. With barely concealed ill-grace water was handed over and the stockpile grew until it was a surly-looking mob that faced Vespasian, each clutching a single amphora.

'Have your men and the lictors recharge their skins quickly, Bolanus,' Vespasian ordered. 'And they should drink their fill and water the horses as fast as possible; we've wasted enough time already.' He turned to the citizens. 'If that confrontation has meant that we don't manage to catch the mutineers in time, we'll have no option but to carry on after them to prevent them fouling the well that will be our next water stop on the way back.'

'And what about us?' It was the same man asking the question, his manner no less aggressive.

'Come here!' Vespasian dismounted, his sword still in his hand, and strode towards the agitator. The crowd parted for him, not wishing to be on the receiving end of any more violence.

Sensing his support fast disappearing, the man edged back further into the crowd; Vespasian followed, his passage unimpeded. With a yelp, the man turned and ran, bursting from the rear of the crowd, straight into the fist of Hormus. Back his head jerked and up his arms flew, flinging his amphora into the air for Hormus to catch as he crashed to the ground.

Vespasian pulled him up by his hair, blood pouring from a split and swelling lip, and dragged him back to his knees. 'Hold his arms behind him, Hormus.'

Hormus placed the amphora on the ground and pulled the semi-conscious man's arms behind him; his head lolled forward.

'This man has caused us to lose precious time and has threat-ened the chances of survival for the whole group. I will not tolerate it; if we are to survive, you will all do as I say without any argument. There will be no dissent; do you understand?'

Vespasian waited; there were a few mutters, some of which could be mistaken for agreement but most just sounded resentful to his ears.

It was the work of a moment; the flash of a sword; the hiss of the blade; the brief, surprised cry of the victim; the wet thud of contact; and the gasp of the crowd as the head hit the ground and rolled, coming to a stop next to the amphora. All eyes were on the blood spurting from the carved-open neck and forming a spume-covered puddle on barren ground.

'I will execute anyone, man or woman, who questions me again; and as the Governor of Africa, I have the legal power to do so.' He pointed to his lictors, who represented that power, as he searched the eyes of the crowd. 'Do I make myself clear?'

This time there was a far more positive answer to his question as Hormus let go of the arms and the corpse slumped down.

'Good.' Vespasian wiped his sword on the dead man's loin-cloth and walked back through the crowd, looking around and defying anyone to meet his eye; none did. 'Just follow our tracks and you will all be all right.'

'What about me?'

Vespasian rounded on the questioner to come face-to-face with Decianus. 'What do you mean: what about you?'

Decianus seemed almost apologetic. 'Well, what about me? Who do I go with? Surely I must come with you?'

'You can if you want but we'll have left you behind before we've gone a mile.'

'Then I'll commandeer one of the Numidians' or lictors' horses and they can have my mule; that'll be much more satisfactory all round.'

'You can try, Decianus, but I wouldn't give much for your chances of survival. In fact, give it a go; I'll enjoy watching.'

Decianus glanced over to the Numidians and lictors who were busy watering their horses, and then back to his forlorn-looking mule and then spared Vespasian a look of deep loathing.

Vespasian smiled in genuine amusement and walked away.

*

It was an hour before any evidence of the mutineers was seen; an hour of scorching sun in which they had covered a fair distance refreshed, both man and beast having drunk deeply.

The horse was lying on the track, its eyes closed, its chest heaving irregularly; of its rider, much to Bolanus' disappointment, there was no sign.

'They're weakening,' Vespasian said, looking down at the dying animal. 'How much further to the dump, decurion?'

Bolanus looked ahead, shading his eyes. 'There.' He pointed slightly east of north to the jagged outline of a hill on the horizon. 'It's about level with that; so, twenty miles or so. Three hours if the horses hold out.'

Vespasian gauged the height of the sun. 'It should start getting cooler soon; we have to press on as fast as we can. If anyone's horse drops out then so be it; they can follow on foot with the others.'

The second horse they came across was already dead.

Next to the carcass, two Numidian troopers knelt, their arms outstretched in supplication, beseeching Bolanus in a mixture of their own language and bad Latin. He dismounted and walked towards them, drawing his sword; he ordered his men to water their horses but indicated to two of them to follow him.

'Tell me why I should spare treacherous lives?' Bolanus placed the tip of his sword under the chin of one of the mutineers and forced his head up as his men took positions behind them both to prevent an escape. 'What's your name, trooper?'

'Mezian, sir.' He looked with wide-eyed terror at the blade.

'Look at me, Mezian, not my sword. Why did you allow yourselves to be talked into mutiny?'

Mezian swallowed before letting fly a stream of his own language. Although completely unintelligible to Vespasian it was obvious from the tone that it was everybody else's fault other than Mezian's and, judging from the outraged looks of his comrade and his cries of protest, it was his fault in particular.

Bolanus looked at the other man. 'Is it true that you persuaded them to mutiny, Lahcen?'

'No, sir,' Lahcen replied in heavily accented Latin. 'Nepos, he say not enough water for many hundreds of people. He speak our language after time in Garama. We better off going now with few people. Better we live than all die. We all say yes; all of us. Mezian lie, he no honour as I share my horse when his fall.'

Mezian shrieked his denial.

Bolanus withdrew his sword from Mezian's throat and, with a snake-quick lunge, skewered his comrade's chest; Lahcen stared at the blade for a few moments in surprise, spewed a gobbet of blood onto it and then collapsed back, dead on the sand.

Mezian fell forward, grabbed Bolanus' ankle and kissed his foot.

Bolanus looked down at the cringing form in disgust. 'How long have you been here?'

Mezian answered in his own tongue.

'Hold him flat on his back,' Bolanus ordered the two dismounted troopers.

Mezian screamed and squirmed as his erstwhile comrades grappled with his legs and wrists, twisting him over.

'Lahcen was here because he tried to help you,' Bolanus said, once Mezian had been restrained, 'and you repaid him by putting the blame for your actions onto his shoulders. His reward for his honesty was a quick death.' Again, snake-quick, his sword flashed but this time it did not pierce, this time it came to rest between Mezian's legs. 'Your double treachery gets you the opposite.'

The Numidian howled like a harpy as with a couple of flicks of the wrist Bolanus cut through the loincloth and sliced away the genitals.

'You'll have time to contemplate your lack of gratitude as you bleed out, Mezian.' Leaving the castrated man screaming on the ground, writhing and clutching his wound, Bolanus leapt back into the saddle and grinned at Vespasian. 'That feels much better; hopefully the vultures will begin their banquet whilst the arsehole is still alive.'

Vespasian looked down at Mezian. 'What did he say?'

'Oh, no more than the sun moving the breadth of two fingers in the sky, less than half an hour. If there wasn't a heat haze we'd be able to see their dust by now, I would guess; but it will be tight beating them to the dump.'

'We'd better get going then.'

And it was tight; very tight. Despite knowing that they had almost caught up with their quarry and were therefore able to exert their horses more than perhaps was prudent, the marker-hill was very close by the time the mutineers could be discerned through the shimmer.

'They're not mounted!' Vespasian shouted over to Bolanus. 'They must be at the dump.'

The realisation that, even now, the stock might be in the process of being destroyed made Vespasian urge his flagging horse on as fast as it could go for the final few hundred paces. The Numidians surged after him, ululating cries rising from them along with the dust they kicked up. On Vespasian galloped as the mutineers became aware that they had been caught and began scrambling for their horses. But the urgency in the hearts of the Numidians seemingly transferred itself into the equine minds of their mounts, for they too appeared to realise that life depended on this final charge; they swelled their great chests and forced their aching muscles to work through the pain as they vied with one another to be the swiftest. No sweat did they secrete for their fluids were low, but their speed they maintained and even increased and, as they thundered past the water dump, Vespasian could see that it had been dug up and had a brief glimpse of fractured earthenware, wet and steaming.

'I want Nepos alive!' he shouted, wrenching his sword from its scabbard and praying to his guardian god, Mars, that his horse would hold out for the final few hundred paces. And Mars heard the prayer, for within a hundred beats of the beast's great heart Vespasian's blade sliced into the skull of the rearmost mutineer, whipping off the crown to spin high in the air, flecking gore, as the rider carried on, open-headed, for a few moments before collapsing and falling from his racing horse in a flurry of spilt brains. And Bolanus with his Numidians swarmed through their former comrades' small formation, hacking at them from behind and bringing them down one by one. Vespasian pulled up his exhausted horse to let other, younger men do the killing and it did not take them long to dispose of fifty or so lives. To the shrieks of the dying and the pounding of hoofs, they dealt death to the men who would have consigned them to becoming dried husks on the desert floor with no hope of a burial, no dignified transfer to the afterlife; a real death, an ultimate death. And it was with the rage of men who had been threatened with such a death by former comrades, traitors to their brotherhood, that the Numidians slew and Vespasian watched with joy in his heart and relief in his belly.

But that sense of relief soon disappeared as he recalled the state of the water dump as he had flashed past it; he turned his horse and walked the weary beast back to where Magnus, Hormus and the lictors were standing next to a pit dug in the sand.

'It ain't looking too bad,' Magnus said, wiping dust from his face with the back of his hand. 'But it's not brilliant either; the bastards did some damage all right.'

Vespasian dismounted and walked to the edge of the pit; planks were discarded to either side having originally provided a roof for the dump that had been covered by just a thin layer of sand. Within were scores of amphorae, some whole and some shattered; precious water soaked into the sand into which the sharp ends of the amphorae were buried to keep them upright.

Vespasian counted them: twenty-five across and twenty up. 'I'd say that of the five hundred there must be about three hundred left.'

'Three hundred; then it's just as well that the mutineers and the rebel slaves did some thinning out of our numbers, I should say. Five hundred wouldn't have been enough for all of us and the caravan. Perhaps Nepos had a point.'

Vespasian slumped down on the ground suddenly feeling the exhaustion. 'I'm getting too old for this.'

'*You're* getting too old; what about me? It's got to the stage where every day I have to make a choice between fighting or fucking because I can't do both.' Magnus joined him sitting on the ground, looking at the depleted dump and shaking his head. 'Will it be enough?'

'It will have to be. Let's see what we can save.'

'No, sir,' Magnus said, breaking into a grim smile. 'I think there's a higher priority.'

'What's that?'

'I think you might like first to ask Nepos some searching questions, if you take my meaning?'

Vespasian turned to where a couple of Bolanus' men were leading Nepos, bloodied and bruised having fallen from his horse, back for justice. 'I do, Magnus, I do; but what would I learn that I don't already know?'

'What!' The answer to that question took Vespasian by surprise. 'I don't believe you.'

Nepos, on his knees, stared up at Vespasian with unyielding eyes. 'Count the bodies then and you'll see that I'm telling the truth.'

Vespasian turned to Bolanus. 'Have your men counted the dead?'

The decurion nodded. 'We did as we stripped them of all their food; fifty-four. With the two we've already caught that means there are four missing.'

Nepos' smile was mirthless. 'Do you think I'd have been so foolish as not to give myself some insurance? Four troopers, with a good supply of water, went straight onto the well with orders to foul it if they don't see me and their comrades approaching. I told them I would come in daylight so there can be no mistaking me; they'll take any attempt to approach the well by night as hostile and foul it immediately. So you see, you do need me alive.'

'What have they got to foul it with?'

'A couple of sacks of decomposing body parts; not very nice to transport, I grant you, but even nastier in a fresh-water well.'

'We'll catch them before they get there; they can't be more than a couple of hours ahead.'

'Look at the state of your horses, they're exhausted; you won't be able to leave for at least a few hours, by which time my men will be well away.'

'Their horses are just as exhausted as ours; they'll have to rest up too.'

'Can you afford to take that gamble? They haven't just fought a skirmish in the heat. You need me, Vespasian; face it.'

Vespasian cursed, knowing that the treacherous slave-keeper was right; he sheathed his sword. 'Very well; you live. But I only need you as far as the well; once we're there your usefulness will be over.'

'We'll see, Governor,' Nepos said, heaving himself to his feet. 'We shall see.'

Vespasian wanted to dismiss that remark as mere bluster but Nepos was cannier than he had given him credit for. 'Get this bastard one of the dead troopers' horses, Bolanus; and have four of your lads around him all the time. We're going onto the well with fifty-four men in total; the others can stay here and rest whilst they wait for the citizens. Have six more of the captured horses loaded with reserve water. Feed and water the men and horses who are coming with us first; we'll move out soon after dark. What time does the moon rise?'

'The third hour of the night, sir.'

'We'll leave then; we can all get a couple of hours' sleep.'

Two hours was not nearly enough and Vespasian felt even more tired when he was woken than he had done as his head hit the pillow of his rolled-up cloak; but he was well aware that the lack of sleep that they all suffered from now was a small price to pay to stand a chance of avoiding a parched death in the very near future.

And so it was with dour determination, and a couple of open-palmed slaps on his cheeks to ward off the tiredness, that he led the reduced column north, as fast as they could travel by the light of the newly risen half-moon.

'I'm starting to get the impression that this is becoming even more complicated than it was originally meant to be,' Magnus observed, riding next to him.

Vespasian massaged his temples with the thumb and ring-finger of one hand. 'Yes, and I think I've worked out how Nepos plans to make it even more so.'

'What do you mean?'

'Well, he seems to think that I will have another reason not to kill him when we get to the well.'

'He might just be planning on making a run for it.'

'Where to? There's nowhere to hide and he wouldn't be able to outrun us, and besides, he hasn't got any water himself, I made sure of that; he has to rely on the water carried by the six pack-horses.'

'Perhaps he's planning on stealing one of them.'

'No, he didn't know we were going to be taking pack-horses with us when he implied that I wouldn't kill him at the well. No, he had this planned out already and it's all about what he told his men to do. He said that they would poison the well if they didn't see him and their comrades approaching; in other words if they saw *us* approaching.'

'Yes, and?'

'And then what would they do? Wait for us to come and kill them?'

'No, obviously they would ride north as fast as they could and hope to get to the next dump before we catch them.'

'Exactly.'

'So?'

'So what would their orders be if they did see Nepos and their comrades arriving?'

Magnus thought for a few moments. 'Ah!'

'Ah, indeed. They'd do the same: keep one stage ahead just in case we were right on Nepos' tail or we had already got him; as we have now. And Nepos is not going to signal to them to poison the well because he needs it fresh just as much as we do.'

'That could go on all the way to Leptis Magna.'

Vespasian glanced back down the column to where Nepos was riding surrounded by his four guards. 'Which gives Nepos reason to believe that I won't kill him for quite some while.'

'And the closer we are to Leptis Magna the more chance he has of making a break for it and being able to make it to some sort of habitation.'

'Exactly. So we've got to put an end to his clever little scheme as we reach the well.'

'And how do you plan to do that?'

'As I said, he didn't count on us taking pack-horses.'

For the remainder of the night and the first few, cooler hours of the following morning they rode north as fast as they dared, hoping that their fresher horses would gain on those of the four surviving mutineers who not only had had little or no rest but also had to bear the weight of their own water.

It was with this in mind that Vespasian ordered the water on the pack-horses to be consumed first when they halted for a rest during the burning hours of the day. By the time they struck camp, in the cooling afternoon of the second day, the pack-horses did not live up to their name as they had nothing at all loaded on them other than their saddles.

'No, Bolanus,' Vespasian said when questioned upon the subject by the decurion, 'we leave them as they are.'

'But they could take a lot of the weight off the other horses and keep them from tiring quite so quickly.'

'Marginally; whereas those six stay much fresher and they'll be more use to us like that, believe me. Just make sure they have their saddles on securely and there is a full holster of javelins on each one.'

The decurion shrugged but did not pursue the matter any further.

Vespasian retreated into his own thoughts for the next couple of hours until the sky glowed red in the west as the sun slipped behind distant mountains and a warm breeze sprung up out of nothing.

'How much further to the well, would you say, Bolanus?' Vespasian asked, pulling up the cloth that covered his mouth and nose.

'We should be there by morning.'

'Then we need to slow down.'

'But the mutineers are ahead.'

'And we won't catch them before they reach the well; in fact, it wouldn't surprise me if they're already there. What we cannot afford to do is to arrive there at night, otherwise they'll foul it.

They have to be able to see Nepos in daylight so we'll go slower, conserve the horses' energy; we'll stop for the last three or so hours of the night and then press on at dawn.'

And so it was, as the east took its turn to burn golden with the rays of a new sun, that Vespasian found himself staring ahead with Bolanus, straining his eyes and just making out the small group of men and horses in the far distance that was as yet unobscured by the heat rising from baking ground. 'Have Nepos and his guards lead the column, Bolanus,' Vespasian ordered. 'We'll approach slowly; we don't want to startle them into thinking that we've got people in close pursuit.'

'Better to be going at some speed, surely?' Magnus said as Bolanus issued the orders and Nepos was brought up by his guards.

Vespasian shook his head. 'If they're going to do what I think they will then it's just possible that they'll be a little slower if they see we're in absolutely no rush. They think we're their comrades, after all.'

'Fair enough.'

'You stay with the column and deal with Nepos.'

'Where are you going?'

'To get a nice fresh pack-horse. Bolanus, I need you and four of your best men.'

Keeping back from Nepos, Vespasian, Bolanus and their men edged out to the side of the column. Ahead, one of the mutineers had mounted his horse and was coming forward whilst the other three remained by the well. At a mile distant the scout stopped and raised both his hands in the air. Nepos raised both of his in reply and the scout turned and cantered back to his colleagues.

'Ready,' Vespasian said, more to himself than his companions. He watched the scout approach the well and caught the faint sound of a shout. The three other mutineers mounted their horses and, as the scout passed them, joined him heading north at speed. Vespasian turned to Bolanus. 'I knew it; Nepos has organised it so that they are always ahead of us in case he was captured. He thinks we need him to approach every water dump or well.'

He waited a hundred heartbeats for the mutineers to be far enough from the well to be past the point of no return. 'Now!' he cried, pushing his fresh horse into action; the beast almost reared, shocked by the suddenness of the command, but responded to his will nonetheless. Bolanus and his men followed, accelerating away, drawing a look of fearful surprise from Nepos as they passed him and raced after the fleeing mutineers.

The warm desert wind whipped dust into Vespasian's eyes and pulled at his hat, eventually dislodging it so that it flapped behind him, its leather strap about his throat; he leant forward, low, so that his head almost rested on his mount's neck. Sure-footed, the beast thundered across the wasteland, some deep equine sense planting its hoofs on flat ground and avoiding leg-breaking loose rocks or cavities. The pounding of his and the other five horses behind him and the clatter and rattle of the javelins in the holster hanging from his saddle filled Vespasian's head and determination to rid himself of the threat to his life steeled him, driving him on in fleet pursuit of the mutineers, no more than half a mile ahead. Hard he pressed his horse, knowing that he had only one chance to take the fleeing enemy whilst the animal was still fresh and that would not last for long. Another couple of hundred paces and the distance between the two groups had begun to narrow. Vespasian urged his mount to even greater effort and he felt a slight acceleration as if the beast, its ears flat, understood the potential life-and-death urgency of the situation. On it galloped, its great heart booming beneath Vespasian, its mane flying in his face; flecks of foaming saliva issued from its mouth. Ahead, Vespasian was aware that the four mutineers had now started to glance back, intermittently, over their shoulders; their horses' exertions seemingly laboured as the distance covered did not appear to equate to the effort involved.

'They're tiring already!' Vespasian shouted over his shoulder; his companions were right on his tail.

Another two hundred paces and Vespasian felt no fatigue as yet in his horse as they were now visibly gaining with every stretched-muscled stride. The glances back from their prey became more frequent. Vespasian reached behind him and pulled a javelin from its holster. Keeping his body's movement fluid, so that it blended with that of the horse, he fiddled for the leather loop halfway down the shaft and inserted his forefinger in it. A quick look back showed him that Bolanus and his men were now similarly armed. He now concentrated on gauging the distance between them and the mutineers; and down the distance came, even as he felt his mount begin to tire, but the horses ahead were tiring at a greater pace. He could now hear the shouts of the chased; he guessed what was to happen. 'Bolanus! They're going to split up! You go left with two of the lads; I'll take the others to the right.'

As he finished the order the mutineers suddenly diverged as he had predicted; swerving his horse he chased the two who were now heading just east of north. The manoeuvre had caused a slight loss of rhythm and momentum for the mutineers and they were now less than a hundred paces ahead; Vespasian could see the tiredness in the horses' limbs as they tried to regain their former pace. One of the beasts gave out an equine bellow as its right front leg buckled beneath it, fractured on an unstable, loose rock; down it crashed, its chest and then its head ploughing into jagged ground, gouging flesh and clouding dust above, as its rider, leaning back against the horns of his saddle, struggled to get a leg over the animal's neck in order to jump clear. With hide ripping and bones cracking the beast hit a small boulder, snapping its neck into an unnatural angle and bouncing onto its side, throwing its rider clear to sprawl on the ground, his face a grated mess. After signalling to both his men to ignore the casualty and follow him, Vespasian made ready to cast his javelin; gripping the flanks of his mount with his thighs, he pulled his right arm back and mentally measured the distance, sixty, fifty, forty. With a mighty heave of his arm and a flick of the loop with his forefinger he loosed the weapon at thirty paces out; away it soared, its trajectory true, flying through the air to pass just over the rider's shoulder and slam, vibrating, into the parched earth. Two jave-lins from behind fizzed over his head, one falling short of the mark and the second just wide as the mutineer swerved his mount at the last moment. Another missile in hand, Vespasian steadied himself; hurling it forward he watched it fly past the rider and narrowly miss the horse's head, as again it shifted its course, to punch into the ground just before it. With no time to react, the animal rammed into the juddering end of the javelin, taking it full on the chest, crushing bone as the shaft snapped into pieces. Up flew the beast's hind legs, catapulting the rider to send him somersaulting through the air as the horse crashed down vertically, its legs thrashing and its eyes rolling. One look at the mutineer as he pulled his horse up next to him told Vespasian that the man was dead from a broken neck.

He spat at the vacant-eyed face and then slipped from his mount, drawing his sword. The injured horse was shaking, limbs twitching, breathing irregularly, its one visible eye staring at Vespasian, registering terror and pain in equal measure.

'Go and deal with the other rider and get his bag of supplies,' he ordered the two troopers accompanying him.

Kneeling next to the horse's neck, Vespasian put one hand on its muzzle, stroking it, as he placed his blade next to the throat. With a sharp jerk he sliced through flesh and muscle, releasing a gush of blood that seeped into the earth, taking the animal's life with it as two shadows passed gently over the body, cast by circling birds above come to feast on man and beast alike.

Unhooking the bag of supplies from the saddle, Vespasian left the vultures to their meal.

CHAPTER VI

'THERE THEY ARE!'

The cry made Vespasian open his eyes and stir from the somnolent state that had been the norm for the past four days. He focused on the awning rigged above him, flapping gently in the warm breeze, which provided a small amount of protection from the relentless attention of the sun, now three hours old.

'Looks like they made it, sir,' Magnus said, stooping into Vespasian's shelter. 'A good amount of them, too, I'd say, judging by the cloud of dust they're sending up.'

'Good.' Vespasian tried to sound enthusiastic as he raised himself up on his elbows but the lethargy into which he had sunk, whilst waiting at the well for the freed citizens to catch up, precluded any degree of animation. 'I'll give them the remainder of the day to rest and then we'll leave soon after dark.'

'We should be back in time for the last day of the Saturnalia.'

'With luck.' Vespasian yawned, got to his feet and ducked out from under the awning; immediately the sun began pounding his bald pate. 'Bolanus!'

'Yes, Governor,' the decurion said, his hand shading his eyes as he looked south towards the column, small in the distance, emerging from the heat haze.

'Have your men keep order at the well; I don't want any fighting for water.'

'Yes, sir.'

'Oh, and keep them away from Nepos.' Vespasian indicated to where the treacherous slave-keeper had been staked out, naked, in the sun a hundred paces away from the well; the occasional twitch, as one of the half-dozen carrion birds pecking at him managed to rip off a shred of flesh, the only indication that any life still remained in him. 'I don't want anyone finishing him off out of misguided vengeance; he still has a bit more suffering to do.'

Bolanus turned and grinned at Vespasian. 'We can't have him missing out on any of that; especially not after all the trouble we went to ensuring he received justice.'

Vespasian smiled back. 'A very pleasing form of justice it is too.' And it was: Vespasian had particularly enjoyed the first day of the sentence when Nepos had pleaded for, first of all, his life and then, as the thirst set in, a quick death; he had been granted neither. His pleas gradually faded as he weakened and, as he lost the ability to struggle, the birds had become braver; he had lost the first of his eyes the previous day. The second had followed soon after. 'How long before we can expect to see the advance party again?'

Bolanus thought for a moment. 'If they managed to travel swiftly then they should arrive in Leptis Magna tomorrow; so, give them a day to get the supplies, then we should see them in three or four days' time.'

'It'll be tight. Have your men ready to leave at the second hour of the night.'

And so it was for the next four nights the ragged column crept north at the pace of the weakest, walking component. The very weak and the few children that had made it thus far were given places on the backs of the spare horses and the four mules, Decianus having commandeered a horse and Urbicus and Lupus having been given one.

But it was not who had horses and who did not that occupied Vespasian's mind as they moved forward: it was food. The Numidians were, understandably, unwilling to share their meagre supplies with the citizens as they had just enough to see them home with tightened belts. The bags retrieved from the dead had contained a fair amount of twice-baked bread and dried meat, but not nearly sufficient to keep the two hundred and fifty citizens strong enough to complete the journey now that the small amount of food given to each one had been almost entirely consumed and the rest of the provisions lost with the caravan. Steaks had been carved from the dead horses and dried in the sun as they had awaited the arrival of the column but not nearly enough to see them through.

It was therefore with relief that the advance party, which Bolanus had sent off after the capture of the well, was sighted on the evening of the fifth day, just as they readied themselves to march. But that relief soon disappeared as the decurion commanding the turma made his report to Vespasian and Bolanus.

'What do you mean: you've hardly brought anything with you?' Vespasian's face was incredulous.

Bolanus was equally disbelieving. 'You had strict instructions to bring as much food as you could each carry.'

'I know, sir; but we didn't have the money.'

'The money! Of course you didn't have money; you were meant to get ... wait.' Vespasian could suddenly see what had happened. 'The Suphetes refused to issue you with anything, didn't they?'

'Yes, Governor. They said that they wanted cash for any supplies that they gave us seeing as you were still out in the desert and there was no guarantee that you would make it back to Leptis Magna alive to make good your debt.'

Vespasian was finding it hard to contain himself. 'And how are we meant to survive without aid? Did they have anything to say about that?'

'I don't know, Governor. I didn't talk to them personally; it all happened through an intermediary.'

'They refused to see you? My representative. A messenger from the Governor himself.'

'Yes, Governor. I tried to see them for a whole day but they refused and said that I would do better just getting back to Carthage and forgetting that this ever happened. I decided that it was best to report back to you, though, so that you would know the situation.'

'Do they know you came back?'

'No, Governor. I got the feeling that they would try and prevent us from doing so therefore I headed west as if going back to Carthage and then cut back south into the desert once we were well away from Leptis Magna.'

Vespasian nodded, approving of the decurion's actions. 'Have your men water their horses and get something to eat; you're coming back to Leptis Magna with me.' He turned to Bolanus. 'I think it's time to pay the Suphetes a visit; we'll take all the cavalry with us and tell my lictors to be ready to leave within the hour. And find Urbicus and Lupus, they're coming with us too.' He paused for quick reflection. 'And bring Decianus; I'd rather keep him close than run the risk of him slipping away as we get near the coast.'

The south-facing walls of Leptis Magna, just two miles distant, were not formidable for, historically, there was no threat from that direction; the port-city's defences were concentrated on its seaward side, as Vespasian knew from his previous visit. What had changed now, however, was that the walls appeared to be manned.

'It looks like they're expecting someone who they don't particularly want to see,' Magnus said as it became apparent that the south gate was closed even though dawn had broken a couple of hours previously.

Vespasian could not suppress the wry grin of a man who had just had his suspicion confirmed as he peered from within a palm-studded oasis whose water irrigated the surrounding farm-land. 'I imagine it's rather a shock for the Suphetes to see anyone come out of the south as they must have thought they'd signed our death warrants when they refused to hand over any supplies. At least, I assume that was their motive in denying us provisions.'

'But what would make them so keen to ensure that we didn't return?' Bolanus asked. 'After all, they did co-operate with the water dumps eventually.'

'Yes, they did. But not until after I had to threaten them; but even that wouldn't make them fear my return. If anything, you'd have thought that they would want to ingratiate themselves with me so I would forget the incident.' He looked over to Urbicus and Lupus. 'I rather think that the Suphetes must have realised that there was a fair chance of finding one or two of the men of the Third Augusta they had sold into slavery and were trying to avoid having to answer some very tricky questions.'

In the two days they had taken to make the final stage across the desert to the coast, Vespasian had pondered on why the Suphetes had been so short-sighted as to refuse the Governor's request for aid as it seemed to make no sense unless they had been actively trying to prevent his return. It had been this realisation that had made him look for a reason why they should fear his reappearance, and now seeing the walls manned against him and the gate shut he was convinced he had hit upon the cause.

'If I'm correct, there is no way that they'll let us in without us resorting to violence.'

Magnus saw no problem with that. 'Then resort to violence; after all, it's only a civic militia on the walls and they ain't going to stand for long.'

'And we've only got cavalry.'

'Take them off their horses and make them climb the walls once it's dark.'

'Yes, I could do that. But how would it look when I get back to Rome? Or, rather, how could it be made to look?'

Magnus thought for a few moments. 'Ah, I see. You're worried that certain people in Rome might try and present your having to take Leptis Magna with troops as proof that you pushed it into rebellion so soon after it had been made a municipality by Nero.'

'I think Poppaea Sabina could persuade her husband that I'd undone any good that he might have done and that I was an unreliable governor.'

'And that would be the end to any hopes you have of another province in the near future?'

'Exactly.'

'So how are we going to get in without a fight?'

'Well, for once I'm pleased to have Decianus' company.' He turned back to where the former procurator stood, soothing his feet in the cool water of the pool. 'He's the perfect liar and very convincing, I'm sure, under threat of death. He can talk a small party of us through the gates and then we'll get the rest in tonight.'

'We had almost completely run out of food and were very low on water,' Decianus shouted up at the Suphetes' intermediary, standing above the south gate of Leptis Magna. 'Governor Titus Flavius Vespasianus tried to address the citizens whom he had rescued from slavery in the Kingdom of the Garamantes but they turned on him and, alas, he was murdered despite the bravery of his lictors, all of whom also perished along with a lot of the auxiliary cavalry. As you can see, we number a mere dozen out of the two hundred and fifty that set out in November. It then fell to me, Catus Decianus of equestrian rank and the former procurator of two provinces, to take command. We abandoned the surviving ungrateful citizens to their fate in the desert and are now on our way first to Hadrumetum, my home town, and then on to Carthage.'

'And what were you doing there, in Garama? I don't recall you being a part of Vespasian's party as he passed through here last month.'

Decianus cast a nervous look at Vespasian, obscured under his wide-brimmed hat and covered with a battered travel cloak; now came the crucial part of the deception. 'I had been held as a slave too in that kingdom, having travelled from Hadrumetum to trade slaves for wild beasts. They took my stock and enslaved me.'

The intermediary could not conceal his surprise as he looked down at Decianus, still portly despite his time in the desert. 'A very well-treated slave.'

'I was of use to the king. He valued my accounting skills.'

'So, you say that Governor Vespasian is dead as well as his lictors and that none of the other former slaves will make it out of the desert alive?'

'That is correct; and all we want is to purchase food and rest up a couple of days in safety before we continue our journey.'

The intermediary turned and began to have a conversation with someone out of sight, behind the gate.

Vespasian held his breath as he looked, from beneath the wide brim of his hat, along the lines of civic militia armed with javelins and bows, aiming their weapons at the small group of cavalry waiting outside the gate; the rest remained, along with the lictors, concealed at the oasis.

After a short discussion the intermediary looked back down at Decianus. 'Very well, you may enter; you have leave to stay for two days in the municipal barracks.'

Vespasian breathed a sigh of relief as the gates began to open.

Vespasian peered through the crack in the door, out into the parade ground at the centre of the barracks; on the far side, guarding the gate, stood two men with a sword, helmet and shield each but nothing more in the way of uniform, implying that they were merely civic militia rather than professional soldiers. 'Ready, Magnus?'

'As I'll ever be at my age,' Magnus replied, cracking his knuckles.

'Well, you said it was now a choice between fighting or fucking each day and I don't believe you've done the latter today, so you should be fine.'

'What a piece of luck that was, eh?'

'Leave two men here with him, Bolanus,' Vespasian said, pointing at Decianus and then opening the door fully. He stepped out into the warm night air and, with Magnus following, strode across the parade ground as if he had every right to be there.

'Where are you going?' the taller of the two guards demanded in Greek as Vespasian and Magnus approached the gate; his hand went to the hilt of his sword.

'To find some whores and a decent jug of wine,' Magnus informed him. 'Do you want to come?'

'You're not allowed out of the barracks.'

'Says who?'

'Orders.'

'Whose?'

'The Suphetes.'

Vespasian stood close up to the guard. 'Are you saying that the Suphetes have made us prisoners?'

'I'm just saying that we have orders not to let anyone out.'

Vespasian took off his hat. 'You may or may not have seen me when I was here in November.'

The guard stared at his face, half illuminated by the waning moon. 'No, but what of it?'

'Because he's the Governor of Africa,' Magnus said.

Vespasian took a step back. 'And as Governor of Africa, the Emperor's representative here, I far outrank your Suphetes. Now, lad, you can either try to stop me leaving the barracks, in which case the chances are that we will kill you, or you can obey your Governor's command and open the gates.'

'Open them,' the second guard said. 'He's telling the truth, that's Governor Vespasian, I recognise him from when he was here.'

'But Vespasian's dead, the leader of the auxiliaries said so when he arrived this morning.'

Vespasian shrugged. 'He lied; he always does. Now open the gate and no harm will come to you.'

Magnus cracked his knuckles again and gave a smile that did not reach his eyes.

'I've got no wish to die for the Suphetes,' the second guard said, turning and lifting the bar across the gates.

The first guard looked from Magnus to Vespasian and then nodded; he put his hand into a recess in the wall next to him and pulled out a huge key, as long as his forearm.

'That's a very sensible decision,' Vespasian observed, turning and signalling for Bolanus and his men to come.

The key clunked in the lock and, using their combined strength, the guards pulled open one half of the gate.

Vespasian took the key from the lock. 'Bolanus, tie these men up, but not so as they're uncomfortable, and leave them with the lads guarding Decianus.'

Once the guards had been secured, Vespasian stepped out into the street, which was dark and deserted; the shadowed hulk of the theatre rose on the other side. Turning left, he led his small party past the colonnaded market, as yet to start stirring for the new day, still four hours hence. As they neared the main street, the Via Triumphalis, which ran from the forum, near the harbour, all the way down to the south gate, it grew more populous. Late-night revellers lurched in and out of the shadows, frequenting the few brothels and taverns still open.

At the Arch of Tiberius, Vespasian turned right onto the Via Triumphalis. 'Split up into small groups,' he ordered. 'We don't want to attract the attention of the local Vigiles, if they have such a thing here.'

Avoiding staggering drunks and inert bodies lying in the gutter and ignoring the offers of various forms of delight from the cheaper whores who worked the street rather than being part of a respectable establishment, Vespasian made his way south, into the main residential area of the city. Here the noise grew as the poor of Leptis Magna, packed into insanitary accommodation almost as tightly as back in Rome, struggled and argued with one another in a continual fight for survival against very high odds.

Trying to keep to the raised pavement and paying attention not to step in anything too disgusting, Vespasian kept going straight south, with Magnus next to him and Bolanus and his men following in groups of twos and threes.

'There it is,' Vespasian said to Magnus as the torches burning to either side of the south gate came into view; a group of guards lounged in their flickering light, passing round a wineskin. 'We need to head east.'

Turning left into the second-to-last cross-street before the gates, Vespasian hurried along its dark length, his footsteps, and those of the men following, clattering on the stone paving slabs and echoing off buildings. Coming to a junction he turned right; a hundred paces ahead he could see the city walls.

'Just a couple,' he whispered to Magnus, whilst looking at two silhouetted men patrolling the walkway. He turned to Bolanus, coming up behind him. 'Have them dealt with, but don't harm them more than necessary.'

Bolanus nodded, leading three of his men off.

Vespasian watched as they crept close to the wall; they waited until the guards had passed the head of the stone steps leading up to the walkway and then edged up them. At the top they stole forward, taking care with every step not to make any sound. Ten paces behind the guards, Bolanus dashed forward, his men in his wake. Reacting to the sudden noise, both guards turned; too late did they see the fists crashing into their faces, punching their heads back, overbalancing them so they collapsed onto the stone-hard ground with their attackers fast upon them. Two more blows each and they were still; not a sound had issued from their throats in warning.

'Come on,' Vespasian said, running forward. Taking the steps two at a time, he clambered up to the walkway and looked over the wall out into the night. The moon was close to setting, its light faint, but even so he caught a movement, no more than the twitching of a shadow. 'They're there; get ready.' He raised his arms, crossing them at the wrists as Bolanus and his men joined him. From out of the night came a running group; quickly across the open ground before the wall they came and as they reached its base they cast up ropes, four in all. Catching one, Bolanus wrapped it about his body and braced himself; his men dealt with the remaining three. After a few moments of straining, Hormus appeared on the wall, a leather bag over his shoulder; further along, Vespasian's lictors began to scramble up, all with bags and with their fasces strapped to their backs. Once all eleven were over, the ropes were hauled in, all bar one.

'Be there at dawn, Bolanus,' Vespasian said as the decurion climbed onto the wall holding the last remaining rope.

'We'll be there, Governor.' Bolanus descended the twenty feet to the ground and was soon lost in the night. In the distance a horse whinnied.

'I have everything you asked for, master,' Hormus said, putting his bag down, rummaging in it and pulling out a pair of red-leather senatorial shoes followed by a white tunic with a thick purple stripe down the front and then lastly a folded, senatorial toga.

'Well done, Hormus.' Vespasian began unlacing his sandals whilst his lictors unpacked their togas from their bags.

'I'll get going with the lads then,' Magnus said.

'And take the guards with you,' Vespasian said, indicating to the two unconscious bodies still slumped on the ground. 'If they come round before dawn ...'

'Don't worry, they won't have the chance to make any noise; they'll be enjoying a deep sleep for the rest of the night, if you take my meaning?' Magnus grinned and then went off down the steps taking Bolanus' men with him, leaving Vespasian and the lictors to change.

The guards on the south gate roused themselves from their drunken slumber as the first rays of the sun hit a high-altitude, rippled cloud, brushing it with deep reds and violets. Within the city the sounds had changed; the inebriated roistering and violent arguments had been supplanted by the calls of tradesmen and market-stall-holders as they set up for the day's business, many of them on the Via Triumphalis, close to the gate. A man whom Vespasian took to be the captain of the ill-disciplined guard rang a bell next to the gates; his men began the process of opening them. From the confines of a narrow alley, Vespasian, with his lictors, watched the gates swing open and the first carts of the farmers bringing their produce to sell in the markets trundled in, each paying a small coin to the captain of the guard for the privilege.

A dozen carts had rolled in before the captain looked south through the gates and then did a double take. 'Close them! Quick!'

As he shouted, Magnus and Bolanus' men emerged from the crowd; within a few moments the guards had been overpowered and the gates remained open.

Vespasian looked behind him to the senior lictor. 'We're off.'

The lictors moved forward, passed Vespasian and turned right, out onto the Via Triumphalis, as Bolanus and his cavalry trotted through the gate. With his lictors preceding him in two lines, led by the senior on his own at their head, and the auxiliary cavalry, four abreast, behind, Vespasian processed, attended by his freedman, up the Via Triumphalis with all the dignity of a governor of an imperial province. The citizens of Leptis Magna paused in their tasks to watch their Governor, cheering him for no reason other than such a showing of Roman magisterial dignitas with a bodyguard of almost two hundred cavalry drew automatic admiration from those so far beneath that station.

And, as the sun rose, quickly warming the cool dawn air, Vespasian smiled inwardly at the scene he had created. 'The Suphetes won't be able to try to dispose of an awkward governor asking tricky questions now, Hormus,' he said out of the corner of his mouth, keeping his nose in the air and looking straight ahead. 'Not now the whole city is witnessing my arrival.'

Hormus kept his countenance equally as dignified. 'I'm sure they will be most polite, master.'

'Too late.'

By the time Vespasian had got to the forum, a massive crowd was following the procession, eager to know what the Emperor's representative in their province wished from them and their Suphetes. News having travelled quickly, numerous people were coming up from the harbour below, in which many of the merchant vessels that provided the city with its wealth were sheltering until it became safer again to risk the crossing to Italia. One small vessel, Vespasian noticed, was braving the season, slipping out of the harbour mouth, and he wondered if he would risk the shorter sea journey, hugging the coast, back to Carthage. The lictors carried on, across the forum to a building on the far side; elegantly colonnaded, painted in bright shades of red and yellow and framed by the blue sea sparkling in the winter sun, it housed the thirty-strong member-ship of the Leptis Magna Senate, many of whom now stood on the steps of the building.

The lictors, fasces held upright in both hands before them, lined along the bottom of the steps; Vespasian stood behind them as the cavalry drew up in ranks to his rear.

Once the clatter of many hoofs had stilled and the only sound was the buzz of the curious murmuring of hundreds of specta-tors, the senior lictor raised his rod-bound axe, the symbol of the magistrate to be able to command and execute. 'The Governor of this province of Africa demands that the Suphetes, Agathon and Methodios, come forth!'

The members of the local Senate muttered together before a man, whom Vespasian recognised as being the intermediary from the previous day, stepped forward. 'What does the Governor wish from the Suphetes?'

Vespasian cleared his throat. 'That will become known when they answer my summons and appear before me. If they do not show themselves very soon then I'll have no choice but to have my cavalry search the city until they are located.'

That very real threat galvanised the local senators; before he had a chance to respond, the intermediary was pulled back into their main body to be kicked and punched to the ground. Half a dozen of the younger men ran back up the steps and disappeared into the building. It was with great pleasure that, a few moments later, Vespasian saw them dragging out two bearded old men, protesting and struggling feebly. 'Bring me a chair,' he demanded as the Suphetes were brought down the steps towards him.

The senior lictor instructed four of his colleagues to seize the Suphetes; their stream of protests and pleas were cut off by hands clamping over their mouths. All was quiet as a slave appeared with a curule chair from within the Senate House. Vespasian sat, arranging his toga to his satisfaction; resting his chin on his right fist, his elbow on the chair's arm, with one leg extended and the other curled beneath the chair, he looked at the two men who had tried to end his life.

For a few score heartbeats he contemplated them; around the forum the murmuring ceased and, apart from the occasional stamp or whinny from one of the horses, silence was complete. Vespasian motioned the lictors to let go of their charges.

'We're so relieved to see you safely back, Governor,' Agathon said, his reedy voice brimming with conjured enthusiasm.

'Our prayers have been with you,' Methodios asserted with equal insincerity.

'Daily.'

'Twice a day.'

'Morning and night.'

'With rich sacrifices.'

'The whitest lambs.'

'Rich in blood.'

Vespasian continued contemplating them, the fingers of his left hand drumming on the arm of his chair, as their professions of piety grew weaker and then eventually died in their throats and they became silent.

The Suphetes had both begun to sweat under the intensity of Vespasian's gaze and, despite their eminent position in the city, they wrung their hands and shuffled their feet as if they were errant pupils being disciplined by their *grammaticus*.

And still Vespasian contemplated them.

Methodios broke first; he fell to his knees, extending his arms in supplication. 'Forgive us, Governor; what we did was for our city.'

Agathon also knelt. 'We didn't think that we could cope with the influx of all those people. We are a small city and there would not be room for them; nor would there be sufficient work.'

'And we wouldn't be able to feed them out of public funds.'

'So we obstructed—'

Vespasian held up the palm of his hand to stop them. He contemplated them for a few more moments. 'Obstructed!' The word echoed around the forum. 'Your refusal to send us supplies could have meant the deaths of me, my lictors, over two hundred auxiliary cavalry and may still, even now, condemn almost two hundred and fifty Roman citizens struggling to cross the desert.'

'We will send them whatever they need, immediately.'

'No you won't; I will requisition what they need and have my cavalry take it back to them as soon as I've finished here. You will be doing nothing in future – if you're sensible.'

'What do you mean, Governor?' Agathon asked, having shared a puzzled look with his colleague.

'Just this.' Vespasian signalled behind him and two riders dismounted; walking forward they stopped behind Vespasian's chair. By the looks in the Suphetes' eyes, Vespasian could tell that they recognised them. 'What do you have to say about these men?'

The Suphetes said nothing, their eyes downcast.

Vespasian turned to Urbicus. 'Are these the men who sold you and your comrades?'

'They are, sir.'

Vespasian addressed the Suphetes. 'You sold legionaries in the Emperor's service as slaves! Do you deny it?'

The Suphetes slowly shook their heads.

'The punishment for selling a citizen into slavery is severe; but I shall be merciful. I will give you a choice: seeing as the Emperor has recently conferred upon you citizenship you can either travel with me, when I return to Rome, so that you can face trial before Nero, or you can elect for a quick execution by decapitation here.'

There was a sharp intake of breath from all the local senators assembled on the steps and the Suphetes looked at Vespasian in shock.

'I would consider carefully as you may find that the Emperor is not nearly so merciful as I am.'

Agathon got to his feet. 'You do not have the power to order our execution.'

Vespasian pointed at his lictors. 'The fasces, Agathon; they represent the power to command and execute.'

The Suphetes swallowed and looked down at Methodios; they came to a mutual decision. 'We will appeal to Caesar.'

'Very well, but I warn you, Optio Urbicus and Legionary Lupus will be coming with us as witnesses against you. We leave once the citizens have arrived in two or three days. You will be kept in custody until then and also on the journey. Bolanus, take them to the barracks.' Vespasian rose to his feet and headed up the steps of the Senate House. 'I will now address the Senate.'

'And so, therefore, you will choose two from your number, before I leave, to replace your discredited leaders and I will endeavour to forgive the Municipality the wrongs it has done me personally.' Vespasian sat back down on one of the two chairs reserved for the Suphetes at the far end of the chamber. The senators, looking suitably chastened after what had been a stinging attack on the civic government of Leptis Magna, applauded him.

The intermediary stood, his face bruised and his clothes tattered; Vespasian motioned for him to speak, interested in how such a staunch supporter of the Suphetes would try to worm his way back into favour. 'Colleagues, we have all been at fault in this matter; I perhaps more than any other. I would like to propose a vote of thanks to the Governor for his forbearance and willingness to forgive.' This sentiment was greeted with enthusiastic cheers. 'I also propose that we offer the Governor a gift, if this would be acceptable to him.' The senators vocalised their agreement to this sentiment. 'What would you wish from us to help ease your forgiveness?'

The image of the ship leaving the harbour earlier came immediately to Vespasian's mind. 'My freedman, Titus Flavius Hormus, will be remaining here for a while to set up a business which will add to the prosperity of the city; he will have need of a good-sized merchant vessel.'

There were a few moments of silence as the senators calculated the great cost of the request.

The intermediary cleared his throat and looked around his colleagues who muttered their assent. 'I think we can all contribute to purchase you that reasonable request, Governor.'

'That is a wise decision as it will guarantee my forgiveness. I will emphasise to the Emperor that the Suphetes acted alone so that there will be no imperial repercussions for Leptis Magna.' That announcement was the cause for many expressions of relief and gratitude. 'Furthermore, my freedman will need a crew and also workers on shore as he intends to import camels and breed them. He will be able to employ a considerable number of the citizens currently on their way here, which will go some distance to allaying your fears about the influx of refugees.'

The intermediary opened his arms and looked to the ceiling of the chamber. 'The Governor shows that he is sympathetic to our problems. I propose that in addition to the gift of the vessel we should vote him a bronze statue out of public funds. I call a vote. Those in favour?'

It was unanimous.

Vespasian stood. 'I would be honoured. Now I must see to the supplies that need to be sent back to the column in the desert and once that is done I will hold a court to hear petitions and cases.'

Feeling pleased with the morning's work, Vespasian strode from the chamber and out into the sun to find Hormus and Magnus waiting for him. 'You heard all that?'

Hormus nodded. 'I did, master; and if it's your will, I'll stay here and set the business up.'

'You'll need no more than a year.'

'Indeed, master. But tell me, where will the money come from? I don't believe that you made any from the Garama deal.'

'Ah, well, that's where you're wrong.' Vespasian reached into the fold of his toga and brought out a bag the size of a large apple; he lobbed it at Hormus. 'Take a look in there.'

Hormus' eyes widened as he loosened the drawstrings and peered inside.

'Forty of them; the biggest, blackest pearls of the whole batch; the pearls that I took as a commission, shall we say, and the twenty that Decianus had taken for himself. They were my price for allowing Decianus to come along. That's why I had to wait for him to bring out the slaves from the city.'

'Lucky he gave them to you already,' Magnus said, taking out a pearl and admiring it.

'Why do you say that?'

'It's just that he's disappeared; we were looking for him whilst you were dealing with the Senate and we can't find him anywhere. The two lads who were guarding him have disappeared too so it would seem like he's offered them a good bribe.'

'Well, he can't have gone far.'

'No? Bolanus sent out a few search parties and it would seem that he was last seen down at the port.'

The image of the ship came again to Vespasian's mind. 'Shit!'

'I'm afraid so, sir. It looks like he was on that ship that sailed a couple of hours ago.'

And Vespasian knew that to be the truth of the matter and cursed himself for not being more vigilant. His replacement as governor would not arrive in the province for at least another four months so he could not expect to be back in Rome for five months at the earliest. Five months that, Vespasian feared,

Decianus would utilise fully to tell his side of the story of what happened in Britannia and here in Africa.

And Vespasian knew all too well that it would not be a story that would reflect favourably upon him.

PART II

✤ ✤

ROME, JUNE AD 64

CHAPTER VII

'I VERY MUCH REGRET, dear boy,' Gaius Vespasius Pollo boomed, 'that Decianus has concocted a very viable narrative since his return.'

Vespasian groaned inwardly at his uncle's pronouncement, although the news did not surprise him in the slightest after six months of contemplating Decianus' possible strategy. 'He's blamed me for stealing Boudicca's silver and gold thus pushing the Iceni into revolt and making me responsible for the deaths of eighty thousand Roman citizens?'

'What, dear boy?' Gaius was momentarily distracted by the arrival of a platter of honeyed cakes brought to the table, shaded by a rigged awning in the corner of his courtyard garden, by an uncommonly attractive youth in his early teens. The smell of fresh baking blended with the scent of lavender hanging in the still air.

Vespasian took a sip of his chilled wine, enjoying its coolness in the burning heat of an unseasonably hot June, and then repeated his assertion once the lad had left the garden and the sight of his barely concealed buttocks no longer commanded Gaius' full attention.

'Far worse, I'm afraid; far, far worse.' Gaius helped himself to a cake and took a large mouthful. 'Decianus has claimed that you had taken the money for yourself and that it was only his intervention that stopped you. At great personal risk, he managed to get it safely to the Cloelius Brothers and have it sent to Rome where he would have returned it to Seneca as soon as he got back.'

'But that's rubbish.'

Gaius shrugged and consumed the other half of the cake, reaching for a replacement as he did so. 'Of course it is and both

Sabinus and the then Governor of Britannia, Gaius Suetonius Paulinus, have said as much in the Senate. But it doesn't matter what the Senate believes – and in general they support you – what's important is what the Emperor thinks and that is, to an ever-growing extent, in the hands of the Empress; or any other part of her anatomy, for that matter.'

Vespasian slammed the palm of his hand onto the stone table-top. 'What is it that she's got against me?'

'Well, that's the interesting thing.' Gaius paused again for another mouthful of cake, leaving Vespasian waiting with rising impatience. He had not been in the best of moods since arriving back in Rome that afternoon, a month later than he had hoped due to his replacement's insistence that the sea-lanes were not absolutely safe for passage until the latter part of April and so had therefore failed to arrive in Carthage until the beginning of May. And yet, Vespasian knew, Decianus had made the crossing much earlier, although how the ex-procurator had been able to afford the huge expense of hiring a ship at that time of year, he did not know.

'The rumour is,' Gaius continued as soon as his mouth was clear, 'that Nero granted Poppaea Sabina a favour just before she married him, a favour that he was only too pleased to grant.'

'Go on,' Vespasian urged as Gaius once again crammed his mouth full of honeyed cake. Again he felt his irritation rising and had to force himself to sit still. It was a ritual that he always went through upon his return to Rome after a long absence: he would call immediately upon his uncle who would impart all the latest news and gossip to him whilst devouring a copious amount of his favourite snack. Vespasian knew he just had to wait for Gaius' mouth to be empty enough to speak without spraying too many crumbs over the table.

'Well, she asked for Pallas to be either executed or forced into suicide.'

'It was her who demanded Pallas' death?' Vespasian could not hide his surprise. 'Why?' He brushed some freshly ejected crumbs from his forearm, considering just why Poppaea would wish for the death of the former imperial secretary to the

Treasury, as Gaius finished his mouthful. 'He may have been Agrippina's lover, but once Nero had committed matricide and got rid of her he had very little influence remaining. What threat was he to her?'

'Exactly, dear boy; what threat indeed? None. So therefore we have to look at the other motivation for wishing someone dead.'

'Revenge.'

'Precisely.'

'But what could Pallas have done to Poppaea? He had been forced out of Rome before Nero had even met her.'

'Revenge has an exceedingly long memory, dear boy. Now, if I were to tell you that Poppaea has also tried to have Corbulo recalled to face treason charges for his taking command of Paetus' legions, what would you say then?'

'Me, Corbulo and Pallas?'

'Bearing in mind that the Lady Antonia, Claudius, Narcissus and the former consul, Asiaticus, are all dead.'

It did not take more than a couple of moments for Vespasian to make the unpleasant connection with one of the most shameful deeds of his life. 'The murder of Poppaeus Sabinus!'

'That's what your brother and I think; you all conspired in her grandfather's death. If I recall correctly, his daughter, Poppaea's mother and namesake, came flying into Antonia's garden, spitting and hissing, as only a woman can, soon after Poppaeus' body had been discovered in his litter, and accused Antonia of ordering her father's murder.'

Vespasian never liked to be reminded of the incident that his former patroness, the Lady Antonia, the mother of Claudius, grandmother of Caligula and great-grandmother of Nero, the most powerful woman in Rome of her time, had instigated. It had been a political move necessary for securing her family's grip on imperial power and consequently the murder had to be made to look like natural death; so they had drowned Poppaeus and then drained his body of all the water. However, Claudius, who was never known for his subtlety, had hit Poppaeus after he had mocked him and called him a fool; this had resulted in a cut lip and Poppaea had, rightly, concluded that this was a sign of a struggle and that her father's death was not natural after all. She had correctly guessed who was behind the deed and had sworn revenge on Antonia and her associates there present in the garden. 'So Poppaea Sabina brought up her daughter to have vengeance; but why didn't she do it herself?'

'How, dear boy? She was married to a nobody: Titus Ollius; once her father had died she had no influence anywhere. Had he not died when he did, Poppaea may well have ended up as empress so she had a lot to be bitter about. And yes, I believe that she did bring up her daughter to seek revenge on the people that she thinks deprived her of such a prize.'

'That's not a happy thought: the Empress wanting revenge for the death of her grandfather. I've always been afraid that such an ignoble deed would come back to haunt me.' But then a thought struck Vespasian. 'You and Sabinus were also in the garden when Poppaea came screaming in; why hasn't she made any moves against you two?'

'We weren't involved, dear boy.'

'How did she know that?'

'I've no idea; I'm just pleased that she does. The real question is: how are we going to keep you safe? Seneca is out of favour and Epaphroditus resents you for forcing him to recommend you for Africa without him receiving a sesterce in return. And as for the prefects of the Praetorian Guard—'

Vespasian waved a dismissive hand. 'Tigellinus hates everyone – it would be pointless to go crawling to him; and Faenius Rufus is honest and would support me but lacks influence with the Emperor.' He took another sip of his wine in contemplation. 'Surely my getting all those citizens out of Garama must count for something with Nero?'

'Ah, that's the other thing.'

'What other thing?'

'The other thing that Decianus has managed to put about: he's claimed that he took it upon himself to travel all the way to Garama to negotiate the freedom of the Roman citizens there in order to show his complete loyalty to Rome and Nero.'

'What!'

'And when you arrived he had already secured their release and they were all ready to leave.'

Vespasian looked at his uncle, aghast, his hands gripping the arms of his chair as he leant forward. 'But that's so far from the truth as to be totally unbelievable.'

'Not if he repeats it enough.'

'What would have possessed him to make such a journey in the first place? He was right in the north of the Empire and he travels all the way to beyond its southern border without going to Rome to sort out the financial mess he seems to have got himself into; bollocks!'

'Of course it is; but Poppaea likes to believe it, or rather, pretends to believe it. And Epaphroditus is convinced that it's perfectly reasonable that Decianus should have made such a journey unprompted and out of the goodness of his heart and so it must therefore be the truth. Nero just wants to know one thing.'

'What's that?'

'Just where are his pearls?'

'His pearls? I gave them to King Nayram, of course.'

'I'm sure you did; but according to Decianus' version of events—'

'I didn't even meet the king so therefore I must have kept the pearls.' Vespasian groaned and massaged his temples with a thumb and forefinger. 'The bastard! How can I prove that I didn't keep them?'

'It's his word against yours.'

Vespasian suddenly brightened. 'And my lictors! They were there, obviously, when I presented myself to Nayram and handed over the pearls. They could swear to it, although I've surrendered them now I'm back in Rome.'

'Let's hope so, dear boy, because if Nero notices you this evening I think he's going to want an explanation.'

'Why should he notice me this evening? I intend to spend it with Caenis.'

'I'm afraid that won't be possible. Tigellinus is holding a banquet for Nero at Agrippa's Lake and all the Senate are expected to attend; the way things are, it's far too dangerous to upset Nero by not going as he'll see it as a personal snub, especially as the feast is in honour of his first public appearance in a theatre.'

Vespasian was horrified. 'Performing in a public theatre? Surely not?'

'Unfortunately so; a few days ago. He's lost all dignity now. At least he chose Neapolis to flaunt himself and not Rome; but it can only be a matter of time before his shame is exposed here. And talking of shame and exposure, I think you ought to brace yourself for the usage that Nero makes of other people's wives; as he considers everything in Rome to be his personal property and the entire city to be his private house. He has become very Caligulan in his outlook.'

'Well, I've no intention of taking Flavia this evening.'

'Even if you did have, you couldn't.'

Vespasian looked at his uncle, confused. 'Why not?'

'Because, along with all the wives of the senatorial class, she's already there.'

It was with much trepidation that Vespasian arrived with Gaius, not long before sunset, at Agrippa's Lake on the Campus Martius; it had been designed to be the reservoir holding the water to feed the Baths of Agrippa and, now also, the newly constructed Baths of Nero, between which two complexes the lake was situated. Gaius dismissed his escort of four thuggish-looking men, members of the South Quirinal Crossroads Brotherhood, whose patronus, Tigran, was a client of his, with orders to return by the third hour of the night to wait to escort them back again. Passing the cohort of Praetorian Guards and a century of Germanic Bodyguards that signalled the presence of the Emperor, Vespasian beheld a lavish spectacle, for the banquet had not been prepared in the spacious colonnade around three sides of the lake, as he had assumed it would be, but, rather, on the water itself. Rafts had been built, half a dozen of them, and spaced around the artificial lake, which was one hundred and twenty paces long and sixty paces wide. Purple cloths bedecked them and dining tables, each with many couches set around, were arrayed upon them; three of the rafts were already full of reclining diners. Each raft had two boats attached to it, with a dozen oarsmen apiece, towing them gently around the lake so the diners could survey the treats languishing within the colonnades and also receive service at the open, northern end of the rectangle; here kitchens had been placed whose aromas filled the setting with the mouth-watering promise of the finest cuisine. A group of musicians, all masters of their instruments, completed the beauteous assault on the senses.

'Tigellinus spent days getting the oarsmen together,' Gaius informed Vespasian as they stood waiting to board a raft; around them, scores of other senators chatted with forced animation as if this were an event to be enjoyed despite what most, knowing their Emperor, suspected to be the truth.

'How come?' Vespasian replied, distracted by the naked whores writhing their way, in a variety of suggestive styles, through the senatorial group.

Gaius paid them no heed, eyeing instead the oarsmen in the boats nearest to him, all of whom were made-up and coiffured with great care; flowers were laced in their hair and jewels hung from their ears and about their throats. Their attire was the sheerest of tunics. 'They're the finest whore-boys in the city; they're all sorted by age and areas of expertise.' His gaze roved over a crew in their very early teens as they shipped their oars, bringing their raft gently to land. 'I wonder what they're good at.'

'I wouldn't like to guess; everything, I would have thought.'

Coyness was not in the whore-boys' repertoire and they competed against the naked whores for the senators' attentions with lewd gestures that showed graphically what that boat specialised in.

Vespasian grimaced in disgust; Gaius winced.

Stepping with care onto the gently bobbing raft, an obliging steward supporting his elbow, Vespasian found it remarkably stable, even as it took the full force of his uncle's weight, and he had no difficulty in walking to the table in the furthest corner. It was then he realised the function of the naked whores as one followed him and began to divest him of his toga; this done, she knelt before him to remove his shoes, although the lascivious light in her eyes as she glanced up at him showed that she was willing to remain in that position for a while longer, should he wish. Refusing the kind offer, Vespasian put on the slippers she retrieved from under the dining couch and reclined as she spread a napkin out before him and then wiped his hands with a warm, damp cloth.

'Over here!' Gaius shouted, waving towards the shore, glad to be distracted from the attentions of the nude female fussing over him.

Vespasian looked over in that direction to see his brother making his way through the crowd, his status as prefect of Rome easing his passage as many deferred to him.

'Oh, so you're back,' Sabinus muttered as he drew close to Vespasian. 'It's a shame you didn't stay away a little longer.'

'It's lovely to see you too, brother.'

Sabinus allowed his toga to be unwound. 'No, I mean it; you should have stayed away longer.'

Vespasian frowned at his brother's lack of welcome. 'Piss off, Sabinus.'

Sabinus looked at Gaius as his shoes were removed. 'You haven't told him, have you?'

'Now, dear boy, it's not for me to know exactly what is going on here. Let alone speculate upon what may happen.'

'May happen? *Is* happening.'

'What is happening?' Vespasian asked as Sabinus took a place between him and Gaius.

'Look around you, brother; what do you see in the colonnades?'

Vespasian had already glimpsed little tableaus of sexual activity within the shadowy interior of the colonnade, but as the light was fading it had been hard to make out the details. Now, however, slaves were circulating, lighting torches, and the tableaus started to glow with soft orange light, their details becoming clear. 'Whores and their clients,' he said in an offhand tone.

'No, brother. Firstly the men are not clients because that implies that there has been some sort of financial transaction; they're doing whatever they choose to do without paying. Secondly, the women aren't whores.'

As more torches were lit, Vespasian's eyes grew accustomed to the light and he could make out the women in detail; he gasped. They wore the finest garments – those who still retained such items – and their hairstyles were of the latest fashion and richly decorated. 'Gods below, they're—'

'Yes, brother; they're our wives and daughters and they're commanded by the Emperor to refuse no man anything for the duration of the banquet, whatever his station.'

'But ...' Vespasian was going to say that Nero could not do that, yet as the words formed in his head he knew them to be false: Nero could do whatever he liked. As the raft was pulled out into the lake he scanned the various couples and groups unable to stop himself from seeking the sight he wished not to see.

And then, of course, he saw it: there she was, Flavia, his wife, kneeling before a seated man as he held her head, his fists gripping hunks of hair, and pleasured himself at her oral expense.

Sickness rose within Vespasian but it was not so much at the sight of his wife fellating another man, although that was bad enough, as were the thoughts of the other acts that she had already performed or would in the near future be forced into; no, it was not that: it was worse, for as he stared at his wife the man let go of her head with one of his hands and gave him a cheery wave. Vespasian looked into the hated eyes of Marcus Valerius Messalla Corvinus. 'I'll kill him! I'll ... I'll ...' Vespasian jumped to his feet, causing the raft to rock, toppling a couple of goblets on the table, such was his fury; he bounded towards the water and was about to leap when he was yanked back by a fist clasping his belt.

'That, brother, is exactly the sort of reaction that's being looked for. That would have been the last defiance of a condemned man.'

Vespasian turned to look into Sabinus' eyes. 'I'll have vengeance; I will kill the cunt.'

'I'm sure you will, Vespasian; but not here and not now.'

'But look, he's … he's … How? How did it … how did it …' Vespasian trailed off, feeling the impotence of his position. Corvinus, who had once promised to conduct himself as a dead man in Vespasian's presence in return for Vespasian saving his life when Corvinus' sister, the Empress Messalina, had been executed by her husband, Claudius, was now committing an outrage upon Flavia that had the sanction of the Emperor himself. There was nothing that he, Vespasian, could do. Sabinus was right, he could not dive into the lake, swim for the shore and drag Flavia away from Corvinus without specifically going against the will of Nero because Vespasian knew that in Nero's city, Nero's will was all; death came to those who opposed it. He could not blame Flavia for what she was doing as she was just one of hundreds of women forced into the same degradation for all to see around the lake. Many of the women he recognised as the wives or daughters of friends or acquaintances; all were involved in trysts of various descriptions and numerical variety. Some looked to be enjoying themselves, vocalising their pleasure and grinding their hips, whilst others stared blankly as they received the attentions of strangers of all ranks or even, as in Flavia's case, rivals of their husbands intent on taking advantage of the situation for petty revenge.

Corvinus was not the only man of senatorial rank sampling the delights of the most distinguished women in Rome and Vespasian cursed each one for their encouragement of Nero's depravity. And yet, as he looked around the diners on the rafts he could see no trace of outrage nor, indeed, any acknowledgement that their womenfolk were being abused by anyone who cared to. No, all he saw were men, chatting to one another whilst eating and drinking without, seemingly, a care in the world; for that was the safest way to survive the evening. All were well aware of the Praetorian Guards nearby ready to quell any dissention to the entertainment arrangements at the banquet organised by the Praetorian prefect in the Emperor's honour.

'My daughter is in there somewhere,' Sabinus said, his voice tight with rage.

Vespasian stared at his brother for a few moments and then the shock hit him as he thought of his own daughter. 'Domitilla?'

Sabinus nodded.

Vespasian choked down a sob; his head fell into his hands. He could say nothing as he tried not to think of the indignities being forced upon his daughter.

'My dear boy,' Gaius said, laying a soothing hand on Vespasian's arm, 'I'm sorry, I should have warned you; but I had no idea that it would be this bad.'

'What did you think then, Uncle?' Vespasian hissed, trying not to let his anger show.

'Well, I suppose I just thought that they would be … well, I don't know what I thought, really; I certainly didn't think that they would be forced into doing … doing, well, this sort of thing with the lowest type of person.'

'Or Corvinus!'

'Or Corvinus; indeed not. We haven't seen this sort of outrage since Caligula.'

Vespasian scrunched up his napkin in a white-knuckled fist. 'Caligula forced senatorial wives into prostitution; people had to pay. He was motivated by a hatred of the Senate for being complicit in the gradual extermination of almost his entire family and to show them that they were unwilling to deny the ultimate donator of patronage anything. Admittedly that was bad enough; but this? This is worse, much worse: no one even has to pay for the pleasure of fucking my wife and daughter; not that it would make it remotely acceptable anyway. And what is Nero's motivation for this? He's doing it just because he can; because he knows that he can get away with it. In fact, it hasn't even occurred to him that he might not be able to get away with it.'

'Perhaps this time we should make sure that he doesn't get away with it.'

Vespasian could not identify the voice; he looked in its direction hoping that he had not been expressing his thoughts so loud that many people had overheard. Settling down on a couch next to him he recognised Gaius Calpurnius Piso. 'What did you say?'

Piso leant forward and kept his voice low as he addressed the Flavians. 'You heard perfectly well, Vespasian, and so did you two, Gaius and Sabinus, so I'm not going to repeat it. All I will say is that my wife and daughters are somewhere in the colonnades too, although I have been fortunate enough not to see them and do not intend to make too close a study of the activities in there for fear of spotting them. And I recommend that you do the same. I for one will try my hardest to pretend that this is just another imperial dinner. But think on what I said.'

Vespasian did not answer but looked sidelong at his uncle and brother.

Gaius shook his head. 'That's not a subject that I like to hear discussed or even be aware that it's being discussed.'

What Sabinus thought, Vespasian could not tell as horns blared a fanfare from the open bank of the lake and brought all conversation to an end, making it harder to ignore the sound of mass rutting from the other three sides.

Vespasian looked to the fourth bank; a score of stakes had been set up in front of the kitchens, and to them struggling people of both sexes were being tied, two to each, their shouts of protest mingling with the sexual dirge emanating from the colonnades. He was not surprised to see that they were naked, nor was he surprised by the arrival of the *gustatio*, the opening course of the meal, as if there was nothing untoward happening at all. He looked without appetite at the beautifully prepared array of dishes being set down on the table by slaves under the direction of the steward of the raft. Gaius immediately tucked into a sausage as another slave came round filling their cups with wine. On the shore the stakes continued to be filled and more torches were lit to ensure that each one was well illuminated.

'We're not going to go back to Caligula's habit of having executions during dinner, are we?' Gaius muttered, helping himself to a second sausage. 'It's so bad for the digestion.'

Vespasian did not comment as he watched a cart containing a cage being wheeled towards the stakes; next to it strode the unmistakable figure of Tigellinus, the Praetorian prefect, flashing his rabid-dog snarl of a smile as he waved to the diners on the rafts. As the cart passed close to a torch the outline of some beast of a good size could be made out in the cage and Vespasian thought that his uncle may well have been right. The sight of the cage and its contents brought a fresh round of screaming from the victims as the cart stopped and its tailgate was lowered; from the cage issued a rumbling growl.

Forced jollity sprang up from the assembled diners as if the dismemberment of restrained prisoners was just what all present had craved to go with their first course.

With surprising casualness, for one so close to a deadly creature, Tigellinus unbolted the cage's grille and swung it open, freeing whatever lurked within. The screams of the prisoners now reached a new pitch, drowning out other noises.

A shadow moved inside the cage; Vespasian held his breath. Whether the beast roared as it leapt out with a bound, none could hear above the terrified victims shrieking to absent gods. It landed on all fours, a thing of indistinguishable shape, covered in fur of different hues in the flickering light; for a few moments it surveyed its prey, shaking as if with great excitement. Then it pounced, its forelegs outstretched, straight at a horrified youth barely in his teens. But it did not pounce high, going for the throat as Vespasian had seen many times in the circus, but, rather, stayed low so that the paws landed on the youth's genitals. His howls were great as the beast tore and ripped at him, sometimes with claw and sometimes with tooth, until a bloody mess was all that remained of his loins and it moved on to its next shrill victim, a woman this time. And it gnawed on her, as if ravenous, ripping at the soft flesh of her pudenda, uttering bestial snarls moistened by saliva and blood; she stared down at it, catatonic in her terror and pain.

Vespasian was transfixed, mouth agape, as he surveyed the scene in all its hideousness. Despite its repellence he could not tear his eyes from it, not because he appreciated the horror or enjoyed the suffering, far from it; it was for another reason: something was wrong. At first he could not put his finger on it; it just felt as if somewhere there was a mismatch. Something did not fit. Then, as the beast left its second victim, ripped and torn, and barrelled towards the next stake, something in its movement caught his eye; and as it sank its teeth into the scrotum of a shrieking greybeard, Vespasian understood. It was not a beast that they were witnessing; it had run, crouching over but not using its forelegs, just its rear two. He looked more closely and could see that its hide was nought but skins that were now coming loose as the thing exerted itself in violent genital mutilation; its claws were not claws at all, they were fingers, pale and stubby, and its face, as it flung its head back with a thing of horror clamped in its jaws, was now exposed, the fur having been scraped off. And it was a face that all present knew, despite the indistinct light, despite the sheen of blood and gobbets of flesh covering it and despite the unnatural set of its features as it explored the boundaries betwixt human and bestial; for who could fail to recognise the countenance of the man they were all subject to? Who would not know Nero?

Vespasian gagged and had to swallow his vomit and then gagged again and failed to contain it; the wine that he had shared with Gaius earlier sprayed, through his fingers, over the table, fouling much of the gustatio and causing his companions to look at him in alarm.

'Dear boy,' Gaius said, putting an arm on his shoulder, 'was it something you ate?'

Vespasian spewed again, unable to answer as, on the shore, fresh screams indicated a new victim was experiencing the teeth and nails of the Emperor. And now, these new screams were the only sound to be heard, for all within the confines of Agrippa's Lake, be they on the water or in the colonnades, had now realised what was happening and were staring in disbelief at the man who ruled the greatest Empire in the world. The oarsmen ceased rowing and all on the lake became still.

Victim after victim he ravaged, always in the same manner, leaving them ruined, hyperventilating, eyes rolling, and all who witnessed it remained motionless, shocked by a barbarity that not even Caligula nor his uncle, Tiberius, had ever displayed – at least not in public. And all the time Tigellinus looked on, his teeth bared in his snarl of a grin, every now and then nodding in approval at his master's actions.

Finally, with three or four stakes still untouched, Nero's lust for genitalia was sated; for a while he lay upon the ground, breathing heavily and licking his fingers and looking up at the sky. The buzz of conversation began to rise with very gradual increments as the guests explored subjects such as the gustatio, delicious; the weather, unseasonably hot; the upcoming games, hopefully lavish; anything, just anything. Any subject but the horror they had just witnessed their Emperor perpetrate or the degradation of their womenfolk around them that had now started up again in earnest.

Vespasian could bring himself to say nothing as Gaius cheerfully ordered the steward to clear away the table and bring a fresh one complete with another serving of the gustatio. He could not understand what had made him so sick; he had seen people being ripped apart in far more explicit ways in the circus on numerous occasions and had witnessed wounds on the battlefield that would make the most ardent beast-hunt aficionado blanche. He remained on the couch staring into the middle-distance, his expression blank, as a group of Praetorian Guards went around the victims, putting an end to their misery and cutting the corpses down. Those who had avoided Nero's attentions were summarily despatched nonetheless, no doubt to their great relief rather than wait for the Emperor to get a second wind.

And then it came to Vespasian: it was not the act itself that had so revolted him; it was everything in conjunction. Having been away from Rome for over a year he had come back to find it even darker and more degraded than before. Nero buggering and then murdering his adoptive brother, Britannicus, at a dinner and then going on to commit incest with his mother and ordering her death, before following that deed with the execution of his wife and then presenting her head to his new Empress as a wedding gift, seemed to be mild in comparison to what Vespasian had returned home to. Now Nero was not just confining his malice to the inner circle on the Palatine Hill; now it was different. Now it was all the élite who would suffer and soon it would start spreading down through Roman society, until, somehow, all the citizens of Rome would feel the effect of the man who knew no restraint; a man who did not even acknowledge the need for restraint because he considered everything and everyone to be his and within his power. Vespasian allowed himself a grim smile; the time that he had predicted was surely now approaching.

'What is it, Vespasian?' Sabinus asked, picking up on his brother's expression.

Vespasian wiped his lips and then leant across so that only his uncle and brother could hear his words. 'This has to be close to the extremes of tolerance, even in our hardened times. Caligula couldn't surpass this.'

Gaius' jowls wobbled in alarm. 'What do you mean, dear boy?'

'You know perfectly well what I mean, Uncle. Piso is already openly looking for support; the time is coming when the idea that the Emperor has to come from the Julio-Claudian bloodline is going to disappear, because look at the way they behave. We must take care in the next year or so; we must swallow our pride and take whatever humiliations are heaped upon us because, whatever we do, we must not join – or even be associated with or remotely implicated in – any conspiracy to rid Rome of Nero.'

Sabinus glanced over to Piso who was deep in conversation with Seneca's nephew, the poet Marcus Annaeus Lucanus, and Senator Scaevinus, one of this year's praetors. 'And why not, brother? A figurehead is needed and he's as good as any.'

'Because, Sabinus, Nero's hold over the Praetorian Guard is still strong, so any conspiracy is doomed to failure at the moment. We wait; but I can assure you that the time is coming.' He looked over to where Nero was starting to stir. 'He still has no heir; we just need to survive a couple more years, perhaps three, and then we shall see. With you as Urban prefect we might find ourselves in a very interesting position.'

Gradually Nero began to get up; he gazed around as if he were unsure of his whereabouts and then looked in surprise at the skins that remained attached to his person as though he had no concept of just how they might have come to be there. Tigellinus approached him from behind and, with surprising gentleness, helped him to his feet, whispering in his ear as a group of slaves erected a tent just near him. Suddenly Nero was animated, ripping the remaining skins from his body before walking forward with purpose and plunging into the lake. As the Emperor washed the blood from himself a Praetorian centurion stood above him shouting at the oarsmen not to restart their efforts; when Nero was done, the centurion hauled him out and escorted the naked Emperor to the tent. None in the gathering affected to notice Nero's nudity let alone comment on the sagginess of his buttocks or the girth of his stomach; all carried on making a show of enjoying the banquet as the group of musicians struck up again and the oarsmen began to slowly circulate the rafts around the lake once more.

It was as if he were making his entrance for the first time that Nero emerged from the tent, not long later, resplendent in the regalia that was now associated with the Emperor: all purple with gold trimmings. With no sense of irony, the company broke out into rapturous applause, hailing their Emperor as he stood before them, his arms open wide, basking in their conjured adulation.

Vespasian joined with the rest, knowing that informers were everywhere and it would not do to be seen to be sparing with imperial praise; but now, more than ever, as dissent became more open, he understood the importance in being seen to support Nero; in that lay safety, whereas association with the likes of Calpurnius Piso was a sure route to death.

Despite how dark his world had become, Vespasian was certain that if he could just survive Nero then things may well be different; and if the prophecy, made at the time of his birth, was anything close to what he thought it might be then things could be very different indeed. And it was with thoughts of the future rather than of the present that Vespasian ceased applauding as the Emperor signalled for silence.

'My friends,' Nero declaimed, striking a pose with his left arm across his chest and his right stretched in the air before his face, his hand cupped, 'I bring news that will sadden you all.' He paused for pleas from his audience to spare them grief but was unmoved by their entreaties. 'It cannot be helped, my friends, for I have other charges who must benefit from my presence. I refer to the people of the second greatest city in the Empire: Alexandria. I plan to share with them the glory of my presence and my talent. Do not weep, my friends, for I shall not be away for long.' There were many cries begging him to remain but there was not one of the guests who did not feel joy and relief: the fear that held sway over them was to be removed from Rome for at least a short while. 'Because I am not, as you all know, insensible to your feelings I shall give you cause for celebration before I leave. Once again, I intend to marry.'

There was a stunned silence as all present considered the fate of the Empress Poppaea Sabina.

Vespasian felt a surge of relief at what had to be her fall from favour.

'So join me tomorrow, my friends, and help me to celebrate my joy at taking a husband.'

Another silence as all tried to make out the meaning of what they had just heard, wondering if they had caught the final word correctly. After a few moments, Tigellinus called out his congratulations to the Emperor, thus releasing a flood of felicitations.

Vespasian found himself cheering with the rest; he looked across to his brother and uncle. 'Is there no taboo he won't break?'

CHAPTER VIII

ROME WAS STILL sweltering, despite the fact that it was approaching the fourth hour of the night when Vespasian and Gaius said goodnight, at the Gate of Fontus, to Sabinus who headed towards his house on the Aventine preceded by his lictors.

With their crossroads brethren surrounding them, Vespasian and Gaius sauntered up the Quirinal Hill, alive with the rumble of carts and wagons and the shouts of the drivers doing their night-time deliveries – they had been banned in the city in daylight hours since the time of Julius Caesar.

Gaius sweated profusely and wheezed with every breath as he dragged his copious bulk up the hill to his front door. 'Will you go home to Pomegranate Street, dear boy?'

Vespasian shook his head. 'No, I'll go to Caenis' house. Flavia didn't know that I'm back but I'm sure Corvinus would have told her as he, well … I'll give her some time to master her shame. I expect that there are going to be a lot of very difficult conversations going on around the city for the next few days.'

'I'm sure you're right, dear boy; it makes me very relieved that I've never ventured into matrimony. Mind you, if Nero sets a new fashion I might very well be tempted.'

'I wonder who the unfortunate man is.'

'Doryphorus,' Caenis said, laying her head on Vespasian's shoulder and stroking his broad chest. 'Nero has been infatuated with him for some time now, or so Seneca tells me; he's an imperial freedman, which makes it even more scandalous.'

Vespasian frowned in the dark, his brow still moist from the sweat of sex on a steamy night. 'Yes, I know him; he was the one who held Britannicus down as Nero raped him. But what has he got to gain by marrying him?'

'Apparently, and don't laugh, he has always wanted to be a bride. Seneca says that he's had a wedding gown made and a wig dressed in a bridal manner. And to add sacrilege to farce he's going to have the ceremony conducted in the Temple of Vesta on the basis that the Sacred Flame has been considered the hearth-fire of the Emperor since Augustus' time and the bride takes a torch lit from her father's hearth-fire to ignite that of her new husband.'

Vespasian chuckled at the absurdity of it all. 'And where does Doryphorus live?'

'That's easy to guess.'

'In Nero's palace on the Palatine?'

'Exactly.'

'And we've got to bear witness to such a mockery.'

'Indeed, my love; and then we will toast the happy couple and wait around whilst the marriage is consummated.' This thought was too much for Caenis and she disintegrated into a fit of giggling.

Vespasian, too, could not help himself. 'I wonder what colour the stains on the sheet will be when they bring it out to prove that the bride was a virgin?'

Laughing in the dark with the woman he loved, having made good and strenuous love, gave Vespasian a feeling of ease that he had not had since he had begun his journey south to the Kingdom of the Garamantes; here in the small sleeping cubicle in Caenis' house, not far from his and his uncle's residences on the Quirinal Hill, he felt insulated from the folly and depravity that so darkened the lives of Rome's élite. In the slow descent into maniacal insanity that had been the journey of the Julio-Claudian emperors since the final years of Tiberius, never had the fear enveloping the city felt as heavy as it had done that evening; and yet here, in Caenis' chamber, he was protected from it. He held her close and nuzzled her hair, revelling in its scent. 'I love you,' he whispered, feeling the emotion just as strongly as he had when it had been new thirty-eight years previously.

'And I love you too, my love,' Caenis replied, her voice gentle and soothing.

Vespasian smiled to himself, closed his eyes and, banishing the memories of a hideous evening, relaxed into sleep.

It was with a sense of holiday that the people of Rome turned out, ten to twelve deep, along the route, to cheer their Emperor as he processed, regaled as a virgin bride, down from the Palatine to the circular Temple of Vesta at its foot on the edge of the Forum Romanum. The conical hair arrangement, the flame-coloured shoes and matching palla were all as they should be; there was nothing to suggest that this was anything other than a bride, except, perhaps, the beard, visible intermittently as the veil swayed with Nero's exaggeratedly feminine gait. But the people of Rome seemed not to notice such a small detail and cheered their Emperor until they were hoarse. If he wanted to marry a man then let him, was the general opinion of the lower orders, as then, if it gave him joy, he was more likely to flood them with generosity. Nero had never been parsimonious in his willingness to purchase the love of the people and they, in turn, were ever happy to be bought and they loved him for it more than they had loved any emperor before. And evidence of Nero's willingness to secure his position with the love of the people had appeared all over the city in the form of kitchens and tables in preparation for the wedding feast to which the happy couple had invited the entire city. Thus it was with the aromas of roasting pork and baking bread wafting around him that Vespasian, with a very taciturn Flavia next to him, watched the Emperor arrive at the heart of Rome: the temple in which resided the flame that would burn eternally, preserving the city from all harm.

The chief Vestal, the elderly Domitia, met him beneath the portico with her five subordinates, arranged in seniority down to the beautiful teenager, Rubria, and then the seven-year-old new intake, Cornelia, behind her. Their veils, leaving their eyes exposed, failed to completely mask the disgust that they felt at such sacrilege but if Nero noticed their thoughts he made no mention of it; he followed the priestesses through into the goddess's presence, there to await the arrival of his husband to be. It was only a few of the senators' wives, Flavia amongst them, who entered with the Emperor, all in a very sombre mood after the ordeals of the previous evening; the men remained outside in the rising temperature as the heatwave that had afflicted the city for the past half month tightened further its baking grip.

Once again there was a forced air of joviality amongst the senators as they awaited the arrival of the groom and his party; however, the normal bawdy remarks were overlooked for fear of exposing the farce through humour and the entire wedding party dissolving into unrestrained mirth at the ludicrousness of the situation.

Vespasian managed to keep his expression fixed as one of pleasure and stood, unlike Gaius who was keen to be seen enjoying the festivities, on the edge of the crowd of senators, uneager to be too conspicuous for fear of coming to the attention of the bride who might remember his pearls.

'A most unusual ... now what should I call it? Ah, yes, event; a joyous event, that's just the word for it: an unusual joyous event,' Seneca said, sidling up to Vespasian, his look solemn. 'I imagine it's the first of its kind; I can certainly find no record of anything similar in the annals of the city.'

Vespasian looked at Nero's former tutor and advisor, wondering if he was being serious. 'A joyous event.' Vespasian's tone was dry.

'As everybody here would agree.' Seneca's porcine eyes sparkled with mischief but his expression remained serious. 'Let us hope it's the last such event that we witness.'

'What do you mean, Seneca?'

'You know perfectly well what I'm implying.'

'You too?'

'What have I to lose? It's a matter of time until I'm told to, er ... how shall I put it? Yes, make an appointment with the Ferryman. Yes, I shall be forced to greet him, having left my fortune, what remains of it, to Nero. What have I to lose, Vespasian?'

Subdued cheers, as the groom and his party arrived, inter-rupted the conversation. Tall and muscular with startling green eyes and manly, rugged features, the freedman Doryphorus swaggered through the crowd, grinning with a smugness that nauseated. His escort, lowlife sycophants with disreputable morals whom Nero kept solely for the purpose of buggery, so Seneca informed Vespasian, played their part and shouted the requisite ribald remarks as Doryphorus disappeared into one of the most sacred buildings in Rome.

'What have any of us to lose, for that matter?' Seneca continued once Doryphorus had gone to claim his bride. 'Look at the sacri-lege that my former charge is committing, here at the heart of Rome before her Sacred Flame. How can the city avoid disaster if this is to go on? It is our only hope; our duty even.' Seneca's voice was low but steeled with vehemence. 'So tell me, what have you to lose?'

'My future.'

'None of us have a future.'

'That's where you're wrong, Seneca: it's just the people who plot against Nero who don't have a future. I intend to keep out of it.'

Seneca looked at Vespasian, disappointed. 'And what of honour?'

'Honour? We all lost that last night as we watched our wives get fucked by whoever and did nothing about it; my wife has not said a word to me since, not this morning or on our way down here. She can't even look me in the eye. So don't talk of honour, you who wouldn't even lend money to your own grandmother at less than twenty-five per cent interest.'

'Let's not get personal, Vespasian; how I make money has nothing to do with the subject, except, perhaps, that you might need my services very soon.'

'How so?'

'Do you know how much those pearls that you took to Garama were worth?'

'What's that got to do with it?'

'Over a million sesterces, although I'm told that Nero has

exaggerated the value to two million now that Decianus has claimed that you've brought them back to Rome.'

'You know perfectly well that Decianus is lying; I gave them to Nayram.'

'Decianus is a slippery snake, I grant you that, but he can be most convincing. Especially when he's saying something that Nero wants to hear. Join us and I'll lend you the money, interest free, and you can buy your way out of that particular difficulty.'

'I don't need it; I'll explain to Nero exactly what happened with the pearls.'

'And you think that he'll want to believe you? You need the money and we need you.' Seneca fixed him with his porcine eyes.

Vespasian frowned, shaking his head, wondering if there was more to this than Seneca was letting on. 'Why? Why am I so important?'

'We need someone to convince your brother to join us and we believe that you are the man to do it.'

Vespasian finally understood. 'You need the prefect of Rome because with him come the three Urban Cohorts and the Vigiles as well as the authority over the business of the city.'

'Exactly.'

'Then ask him yourself.'

'I already have.'

'And he gave you a sensible answer, evidently.'

'No, he gave me no answer; he said he wanted to consult with you upon your return. And now, here you are.'

'Well, he hasn't asked me but I made my views perfectly clear last night. And besides,' Vespasian gestured around the seemingly endless sea of adoring faces of the common people, 'look at them; they love him. Do you think they love us in equal measure? Of course they don't; what do we give them in comparison with Nero? They'll tear whoever harms him apart; you wouldn't stand a chance, Seneca. Not until the people turn against him. That's my answer.'

Seneca gave a thoughtful nod, pursing pudgy lips. 'Very well; I hope you don't come to regret your decision.' He turned and was gone as shouts of 'Hymen, Hymenaeee!' rose from the front of the crowd and Doryphorus appeared at the top of the temple steps, pulling Nero's arms as Domitia, playing the part of the mother of the bride, tried to prevent her 'daughter' being taken from her. As this ritual, which went back centuries to the abduction of Sabine women in Rome's first years, was being performed the crowd threw walnuts in the air, symbolising fertility – although there was little chance of that in this union, no matter how vigorously the newly-weds tried, Vespasian reflected as he scanned the assembly for his brother.

Nero squealed as Domitia, her face thunderous, let go of the bride, who fell, with coquettish flamboyance, into the strong arms of her new husband before shamelessly rubbing her crotch up and down his thigh like a rutting bitch on heat. Doryphorus' companions shouted lewd observations as the three young boys who would escort the bride, all of whom had both parents still living, looked on with unconcealed bemusement. And then the torch kindled in Vesta's Flame was brought out and more torches were lit from it until all of the groom's companions bore offspring from the bride's hearthfire. Led by Domitia and her five colleagues, the women who had witnessed the ceremony lined up behind the groom's escorts. Now the wedding party could set off for the Palatine, Nero proudly bearing the spindle and distaff presented to him by his 'mother', symbolising his role as the weaving wife and everyone else lobbing walnuts in the air and shouting 'Talassio!', the ritual good-luck greeting for a bride whose meaning and origin were lost to time.

And how the people of Rome greeted the newly-weds and how the bride blushed, making shows of modesty and coyness, having restrained herself after her earlier lapse in the strong arms of her husband; that passion was now being saved for the marriage bed. Now, in public, Nero presented the picture of the demure Roman bride being led to her husband's house to consummate the marriage. Such was the bride's happiness that tears rolled down his cheeks and wetted his beard; Nero caught a couple on his finger and showed them to those closest to him and all marvelled at the joyousness of the occasion.

Vespasian moved through the crowd, seeking his brother, to no avail, as the procession made its way up the Palatine, cheered all the time by the throng to either side of the route, keen to feast upon the Emperor's largesse.

Upon arrival at the palace, Nero rubbed oil and fat into the doorframe and then draped spun wool around it to announce, without a trace of irony, his arrival to the household gods within; his gods, to whom he had sacrificed that very morning.

Taking care not to trip, Nero stepped over the threshold and then clasped Doryphorus' hand. 'Where you are Gaius, I am Gaia.' He spoke the ritual words in a soft, high voice that could almost be mistaken for that of a woman.

Doryphorus gazed at his bride with love and gently caressed his cheek and stroked his tear-soaked facial hair. 'Where you are Gaia, I am Gaius.'

In filed the wedding party, into the atrium, high and elegant with tall marble columns and intricate mosaics; built by Augustus, it had been designed to put visitors in awe of the grandeur of Rome. But now the grandeur of Rome was but a sham as the great-great-grandson of the first Princeps, the First man in Rome, was led away by the matron of honour – who was meant to be a woman married only once to a husband still living and who was the incarnation of a faithful wife, but was in reality the thrice married wife of the new bride, Poppaea Sabina – to the bridal chamber to pray with her husband and prepare him for the arrival of his husband. Assisting her was a youth of striking beauty bearing a remarkable resemblance to Poppaea, who Vespasian had seen before but could not place.

'It seems to get more complicated all the time,' Sabinus whispered in Vespasian's ear. 'That's Sporus helping the Empress to prepare the bride.'

'Sporus? As in "seed" in Greek?'

'"Spunk", more like. He stood in for Poppaea at the consummation of her marriage to Nero due to her advanced pregnancy at the time.'

Vespasian recalled the youth, uncannily dressed and made-up in the image of the Empress. 'Of course, that's where I've seen him before.'

'Apparently Poppaea is as keen on him as Nero is, so I imagine he's rather a busy boy.'

Vespasian did not want to think about it. 'Where have you been? I've been looking for you.'

'I've been trying to talk some sense into my son-in-law, Paetus; although I wonder whether he hasn't actually talked some sense into me. I had to restrain him from,' Sabinus leant closer to Vespasian so that no one could possibly hear, 'from bringing a dagger to Nero's wedding after what happened to Flavia Tertulla, his wife, last night. Suffice it to say, she's still losing blood.'

'That's terrible; will she be all right?'

'I hope so; but the doctor can't say for sure. You can imagine how Paetus is, and I expect that there are many more like him.'

'What did you mean when you said that he might have talked some sense into you?'

Sabinus looked around to make sure that no one was too close. 'He's insistent that Nero has to go, and after seeing my daughter lying in bed, faint from loss of blood, I'm inclined to believe him.'

'No, Sabinus; we step back and let others do that.'

'I've been approached by Seneca.'

'I know; he was trying to get me to persuade you to join his cause just now. It's too dangerous; a plot like that can never be kept secret. Nero or Tigellinus is bound to find out. And anyway, the people wouldn't let the assassins get away with it; what do they care for the honour of our women when Nero feeds and entertains them?'

Sabinus gritted his teeth. 'But look at this; how can it go on? As you said last night: "Is there no taboo he won't break?" What next?'

An outbreak of more ribaldry and coarse humour announced Poppaea Sabina opening the door to the bridal chamber. She signalled to the groom that all was ready inside and his bride awaited him. Doryphorus grinned and made his way at speed to the room, just off the atrium, raising clenched fists in the air, pumping them up and down as if warming up for strenuous exercise; an image that Vespasian tried to banish from his head as soon as it appeared.

'Look at it this way, Sabinus,' Vespasian continued as the wedding party settled down to await news of the happy coupling, while slaves began to circulate with drinks. 'They're being far too open about it already. Seneca approached both you and me in a very direct manner. Last night Piso made no secret of where he stood and then proceeded to have intense conversations with that poet, Lucanus, and what do you know of him?'

Sabinus shrugged. 'Other than he's Seneca's nephew? Only that Nero has forbidden him to publish any more of his poems out of jealousy and therefore he has personal reasons for hating Nero.'

'I didn't know that. But I meant what do you know of his character?'

'That he's a terrible gossip?'

'You have it, brother; do you want to trust your life to a conspiracy with someone like Lucanus involved?'

Sabinus did not have to think about that at all. 'All right; so we keep out of this one. What about after that? How do we free ourselves from this? How do we ensure that things like last night never happen again?'

'It has to come from outside the city, from the legions; and it has to be when the people are losing their love for Nero.'

'But the conspiracy against Caligula was hatched in the city.'

'Yes, but that came, mainly, from within the Praetorian Guard and they were replacing one Julio-Claudian with another. This time it's about getting rid of that family completely; the Guard will never support that as they will fear that their own extinction will follow. Besides, Tigellinus knows that he is nothing without Nero so he would never be a part of it, and the other prefect, Faenius Rufus, is too timid and too honest. It needs someone with legions behind him to march on Rome and cow the Guard into submission. Parade-ground soldiers like them would never stand against veteran legions.'

'Corbulo?'

'He's the obvious choice.'

'But what about—' Sabinus stopped himself abruptly.

'I know what you're thinking, Sabinus; and I've been thinking it too. But if you won't tell me the exact details of the prophecy then how can I know what to do?'

'You know that I'm sworn not to reveal anything to you.'

'Under the terms of the oath our father made us both swear, you can.'

'But only when the time is right and you need help making a decision; and I can tell you that the circumstances at the moment are not right.'

'And will you tell me when they are?'

'I will, Vespasian; I've been sworn to.'

'Thank you, Sabinus; that's all I need to know.' He paused as a high squeal, somewhere between pleasure and pain, cut across the atrium; the groom's companions cheered. 'In the meantime I'm going to write to Corbulo and suggest a marriage alliance between the families. His eldest daughter, Domitia, was married last year but his youngest, Domitia Longina, is coming up to eleven, just two years younger than my Domitian. I've been contemplating it for a while.'

Sabinus did not look so sure.

'He's my son, Sabinus, whatever his character. It's my duty to see that he is well married and who better than the daughter of the general in command of four legions in the East?'

The squeal repeated but this time longer and more pleasurable; it then rose in tone and turned into a series of high-pitched ejaculations that became quicker and quicker, leaving no one unsure of what was occurring. The groom's companions clapped in time to each one as the more staid male members of the company made small talk whilst trying to ignore the reality of the situation. The women, most of whom were still suffering from the previous evening's indignities, stood in small groups looking uncomfortable at this parody of female pleasure; for Domitia, the chief Vestal, it was too much and, without ceremony, she turned and led her five colleagues from the building.

'That will reach Nero's ears,' Sabinus observed.

'I don't think he can hear anything at the moment,' Vespasian quipped.

'So you think you're funny, Bumpkin,' an unpleasant voice drawled.

Vespasian turned to see Corvinus sneering at him, looking down his long nose. 'I should kill you now, Corvinus.'

'You tried to once but I came back, remember?'

'Because you have no honour and went back on an oath you made after I had your life spared.'

'Yes, it was stupid of you. She loved it, you know.'

Vespasian flew at Corvinus who stepped aside, avoiding a slashing fist; Sabinus grabbed his brother's shoulders and hauled him back, restraining him.

'Such rustic manners, Bumpkin,' Corvinus said, adjusting the folds of his toga. 'Fighting at a wedding, really. Still, I suppose it's to be expected from someone brought up in the company of mules.'

Sabinus held tight to Vespasian. 'That's the last time you insult my family, Corvinus.'

'Is it, Sabinus? I doubt it.' Corvinus turned to leave and then looked back over his shoulder. 'Oh, by the way, Bumpkin, Flavia mentioned – when she was able to talk, that is – that she would be willing to see me again for a financial consideration; quite a large financial consideration, actually. She didn't know that you were back, you see; not until I told her, that is, and pointed you out to her. She begged me not to say anything to you but, well, you know what I'm like. Anyway, I thought that you might be interested to know that your wife was willing to whore herself to me because she needs the money; my guess is that she's been spending rather lavishly whilst you've been away. I doubt that you can even afford to buy the Emperor a wedding gift on this happiest of days.' He grinned with easy malevolence and strode off as a prolonged howl of pleasure combined with a very masculine roar of triumph issued from the bridal chamber.

'He's lying,' Sabinus said, still holding Vespasian firmly, both ignoring the successful climax of the consummation. 'Flavia would never do a thing like that.'

Vespasian struggled for a few moments, before realising the futility of it: there was nothing that he could do to Corvinus in this company. 'I'll have him, and I'll have him properly this time.'

'Why didn't you just let him be executed in the wake of Messalina's fall?'

'Because I thought it would be more painful for him to have to acknowledge that in my eyes he was dead and had no meaning for me; but that only works with a man of honour. Next time I won't play silly games.'

A loud cheer announced the arrival of the bridegroom, naked and fresh from his labours; he thumped his fist in the air repeatedly and his companions took up the beat, clapping in time. Behind him, Poppaea Sabina supervised the women bringing out the bloodied sheet which proved, miraculously, that the bride's hymen had been intact. And this was cause for yet more rejoicing and shedding of blissful tears on this gods-blessed day.

Overwhelmed as he was by the reception and celebration of the news that the marriage had been consummated, Doryphorus managed to hold himself together for the final announcement of the proceedings. 'The public feasts will go on for the remainder of the day; but, dear guests, my wife and I invite you all to our wedding banquet, tomorrow, where we shall be pleased to receive your gifts. Until then, we shall be fully occupied.' With an obscene gesture with his fist, he turned and walked back to his wife and the reception began to break up.

Sabinus sighed, rubbing the back of his head and closing his eyes. 'Wedding presents? I heard someone say something about them but I didn't think that we'd really be expected to come up with anything as it's not a real wedding, surely?'

'In Nero's mind it is, and that's the only thing that counts. And besides, he's got to cover the expense of this extravagance somehow; so who better to pay for it than everyone here?'

'Seneca and Piso are becoming more and more appealing.'

'Don't even joke about it, Sabinus.'

'Who said I was joking? I'll see you here tomorrow with what-ever cash I can get from the Cloelius Brothers' banking business;

I imagine they're going to be rather busy today.' Sabinus gave a curt nod and walked away.

With financial gloom descending on him, Vespasian stood and waited for his wife as she made her way, eyes downcast, through the dispersing crowd towards him.

'I said no such thing, Vespasian.' Flavia was insistent.

'Well, at least you're talking to me now.'

'What option do I have when I have to defend myself against such calumny?' Still she would not look at him but, rather, kept her eyes fixed on the pavement as they made their way across the Forum Romanum. 'It's bad enough what happened last night; the things that we, the most respectable ladies in Rome, were forced into! Where now is our dignity? To have to undergo that sort of humiliation in public so that one's own husband can see the degradation one suffered is, in itself, intolerable. I heard today that at least a dozen of the women have taken their own lives already, and with Corvinus ...' She spat on the ground, in a very un-Roman-matron-like manner. 'With Corvinus lying about what I said to him whilst he was abusing me, makes me think that I should perhaps do the honourable thing as well.'

'No, Flavia; think of Domitian.'

'Domitian! Domitian wouldn't realise for a month or two that I was dead. And only then it would be because he'd notice that he's not shouted at so much.'

Vespasian put a hand on her arm; Flavia shook it off immediately. 'Flavia, I don't blame you for what you were forced into last night; nor will I let it stand between us.'

'But that's just it, you fool! It *should* come between us; you should be madly jealous and swearing all kinds of retribution. You should be defending my honour; instead you just say that it won't affect our relationship. I was raped last night, Vespasian; raped! Repeatedly! I was even raped in a way that I've never been taken before; do you understand? In a way that I have never even experienced with my husband and you say that it won't stand between us? How can you? I'm the mother of your children and yet you react as if it were one of our slaves who had the misfortune to get caught out late at night. In fact, if it were, you would probably seek redress from the culprit for damage to your property.'

'Flavia, please, don't do this in public.' Vespasian tried to calm her as she became shriller, gesturing with his hands to keep the volume down as they crossed into the Forum of Julius Caesar.

'In public! After I've been forced to have sexual relations with half of Rome in public you worry about me making a bit of noise in public? I demand that you show some anger in public; some jealousy, some outrage, anything. Just never tell me that my ordeal doesn't matter and it won't affect us, because I tell you, husband, the way I'm feeling now I would never let another man touch me again and just how would that affect our relationship, eh? Or would you just spend even more time with Caenis like you did last night whilst I spent hours washing myself and crying?'

'Flavia, I'm sorry, truly sorry for what happened, I really am. And yes, I felt rage when I saw you with Corvinus; I felt rage at Nero for allowing such things and at Corvinus for taking advantage of them and I swear that I will have revenge on him. I will kill him.'

'Who?'

'Corvinus, of course.'

'And what about—'

Vespasian just managed to get a hand over Flavia's mouth before she said the Emperor's name. 'Hush, woman. You forget yourself.' He lowered his voice to a hiss. 'What can I or anyone else do? We all have the same problem but who can you trust? Eh? Who *can* you trust? I want to survive Nero and that means caution. I know of a conspiracy but there is no way that I would join it even after what happened to you. I must wait and you must forgive me for doing so.'

For the first time that day Flavia looked directly at her husband. 'For how long?'

'Until the whole world wants rid of him and the legions take action.'

'Never, in other words.'

'No, Flavia, it will be soon but not quite yet.'

Flavia gave a slow, sad nod of understanding and walked on up the Quirinal Hill. 'You're all cowards.'

Vespasian followed. 'Perhaps that's so, Flavia, and I can offer no excuses.'

'You're no better than Corvinus.'

'At least I don't tell all those lies about you as he does claiming that you'd do anything for money.'

'He's almost right in that respect, although I never offered to prostitute myself, to him or anyone else. But yes, I am desperate for money, though I don't know how Corvinus found out.'

'What do you mean, Flavia? Why are you so desperate for money?'

Flavia stopped and faced Vespasian. 'Because we need it.'

'You've spent it! Haven't you?'

'Not me, husband; at least not all me. It would have been all right if it had been just my spending.'

'Who then?'

'Not who but what.'

'What?'

'Blackmail, Vespasian; blackmail. I'll show you at home.'

'There,' Flavia said, handing Vespasian, across his desk in the *tablinum*, a small wooden box, no bigger than the palm of his hand. 'Open it.'

Vespasian did as requested and took a sharp intake of breath. 'Decianus!' He reached into the box and pulled out a single black pearl. 'When did you get this?'

'Just over a month ago. A note came with it but it was anonymous; you seem to know who's responsible, though.'

'Catus Decianus, I would assume; I'll tell you about him later. What did the note say?'

'It said that when you returned from Africa you would immediately be in serious, life-threatening, trouble with the Emperor. The only way that you would be able to reprieve yourself is by purchasing four hundred and sixty black pearls from the writer so that you can put them together with the twenty that you stole and the twenty you extorted from the writer and therefore be able to return all five hundred to the Emperor when he demands them. Did you steal or extort forty pearls, Vespasian?'

He could not help a bitter laugh. 'Forty pearls! But that's nothing; Decianus stole four hundred and sixty and I never knew it. That must be how he bribed his guards and managed to hire a ship out of season; I should have realised. How much does he want for these pearls?'

'Two million sesterces for the remaining four hundred and fifty-nine; we can keep this one as a show of good faith.'

'Very kind, I'm sure. Two million, that's twice what they're worth and more; the bastard thinks that I'll pay a premium of over a hundred per cent to get them back. If I did, not only would he come out of the deal very wealthy but he'd also be spared trying to sell them without someone close to Nero noticing.' Vespasian slammed the pearl down on the desktop. 'Well, I'll not do it.'

Flavia looked at him, her eyes widening in surprise. 'But you must.'

'Why must I?'

'Well, to make yourself safe of course.'

Vespasian picked up the pearl again and rubbed it with his thumb, admiring its lustre. 'I don't need them to make myself safe; I could just pay Nero the two million directly if he refuses to believe me when I swear that I gave them all to Nayram.'

'This is what I'm saying, husband: you can't do that; we haven't got the money.'

'Because you've spent it?'

'No, Vespasian; because I've already paid the two million.'

'You've what? How? You don't have access to that sort of money.'

Flavia looked contrite, one hand twisting in the other. 'I, I had to forge a banker's draft in your name; I managed it using an old seal of your father's. I told the Cloelius Brothers that you'd sent the draft to me from Africa, which is why it was a bit damaged. They believed me and handed over the money, which I then passed on to a freedman of the blackmailer. I was desperate, Vespasian. The fact that the blackmailer had given me a pearl worth so much convinced me that it was true, and if you came back and couldn't produce the rest of the pearls then you may well have been executed and all your property confiscated and then where would that have left me? I would have been destitute; I've seen it happen to too many women and it's not a nice thing to witness, let alone suffer personally.'

'Why didn't you wait until I got back?'

'Because in the blackmailer's note, Decianus you said, he had promised that Nero would summon you immediately on your return.'

'But luckily he was busy with the banquet and his wedding.' Vespasian let out an exasperated sigh, his expression more tense than was normal. 'So where are they then, Flavia? You said you passed the money on.'

'I did; Decianus wrote again saying that a freedman would call, bringing the pearls with him, which he would exchange for the money.'

One look at Flavia told Vespasian that the news would not be good. 'And you gave him the money but he didn't give you the pearls.'

'No, he gave me the pearls and left with the money; it was all fine. And I hid them here, in your study.'

Vespasian looked down at the floor at the foot of the bookshelf that housed a secret compartment in which he stored valuables. 'So what's the problem?'

'The problem is that when I came to fetch them the next day to take them to the Cloelius Brothers for safekeeping, they were gone.'

CHAPTER IX

'THAT'S WHERE TIGRAN'S lads say he's been staying,' Magnus informed Vespasian as they walked past a substantial residence close to the summit of the Aventine; it was not far from Sabinus' house as well as that of Vespasian's daughter, Domitilla, and her husband, Cerialis. 'It took a while to trace him to here as he don't seem to go out much. It was Marcus Urbicus, the optio from Africa, who spotted him a couple of days ago, on the Campus Martius, coming out of Nero's new baths but then he lost him as they started to climb the Aventine. The lads didn't pick him up again until this morning.'

'Urbicus?'

'Yes, how else could we have found him? Urbicus and his mate, Lupus, knew what Decianus looks like so I introduced them to Tigran and they've joined the brotherhood whilst they wait here to testify against the Suphetes.'

'Well, I'm very grateful,' Vespasian said, staring at what was purported to be Decianus' home in Rome. 'Now I suppose we have to work out how to get in and where he would keep anything valuable; assuming that the pearls are even there, that is.'

Magnus indicated with a nod to a couple of hard-looking men lurking in the shadows of a side street just opposite the house. 'Tigran's on to that; he's having the place watched day and night to see what the routine of the household is. Once we know that, it would be just a question of choosing which member would be most likely to give us the information we need, whether through fear or a financial incentive.'

'How long will that take? It's been more than half a moon already.'

'They'll be as quick as they can.'

Vespasian grunted to make clear his impatience. It had indeed been more than half a moon since Flavia had told him of the pearls and it was now the ides of July. His impatience stemmed from the fact that Nero, having celebrated his wedding banquet at which he had received a fortune in gifts and thus, financially satisfied for the time being, had retired to his villa down on the coast at Antium to escape the burning heat of Rome and to spend time with his new husband as well as changing roles now and again and enjoying the charms of his wife. But Vespasian knew that although he had been lucky with Nero's distractions the issue of the pearls would come up as soon as the weather broke and the Emperor returned, having satiated himself with his various spouses. Before that happened Vespasian intended to have the pearls in his possession and, if possible, their current owner dead. He was in no mood for compromise even if he had felt that Decianus was a reasonable man; no, Decianus' serial treachery had taken the issue way beyond that. And besides, his mood had not been helped by the fact that he had been forced to give up his last remaining reserves of cash to Nero as a wedding gift and was facing financial ruin unless he could find a source of more.

Vespasian and Magnus continued up the hill towards Sabinus' house, the heat of the afternoon almost unbearable. Vespasian looked down onto the Appian Aqueduct, which terminated on the Aventine, to see its flow had reduced to hardly more than a trickle. 'If it goes on like this there will be an even more acute water shortage and that will only lead to disturbances. Once this business is over I'm going to get out of the city and spend some time on the estates, if you fancy coming, Magnus. You could bring Caitlín if you want and see how Castor and Pollux are after being so long away from them. I've already sent Flavia and Domitian off to Aquae Cutillae; I'll probably go there first and then spend some time up at Cosa with Caenis.'

'It would be good to see the dogs again. Yes, I'd be glad to; I've never known the city so hot.' Magnus wiped his brow as if to prove the point as Vespasian halted abruptly. 'What is it?'

Vespasian pointed to the house two up from that of Decianus. 'That house.'

'What about it?'

'It belongs to Corvinus; I know because he lives close to Sabinus on the Aventine and it was him that used one of the Aventine brotherhoods to try to kill me on the night that I was meeting Narcissus in your tavern.'

'When my tavern was burned down and I was forced to retire as patronus of the South Quirinal; I remember it well, or not so well, if you take my meaning?'

Vespasian carried on walking. 'So that would explain how Corvinus might have known that Flavia was in need of money; he and Decianus are neighbours and I can imagine them having some nasty little chats together. I wonder what they've been up to. When Tigran questions the chosen member of Decianus' household ask him to see if he can find out anything about his relationship with Corvinus.'

'I will do; and I'll tell the lads on lookout to report if they see the two together and to follow them to see where they end up.'

Vespasian slapped Magnus on the shoulder and grinned at his friend. 'That is a fine idea; I'm glad to see that despite your very advanced years you can still do a bit of thinking.'

Magnus affected a hurt expression, which was not entirely successful as his false eye was staring in a direction of its own volition. 'Now you're mocking me again, sir. As I've always said: there's plenty of fight and fuck left in me, just not both on the same day.'

'I'm sure you're right, my friend; let's hope for Caitlín's sake the former runs out before the latter.'

'No, Vespasian, I won't.' Sabinus was adamant.

'Sabinus, it won't be for long,' Vespasian insisted. 'Just until I can sell this year's new batch of mules and perhaps get some income from the camel importing and breeding business that I'm having Hormus set up in Africa.'

'No, Vespasian.'

'But my steward has told me that this year we have more foals than ever before and what with the continuing operations in Britannia and the need to replenish all those lost last year by your son-in-law in Armenia, the price is at a premium. By the end of the year I'll easily have the money to repay you.'

'No, Vespasian.'

'But why not? You make fortunes out of being the prefect of Rome.'

'I'll tell you why not, you parsimonious little shit. Because of all that trouble you gave me about taking a loan from your old friend, Paetus; do you remember? You said that no one should ever take out a loan and you asked me how I could sleep at night and then you went on and on when you found out that I hadn't paid it back after Paetus had been killed. All that disapproval that you heaped upon me for so long was very unpleasant and having suffered it I want to protect my little brother from the same thing. So for your own sake, Vespasian, I am not going to lend you three million sesterces.'

'Don't you turn it round on me, Sabinus; you're just doing this out of spite.'

'No, I'm doing this because you genuinely said that no one should ever take out a loan and I'm holding you to that.'

'But I need some liquidity to run the estates until the foals are sold; you know how expensive that is. The steward has written to me saying that he urgently needs cash; plus, what if I can't recover the pearls and Nero calls in the two million and I can't produce it right away? What then?'

'Then you'll be in a very nasty situation.'

Vespasian looked at his brother, unable to believe what he was hearing. 'After all I've done for you: saving your life when you were part of Caligula's assassination; coming to find you when you had been careless enough to let yourself be captured by druids, and you won't even let me have the cash that might save my life.'

'I never said that.'

Vespasian was speechless for a few moments, frowning; his mouth opened and then closed. 'What did you just say?'

'That I wasn't going to deny you the cash that might save your life nor was I going to deny you the cash that you need to keep your estates going until the mules are sold.'

'But you've just flatly refused to give me a loan.'

'Of course I'm not going to give you a loan, you hate them.'

Vespasian slumped down on a couch utterly confused. 'So what then?'

'We'll draw up a legal document whereby you mortgage one of your estates to me – and I don't care which one – for three or even four million, it's up to you, and then you'll get the money.'

'But we're brothers.'

'That's why I'm doing you this favour. But it won't be a free loan like you were expecting, not after all the self-righteous nonsense you forced on me. Agreed?'

Vespasian choked back his anger, knowing that his brother did have a very good point: he had involved himself with the loan that Sabinus had taken when Paetus had offered it and he had threatened to tell the younger Paetus, Sabinus' now son-in-law, about the loan when it became apparent that Sabinus had not repaid it. 'I'm sorry, Sabinus. Looking back, I realise just how sanctimonious I was.'

'You certainly were. Now, do you agree to my terms?'

'I do, brother; I need the money.'

'And, at that time, Vespasian, so did I.'

Vespasian strode with purpose, behind his steward, into the atrium of his house to see Magnus along with a man, in his sixties, of eastern appearance with a blue-tinted beard, embroidered trousers and a long-sleeved tunic coming to below his knees, standing by the *impluvium*; the fountain trickled pitifully into the pool made shallow by the worsening water shortage. Behind them, waiting just inside the vestibule was a middle-aged man who, on first sight at a distance, Vespasian could tell was about as trustworthy as a Greek slave-merchant.

'That is Drakon, sir,' Magnus said, keeping his voice down and indicating to the man. 'He's a freedman of Decianus' but, unfortunately, seems to have a few grievances; at least that's what he has assured Tigran.'

'He was very insistent on the point,' the easterner confirmed.

'Was he now, Tigran? Drakon, you say?' Vespasian said to confirm that he had heard correctly and thinking the man well named for he looked very much like a slithering reptile. 'How did you find him?'

'He's dealing with the possible sale of the pearls for his patron should you not submit to Decianus' blackmail, senator; that's how we got interested in him.'

Vespasian was intrigued. 'Go on.'

Tigran looked at Magnus who took up the story. 'Well, it was like this, sir: it occurred to me that Decianus might well be seeking to negotiate the sale of the pearls to another party in the event that you don't submit to his blackmail; after all, they're the only collateral that he has as he brought nothing else out from Garama.'

'That we know of.'

'Yeah, well, he only had that cloth bag with him, which he used as a saddlecloth on his mule and which must have contained the pearls, so it's a fair bet that there was nothing else of value. He's renting that house and, as you know, a house near the summit of the Aventine ain't cheap; and then he's got to run it. He'd already lost all the money that he stole in Britannia and, although he maybe had a bit more deposited here in Rome, it was likely that after having nothing to show for the last few years other than four hundred and fifty-nine pearls he would be looking to cash them in as soon as he could, should you refuse him. So negotiations were probably already happening because he needs money quick.'

Vespasian smiled at his friend's reasoning. 'And therefore the person negotiating on Decianus' behalf would have knowledge of the whereabouts of the pearls.'

'Exactly, sir. So I mentioned it to Tigran.'

'I know of almost all of the people in the city who would be interested in such a purchase,' Tigran said, 'so I just had my men monitoring the household report any member of it who approached one of the dealers; and that led us to Drakon. All we had to do then was get him to come to me, which was simple enough seeing as it's no secret in the underworld that the brotherhoods are always interested in such purchases.'

'And it didn't take long before we could sense his hostility to his patron,' Magnus affirmed, 'and now you know the rest. We're just going to have to persuade him to hand over the correct information.'

Vespasian was satisfied. 'We are and I'm indebted to you both; obviously there'll be a substantial consideration for your services once I'm clear of this predicament. He had better come in.' He turned to his steward. 'I'll see the gentlemen in the tablinum, Cleon. Have chilled wine served.'

'Yes, master,' Cleon said, bowing his head as Vespasian turned on his heel.

'He has made many promises of advancement to me but never has he kept one,' Drakon said in answer to Vespasian's question. 'He has promised financial aid so that I can set up a brothel, as well as introductions to the local magistrates on the Aventine to get the licence to do so and make the business run smoothly, but they are empty promises. Instead, he has me scurrying after him, doing menial tasks that benefit only him and it makes me look like a man of no worth whatever.'

'Well, that's terrible,' Vespasian said, rolling his wine cup in his palms and thinking that it would not take much to make Drakon look like a man of no worth. 'And for how long have you served him?'

'I was his slave since an early age; I must have been about eight when I was purchased into his household. He freed me seven years ago after serving as a slave for twenty-five years. Seven years ago!' Drakon's pinched face screwed up in outrage at the injustice of his treatment; his eyes, which could not quite meet Vespasian's, betrayed the hardness of one who has had little in life and was determined that things should not remain so. 'For seven years I have been little better than a slave in status. Seven years!'

'Seven years? That is shocking,' Vespasian crooned in his most sympathetic tone, shaking his head and his eyes widening with incredulity. 'How ungrateful can a patron be to his freedman and client? Have you ever heard of such a thing, Magnus?'

'I can't say that I have, sir. I'm speechless; absolutely speechless. Speechless! Just the thought of such injustice makes me boil up with fury at a man who shows such little regard for those who serve him. As you can probably tell, I'm speechless; I don't know what to say. The cruelty of it.'

With a slight frown at the melodrama of Magnus' reaction, Vespasian cut in. 'So, Drakon, you came to Tigran for advice, did you?'

Drakon's eyes flicked around the room as he thought about the question, assessing it for any traps; he found none. 'He invited me to come and see him on other business; recently I have been looking into the sale of certain items for my master and Tigran had got to hear of this and suggested that we might do some business together.'

Tigran nodded his head in slow agreement. 'Drakon's unhappiness came out quite by chance in the course of our negotiations and so I suggested that perhaps he might like to share his burden with you, senator.'

'When it was suggested I was only too pleased to come; especially as your brother is the Urban prefect and you are a proconsul of considerable influence.' Drakon leant forward and spoke in a confidential tone. 'The items I was referring to are pearls, black pearls; the ones that your wife had purchased from Decianus and were then subsequently stolen from your study.'

'By you?' Vespasian asked, resisting the urge to throttle the man.

'By acquaintances of mine on Decianus' orders; I had no choice in the matter and now regret it thoroughly.'

'And how did these "acquaintances" know where to look?'

'That would be betraying a confidence.'

Vespasian just managed to refrain from asking if Drakon was always so sensitive about betraying confidences. 'I see; so I have a traitor in my household.'

Drakon neither confirmed nor denied this.

Tigran broke the silence. 'I saw immediately that there was a mutual interest here, senator. It seems perfect, seeing as I know you to be a man with an acute sense of justice; and I think that we can all agree, a man with such a sense of justice is exactly what is needed in this situation.'

'Indeed, Tigran,' Vespasian concurred with solemnity, placing his cup back on the desk. 'This is a situation that demands a sense of justice and I shall be only too pleased if, somehow, by my actions I can help right this wrong done to you and at the same time avenge myself.'

'If you could, senator,' Drakon said, picking up no irony in Vespasian's voice for there had been none, 'then I would serve you faithfully as your client.'

Until someone paid you to betray me, you snake, Vespasian thought as he smiled. 'I would be honoured. What would you have me do to help?'

Drakon was not short of ideas.

'Obviously we can't trust him,' Vespasian said soon after Drakon had been shown out by Cleon, 'but can we believe what he just said?'

'That he'll tell us where about in Decianus' house the pearls are hidden once you've got Sabinus to issue the appropriate licence for him to set up his brothel? I very much doubt it,' Tigran said, replenishing his cup.

'Yes, so do I.'

'The thing is, he's well aware that if he and Decianus are the only ones who know their whereabouts and we go in and steal them, it will be pretty obvious to Decianus where the information came from. So then Drakon's better off stealing them himself as Decianus will be out to kill him either way.'

'There must be slaves in the household who have seen Decianus or Drakon taking the pearls out.'

'There may well be but there may not. I don't think Drakon's stupid by any means, so he won't bank on there being anyone else who knows the hiding place and therefore he won't give us the real one.'

Vespasian was forced to agree. 'Yes, it seemed too easy; what he's done is open negotiations with us. Still, what he has confirmed is that they are in the house, somewhere; if they were with one of the banking firms he would have said so because it's best to tell the truth if it does nothing to weaken your position. The questions are: how do you pressurise Drakon into giving the correct information? And when do you retrieve the pearls before Nero comes back to the city for the three days of racing that conclude the Victorious Caesar Games at the end of the month?'

Magnus was in no doubt. 'As soon as possible; we go in tonight.'

'Tonight?'

'Yeah, Sabinus' house is close by; we'll use that as a base.'

'But why tonight? I know it has to be done soon, but this soon?'

'It stands to reason, don't it? Today is three days after the ides of July; it's a Black Day.'

'And?' Vespasian knew well that it was the anniversary of Rome's defeat by the Gauls just over four hundred and fifty years earlier.

'Well, nothing happens today as it's considered really bad luck.'

'So wouldn't it be really bad luck to try to break into Decianus' house and steal the pearls on such a day?'

'That's what anyone would naturally assume, isn't it? But in reality it's one of the best days to do something like this because that is just what everyone thinks. People just can't wait to get the day over with so what do they do? What does everyone do on a Black Day?'

Vespasian shrugged. 'Go to bed early?'

'Exactly; and at this time of year when the night hours are half as long as the day ones people have no trouble going to bed as soon as it gets dark. No one has late dinner parties or anything like that; they're all tucked up in bed with their favourite slave or perhaps even their wife.'

Vespasian could see the logic of it. 'You're saying that it's far more unlikely that there'll be no one around?'

'No, I ain't saying that; I'm saying that the chances are better of getting in, retrieving the pearls and then getting out without being seen. And besides, the Dog Star rises tonight a couple of hours before dawn and that, for me, has always been a lucky night.'

'That's all very well, but we don't know where the pearls are yet.'

'I wouldn't worry about that, sir, we will do within the hour. Drakon ain't going to make it all the way back to the Aventine; in fact, I should say that right about now Sextus is escorting him very politely to Tigran's tavern.'

'You could have just taken him there in the first place.'

Tigran wagged a finger. 'No, no; we were hoping that he would be a little more forthcoming with us here first, because we'll have no way of checking what he tells us as he'll be dead.'

'Dead?'

'Of course; then Decianus will think that his freedman has run off with his pearls and won't realise that you've got them back.'

Vespasian rubbed his hands and then clapped them once, grinning. 'That's a most excellent idea. But, before you finish off the snake, ask him who the traitor is in my household.'

Still there was no sign of the heatwave abating as Vespasian and Magnus made their way back to the Aventine, across the Forum Romanum and around the base of the Palatine, past the Temple of Vesta whence came the signs of activity.

'What are they doing on such a day?' Magnus wondered as the six priestesses processed out, Domitia holding a lantern containing an offshoot of Rome's Sacred Flame shielded from the breeze by thin strips of horn that glowed warm in its light.

'More to the point, what's he doing there? He went down to Antium with Nero,' Vespasian asked as Domitia presented the flame to Nero's freedman, Epaphroditus.

'Perhaps he wants to rekindle Nero's hearth-fire in readiness for his imminent return.'

'He would have sent a slave to do that; he's far too aware of his own importance to do that himself.'

Magnus spat and clenched his thumb to avert the evil-eye. 'Still, it seems a strange thing to do on a Black Day, rekindle a hearth-fire; no good will come of it, Dog Star rising or not.'

Vespasian found comfort in that thought, if it really were what Epaphroditus was doing; but somehow he doubted it. He put it from his mind as they passed by the baking hulk of the Circus Maximus; its great wooden gates at its flat end were closed as were most of the shops within its precincts due to the blackness of the day. However, as they walked along its length, still bustling with folk going to and fro, it became apparent that some shop-owners thought more of profit than superstitions and used the lack of competition to bolster their takings. The smell of fresh bread wafting from a bakery at the far end of the huge construction proved too much for Magnus to resist.

'I ain't ever been in this one before,' Magnus said, coming out with his purchase; he broke the loaf in half and then ripped off one of the pre-shaped segments. 'It's new, apparently; just opened yesterday, which is why they didn't want to close today, according to the slave who served me.' He took a bite of the bread, chewed a bit and then frowned as they headed around the curved, southern end of the circus hemmed in by many tenement blocks, pushing their way through a group of young boys playing at gladiators whilst their sisters and girl-cousins played a shrieking game of tag. 'Well, I'd say that whoever is in charge of the baking needs to take a few more lessons; that's pretty chewy on the inside.'

But it was not the standard of the local bakeries that concerned Vespasian as they ascended the Aventine with the sun beginning to fall towards the western horizon before them. 'Just make sure that none of your lads let on to Sabinus what you're about tonight. You're all only here to escort me home once Sabinus has read this contract, all right.' He produced the mortgage contract from the fold in his toga to emphasise the point. 'Obviously, he'll not sign it today but tomorrow, if it's acceptable to him.'

'Don't worry, sir; the lads know when to keep their mouths shut. With luck they should be here soon after dark. I can't imagine that it would take Tigran long to get what he needs out of Drakon; he's very good at encouraging a bit of chat, if you take my meaning?'

Vespasian only half heard the remark, his mind occupied with the dishonourable deeds that he seemed forever to be forced into. Through the heaving maze of tenement buildings they went until they passed beneath the Appian Aqueduct, which acted as the demarcation line between the crowded squalor of the lower Aventine and the sumptuous villas towards its summit. Coming into the less densely populated neighbourhood of the hill, Vespasian stopped and turned to look out over Rome across to the imperial residences on the Palatine, on the opposite side of the Circus Maximus, with the beauteous marble-colonnaded edifice of the Temple of Apollo behind them and the new Temple of Claudia Augusta next to that. His gaze then moved on to the Esquiline beyond, with its villas encircling its summit which was crowned with the tranquillity of the Gardens of Maecenas. There, in its midst, stood the three-storey tower that Caligula had had built so that he could oversee his city when in residence at the gardens that had been bequeathed to Augustus by his friend and canny political advisor. The hubbub of humanity rose from the tenements below in striking contrast to that imperial oasis of peace.

Vespasian turned his gaze northeast to the Capitoline Hill, supporting the Temple of Jupiter; the heart of Rome, glowing golden in the deepening light. Behind it lay the baths, theatres, temples and other public buildings on the Campus Martius with the Gardens of Lucullus and Sallust to their east and the ribbon of the Tiber to the west and north. And then in the distance lay the conical-roofed Mausoleum of Augustus, the man who had claimed that he had found a city of brick and had left one of marble.

Vespasian recalled the first time he had set eyes on the mistress of the world thirty-eight years ago, a lifetime ago. He had been on the other side of the city, on the Via Salaria, travelling to Rome for the first time, with his parents and brother. Overawed by her sheer scale as she perched upon her seven hills crowned with the pall of brown smoke from the tens of thousands of fires that warmed and fed her, it had been at that moment he had vowed that he would serve her all his life.

Vespasian smiled at the naïvety of his youth in thinking that Rome was a noble cause; he had seen enough to know that there was nothing noble in the ambition that drove men to serve her. No, the motives were not the pure ideal of serving the state for the common good as he had imagined, looking down upon the city with his father next to him; they were far different: they were power and position received through the patronage of one man, the Emperor. And now that Emperor, Nero, was disporting himself in a way that no Roman of noble birth should: singing in public, having never once taken the field with one of his legions – even his uncle, Caligula, had had some experience of the campaign tent; an experience that his crippled predecessor, Claudius, could also boast, just. Even now Nero was probably either gorging himself with food and drink or filling himself with his new husband. Would he, Vespasian, have entered into the public service of Rome had he known how low it would fall?

It was a question that he had asked himself many times and he had always contemplated the alternative when considering the answer: would he have been satisfied staying on his estates where – as his brother had once put it – the only way to differentiate between the years would be to note the quality of the annual vintage? He knew such an existence would not have been for him despite the fact that before he had beheld Rome a quiet life as a country farmer had been all he craved. But now, no; now he could not imagine tolerating such a dull reality even though he had the opportunity to go back to it at any time. So it was that he would continue on his course: he would authorise a burglary in order to retrieve goods that had been stolen from him, using the information of a recently murdered man. And why was he doing all this, wallowing in dishonour? In order that he would have a better chance of surviving the reign of Nero. Not for the good of Rome but for himself alone. And it did not surprise him; after all, he had stooped even lower in his time: the murder of Poppaeus which seemed to forever haunt him; his involvement with Nero's matricide and many other acts of which he could be less than proud. Each one, however, had helped to secure his survival and his rise in the pool of cess that was the Rome of the Caesars; for the time being, at least, Vespasian reminded himself; at least for the time being.

Could life for the élite improve under a new regime? What was certain was that it could not get any worse than it was now. And so, as the sun fell into the west, casting the greater part of the city into shadow, Vespasian wondered what it would take to cleanse the city of the malaise that blighted it and as he did so his eye fell upon the mighty edifice of the Praetorian camp right across the city, just without the Viminal Gate. There was the key to it all; there was the power that kept this most unmartial and effeminate of men upon the throne. This man who affected great artistic talent as if it were a thing of equal import as military prowess or firm, enlightened leadership and yet still failed to live up to the standards he had set himself, such were the limits of his abilities.

Shadows still lengthened; candles and lamps were lit, turning the city into a mini earthbound cosmos as soft points of light became myriad. Such was Rome on this evening of the third day after the ides of July, one of the blackest days in her calendar; tinderbox dry after almost two months without rain so that there was now but a trickle of flow in the Appian Aqueduct below.

'Beautiful, isn't she?' Vespasian muttered as he took in the view. 'The greatest city on earth but dominated by the greatest mediocrity the world has ever seen.'

'Can you have a great mediocrity?' Magnus asked, genuinely interested.

Vespasian laughed. 'I suppose not; but you know what I mean.' He turned and continued up the hill as the sun set on the city he loved.

It was as Vespasian and Magnus approached Sabinus' house that the news they had been waiting for arrived in the form of Sextus accompanied by Marcus Urbicus and Lupus carrying a couple of ladders between them.

'Well, Sextus?' Magnus asked.

Sextus screwed up his eyes in a struggle for recollection; it took a few moments but it came. 'Under the lilies in the pond at the centre of the courtyard garden, Magnus.'

'Good man, Sextus; did he say exactly where?'

'Yes, Magnus.' There was another pause for a bout of recollective exertion. 'The corner closest to the Forum Boarium.'

Magnus clapped the bovinesque brother on the shoulder. 'Well done, Sextus; you and the lads go and keep an eye on the house, and keep out of sight, we don't want anyone asking what them ladders are for, do we?'

'No, Magnus, we don't; that would be ... er ... awkward.'

'It would indeed. I'll join you in half an hour or so.'

'Yes, Magnus.'

'Sextus,' Vespasian said as the brother turned to go, 'did Tigran give you an answer to the question I asked him to put to Drakon?'

'Oh, I'm sorry, senator, it slipped my mind what with all the other stuff I had to remember. Here.' He pulled a wax tablet from his belt and handed it to Vespasian.

Vespasian peered at it but could make nothing out in the faded light; he placed it in the fold of his toga. 'I'll look at it when we get to Sabinus' house.'

'Just what are you doing bringing me the contract on a Black Day, Vespasian?' Sabinus said after Vespasian had explained his excuse for the visit.

'And it's very nice to see you too, Sabinus. Of course I don't expect you to sign it today but I thought that you might like to look at it and then sign it tomorrow, as I'm eager for the money.'

Sabinus grunted grudging acceptance. 'I was just about to go to bed but I'll have a look at it if you wish over a jug of wine. Magnus?'

'Er ... no thank you, Sabinus; I've got a little bit of business to do whilst I'm in the area. I'll come back when it's done with a few of the lads and escort Vespasian home.'

*

'What are you really doing here, Vespasian?' Sabinus said as he placed the contract on his desk in the tablinum. 'It's a perfectly straightforward contract that doesn't need anything added to it before signing and you know that very well.'

'Hmmm?' Vespasian looked up at his brother, tearing his eyes away from the name written in wax that he had been staring at, his guts crawling.

Sabinus repeated the question.

'As I said.' Vespasian's throat was dry and he could barely talk such was the shock of the betrayal.

'Bollocks, brother. You turn up under some false pretext and Magnus just happens to have a bit of business in the area? Do you think I'm stupid? And you've been staring at that wax tablet as if it was your death warrant, so you've evidently just received it, therefore you must have met with somebody on your way over here; associates of Magnus, would be my guess.'

Vespasian looked again at the name on the tablet. 'I don't want to talk about it, Sabinus.'

'As you wish.' Sabinus poured them both a cup of wine and passed one over to Vespasian; he contemplated his brother for a few moments before changing the subject. 'I don't mind telling you but since Nero's latest wedding I've been getting some very strange enquiries.'

'What sort of enquiries?'

'Well, you know: how am I enjoying my position as prefect of Rome? Questions left half asked as if it may be possible for me to rise higher; hints at better times in the future should I wish it and that sort of thing.'

'Don't get involved with Piso and Seneca, I've told you that already.'

'It's not from Piso or Seneca, or Lucanus for that matter; it's others: Scaevinus, one of this year's praetors, the grain merchant, Antonius Natalis and Senator Afranius Quintianus to name but a few, all of whom are associated with Piso. Scaevinus was sharing a couch with him at the banquet on the lake, for example. The problem is that at the moment everything has been vague, but if it carries on then they'll be forcing me into a situation whereby if

I don't report them to Nero it'll look as though I support them, and if someone else reports them to the Emperor and he finds out that they have been talking to me then my life will be as worthless as theirs.'

'Just make sure that you are never in private with these people and certainly make sure that you don't know what their ultimate objective is.'

'Well, to get rid of Nero, obviously.'

'Obviously, but what I mean is make sure that you don't know who they plan to replace him with.'

'That's just the point; I think they are sounding me out as their figurehead. Perhaps they don't think that Piso is up to it, but I get the impression that they would be willing to offer the throne to me.'

'To you!'

'I would seem one of the obvious choices seeing as I'm the prefect of Rome and Piso is just a senator from a very good family.'

Vespasian could see the logic of it and the extreme danger. 'Don't be tempted, Sabinus.'

'I don't have the troops behind me who would secure me in place or the money to buy them, so of course I'm not tempted.'

'Good.'

'Why? Because you want the ultimate prize for yourself?'

'Don't be stupid.'

'Come on, Vespasian, we both know what I'm talking about.'

'Do we? You've never revealed the nature of the prophecy.'

'But I've hinted at it once or twice and you know that to be ...' Sabinus paused and sniffed the air. 'Patroculus!'

The slave waiting outside the room stepped in.

'Is the hearth-fire smoking?'

Patroculus went to have a quick look and soon returned. 'No, master.'

'Well, something is, I can smell it. Go and have a look around the house.'

With a bow, the slave departed as a commotion erupted in the atrium.

Sabinus stood in alarm. Magnus dashed into the room.

'What's wrong, Magnus?' Vespasian asked, getting to his feet as well. 'Was there a problem?'

'I'll say there was, sir; the lads were in and then it was like someone had poked a stick in an ants' nest. The boys just managed to get out in time, but empty-handed unfortunately.'

'Why?'

'You'd better both come and have a look. I reckon you're going to have a busy night ahead, Sabinus. The Circus Maximus is burning.'

CHAPTER X

'THAT'S THE WHOLE southern end on fire,' Sabinus exclaimed, incredulity in his voice.

'And it's already spread to two of the tenement buildings next to it, by the looks of it,' Vespasian said, thinking of the children who had been playing in that very place as he had passed it a little over an hour previously and hoping that they had been taken to safety.

'It spread really fast,' Magnus informed them, 'it was half that size when we first saw it from Decianus' place.'

Sabinus gave Magnus a quick quizzical glance but his mind was more focused upon his duty. 'I'd better get down there and take charge.'

Vespasian followed his brother down the hill at speed until the streets became choked with terrified people fleeing the ever growing conflagration that now, with flames clawing at rising, billowing smoke, lit the entire quarter. Their passage was made even more gruelling by knots of spectators from the surrounding areas whose properties were not yet threatened and had no concept of the danger that lurked.

'Get back to your homes!' Sabinus shouted to the onlookers, as Magnus, Sextus and the two other South Quirinal brothers beat a path through the crowds in lieu of Sabinus' lictors whom he had dismissed for the day. 'Get back, the Vigiles will need easy access if this isn't to spread too far. Your homes could be next.' The authoritative voice of the Urban prefect, conspicuous in his purple-bordered toga, warning them of imminent danger to their property brought a sense of reality to many and it was with urgency and rising horror on flickering faces, at the thought of losing everything, that the curious dispersed.

Still fighting against the tide of panic as people, carrying or dragging possessions or clutching babes or small children's hands, struggled to get clear of the heat emanating from what were once their homes, Vespasian and Sabinus struggled forward with Magnus and the lads doing their best against the throng. Even as he glanced up at it, the tenement next to the two already burning burst into flames that leapt from windows as if the place had been torched by fire-razers. Out ran the inhabitants who had been clinging on until the last moment in the hope that their squalid abode would be miraculously spared; but it was not to be. So quick was the building engulfed that Vespasian did wonder, briefly, whether there had been foul play, but all extraneous thoughts were soon banished as the scale of the blaze, compared to the lack of effort to counter it, became apparent. The entire rounded end of the circus was being consumed by flames that seemed to spring from the very stones themselves rather than just the thick wooden beams upon which the edifice had been constructed. Facing the fire were two pathetically weak hand-pumps, whose jets of water spurted irregularly and barely made it twenty feet into the air, and four bucket-chains of twenty or so sweating Vigiles conveying water from a nearby cistern.

'Where are the rest of your men?' Sabinus shouted at the Vigiles centurion overseeing the pitiful attempt to douse the flames.

'Coming, prefect, I hope,' the man replied, recognising Sabinus at once.

'You hope? What's taken them so long?'

'Confusion, sir; orders and counter-orders came as we left our barracks. Some of us were told to turn back and wait in reserve.'

'Reserve! Reserve for what? Reserve for when the whole city is ablaze because we only tried half-heartedly to put out the fire?'

'I don't know; all I know is that it seemed stupid so I came with my century anyway.'

'You mean you're only here because you disobeyed orders?'

The man gave a nervous nod of his head. 'Yes, sir.'

'And whose orders did you disobey?'

'Nymphidius Sabinus', sir.'

'The prefect of the Vigiles himself ordered you not to attend this fire?'

'Er … yes, sir; that would seem to be about it.'

'There must be some mistake.'

'That's what I thought and so I came anyway.'

Sabinus flinched back as the next portion of the circus caught and spewed forth a searing jet of flame, scattering the bucket-chains as the temperature became unendurable; literally blistering.

'It's too late to fight it,' Vespasian said, recoiling and pulling an arm up as if he could ward off the heat. 'Even if we had all the Vigiles from this area's cohort and those surrounding, it would be impossible.'

'You're right; everything is so dry because of the heatwave,' Sabinus agreed. 'It's containment that we need.' He looked back to the centurion. 'Do we know where it started?'

'In the bakery just around the corner.'

Vespasian knew it at once. 'The one that only just opened yesterday?'

'That's the one, sir; how did you know?'

'It doesn't matter.'

Sabinus was not interested in that detail either. 'Get your men making fire-breaks, centurion; pull down every building in its path, starting with that one there.' He pointed to a four-storey tenement that stood next to one that had begun to smoulder. 'And then pull down the one next to that and work in; I don't want it spreading up the Aventine.' He did not add that it was because his property lay at the hill's summit. 'Get started and I'll have as many Vigiles Cohorts and all three of the Urban Cohorts come to aid you as soon as I can.'

The centurion snapped a salute, evidently pleased that he had orders that he could obey. 'Yes, sir.'

'And as soon as more men arrive have some of them start wetting down the circus to try to prevent that from spreading.'

'That will be difficult, prefect.'

'Difficult! Of course it will be difficult, man; but do it anyway.'

'Yes, sir; but it will be very difficult without water.'

'He's right,' Vespasian said. 'On the way up here I noticed that there was only a trickle in the Appian Aqueduct.'

Sabinus punched his fist into his palm. 'This fucking weather! What about the cisterns and water butts, centurion?'

'All of them almost empty; we were struggling as it was.'

'We'll just have to fetch it from the Tiber. I'll mobilise every public slave we have and put pressure on people to lend their personal slaves; this has got to be halted.' He looked up to the imperial residences on the summit of the Palatine, glowing golden in the radiance of fire. 'At all costs, it must not be allowed to spread to the Palatine or my life will be worth nothing and I might as well jump into the flames now. Get on with it, centurion.' He turned to Vespasian. 'Come, brother, we've got work to do, starting with a polite enquiry of Nymphidius Sabinus as to just what the fuck he thinks he's doing.'

'How long has he been prefect of the Vigiles?' Vespasian asked Sabinus as they hurried towards the Forum Romanum, still feeling the warmth of the blaze on their backs despite being at least three hundred paces from it.

'Hmmm? Oh, he was appointed towards the end of last year, whilst you were in Africa; needless to say, he's Tigellinus' friend.'

'And he's no friend of ours.'

'What do you mean?'

'Don't you recognise the name? He was the prefect of the auxiliary cavalry ala that accompanied Decianus to Boudicca's settlement. He acquiesced in leaving us to her mercy.'

'Was that him? Are you sure?'

'Pretty sure; I'll know when I see him.'

'We haven't got time for personal feuds at the moment.'

'Indeed not, Sabinus; but it's always good to know where old friends can be found.'

'Very true, brother. Once we've fought the fire I think we should make life even hotter for the bastard. I'm in a very good position to make Rome exceedingly dangerous for the prefect of the Vigiles.'

Vespasian looked back over his shoulder to where the fire was noticeably growing. 'If there is any Rome left, that is.'

'What do you mean, he won't come before the Senate?' Sabinus roared. 'I want him here to explain why he ordered his Vigiles to do next to nothing about the fire.'

'He says he's too busy fighting the fire to come and talk about it,' the senior consul, Gaius Licinius Mucianus, said. 'I sent a message for him to present himself to the Senate as I rushed over here; that was his reply.'

There were rumblings of outrage around the shadows of the Senate House; at least two hundred senators were now present with more coming through the doors all the time as, beyond, the southern half of the circus was almost entirely engulfed. Public slaves bustled about the chamber lighting lamps and candles that had been hastily gathered to illumine this impromptu and most irregular night-time meeting; but such was the urgency of the situation that convention had been set aside as all present wanted the fire halted before it reached their property. Even the customary prayers and sacrifice had been omitted.

'However,' Mucianus continued, 'I believe that we should ask the Emperor to come and take personal command of the fire-fighting effort.'

That met with unanimous mutterings of approval. Vespasian joined in, smiling inwardly to himself. He knew Mucianus very well from when the man had been his thick-stripe military tribune in the II Augusta in Germania Superior and then in the early part of the invasion of Britannia. He had proved himself to be a very capable soldier and an intelligent politician, as he was now showing: to invite the Emperor back to Rome to take charge was a good way of ensuring that Nero could not blame Mucianus for the disaster.

Sabinus realised it would provide him with a certain immunity too. 'I second that. I think that a combined appeal from the senior consul and the Urban prefect would convey to the Emperor the seriousness of the situation and the fact that his advice is desperately needed.' Sabinus looked around the gradually filling chamber and then added: 'Especially seeing as the prefect of the Vigiles seems to be giving contrary orders to his men.'

Again there was unanimous agreement as the process of focusing the blame had begun even whilst the disaster was still growing.

'Very good,' Mucianus said, his eyes roving around the gathering, 'whoever leads the delegation to the Emperor could make that suggestion in a way that the Emperor would understand without it being an out and out accusation.' His eyes rested on Vespasian. 'The leader of the delegation should be of proconsular rank and I would nominate my former commander in the Second Augusta, a man with Triumphal Ornaments, a newly returned Governor of Africa and a hero of the invasion of Britannia as well as playing a crucial role in the suppression of the revolt in that province a few years ago: Titus Flavius Vespasianus. In him we have a man who can represent the full dignity of the Senate and thereby demonstrate to the Emperor just how much we honour him. Who will second the motion?'

As the senators vied with one another to be associated with the proposal, Vespasian turned to his brother in alarm. 'Seeing Nero is the last thing I want to do; can you get me out of it?'

Sabinus shook his head. 'You can't refuse such an honour from the senior consul, Vespasian; Mucianus is doing you a great favour. He doesn't know about the problem of the pearls.'

Vespasian understood and had no option but to comply with the will of the Senate as a vote was called and passed with very little opposition. 'I thank the Senate for the honour it does me and will do my utmost to ensure that the Emperor understands the gravity of the situation and speeds to our aid. I would recommend that the delegation be made up of men of propraetor and proconsular rank; a dozen of each. I propose my uncle, Gaius Vespasius Pollo, as one member; I leave the rest up to you, Conscript Fathers. To save time we should travel to Antium by sea. We will take boats from the Campus Martius at dawn, sail down to Ostia and take a trireme from there.'

*

A breeze had got up and was blowing with increasing vigour to the south as Vespasian and the delegation boarded a small flotilla of river craft at the landing stage on the Campus Martius, next to Agrippa's Bridge, in what would have been the half-light before dawn had the sky not glowed with the force of many dawns, obscuring the rise of the Dog Star after its seventy-day absence from the night sky. Flames leapt high, being driven south, away from the centre of the city by the freshening wind. The small boats pushed out into the current and, combined with its strength, the power of the oarsmen and the wind, sped south. Crowds of refugees had already begun to cluster in the few open places on either bank, looking back at the consumption of what little they owned in this world.

'This is going to turn out very expensive, dear boy,' Gaius observed, steadying his bulk against the rocking of the vessel. 'Those people are all going to have to be rehoused if we're to keep the peace; if the mob was to get resentful it would be at our throats in no time, especially if there is nowhere to stage any games.' He looked at the burning bulk of the Circus Maximus as they sailed past the Tiber Island and came out from under the Fabrician Bridge. Behind the circus the imperial residences on the Palatine looked to be safe for the moment as the wind had taken the flames away from them; but all the tenements crowding between the circus and the Servian Walls were now blazing. The fire-breaks had not worked. The flames now straddled the city walls and ran amok in the tinder-dry shanty town beyond. Each time Vespasian looked there seemed to be a broader front to the fire. The summit of the Aventine still remained untouched but the fire was eating its way around it as the wind gusted and veered from south to southwest and then back again. Within the time it took them to reach the Aemilian Bridge the flaming detritus blown on the breeze had passed over the Laveran Gate, to the southwest of the Aventine, and seeded the area beyond with sundry infant conflagrations that, despite the efforts of countless silhouetted figures scurrying around with buckets, began to link up.

'The granaries will be next, Uncle,' Vespasian said as the sun rose on a city that had little need for more light.

Gaius wiped the sweat from his brow; his handkerchief came away smeared with soot. 'They're full as well; the Egyptian grain fleet arrived shortly before you did. That will be very costly.'

'More to the point, if they go up then they'll take everything around them; all the warehouses, everything. People are going to lose fortunes and that means ... well, chaos.'

'And chaos will mean Nero will be looking for even more money to solve the problem; we'll all be paying for this. Nero will definitely be wanting your non-existent pearls now, dear boy.'

'They're not non-existent, Uncle; Decianus had them all along.'

'Well, that is rather fortunate, dear boy,' Gaius said after Vespasian had explained the details to him. 'What are you doing about it?'

'I've got Magnus and Tigran's lads working on the problem; we know where they are hidden, it's just a question of breaking into Decianus' house. They were in the process of doing that when the fire broke out and they had to get out quickly, without the pearls. Magnus and the lads have gone back to try again or see if they can grab them as they're being moved out of the house if the fire starts to threaten the summit of the Aventine.'

'Which it will. Look.' Gaius pointed to the hill, just within the Servian Walls, bathed with a mixture of risen sun and burning city; the untouched crown of the Aventine had definitely diminished.

'It must be getting very close to Decianus' house. Sabinus' house will be in trouble soon too as will Domitilla and Cerialis'. I sent a messenger to them this morning to tell them to get their valuables over to our houses; Sabinus is doing the same.'

'Thank the gods that we live on the other side of the city.'

'What makes you think that we'll be safe on the Quirinal?'

'Surely the fire can't travel all the way over there?'

'How do you think we're going to manage to stop it? Men with buckets and a few pumps? It's in the hands of the gods, Uncle. If the wind stays in the south then we should be fine and just the Aventine and perhaps the Caelian will suffer; but if it comes around to the east or even northeast to north, what then? Whoosh.'

Gaius' jowls wobbled with the hideousness of the mental image. 'I see what you mean, dear boy; I shall have my boys make preparations for an evacuation as soon as we get back.'

'Let's hope that Decianus is in the process of doing just that,' Vespasian said as he looked back at the burning Aventine; in the foreground the first of the granaries burst into flame and, as they left the city behind them, the smell of the fumes clung to their clothes.

'The Emperor will see no one until he has completed his recital,' Epaphroditus informed Vespasian at the gates of Antium's theatre, adjacent to Nero's newly constructed villa boasting a sea frontage that was eight hundred paces long.

Vespasian took a deep breath in a monumental effort to remain calm. 'Epaphroditus, Rome is burning; the fires are running out of control.'

The freedman shrugged. 'There is nothing that I can do about it; he's given exact instructions that he is not to be distracted until he has competed in this competition. He's determined to win it.'

'Of course he's going to win it; the judges won't dare vote for anyone else. I must speak to him now.' He turned and gestured at the two dozen senators behind him. 'Look at the makeup of the delegation: all proconsuls or propraetors; that's how important the Senate deems the situation to be. The Emperor must be informed immediately.'

'It's impossible, I'm afraid,' Epaphroditus said as a welling up of applause came from within the theatre. 'That's the Emperor being announced, he'll be going on now. If you're quick you can get in before he starts. It wouldn't do to be here and not watch the performance; Nero won't take kindly to that.'

'It looks as if we've no choice, dear boy,' Gaius muttered. 'Although how we're going to report to the Senate that we were forced to sit through a performance of the Emperor's as Rome burned, I don't know.'

'Sit?' Epaphroditus asked. 'Oh no, we haven't got time to get you seats; they're all taken and I can't start moving people now, that would be very off-putting for the Emperor. I'm afraid you'll have to stand at the back.' He pointed up to the top tier of the theatre to a group of men in headdresses and wearing black and white mantels over their tunics. 'You can squeeze in behind the Jewish delegation from Jerusalem; you had better hurry.'

Vespasian could contain himself no longer. 'But the dignity of the Senate cannot be treated like that, freedman! I insist that seats are found for us; we're not being made to *squeeze in* behind some Jews.'

'And I insist that the Emperor is not distracted. It's also for your own good as if he doesn't win this competition he will be in no mood to grant your request.'

'Of course he's going to win it, you fool.'

'Is he? With his voice I'm sure he will but it requires his full concentration so therefore you will have to stand.'

'I have done what I can,' Nero said, addressing the six judges sitting at the centre of the front row. 'The issue will now be in Fortuna's hands. Since you are men of judgement and experience, you will know how to eliminate the factor of chance.'

Vespasian and his delegation looked on in horror, from the very top of the theatre, down onto the stage where the Emperor stood in an ungirded tunic, his lyre poised. And then it happened: he plucked a chord – it was almost melodic – then, with a reedy voice that barely made it to Vespasian's ears, he launched into an epic ode of the Fall of Troy. An emperor performing in public; on he went, as the audience sat as if enraptured, through verse after mediocre verse, never improving. Behind him the Tyrrhenian Sea, speckled with fishing boats and merchant vessels going about their business, glistered as the sun touched its zenith; a warm breeze, laced with salt, blew in bringing with it the gentle, slow crash of breakers from the beach below. The beauty of the setting contrasted so markedly with the chaos left behind in Rome that Vespasian found it hard to believe that there really was a disaster of such a scale occurring in the city until he looked in its direction: there, rising over the horizon, fifty miles away, was the column of smoke that spoke of the reality of the fire; a reality that the Emperor was not yet aware of as he waded on through the Fall of Troy with tears flowing down his cheeks as he sang of her burning towers. Vespasian clenched and unclenched his fists and seethed at the irony but he, like the rest of the world, was powerless to do anything against the young ruler of Rome and her Empire whose dignity was expiring as he performed, so outrageously, in public so close to the seat of his power.

No one could deny Nero.

The judges were evidently of the same opinion and awarded the victor's crown to the Emperor as soon as the applause, almost as long as the ode itself, had died away; and it was with an assumed air of humility and extravagant gestures of relief that Nero congratulated and commiserated with the other performers as he made his way towards the senatorial delegation now waiting for him in the orchestra.

'My friends,' Nero rasped, his weak voice stretched by such a long recital, 'you do me honour to come all this way to witness my triumph. You must stay, there is plenty of room now that my villa has been completed; there are two more days of competition and I intend to enter both of them and would appreciate your support to help alleviate the nervousness of an artiste before a performance.'

'Princeps,' Vespasian replied, 'would that we could. I'm sure that I speak for all here when I say that nothing would give us more pleasure having arrived just in time to witness your performance; none of us has seen the like.'

Nero made a show of modesty. 'You do me too much kindness; I must insist that you stay.'

'Of course we shall if you insist, Princeps. However, before that is decided I must tell you that we are a delegation sent by the senior consul and the Urban prefect to beg you to return at once to the city where we have urgent need of you. I have to tell you, Princeps, that the Circus Maximus, the Aventine, parts of the Caelian, the granaries and the emporium are all burning.'

Nero looked confused. 'What is that to do with me? Surely that is the responsibility of the Urban prefect and the prefect of the Vigiles? Besides, I can't come now. I've got more competitions to enter.'

'I understand, Princeps, but we need your advice and leadership to tackle the blaze; it's spreading out of control. And the prefect of the Vigiles is being less than clear with the orders that he's been issuing.'

Nero was unconcerned. 'My advice is not to let it spread to my property on the Palatine and the Esquiline as well as over the river on the Vatican; that's the best advice I can give. Then once you've secured them I would advise you to make sure that your own properties don't suffer too much damage. Send orders back to Rome to that effect. Epaphroditus!'

'Yes, master,' the freedman said, his voice unctuous as he stepped forward and bowed his head.

'Have rooms prepared for the senators; they will stay for the next couple of days to watch my performances.'

'Yes, master. And what should I say to the Jewish delegation waiting to see you?'

Nero waved the idea away. 'Tell them they'll have to wait now until I have more time to listen to their whining. Procurator Florus had good reason to imprison those twelve priests they're pleading for seeing as they refused to pay a new tax for religious reasons. They were lucky that he didn't order their execution.' Nero turned back to Vespasian. 'You can go back to Rome after the competition, by which time I'm sure that the fire will have burnt itself out.'

'But Princeps,' Vespasian began but then stopped as Nero held up his hand.

'My mind is made up, senator; there is no need to rush. My art must come first; I cannot deprive the people of the town of my birth the chance to share my talent. Rome can wait until my song is sung.'

The food was exquisite, the music soft and sublime and the wine delicate and fine, chilled by snow brought down from the north and stored in the ice cellars beneath the villa.

Vespasian, along with the rest of the delegation made a show of eating and drinking copiously, laughing at Nero's jokes and trying to ignore the fact that he was wearing women's clothes and was more often than not rubbing his buttocks against his new husband's groin as he reclined on the couch behind him. Of Poppaea Sabina there was no sign; however, Sporus, he too dressed in stola and palla and wigged extravagantly, waited on Nero, looking remarkably like the Empress.

'It's bizarre in the extreme, don't you think, dear boy?' Gaius whispered in Vespasian's ear as the boy bent down to serve Nero more wine.

'What, feasting as Rome burns?'

'No, no, although I grant you that shows a remarkable lack of concern on the Emperor's part. No, I was talking about that young lad's resemblance to the Empress. Ravishing.'

'I would have thought that the Empress wouldn't be to your taste, Uncle?'

'That goes without saying, dear boy; but that lad, on the other hand, is completely to my taste. It's what's in the loincloth that counts.' Gaius tore his eyes away from such tempting but dangerous beauty and concentrated his attention on a dish of seafood served with a thick cumin sauce.

'You have an interest in my slave, Senator Pollo?' Nero asked.

Gaius spluttered a half-eaten prawn onto the napkin spread on the couch before him. 'Indeed not, Princeps; at least not a personal one. I was just admiring his ... er, his countenance.'

'Is that what you call it? I call it his arse.' Nero slapped the item in question, causing Sporus to squeal, and broke into a raucous laugh followed by all present, even Gaius who was only too pleased to have a diversion from his embarrassment.

'But that reminds me,' Nero said, controlling his mirth at last, 'coveting things that are not your own.' His eyes went to Vespasian. 'I believe that you still have those pearls that I gave you to secure the release of all the citizens enslaved in the Kingdom of the Garamantes. Is that not so, Vespasian?'

'I do, Princeps; and I shall return them to you at the first opportunity. I have only just returned from Africa, as you know, and you have been so busy celebrating your joyous marriage and covering yourself with glory on the stage.'

'Yes, yes; I understand. Bring them to me when I'm back in Rome.'

'I shall also bring the two former Suphetes of Leptis Magna who sold legionaries into slavery.'

'Have you proof?'

'Yes, Princeps; two of the legionaries in question made it out of the kingdom and are ready to testify against them.'

'Then why bring these Suphetes to me? They should be dead already.'

'They are citizens, Princeps, and claim the right to be tried by Caesar.'

'Then advise them, instead, to claim their citizen's right to suicide, unless they would prefer me to condemn them to the beasts as they should be for such a crime. And as for the two legionaries who became slaves, they're released from service as we can't have the taint of slavery in the ranks. Just bring me the pearls.'

'It will be my pleasure, Princeps.'

This seemed to satisfy Nero and he returned his focus to his wine and some energetic spooning with his husband.

'Was that a wise promise to make, dear boy?' Gaius asked in a whisper.

'What else could I do, Uncle?'

'Nothing, I suppose; you'll just have to pray to your guardian god that Magnus is successful.'

'I'm praying to all of them.'

'As shall I, dear boy, as shall I.'

Vespasian's concern over his predicament was put to one side as Epaphroditus hurried through the door with a Praetorian tribune, dusty from travel, close behind him.

'Master,' the freedman said, 'Tribune Subrius has been sent from Rome with the latest report; he asks to speak with you alone.'

'Alone? Nonsense. Tribune, say what you have to say in front of all. There is nothing to hide; we're certain that all is being taken care of.'

Subrius snapped a very smart salute. 'Yes, Caesar. I've been sent by the prefects of the Praetorian Guard, the senior consul and the Urban prefect. The situation has deteriorated considerably since that delegation left at dawn this morning. The wind has veered around to the northeast and the fire has now taken the whole of the Circus Maximus, parts of which are now collapsing. The entire Aventine and Caelian Hills are burning as is the lower part of the Esquiline.'

'The Palatine?' Nero almost shouted the question.

The Tribune cleared his throat. 'It was still safe, Caesar, when I left but—'

'But what?'

'But Prefect Sabinus told me to tell you that despite all their efforts the Palatine would be burning by the time I reached you. The fire is now threatening the heart of Rome, Caesar; that was his message.'

Nero jumped to his feet, his face a study in horror. 'But that can't be; the Palatine was supposed to be safe. I gave orders that it was to be protected at all costs.'

'It's the wind, Caesar; it fuels the flames.'

Nero looked about him, his chest heaving with barely repressed sobs, tears welling. 'My beautiful things: my clothes, my jewellery! Out! Everyone, out! We leave at dawn tomorrow. I must save my things.'

CHAPTER XI

I T WAS NOT so much the fury of the flames or the strength of
the wind that the furnace was sucking into its blazing heart
on the Aventine that shocked Vespasian and all who accompanied the Emperor, it was the intensity of the heat. Even with
their river craft keeping to the west bank of the Tiber, the
senators flinched at the wrath of it as it pounded their faces,
forcing them to squint and shut their mouths, such was its
might as they passed the granaries and warehouses now lost to
a storm of fire.

Nero whimpered and cowered behind his husband, even
though he himself was now dressed as a man. Peering out from
behind Doryphorus as the boats cleared the Aventine and
approached the Forum Boarium, Nero shaded his face with a
hand and looked beyond the Circus Maximus, its shape now
indiscernible, to the Palatine; but there was nothing solid to be
seen. Flame blended with flame so that the imperial palaces
seemed to be no more than a hill of fire extending up from the
conflagration consuming what had once been the biggest
construction in Rome. Thus the Aventine and Palatine Hills
burned; and then beyond this terrible sight the Caelian, too, was
completely afire.

At the same time hypnotic, magnificent and terrifying, the
combined fury of the blaze on the three southern hills of the city
captivated Vespasian and he could not tear his scorching eyes
away from the sight. It was with some relief that the boats passed
beneath the two bridges crossing the Tiber from the Forum
Boarium for the heat lessened and the eyes were rested. But as
they once again came out into the open the scale of the tragedy
could not fail but draw them back. No one said a word as the

flotilla of twenty small river vessels rowed against the current up the Tiber; all just sat and stared at the horror.

It was not just the visual but also the aural that horrified: above the rush of the wind, the rumble of collapsing masonry, the crackling, spitting and hissing of thousands of tons of timber being consumed together, there was another sound; a sound Vespasian did not notice at first but one that soon insinuated itself into his consciousness: the wail of a million people. Once he was aware of it, Vespasian could not ignore that wail as it seemed to soar above all other sound such was its rawness and desperation. And the people issuing it were everywhere that there was not fire, fleeing from its path; they swarmed over the bridges, they rushed across open ground, they stampeded through narrow alleys and pushed through the city's gates, trampling the frail, infirm and young underfoot. All the while every man, woman and child wailed in despair for the fire was gaining, leaping from one building to the next so that it had now claimed the southern end of the Forum Romanum, and within it, at the foot of the Palatine, the Temple of Vesta was now ablaze.

It was this that had confirmed to all who saw it or heard of it that Rome was lost, for should the Sacred Flame be extinguished then the city would most certainly fall; and where was the flame now if not consumed by the fire, melded with it so that its potency now added to the blaze that incinerated the city it was meant to protect? Who could fight such a fire imbued as it was with the power of Vesta? What was there left to do other than flee?

The whole city wailed in despair; the whole city, that is, with the exception of the Emperor and the senators who accompanied him; they could do nothing but stare in silence. And it was in silence that they arrived at the landing stage on the Campus Martius whence they had departed the previous dawn. There, standing, grim and covered in ash, was Sabinus; gone was any marking of rank for he wore nought but a pair of sandals and a singed tunic; the left-hand side of his hair had been seared away and there were raw blisters on his arms and legs. Mucianus stood next to him, his appearance much the same; their fatigue was evident to all. They caught ropes flung by the crews and the boats were hauled in and secured.

'Hail, Caesar,' Sabinus croaked, his voice dry with fumes and the issuing of orders. 'You return to us not a moment too soon. We have all the Vigiles, the Urban Cohorts and almost the entire Praetorian Guard at work tearing down firebreaks and dousing important buildings in the fire's path with water in an attempt to prevent them from catching. What are your orders, Princeps?' He reached down, extending his arm to help the Emperor disembark.

Nero looked around; panic flickered in his eyes, and he said nothing as he heaved himself up onto the jetty. Vespasian followed, helping Gaius lever his bulk out of the boat as the rest of the party landed. Although there was, as yet, no fire on the Campus Martius, smoke clouded the air. The Capitoline Hill, to the right, was hazed so that only the faint outline of the Temples of Jupiter and Juno, both still untouched, could be made out; they were framed by the glow of the flames beyond. Indeed, the whole sky above the city glowed red as Vulcan's furnace.

'Your orders, Princeps?' Sabinus repeated.

Nero opened and closed his mouth a few times, evidently unable to think of anything practical that could be done that was not already in action. 'I need to see for myself the extent of the flames; we will go around the city to my gardens on the Esquiline Hill. I shall observe from the tower there.'

It was without imperial dignity that Nero made the journey across the Campus Martius through throngs of refugees. There was no imperial litter and no time to fetch one; accompanied by the senators and the dozen Germanic Bodyguards who had travelled with him from Antium, Nero walked through his people, who stretched out their hands in appeal for they had nothing, no food, no shelter and no hope.

Nero made a show of weeping as he walked, displaying his tears to all. 'Your Emperor is amongst you now; he will share your grief and hardship. My home on the Palatine has been destroyed as have yours. I understand your woes.'

'What are we going to do with all these people, dear boys, eh?' Gaius asked as he looked around in amazement at just how many there were; every open space, every temple step, the Theatre of Pompey, the Flaminian Circus, the baths, everywhere, there were people. Nowhere was without a group of wretched humanity, the lucky ones clutching a few possessions but many had nothing; and to have nothing in a city burning to the ground was a very bleak prospect indeed.

'I've no idea, Uncle.' Vespasian was equally astounded by the multitude. 'I thought the Circus Maximus held a lot of people but this is far more.'

Sabinus rubbed his eyes, trying to blink the caustic fumes from them. 'The Subura caught this morning and what with all the southern quarters on fire the people had no choice but to come this way. I think it's the first time that we have become aware of just how many people are crammed into the Subura, seeing them all together.'

'I just don't believe that there could be so many people; where do they all live?'

'Four or five people to a room in four- or five-storey tenement blocks and you soon get the numbers up,' Sabinus pointed out.

'Prefect Sabinus,' Nero said, stopping and turning. 'I must do something for the people.'

'Indeed, Princeps,' Sabinus said, unable to conceal his surprise.

'I will open my gardens by the Vatican Hill and my circus next to them; have a proclamation to that effect read out as soon as possible.'

'Yes, Princeps.'

'That's an uncharacteristic display of compassion from the man who has lived entirely for himself,' Vespasian muttered to Gaius.

'Haven't we all, dear boy, haven't we all; at least for ourselves and our family.'

'There's the difference: we tend not to kill our families.'

Nero resumed his progress. 'I will have a cohort of the Praetorians stationed there to keep order and to make sure that there isn't any damage done and evict those that cause any.'

Gaius chuckled. 'Ahh, that's better.'

*

It had taken two hours to push through the scores of thousands of refugees and make their way around the Servian Walls, across the Via Nomenata at its junction with the Via Salaria, where Vespasian had first set eyes on Caenis on the day of his arrival in Rome. From then on the going became easier and they soon passed between the almost deserted camp of the Praetorians and the Viminal Gate and then, passing the Praetorian Cavalry stables, arrived at the Esquiline Gate; smoke from the fire burning on the lower part of the Esquiline thickened and made breathing unpleasant. But that was nothing to the shock of direct heat as they came through the gate and forwent the protection of the city walls. It slammed into Vespasian as if it were a physical thing and he almost staggered at its impact. Nero shrieked as the force of it hit him and held onto his husband's arm. The party quickly turned to the right and, following a street between two lavish villas whose owners were in the process of loading their contents onto many wagons, came to the gardens.

The Praetorian duty centurion unlocked the gates at the sight of the Emperor. Up through the terraced levels they went, past Maecenas' Auditorium and Library and to the tower at the summit of the garden. With rasping breath they mounted the wooden stairs, Nero in the lead, each too busy with thoughts of what they would see to make conversation. Out into the open they came at one of the highest points in Rome and the sight took Vespasian's already laboured breath away. Below them was a sea of fire, far larger than Vespasian had imagined when he beheld the Aventine, Palatine and Caelian conflagration from the river; then it had seemed like a hill of fire rising high into the sky, impressive in its height but revealing nothing of its true scale. Up here that scale was laid out for all to see, from the granaries and warehouses next to the Tiber all the way to the lower Esquiline where hundreds of silhouetted figures could be seen working within the swirling smoke, pulling down buildings and creating a break. But even as they watched, flames straddled the rubble, blown by the strong wind of the inferno, and attached themselves to a rickety tenement block whose dry timbers welcomed them and submitted to their power. That was the scale from west to east; from south to north it was of a similar size, reaching from the extension of the city outside the city walls to almost the Capitoline Hill. The Subura burned, as did the lower Viminal whilst its upper reaches smouldered.

'It's just the Capitoline and the Quirinal that are safe,' Gaius said, relief in his voice. 'That's very lucky for us; and for Caenis.'

Vespasian shook himself out of the morbid fascination that had held him spellbound in a way that the flames of the hearth-fire can entrance on a winter's night, multiplied a hundredfold and then again. 'We must try to get over there as soon as we can get away from the Emperor. Flavia will be beside herself with worry; I told her that I'd be back yesterday.' He looked back out over the city and shook his head as the heat seared his face. 'I never thought that a fire at the southern end of the Circus Maximus could end up threatening the Quirinal; it's almost as if it's been helped on its way.'

Gaius thought for a few moments. 'What did Nero mean when he said that the Palatine was supposed to be safe and that he'd given orders that it was to be protected at all costs?'

'Just that. He'd told me, as leader of the senatorial delegation, to send orders back to Rome to do everything possible to protect his property.'

'And did you?'

'Of course.'

Gaius took Sabinus' arm and pulled him close. 'When did you receive your brother's message to make sure that the Palatine was preserved at all costs?'

'At what passed for dusk yesterday.'

Gaius looked back at Vespasian. 'You see.'

Vespasian saw immediately. 'Of course; Nero would have known that my message would not have got back to Rome before Tribune Subrius left with the news that the Palatine was going to burn.' Vespasian glanced over to the Emperor aghast. 'He must have been referring to a previous order, one given earlier, before we arrived, before I told him that there was a fire.

Which means …' Vespasian could not bring himself to say what the implication was.

'It would look that way.'

Vespasian was incredulous. 'He wouldn't, would he?'

'Why not? He's done just about everything else.'

'I mean, why would he?'

Gaius shrugged. 'The gods alone know.'

Sabinus looked between his uncle and brother. 'Are you accusing Nero of starting this?'

'Not of starting it,' Vespasian replied, still in shock at the magnitude of the crime that had been committed. 'He personally couldn't have started it as he was in Antium.'

'But he could have ordered it.'

'Yes, Sabinus; and we know he's perfectly capable of doing such a thing if it suited his purposes.' He slapped his palm on his forehead as a thought hit him. 'On our way up to see you on the evening of the fire we passed Epaphroditus receiving an offspring of Vesta's Flame from the Vestals. I didn't think much of it at the time.'

'But then, Epaphroditus was down at Antium when we arrived the following afternoon,' Gaius said.

'To report to his master that the fire had been set in a new bakery that had been opened solely for that specific purpose; which is why he was so calm about us not giving Nero the news until he had finished the performance: he knew that Nero was already aware of the fire and didn't intend to do anything about it, so therefore why disturb him?'

'Nymphidius was in on it too,' Sabinus said. 'Which is why he gave conflicting orders to his Vigiles. You're right; this was arson on a massive scale only it's gone wrong as the Palatine caught. When I went up there after you had left with the delegation, yesterday morning, I found almost half the full force of the Vigiles just keeping as much water on the buildings as possible. Nymphidius was there shouting and kicking; I couldn't get any sense out of him. I certainly couldn't get him to use his men to help make fire-breaks. And, come to think of it, Tigellinus only ordered the Praetorian Guard to help when the Palatine was threatened and not before. He's burnt my house down and for what?' Sabinus leant closer to Gaius and Vespasian. 'Now what are you thinking about Piso and the rest?'

But Nero coming to a decision prevented them from answering. 'Prefect Sabinus, clear everyone out of the city below equestrian rank who is not a member of a senatorial or equestrian household or is in the Praetorian Guard, the Urban Cohorts or the Vigiles; we must prevent looting. No man is even to search the ruins of his own house on pain of death.'

'And the fire, Princeps?'

Nero pointed down to the figures struggling in the smoke. 'Leave that to Nymphidius and Tigellinus; they know what they're doing. I will make this my base; send your reports here. I want to know the extent of the destruction for we must plan a new city, one that will rise out of the ashes of old Rome; a city that will be worthy of my greatness where I can live with space and beauty all around me and not cooped up on a hill. The city I shall build will be the wonder of the world and it shall be called Neropolis.' He flung his arms in the air as if he was expecting a huge ovation but his entourage just stared at him, rendered speechless by the monstrosity of the thought: to change the sacred name of Rome was unthinkable and yet the Emperor had just mooted it.

Nero stared at all the horrified faces looking at him and chose to misread the expressions. 'I astound you with my vision, I can see, my friends. Leave me now to formulate my plans to bring about the birth of Neropolis.'

'I thought you were dead; burnt alive!' Flavia flung herself at Vespasian as he came through the vestibule of his house and on into the atrium. 'Where have you been? Why didn't you send a message? I don't know what to do; the fire's getting so close and the city is full of cutthroats and looters.'

Vespasian held his wife as she sobbed onto his chest, relieved that she had not chosen the more violent reaction that he had been prepared for as he came through the door. 'We'll take everything that we can and go to the Aquae Cutillae estate if and when the fire starts to threaten the Quirinal. I'll have Cleon get the horses and carts ready in the yard at the back.'

'I've already done that,' Flavia said, her voice muffled by his toga. 'And I've also had all our precious things loaded on, as well as your library.'

'My library?' Vespasian felt unusual affection for his wife. 'That was very considerate of you, my dear. Thank you.'

'Domitilla and Cerialis have already gone to their estate; they just stayed here for one night. We're all ready to leave; I was considering leaving earlier seeing as I didn't know what had happened to you, but there is a problem.'

'What?'

'Domitian's missing again. He disappeared soon after the fire started.'

Vespasian sighed; his youngest son's behaviour had always been an issue. 'I imagine he's enjoying the chaos. The Quirinal isn't in danger of being threatened yet; we won't be thinking of leaving for a while. He's got plenty of time to turn up; although when he does he's going to wish he hadn't.'

Flavia looked up at Vespasian. 'Why? What has he done now?'

Vespasian paused, unwilling at first to share what he knew with his wife and then deciding that she had a right to know. 'Tigran questioned Decianus' freedman, the one who did the transaction with the pearls; he also organised the burglary. Before he died he admitted that the person who told him where in the house they would be concealed was our own son, Domitian.'

'Why would he do such a thing?' Flavia asked for at least the tenth time, wiping her eyes as much against the fumes in the air as to stem her tears. 'He's twelve; he surely knows that loyalty to the family is the most important thing in life?'

'My dear, stop going on about it,' Vespasian said, sharper than he meant to, as he sorted through legal documents in the tablinum with an eye to what needed to be saved and what might be better being lost, should the worst occur. 'The fact is that he did and I like it no more than you do, but, at the moment, there are far more important things to worry about than the hideous betrayal of trust by our youngest son. Did Domitilla and Cerialis manage to save much?'

'Only what they and their household could carry and that they very nearly lost to muggers in the chaos; apparently the city is full of gangs taking advantage of people fleeing with their valuables. Cerialis, along with some of his freedmen and a few friends of Magnus' who were helping them, fought them off and killed a couple. They were fortunate in that respect but they had to leave all their furniture behind so that's all gone. Domitilla was in tears as she had only recently redecorated and some of the pieces were very valuable; she'd also just had new frescoes done in the triclinium at great expense.'

'Yes, well, at least they got out in time; furniture is a small expense when compared to the cost of rebuilding the house.'

Flavia wrung her hands and looked up at Vespasian. 'How will we afford it if the fire reaches us?'

Vespasian put down the document he was perusing. 'We'll manage somehow. I'll just have to try to squeeze more out of the estates and, with luck, Hormus' business will do well in Africa; just before I left he wrote to tell me that he had negotiated the purchase of one hundred breeding females and a dozen males from Egypt. They should have arrived by now. Once the locals see just how better suited to the conditions in Africa they are compared to horses, the business should flourish.'

'But that could take years.'

'What can I say, Flavia? The city is burning down around us; people are losing everything. At least we have two estates and a burgeoning business in Africa.'

There was a discreet cough at the entrance; Vespasian looked up. 'What is it, Cleon?'

'Magnus is here, master.'

'Show him in.'

Cleon bowed and a few moments later a very blackened Magnus appeared; the normally luxuriant hair on his forearms had been singed away and his glass eye was smeared with ash. 'I've got good news, sir.'

Vespasian felt his heart jump. 'You've got the pearls!'

'No, not quite; but I know where they are. Decianus wouldn't have moved them yesterday when he left his house, just before the fire took the Aventine, simply on the basis that they were safer in the pond than anywhere else and he could reclaim them once the fire was out.'

'How do you know?'

'Because it's the obvious thing to do, what with all the lawlessness at the moment. It's not too bad here but on the Aventine and the Caelian anyone who looks wealthy was being attacked as they tried to save their possessions; there were huge gangs going around taking anything they wanted; no one was in control. Decianus got mugged like the rest of them. I watched it and he gave up his strongbox happily, which means that there was very little in it. So I think that we might find more than just the pearls at the bottom of his pond.'

'You're right, Magnus; we just have to get there first.'

'Exactly, sir. But I'm afraid that it's going to have to be just you and me; Tigran can't spare any of the lads as the flames are getting very close to a lot of South Quirinal Brotherhood property.'

'Where's Decianus now?'

'I don't know exactly, but he's certainly left the city.'

'In which case, I'm staying, whatever happens. We'll wait for the blaze to die down and beat him back onto the Aventine.'

Smoke hung in the air that had become still since the intensity of the flames had diminished. Whether the flames had eased due to the wind fading or the other way around, no one either knew or cared; the plain fact was that on the evening of the third day of the fire, it seemed to be under control. The destruction was confined to an area not much larger than the sea of fire that Vespasian had witnessed from the Gardens of Maecenas two days previously. Two days in which he had watched the progress of the fire either from his house or Caenis' as it crept closer to the Quirinal, gradually making its way from the Subura, up the Vicus Longus, but, thankfully, never managing to cross the Alta Semita, on the northern side of which lay Pomegranate Street. The combined efforts of the Guard, the Urban Cohorts and the Vigiles, over twenty thousand men in total, had been enough to turn the tide against the fire by pulling down hundreds of buildings and denying it the sustenance it needed. But still there were pockets burning, although they were small and manageable, and Vespasian and Magnus passed many bucket-chains as they made their way through the ruined city as a false dusk dwelt upon it.

Vespasian could but marvel at the completeness of the destruction in certain areas: blackened, smouldering masonry lay on the ground as if it had been levelled by a huge earthquake. Nothing remained intact of the Circus Maximus as all the beams that had supported its huge mass had perished in the flames and the building was now so much rubble in the shape of the circus.

The fire itself had not managed to make it across the Forum Romanum; the Senate House and the Aemilian Basilica next to it were both safe, as were the Tabularium and all the buildings on the Capitoline Hill behind it as well as the Quirinal, and it had been with great relief that Vespasian had watched the threat to his property recede.

The Aventine was a wasteland of jagged forms, charred and wreathed in a pall of smoke and steam. Glowing piles of embers still emitted substantial heat and added to the fumes as the blackened corpses of the old, weak or plain unfortunate began to exude the reek of death and decay. Live human forms flitted here and there through the dim light, sometimes in groups and sometimes singularly or in pairs; none threatened Vespasian and Magnus, as they picked their way through the detritus, for they openly carried, contrary to the law, swords that were forbidden to all in the city other than members of the Praetorian Guard or the Urban Cohorts.

'The Emperor's injunction against all but the élite and their households leaving the city doesn't seem to be holding,' Vespasian observed as a group of feral youths, sacks over their shoulders, appeared out of the miasma, took one look at their unsheathed weapons and scampered off.

'Everyone's too busy fighting the fire to patrol the streets.' Magnus looked about at the rubble strewn all about, underfoot.

'Not that we have streets any more in the real sense of the word, if you take my meaning?'

And Vespasian did, only too well. 'To rebuild this you would have to start right from the beginning; you wouldn't have to keep to the original plan.' The audacity and ruthlessness of what had been attempted struck him with a mixture of shock and wonder. 'You could build anything you wanted in all the areas around the Palatine. Nero's going to have his wish.'

'What's his wish?'

'Neropolis.'

'Neropolis? Do you mean to say that he started this so that he could build his own city on the rubble?'

'That's what it looks like, except that the Palatine was meant to be an island in the flames; although how Nero expected that to happen the gods only know.'

'Well, that explains the strange things that me and the lads witnessed over the last couple of days. After we left you and Sabinus at the Senate House we came back here to wait for Decianus to make his move and also to help your daughter and her husband get to the Quirinal, and all I can say is that there were almost as many people trying to hinder people fighting the fire as there were tackling the flames themselves.'

'That doesn't surprise me,' Vespasian muttered as they passed between the remaining stumps of the Appian Aqueduct, clambering over the still hot rubble of its fallen channel, shattered and brought to the ground, after almost four hundred years, by extreme heat.

'Yeah, well, they was running around saying that they had orders from very highly placed individuals that the blaze was to be allowed to spread in certain directions. I even saw one group preventing some Vigiles from pulling down a couple of buildings for fire-breaks. They were all men of military age and had more than the whiff of the Praetorian Guard about them. Anyhow, once the fire had really caught and the Aventine was completely alight as well as the Subura all these groups started to disappear and, instead, we seem to have more men fighting the fire.'

'Or containing it to the extent that Nero wanted.'

'That's what it seems to look like, now.'

Vespasian knew it to be the truth and wondered just how the Emperor thought he would cover up his atrocious crime, or was he, perhaps, arrogant enough to think that he did not have to? What was certain was that whatever Nero thought would have no grounding in reality as had become abundantly clear with his growing list of outrages.

The shadowy sight through the fumes of a group of half a dozen spectral looters scrambling over the ruins of Decianus' house focused Vespasian and Magnus' minds back to the task in hand. 'We need to get rid of them sharpish,' Magnus said, 'before one decides to have a nice little cool off in the fish pond.

Vespasian did not argue; he strode forward to the rubble and, brandishing his sword in one hand, began to climb using his other to steady himself. Magnus followed, cursing under his breath as the heated masonry scalded his exposed flesh. With smoke oozing from various smouldering piles within the burnt-out house, Vespasian and Magnus' approach went unnoticed as the looters rummaged in the ruins of what had once been a dwelling way beyond their means.

With a cry of triumph one man pulled a copper cooking pot from the wreckage and stuffed it into a hessian sack slung over his shoulder.

'Out! Vespasian shouted. 'All of you!' He moved as fast as the uneven surface would allow towards the group, his sword at the ready for an underarm, military thrust to the gut.

Magnus stooped to pick up a cracked brick before coming on in support.

The group, four men and two women, edged back at the shock of the sudden materialisation of two armed men so close by. They shared quick glances as Vespasian and Magnus advanced and came to a mutual agreement upon seeing that there were just two adversaries trying to move them from their lucrative find.

'Make us,' the man with the cooking pot said, unslinging his sack and swinging it with menace as his three comrades moved towards him, ready to stand shoulder to shoulder, all brandishing improvised weapons in one hand and daggers in the other.

Vespasian was not in the mood to ask twice and Magnus had never seen the point in doing so. The brick hurtled through the air, felling the man, ripping open his right cheek; the women screamed as Magnus came on. Vespasian lunged forward, grabbing a knife-wielding fist and then, ducking under the swipe of a smouldering baton, he rammed his blade, lightning-quick, into the entrails of the looter, pulling him onto it with a jerk of his hand clamped around his wrist. Punching his right arm forward and to the left he pushed the doubling-over, skewered man, grunting gutturally, into the path of a comrade's blade; with a dull thump the tip sliced into a kidney, reversing the looter's direction as he now arched back, pierced both front and back, the low bestial noises morphing into a scream of intense agony. With a swift stroke and a stab, Magnus opened the throat of the fourth looter, spraying blood onto the women who turned and fled along with the last male whose knife remained buried in his dying comrade's back. Angry that it had had to come to this, Vespasian finished off the two wounded men with petulant thrusts to their hearts as Magnus examined their loot.

'Anything?' Vespasian asked as Magnus rummaged through the various sacks and bags.

'No, just cheap rubbish in here, sir,' he said, tipping out a bag, its contents clattering on the rubble. 'Anyway, I would reckon that if they'd found what we're looking for they would have been long gone.'

'Let's hope so.' Vespasian moved forward over the wreckage and down into what was once the rectangular courtyard garden.

Despite it having had no roof other than a colonnade around all four sides, now totally demolished, it still looked as if a ceiling had fallen into it such was the mess strewn about.

'The pond is almost choked,' Vespasian said, looking at the bricks and roof tiles lying in the green water that was much reduced in depth. 'Which corner?'

'The one nearest the Forum Boarium,' Magnus replied, pointing at the northeastern corner.

Vespasian knelt down and began removing the loose remains; the water, what little remained of it, was unsurprisingly hot and each piece had to be grabbed and pulled out with a quick continuous motion. Magnus joined him and together they worked, all the while aware of shouts and screams from round about as others fought over booty in a city whose law and order had completely broken down.

'This'll take both of us, sir,' Magnus said as he tried to lift what must once have been a segment of a column, the last remaining stone in the corner.

Vespasian leant over the rim of the pond and took a firm grip, wincing as the water scalded the soft skin of his wrists and the underside of his forearms. With a quick look between them they heaved; slowly the stone was raised and then with huge effort they pushed it away towards the middle of the pond.

Vespasian glanced at Magnus before looking down into the water, unwilling to reach down into it and feel around for fear of bitter disappointment.

Magnus stuck his hand in and swirled it around; his face suddenly lightened as the atmosphere all around darkened with the sinking of the obscured sun into the west. 'There's something here.' He pulled out a dripping bag.

Vespasian recognised it immediately. 'That's the old saddlebag that Decianus brought out of Garama.'

Magus unclipped a fastener and opened it for Vespasian to explore. He put a hand in; deep down at the bottom he felt many smooth spheres that clacked together as he ran a finger through them. He grinned at his friend. 'You were right.'

'I normally am.'

'Don't move!'

Vespasian and Magnus froze.

'Stand up slowly and turn around.'

They did as they had been ordered and ended looking up at a Praetorian centurion standing on the wall of rubble above them; to either side of him were four Guardsmen with javelin-like *pila* aimed directly at their chests.

'Looting, are you?' the centurion asked in a light manner.

'I'm Senator Titus Flavius Vespasianus and this man here is a part of my household. We have a perfect right to be in the city as the exclusion order did not apply to senators, as you well know.'

The centurion indicated to his men to lower their weapons and crashed to attention. 'Centurion Sulpicius Asprus, sir. I'm afraid that we've had specific orders that the injunction against looting applies to everyone; senators and all. I have orders to round up anyone I catch. But seeing as you are a senator it's beyond me. Come with me, sir; I'm obliged to take you before the Emperor.'

CHAPTER XII

I T WAS A tortuous route to reach the Gardens of Maecenas; they were forced to retrace their steps to the Fora Boarium and Romanum and then pass between the Senate House and the Aemilian Basilica, where much of Rome's business was conducted, before heading along the Argiletum and traversing the Subura on the way to the Esquiline.

'Typical, ain't it,' Magnus said as he surveyed the burnt-out wrecks of tenement blocks to either side of the Argiletum. 'All those with next to nothing lose what little they had and then the premises of people like the Cloelius Brothers in the Aemilian Basilica don't get touched; how does that happen? It ain't natural.'

Vespasian shifted the saddlebag to the other shoulder, its warmth excessive in the conditions. 'I'm afraid that it's one of the most natural things in the world, Magnus.'

'Yeah, well, I'd still like to know how it happens.'

'I don't suppose it's got anything to do with the fact that Tigellinus owns the Aemilian Basilica; that would be far too cynical.'

'Tigellinus owns it?' Magnus was surprised.

'Yes, Nero gave it to him as a present for services rendered a few years back; he makes a fortune out of the rents.'

'I'm sure the Cloelius Brothers pay very handsomely for one of the best addresses in Rome.'

As they passed on through the Subura the devastation was everywhere and, for the most part, complete. It had been here that the fire had burnt strongest as most of the buildings had been cheaply put up, using much timber, and crowded together. The firestorm that had swept through, fed by the wind funnelled between the Viminal and Esquiline Hills, had been so intense that much had simply disappeared, incinerated, so that there was less wreckage than there had been on the Aventine, but it was ankle-deep in the cloying ash that covered everything. The wrath of the flames, burning at such high temperatures, had had the result that the Subura fire had burnt itself out very quickly, in a matter of a couple of days, and now it was just a grey-sanded desert.

Up the Clivus Suburanus, on the Esquiline, the damage was more similar to that of the Aventine on its western side but, as they progressed further up the hill, on its eastern side it was very different: for fifty paces there was just rubble, uncharred rubble. For it had been along the course of this road that the main fire-break had been constructed to protect the Gardens of Maecenas and Nero's property within.

And inside the garden's walls there was no sign of the fire. As Vespasian looked at the lush vegetation, carefully arranged on the garden's many terraces to give such a variety of colour and shape, he could scarcely believe, despite the ash that dusted some of the plants, that had he turned around he would have been presented with a scene of devastation such had never been witnessed before in the eight hundred years of Rome's history.

It was to the long, round-ended building that was known as Maecenas' Auditorium that Centurion Sulpicius led Vespasian and Magnus.

'Wait here with them,' Sulpicius ordered his men as he went in, passing the two Praetorians guarding the entrance who snapped to attention.

'You seem very calm about the whole thing,' Magnus observed.

Vespasian grinned and looked at the saddlebag. 'That's because I've a feeling that I'm going to rather enjoy this.'

A raised voice came from within; it was that of the Emperor. 'Don't ever dare to defy me; you will be recompensed. Now go!'

Magnus sucked the air between his teeth. 'He don't sound in the best of moods.'

Barging past the two guards, Tigellinus came barrelling out of the Auditorium, his face taut with fury and his eyes dark with hate.

Vespasian watched him go, travelling at a walk so brisk as to be completely lacking in the dignity expected of a prefect of the Praetorians. 'I'd say that's a man who has just been ordered to do something that he'd rather not do.'

'Senator, you must come in,' Sulpicius said, poking his head out of the door. 'Your man can stay out here.'

Vespasian steeled himself and then walked into the building; immediately he choked back a cry of surprise. In the middle of the large space Nero stood next to a table, a large table, admiring what lay on it.

Subrius, the same Praetorian tribune who had delivered the message to Nero in Antium, dismissed Sulpicius and led Vespasian forward.

'Senator Titus Flavius Vespasianus,' Subrius announced. 'Suspected of looting contrary to your edict.'

Nero waved his hand in a dismissive manner, unable to take his eyes from the table. 'What do you think of my model, Vespasian?'

Vespasian looked at the model, the model of a city: Rome. Yet it was not Rome as anyone had ever seen it, it was a new Rome, and at its heart stood a building so vast, arranged about plentiful gardens and a rectangular lake surrounded by colonnades, much like the one on which the dinner had been held, only four times the size. The whole complex took up most of the route Vespasian had just walked from the forum. It was a palace to surpass all palaces and with only a cursory glance at the exterior he could see that it would cost a fortune in gold to erect and, knowing Nero's taste in décor, another fortune would be squandered furbishing it.

'Neropolis!' Nero said, still unwilling to take his eyes from the model and the huge statue of himself in its midst. 'With my Golden House at its heart; the house where I will at last be able to live like a human being should. What do you think?'

Vespasian did not know what to think except that the model was so detailed and thought through that it could not have been constructed in the five days since the fire had started and thus made Nero's vision of a new Rome, Neropolis, possible. 'Magnificent, Princeps. Such elegance.'

Nero smiled to himself, with an air of abstraction, in the way that content, fulfilled people do. 'It is; and it shall be a reality within two years.'

Again Vespasian checked himself: to build a palace like that in two years would double the cost, such would be the intensity of the labour and the pressure on suppliers for materials. 'Two years to build such a house, Princeps?'

'The Golden House alone? No, Vespasian, no. Two years to build Neropolis; all of it.'

Vespasian looked at the scale of the model and, as he did so, he noticed an anomaly: there were new buildings where he had seen for himself, within the last couple of hours, there had been no destruction; but nevertheless they were there, where the fire had failed to reach, both at the far end of the Forum Romanum and also on the, as yet completely untouched, Campus Martius. And as he looked at the site of the Aemilian Basilica he saw that the building was of an entirely different design and he realised why Tigellinus had been so unwilling to obey his master's will for he was yet again to become an incendiary.

Vespasian waited, saying nothing, as Nero continued to admire the model from all angles, bending down to look along thoroughfares, leaning over to look down at the gardens within the Golden House, and all the while humming to himself the ode of the Fall of Troy that he had sung in the competition at Antium on the first day of the fire. The tribune looked on, betraying no thoughts, as the Emperor gloried in the new city that he would raise from the ashes of the old whose demise, it seemed certain, he, Nero, was responsible for.

'Subrius, here, tells me that you were caught looting, Vespasian,' Nero said in a matter-of-fact way whilst revolving a dome on the Golden House. 'Well? Were you?'

Vespasian knew Nero well enough to make him the centre of any conversation. 'Only for you, Princeps.'

'For me?'

'Indeed, Princeps; in order that I could keep my word to you. You see, I promised to bring you the pearls at the earliest opportunity but I will confess that I had told you a slight untruth: I said that I still had them but what I really meant was that I knew where they were as they had been stolen from me.'

'Stolen?' This got Nero's attention and he looked directly at Vespasian for the first time in the interview. 'By whom?'

'Catus Decianus.'

'Decianus! But he was the one who told me that you still had them.'

Now was the time, Vespasian judged; now he could put his side of the story. And so he started from the very beginning, from Decianus' seizure of Boudicca's gold that was the initial spark that lit the flames of rebellion in Britannia, which claimed eighty thousand Roman lives, right the way through to handing the saddlebag containing the pearls over to Nero.

'They're short, Vespasian,' Nero said after Subrius had done a tally. 'Forty-one are missing.'

'What can I say, Princeps? The centurion who brought me here will witness the fact that I had only just retrieved the bag when he came upon us; I had no time to sequester forty-one pearls. All I know is that there were five hundred when Decianus stole them from my house.'

Nero stared hard at Vespasian, trying to detect the truth; but as one so cloaked in self-delusion he had no aptitude for it. 'Decianus must have taken them; still, no matter. I'll reclaim their worth from him when I take the two million sesterces that you paid him to return them in the first place. And what happened to the five million in gold and silver he took from Boudicca? I certainly never saw any of that.'

'He claims that Seneca got the Cloelius Brothers to hand it over to him, whilst Decianus was in hiding in Garama, and then he gave it to you. But I don't believe that; I expect Decianus is still sitting on the full five million.'

Nero looked down at his model. 'I'm going to need every sesterce that I can get if I'm to do justice to my genius. I think that Decianus will be able to play his part. Subrius, find out where he is and have him brought to me.'

The tribune saluted. 'Yes, Princeps.'

'He's left Rome,' Vespasian said, trying to be helpful.

Nero continued to admire his model; the new version of the Aemilian Basilica now seemed to particularly hold his attention. 'You can go, Vespasian; you're of no more use to me seeing as you seem to have very little money any more.'

'Indeed, Princeps, thank you.' Vespasian turned and strode out of the building as fast as he decently could and then on down through the gardens with Magnus scampering after him.

'Well?' Magnus asked.

'Well, what?'

'Well, did he take the pearls?'

'Of course he did, but that's all he's going to take from me; I seem to have shifted his attention onto Decianus and in the process managed to conceal my having forty-one of those pearls. Nero's very keen that Decianus should help as much as he can to fund his new building project. I'd call that a good morning's work.'

Magnus grinned. 'Let's pray to all the relevant gods that Nero has got a lot of building in mind.'

'Oh, he has; I've just seen it. He's got the whole city planned out and seems to have done for a while; certainly for longer than the duration of the fire.'

'Do you mean?'

'I do.'

'Are you sure?'

'Yes.'

'Surely not?'

'I'm afraid so, Magnus, and if you want proof …' He pointed towards the Forum Romanum.

Magnus squinted his one good eye in that direction. 'Smoke; so?'

'So, it wasn't burning an hour ago and now it suddenly is and the reason is that there is a brand new version of the Aemilian Basilica and so the old one's got to go; as well as the Senate House and all the temples on the Capitoline and a few of the older ones on the Campus Martius.'

'What about the Quirinal?'

'That still seemed to be residential and commercial in Nero's model rather than public, but I think we should hurry back.' The column of smoke rising from the Forum Romanum had thickened and had now been joined by a couple more. 'I think no one really cares about what gets destroyed any more; if Tigellinus is having to torch his own property then why should he be worried if it spreads uphill to ours?'

'Vespasian!' Caenis exclaimed as he walked into her atrium, which was now almost completely devoid of furniture. 'Have you seen it's started up again, just when we all thought that it had been beaten?'

'I have, my love; and I know for sure that it was deliberate.'

'Deliberate?'

He told her all that he had seen.

'But that's terrible,' Caenis said slumping down onto the sole remaining couch, putting a hand to her mouth.

'No, my love, it's madness; and to make it even worse, I believe it's also sacrilege: I saw Epaphroditus take an offspring of Vesta's Flame just before the bakery was set alight; I think the fire was kindled with Rome's Sacred Flame. Somewhere in the depths of Nero's mind he must think that using the Flame makes it all right. Not even Caligula would have gone this far.'

'He didn't reign long enough to come up with the idea. Perhaps he would've done had he survived.'

'It's possible, but he was more interested in humiliating the Senate in revenge for their complicity in the extermination of much of his family. His bridge across the bay was the grandest scheme that he ever had and that was just to take his mind off the death of his sister, Drusilla. No; this has got to be stopped.'

'And you're the man to stop him?'

'Of course I'm not!' Vespasian breathed deeply. 'I'm sorry. I still find the whole thing so outrageously hard to believe.'

'So what are you going to do?'

'I need to make sure that people get to know the truth.'

'Without the source of that truth becoming obvious.'

'That goes without saying, my love.'

'Well, you know that the best way to appear innocent is not to be anywhere near the scene of the crime.'

'Leave Rome? I plan to anyway in order to squeeze some more money out of the estates; I thought you might like to join me at Cosa.'

'I'll leave very soon; everything is ready and I've hired an escort.'

'I'll be with you once I've spent some time at Aquae Cutillae.'

'With Flavia?'

'Of course with Flavia!' Again Vespasian took a deep breath. 'I'm sorry.' He sat down on the couch next to Caenis and put an arm around her. 'I'll come to Cosa as soon as I can. But if I'm going back and forth between the estates how can I spread any rumours?' He kissed her on the forehead.

Caenis responded by lifting her face and kissing him full on the lips. 'Graffiti, my love.'

Vespasian pulled away, cupping her head between his hands, looking into her eyes. 'Graffiti?'

'Of course; on the first few new buildings that go up have people write on it just who was responsible for the fire; it won't take long for the idea to spread. I'm sure you know who can organise that without you being in the slightest way implicated.'

Vespasian smiled and kissed her with passion. 'You are the most brilliant woman I know.'

'That's not saying much.'

'In the world, then.'

'That's better.'

An urgent knock on the front door interrupted the praise. Caenis got to her feet as the doorkeeper checked who was requiring ingress. 'It's Magnus, mistress.'

Caenis nodded and the door was opened.

'You'd better come quickly, sir,' Magnus said with just the briefest of nods to Caenis. 'The fire is spreading up the Quirinal. Senator Pollo is leaving and Domitian has turned up so Flavia is desperate to go too.'

*

'You go with Gaius, Flavia,' Vespasian urged, looking south to the approaching fire that was now no more than half a mile away; tackling it were men from the Third Cohort Vigiles and they did not seem to be making a very good job of it. 'And take Domitian with you.'

Flavia put an arm around Domitian who immediately shrugged it off. 'What about you?'

'Magnus and I will stay until the last moment; we'll help try to fight it. Better that than just allow the house to be burnt down.'

'I want to stay too,' Domitian insisted.

Vespasian resisted the urge to box the boy's ears. 'You will do as I tell you; go with your mother and try to make up for the distress that you caused her for going missing for five days.' The glare he gave his son silenced any cheek or insubordination that may have been brewing within him.

Domitian turned and mounted his horse as if it were exactly the thing he wished to do at that moment.

'Say nothing to him about the pearls, my dear,' Vespasian whispered as he helped Flavia up into the raeda, the covered, four-horse carriage in which she would travel surrounded by slaves and cushions.

'As you wish. You'll come soon?'

'Magnus is getting the horses ready; we may even catch up with you this evening if the fire carries on spreading this quickly and overruns this whole area. Otherwise I'll come as soon as I know the house is safe.'

Flavia surprised him with a kiss on the cheek. 'Take care, husband; you know I love you.'

'Come on, dear boy,' Gaius called back from his raeda, just in front of Flavia's. 'Put the woman down so that we can be off.'

'I'll see you in Aquae Cutillae, Uncle. And you too, Flavia.' Vespasian returned his wife's kiss as Gaius settled back down into the comfort of his carriage with a couple of his boys for company; the rest of his household joined Vespasian's slaves behind the two raedae as the drivers cracked their whips and the little convoy moved off – the injunction against wheeled vehicles within the city in daylight being universally ignored.

Vespasian watched them go for a few moments before the smell of burning brought his attention back to the fire that he and Magnus must now face.

'Pull back!' the Vigiles centurion ordered his men as Vespasian and Magnus arrived at the face of the fire raging in the Temple of Quirinus, the spear-wielding god of the Sabines.

The eighty men under the centurion's command pulled their pumps back and ran with their buckets as the roof, wreathed in flames, began to buckle. For three hundred and fifty years the temple had stood, brick-built around a wooden frame; now that ancient timber blazed out of control.

'Back! Back!' the Vigiles centurion yelled again, signalling to Vespasian and Magnus to turn about.

Roof tiles cracked and splintered in the heat, sending razor-like, super-heated shards flying in all directions as the blaze raged in the roof beams, now sagging to the point of unsustainability.

'Back! Back!' the centurion repeated, urging his sprinting men past him and then rushing to help two of them wheel the last of the pumps away.

With a surge of incendiary activity bursting from it, the roof collapsed in gradual stages as if Time's chariot had again slowed for the few moments it took, extending them. Thunderous was the shattering of tiles and the cracking of beams hitting the floor as a jet of flame shot through burning doors to explode up the street. With terrified cries, the Vigiles handling the pump were projected forward, such was the force of the eruption. Vespasian felt his eyebrows singe as he shielded his face, bending over, the heat scalding his bald pate.

'Fuck me!' Magnus cursed as he slapped his knee repeatedly to extinguish the burning hem of his tunic.

'Quick!' Vespasian shouted, dashing forward as burning debris fell all about. He cradled an arm over his head as he sprinted to where the pump now burned. Beside it writhed and rolled the centurion and his two men, their tunics afire. Vespasian beat at the flames on the centurion's back as Magnus attempted to help the other two. 'Pull it off!' Vespasian shouted over the screams, going for the man's belt buckle. Roasted flesh and sizzled hair clawed at his nostrils as he pulled the belt free; through his agony the centurion realised what was being attempted and with a fleet jerk pulled the flaming garment over his head, flinging it away. Vespasian beat the flames from the man's hair as Magnus managed to get the tunic from one of the Vigiles; the second was beyond help, a crazed fireball on two legs running about as if a decapitated chicken.

They hauled the centurion and his man away from the burning debris of the temple, leaving their comrade screaming in its midst. Their skin raw and their hair gone, they hyperventilated with the pain.

The rest of their century came running as Vespasian and Magnus dragged, more than led, the injured men back up the hill.

'Two of you, get them back to your quarters to be seen to,' Vespasian ordered. 'The rest of you come with me.'

Such was the authority in his voice that no one, not even the optio, questioned his right to command; besides, he had just saved two of their number from a certain and unpleasant death.

Vespasian addressed the optio. 'Have you got ropes?'

'Yes, back there, sir.'

'Get them. It's pointless fighting it so we'll make a fire-break instead. We'll fall back to the Quirinal Gate, where the walls project in a few dozen paces; we'll do it there.'

Three men lay dead in front of the two houses, heads cracked and bleeding, bludgeoned to death by the clubs of the Vigiles when they tried to prevent them from tearing their houses down. There had been no time to reason with them and Vespasian had given the order willingly seeing as the break was but a hundred paces from his uncle's property and it was the best chance of containing the blaze that he could envisage. Other citizens screamed at them to move the break forward so that their houses would be saved, but Vespasian knew that here, by the Quirinal Gate where the wall pushed into the city, was the obvious place as a third of the work had already been done and the street from the gate to the Alta Semita and beyond was the width of two carts.

Screaming, fleeing citizens raced past, carrying what they could; a few occasionally turning back to search for a loved one or risk a bit of looting before the flames surged forward across another block. Some did not return.

'Pull!' Vespasian roared over the chaos. The four ropes tautened and the eighteen men hauling on each strained their muscles, gritted their teeth and grunted with exertion.

'Keep at it, you whoresons!' Magnus shouted by way of encouragement. 'Pull like you'd pull a Briton off your mother.'

Even amidst the danger, Vespasian could not stop a small grin as he remembered the long-dead centurion Faustus use a similar expression in Thracia; it had been a favourite phrase of his ever since. He glanced at Magnus and his friend grinned back. 'I thought that would amuse you, sir.'

There was a sharp report and the masonry under one of the grappling hooks cracked.

'Keep at it; it's coming,' Vespasian shouted as the whole front wall of one of the houses began to shift.

Feeling their imminent success, the Vigiles renewed their efforts, blistering the palms of their hands on the rough hemp. For four more heartbeats the brickwork held out and then, on the fifth, the walls toppled, breaking in half as they fell, folding back onto themselves, spraying up clouds as they crashed onto the road. Terracotta tiles slipped from the listing roofs as the first floors sagged and then collapsed causing the other walls to shudder, further dislodging the roof beams so that they too came crashing down in a welter of rising dust that billowed as objects fell through it.

'Take two contubernia and get as much of the wood out, and anything else flammable, as you can,' Vespasian ordered the optio. 'I'll take the rest of the lads on to the next two houses.'

Sweat poured from Vespasian and his tunic clung to him; thirst assailed him, his throat dry with ash and fumes, as he urged his men to greater efforts in pulling down the next two buildings. All the while he kept a nervous eye on the fast-approaching flames which, against all logic that he could think of, advanced quicker going uphill.

And it was with desperation that they now worked, hauling at ropes to collapse walls, some sturdily built, others less so, as the optio and his men extracted as much timber from the wreckage as possible. In the hour that it took the flames to travel from the Temple of Quirinus to the gate of the same name, almost two dozen houses fell on the northern side of the Alta Semita, providing a break almost two hundred paces long and, including the street whose path it followed, forty paces wide.

'Will it be enough?' Magnus asked as they watched the flames begin to consume the last buildings before the break.

Vespasian did not answer; it either would be or not and his opinion would not influence the outcome one way or the other. The entire Vigiles century now toiled to remove the wood from the wreckage, although the heat was now so intolerable that each man could only stand a few moments' labour at a time.

'Who's in charge here?' a voice shouted.

Vespasian recognised it immediately and turned. 'I am, Sabinus.'

Sabinus came striding up, he and his lictors all bearing the marks of six days' struggle against the flames; behind him came four centuries of one of the Urban Cohorts. 'What are you doing here, Vespasian?'

'And it's nice to see you too, Sabinus. I'm protecting our family's property is the answer to your question.'

Sabinus walked past Vespasian and approached the fire-break. 'Everyone, back; this area of the city is being evacuated. Out!'

The Vigiles were more than happy to pull further away from the rising heat and complied immediately.

Vespasian ran to catch up with Sabinus. 'We can't evacuate now; who's going to fight the fire if it jumps the break?'

'No one, Vespasian; no one. The Emperor has ordered that everyone should leave; he's set up refugee camps on the Vatican Hill and is feeding the people at his own expense.'

'Create the problem and then be seen to solve it.'

'What do you mean?'

'Just that. Nero's responsible for the fire and now he wants to make the people love him by looking after them.'

Sabinus looked non-committal. 'Well, whatever his motives, those are his orders. The fire has taken the Capitoline and the part of the Campus Martius that adjoins it; this is the last place that it is out of control and Nero wants to just let it burn itself out.'

'That's all very well for him to say when it's not his property.'

Sabinus turned tired eyes onto his brother. 'You can stay and try to fight it single-handed if you want, brother; but I'm ordering everyone out and leaving the Urban Cohort lads here to stop any looting, so yours, Gaius' and Caenis' houses will all be safe provided the fire doesn't get them.' He gestured to the break. 'But I would say that should hold it; so you should be fine. Go, brother; get yourself to Aquae Cutillae. I'll show the centurions which houses to take special care of.'

'What about …'

'What about what?'

'The loan?'

Sabinus shook his head. 'Now's really not the time. The contract was burnt along with the rest of my house. Send me a new one next month and I'll have the money transferred up to you. Now go; I'll send word about how your houses fare.'

Vespasian squeezed his brother's shoulder, turned and then walked away. Magnus followed him; between them they said nothing, not even when they reached their horses. Jumping into their saddles, they urged their mounts up the Quirinal to the Porta Collina and then bore left onto the Via Salaria, hemmed in by tombs and clogged with refugees.

It was not until they had waded their horses through the crush and were able to travel to the side of the road as the tombs thinned out and it began to climb uphill that Vespasian turned to his friend. 'I won't let Nero get away with this, Magnus.'

Magnus looked dubious as he bounced along in discomfort. 'Oh, yes? And just what makes you think that you have the ability or power to punish the Emperor?'

'I don't personally; but I can help start to make the people aware that he deserves punishment. The time is coming, Magnus; and I'm going to need your help.' Vespasian halted and turned his horse to look back on the city from the exact same place as he had first beheld it, with his father and brother, all those years ago; but this time all was different. The Rome that he had entered as a teenager, the Rome that he had deemed to be full of hope but had found to be brimming with darkness and fear, was no more. Perhaps she had been cleansed or perhaps she had been sacrificed.

The mistress of the world still reclined upon her seven hills but now she was but a shrivelled carcass covered by a funeral shroud of thick fumes: the smoke, steam and other vapours that she had exhaled in her final breaths as she writhed in her agony. All about her, her people scurried like so many small ants, witnessing her death throes as the last of the fires extinguished any remaining beauty left to her; their cries rose to the air as they wailed their grief to the gods at the death of their city. And the gods were deaf to them. But the gods needed to do nothing to help for the cause of the catastrophe would also be the saviour of the hour. Nero, still lurking in his sanctuary in the Gardens of Maecenas, overseeing the disaster from Caligula's tower, was going to house and feed all those he had dispossessed and make them eternally grateful to him as he rebuilt the city to satisfy his vanity.

Vespasian winced at the remembrance of the Emperor gloating in the name of Neropolis. 'They have to find out who was responsible for this, and we can help them to do so, Magnus. And once they do know for sure then Nero will not have his dream. There will be no Neropolis.'

PART III

✢ ✢

AQUAE CUTILLAE, APRIL AD 65

CHAPTER XIII

'T HAT'S THE FIFTH one in the eight months that we've been here,' Vespasian said, looking up at the tree on the edge of a wood and then averting his eyes from the grisly sight. It was the same wood on the eastern edge of the estate in which he and Sabinus had hidden, all those years ago, with six freedmen waiting to ambush a group of runaway slaves who had been stealing mules from the estate.

Magnus hauled Castor and Pollux off the pile of fly-infested offal mouldering at the base of the tree to which the eviscerated carcass of a mule had been nailed. 'You don't want to eat that, boys.' The two hunting dogs, sleek and black with shoulders at waist-height and wide, block-like heads that melded with thick-muscled necks, growled at being denied a free meal; their baggy, saliva-drooling lips pulled back to expose yellowed, vicious-looking teeth. 'I don't care what you think, you ain't having it.' Magnus yanked on their leashes again, causing more canine complaint. 'More to the point, sir, that's the second this month; they seem to be becoming more frequent.'

Vespasian turned to Philon, the estate steward since the death of his father, Pallo, two years previously. 'Who found it?'

'Drustan, one of the freedmen, master.'

'That huge Briton I freed just before I went to Africa?'

'Yes, Titus Flavius Drustan,' Philon confirmed.

'Did he find any of the other seven?'

'Just one, master, last year; why?'

Vespasian waved his hand, dismissing the question. 'When I came back from Britannia after the revolt there, three years ago, your father mentioned that there had been a few instances of mules being slaughtered or stolen but he never mentioned anything like this happening.'

Philon shrugged, shaking his head, clearly at a loss. 'I've lived on the estate all my forty-five years and I've never seen anything like it. My father would surely have told you had he witnessed something similar and I never heard him mentioning atrocities such as this.'

Vespasian looked back up at the mule; its front legs had been broken so that they could be pulled sideways at unnatural angles in order for the beast to be nailed to a couple of the lower branches in the tree in a parody of a human crucifixion as if imitating the young runaway, the only survivor of the gang, whom he and Sabinus had crucified nearby. Its rear legs hung free whilst its head lolled to one side on its chest exposing an eye socket pecked empty. 'That's the first one that has been so obviously nailed up; the rest were much cruder.' He turned to Magnus who was having much difficulty in restraining his dogs. 'What do you make of it?'

'Make of it? Well, no one is going to do something like that for fun, at least not without a reason.' Magnus gave up the fight with the straining beasts, releasing them to their fetid feast, and indicated down the slope of rich pasture behind them, rolling from the wood to the gully at its bottom beyond which were hills, covered with rocks and stunted trees, of no use for cultivation. 'But we're right at the eastern border of the estate here; and you know only too well about the outlaws that roam around in those hills.'

'That's what I was thinking about,' Vespasian said with a frown. 'And I've a feeling that it's not random but personal.' This thought had been growing in his mind ever since the third such find had come to light soon after the New Year had been celebrated.

He and Magnus had caught up with the convoy as dusk fell on the day they had left Rome. They had then ridden ahead and arrived in Aquae Cutillae in advance of Flavia, Gaius and the households, giving Philon time to prepare for such an influx of domestic slaves.

Life had quickly settled down into the normal routine he followed when on the estates: a mixture of estate management and hunting. Magnus' reunion with Castor and Pollux had involved much slobber and wagging of tails and the hounds were keen to follow the scent of game all over the estate in the company of their master, who in turn was always keen to get back, after a long day in the open, to be ministered to by his slave, Caitlín, who had travelled up as part of Gaius' household.

Having spent a month in Aquae Cutillae, investing half of Sabinus' loan in new slave-stock and thus greatly increasing the estate's efficiency, Vespasian then went to join Caenis at Cosa for a month. Here he fell into a different routine, which involved seeing a good deal more of Caenis than he had done of Flavia as well as attending to the running of the estate that he had inherited from his grandmother, Tertulla, and spending the rest of Sabinus' loan upgrading its slave-stock. And thus he had divided his time, alternate months on each estate, as the wreckage was cleared from Rome, sent back down, in the barges that had brought emergency grain to the city, to the mouth of the Tiber where it was being used to reclaim marshland. But clearing the city was a long process and with government virtually paralysed there was little for the Senate to do other than tend to their estates; the main administrative work was being done by the Emperor, Sabinus as prefect of the city and the Urban praetors and aediles.

But it was the Emperor, according to the regular reports that Sabinus sent Vespasian, who had come out of the cataclysm as the hero of the mob. He had selflessly deprived the people of Egypt of the chance to witness his talent by cancelling his trip to Alexandria so he could care for the welfare of his subjects. This he did by personally supervising the daily distribution of bread at least once a month and by keeping very clear of the festering city of tents, baking in the late summer heat, that had sprung up in and around his gardens on the Vatican Hill. But it was merely that he had opened his property and was occasionally seen to give out bread that had made him the darling of the people and they would not hear a word said against him. They saw nothing in the fact that he spent most of the time ensuring the clearing of a huge tract of land right at the centre of the city and supervising the surveying and marking out of what would soon be the foundations of the Golden House, which in his mind was the centre of Neropolis and the sole reason for the city to exist at all: how else would his needs be seen to if there were not people around to do his bidding?

And so Vespasian had put all his energies into squeezing as much from his estates as he could; mules were bred and nurtured and then sold on to the army or one of the many construction companies that had sprung up around Rome, eager for a portion of the business generated by the reconstruction. Due to demand, the price of mules was at a premium and by the end of the season as the Saturnalia approached, Vespasian felt a great deal more confident about his financial status than he had upon his return from Africa. The fact that his house, and indeed Gaius' and Caenis', had been spared destruction was also an added bonus sent by Fortuna.

But it was not Fortuna to whom Vespasian sent a prayer, as he contemplated the crucified mule, but to Mars, his guardian god, for a cold dread had begun to gnaw at his belly and he had learnt to trust his feelings. 'Have it cut down and burned, Philon.' He took Magnus to one side away from the wood as Philon gave the orders to the accompanying slaves for the carcass' disposal. 'Do you remember those poachers that we caught last time we were here? The ones who took Domitian hostage.'

Magnus scratched his head. 'The bastards who left an arrow in Castor's leg? Of course I do; a couple of them died very pleasingly unpleasant deaths.'

'Yes; but I let the last one go.'

'Which I thought was very stupid at the time, and still do as a matter of fact.'

'I'd given my word.'

'Bollocks; one's word to scum like that is worth about as much as a Vestal's advice on cock-sucking.'

'Yes, well, be that as it may, I kept my word.'

'And you think that this poacher might be trying to have his revenge for some worthless mates? I doubt it, not after this amount of time; it's been four years or more.'

'I know; but during that period I haven't stayed on the estate for more than a few days at a stretch. This time I've been here for longer visits, much longer; long enough for it to be noticed that I'm around.'

'Then why haven't they tried anything other than slaughter a few mules in a nasty manner?'

'That's what's been bothering me but then I remembered what one of the poachers' last words were; he said that someone called The Cripple would hear of his death and would avenge him.'

Magnus nodded as the dying man's words came back to him. 'That's right; and he said that The Cripple takes his time because he can't move quickly.'

'And he always takes his revenge and shows no mercy because none was ever shown to him.'

Magnus looked back to where the mule had been chopped down and was now subject to the attentions of Castor and Pollux who had tired of entrails. 'And you think that mule being nailed up is a sign that The Cripple has arrived in the area?'

Vespasian shrugged. 'I don't know; but what I would say is that it won't do any harm to be cautious.'

Flavia was outraged; she sat up on the couch she had been reclining on with Domitian. 'What do you mean: I can't leave the house without a couple of freedmen guarding me?'

Vespasian drew a breath and formed his sentence in his head. He knew the sort of situation that he was dealing with very well; well enough to understand that this was no time for a misplaced word. He took a prawn from the dish before him on the triclinium table and shelled it with deliberation. 'My dear.' He paused to crunch the tail flippers. 'I didn't say that you *had* to be accompanied, I just said that I thought it was *best* if you were.'

Flavia snorted and pointed to Gaius, trying to be inconspicuous, next to Magnus, on the third couch around the table. 'And does that apply to your uncle too; or is it just for weak women?'

'I won't be accompanied,' Domitian stated with an adolescent's finality.

Vespasian did not even bother to look at his son. 'You'll do what you're told. Now, Flavia, Gaius is not my legal responsibility but you are. I cannot order Gaius to do anything but I can give him advice from one equal to another and yes, I do advise Gaius not to stray from the buildings without an armed escort.'

'And I, dear boy, will be very happy to take that advice.' Gaius held out his hand for one of his exquisite boys to wipe clean of prawn juice. 'If Vespasian says there may be a threat then I value my skin far too well to ignore it.'

'Especially as there is so much of it,' Domitian muttered and immediately received a sharp slap about the ears from his mother whose annoyance at her husband precluded any easing of the force of the blow.

'And I shall do as I please,' Flavia said, rubbing her hand as Domitian blinked incessantly, his head evidently ringing. 'And if I choose to go on a walk by myself, to get some air, then that is what I shall do.'

Vespasian almost choked on his prawn. 'My dear, you haven't been on a walk once since we've been here. You spend all your time visiting other bored wives in the area in the raeda so you can all complain about your husbands together. And when you do that you always have an armed escort.'

'Because the roads are not safe; but here on our own property? Besides, how do you know what I get up to whilst you're away with Caenis? I might spend all my time strolling around the estate, conversing with country-folk.'

'Flavia, you never tire of pointing out just how much you hate the country and how much the estate bores you. You wouldn't know the difference between an olive tree and a pomegranate.'

'Then perhaps it's time that I learnt.'

'I would be delighted should you decide to take more interest in the estate but would ask you just to take the small precaution of being accompanied. Please, my dear?'

'I ain't going anywhere without my dogs,' Magnus informed them in an attempt to bolster Vespasian's argument.

Flavia's face showed just what she thought of the dogs. 'And you're welcome to them, Magnus. I will certainly not be going anywhere *with* them.'

Vespasian had the distinct impression that Magnus had to check himself from saying that Castor and Pollux had similar opinions; he knew that he would have, had he been in his friend's place. 'We will all be accompanied. I have asked Philon to have Drustan see to it.'

Flavia's face elongated in horror. 'That brute! He's covered in tattoos and smells worse than the pigsty.'

'How do you know? You've never been to the pigsty.'

'I'll not have anything to do with that Britannic savage!'

'You don't have to have anything to do with him, just have him and one of his comrades escort you; they can walk behind you or downwind, whatever you like. Just don't go—'

'Master!' Philon said, hurrying into the room and interrupting without any ceremony. 'I think you had better come and look at this.'

Vespasian, Magnus and Gaius followed the steward out into the courtyard garden; a blazing torch at each corner of the colonnade shone flickering light over the shrubs and central fishpond and cast unstable shadows from the columns supporting the terracotta-tile-covered walkway. The evening air was cooling but still retained the residue of an early spring day as all about the cicadas began to wind down their daytime exertions to make way for the sounds of the night.

Philon led them around the colonnade to the right and then out through a wooden door at the far end, minded by an old slave, that brought them out, between two stable stalls, into the enclosed farmyard that adjoined the main house. To the right was the single-storey freedmen's quarters, forming the western wall of the yard; opposite stood the two-storey slave-block with the field slaves' stables on the ground floor and the more trusted house slaves' dormitory on the floor above. To the east were the workshops, forge and more stabling for horses; in the middle of this wall were the gates, two sturdy wooden constructions. It was in front of these that a group of freedmen had gathered, looking down at something on the ground.

'Move back, lads,' Philon said as they approached the group, 'and hand me a torch.'

Vespasian, Magnus and Gaius stepped forward and looked at the cause of interest as Philon held a flame close to it.

'It was thrown over the gate just now,' Philon explained. 'I sent some of the lads out to see if they could catch whoever did it, but they seem to be long gone into the night.'

'It's a mule's head,' Magnus said, giving the thing a nudge with his toe.

'Yes,' Philon agreed. 'But look closely at it.'

Vespasian knelt down and squinted. 'It's got burn marks and is missing its eyes.' The relevance of the observations sunk in immediately. 'It's the head from the mule this afternoon; someone must have pulled it out of the fire.'

Philon nodded. 'That's what I thought, master.'

'I don't like the sound of that at all, dear boy,' Gaius said, heaving himself upright from the squatting position and passing wind with the effort.

'Nor do I, Uncle. Someone is telling us very clearly that they are watching our every move.'

Vespasian had slept little that night, managing only to snatch an hour or two between organising the arming of the freedmen and those slaves that could be trusted and then keeping up a regular watch on the walls and roofs of the complex. But as dawn had broken nothing further untoward had happened and the estate had roused itself into another working day. The field slaves were given their fodder and then whipped out to their hard labour by their overseers whilst the domestic household worked their far less rigorous routine.

By the second hour of the day it seemed to many of the people of the estate as if the incident of the mule's head was but a fading dream as they became immersed in daily tasks that barely changed from month to month and year to year.

It was something of a relief to Vespasian when Philon disturbed him in the tablinum to tell him of the approach of a rider. 'He's coming from the Via Salaria, master; he must have left it at Reate.'

Vespasian rolled up the scroll of last year's accounts he had been perusing. 'He's from Rome most likely. It's good to know that we're not cut off. Whoever this Cripple is, he hasn't got the manpower to surround us; that makes me feel much easier within myself. Offer the rider a bed for the night if he wishes.'

Philon bowed and retired as, from the atrium, there came the sound of someone being admitted. He was soon back and handed Vespasian a couple of leather scroll-cases.

'Letters, dear boy?' Gaius said, following the steward in. 'Something to relieve the tension at least.' He sat down without being invited and awaited the news.

'Titus,' Vespasian said, looking at the seal of the first letter and then breaking it open. 'He says he's on his way here to discuss a proposal for a new marriage.'

'Is he now? That's quick; his first wife is only just cold in her grave. He should never have taken her out to Asia with him. Surely now that he's back he should be concentrating on becoming a quaestor and getting into the Senate, not getting remarried.'

'Perhaps he sees this match as a way of improving his chances of doing so; after all, at the moment this family cannot even afford the bribe to get Epaphroditus to put him on the list of prospective candidates.'

'You might be right. Whose daughter is it?'

'Quintus Marcius Barea Sura's.' He looked to the steward. 'Philon, go and tell the mistress that we can expect our eldest son in the next day or two. She had better warn the young master that his older brother is coming so that he has time to get used to the fact.' He turned back to Gaius as the steward left the room. 'That could be a very good match for our family. We should be honoured that Sura has suggested it. I assume it's to Marcia Furnilla as I seem to remember the older Marcia getting married some time ago, unless she's been recently divorced.'

Gaius warmed immediately to his favourite pastime of gossiping. 'No, she's still married to Marcus Ulpius Traianus who is serving in the East with Corbulo at the moment; with great distinction, I hear. They've got an eleven-year-old son who you should have your eye on for Domitilla's daughter. There's also an older daughter, Ulpia Marciana, who's made a very good match just recently with Gaius Matidius Patruinus; he, as you know, has more money than he knows what to do with even after he's given interest-free loans to the Emperor.'

'They certainly are a coming family.'

Gaius considered the match whilst Vespasian opened the second letter from Sabinus and began reading. 'I have heard that Sura's brother, Soranus, is a close associate of Piso's.'

Vespasian lifted his eyes from Sabinus' letter. 'How close?'

'They know each other.'

'So? I know Piso; as do you.'

'Yes, but we don't get invited to his dinner parties.'

'We'll discuss it with Titus when he arrives; it's no doubt something that he would wish to raise. He says that he's provisionally said yes, subject to my approval; Sura's very keen to complete the formalities as soon as possible so he suggests that should I have no objections we could meet with Sura and the marriage could take place the following day, auspices being favourable, obviously.'

'Obviously. He seems uncommonly hasty.'

'Titus has only been back from his province for less than a month and finds himself a widower. He's the nephew of the prefect of Rome and my son, to boot; he's a good match as far as Sura is concerned. I'm minded to agree to it if only to make closer links with the Ulpii.'

'As you wish, dear boy; just remember what I said.'

'Of course, Uncle.' Vespasian turned his attention back to his brother's letter for a few moments before passing it across the desk to Gaius. 'This wedding might happen sooner than you think. I don't believe we can avoid it for much longer, Uncle; Sabinus writes to say the Senate House is to be inaugurated during the festival of Ceres this month and the Circus Maximus will be reopened the following day for the traditional races on the last day of the festival. We need to contemplate going back to Rome.'

Gaius glanced at the letter. 'A pity; I was so enjoying being out of Nero's gaze. It's the first long period of time that I have had since the very early days of Claudius' reign when I haven't felt the weight of fear heavy upon me all the time.'

'I know. And, what is more, we'll be going back to an emperor who is, no doubt, in dire need of cash.'

'The provinces have borne the brunt of the financing.'

'And Rome has only just started to rise like the Phoenix from the ashes. Don't delude yourself, Uncle; it'll be the turn of our class again next.'

Gaius threw down the letter in disgust. 'All I've ever asked for in life is to be inconspicuous and to be left alone with my boys and all I ever get is …' He cocked an ear. 'What was that?'

'What?'

Gaius held up a hand. 'Listen.'

And then Vespasian heard it. 'That's a scream; a long way away.'

'That, dear boy, is a man in a great deal of pain.'

Vespasian rushed from the tablinum through the open doors into the garden to almost crash into Magnus, pelting in the opposite direction. 'What is it, Magnus?'

'I don't know, sir; but it seems to be coming from the direction in which we found the mule yesterday.'

Vespasian ran through the garden and on, out into the farm-yard. 'Philon! Philon!' He found the steward coming out of the estate office in the freedmen's accommodation block. 'Philon, get as many freedmen as you can armed and mounted.'

'Yes, master.'

'And then get everyone else inside. Call in all the work parties, understood?'

'Yes, master.'

'And the mistress? Did you find her to deliver my message?'

'I sent a boy out after her.'

'After her?'

'Yes, she had decided to go for a walk.'

Vespasian could have cursed the stubbornness of his wife. 'Now? After all this time she chooses to go for a walk?'

'Don't worry, sir, I made sure that Drustan and one other went with her.'

That news calmed Vespasian. 'Well, get her in as soon as possible whilst we go and investigate who is making such a noise.'

The sun was swallowed by grey clouds blown in on a strong wind gusting from the east; Vespasian felt the first drops of moisture brush his face and forearms as he, Magnus and eight available freedmen galloped through the gates without waiting for them to fully open.

The scream had become more of a wail and was now sporadic, as no one, no matter how much agony was being inflicted upon them, would be able to keep up such a noise incessantly.

Vespasian urged his horse on, eastwards, in the direction of the macabre sound, shouting to anyone within hearing in the fields to retire to the safety of the farm complex. Chained gangs of field slaves shuffled as fast as possible back along tracks, brutally encouraged by the lashes of their overseers in their anxiety to see themselves to safety.

On Vespasian and his companions raced across rolling grazing-pasture interspersed with fields of vines and olive groves; the droplets in the air thickened into a drizzle and the wind, blowing directly into their faces, flapped their cloaks behind them. Impervious to the worsening weather, herds of mares grazed as their mule offspring, bandy-legged and with oversized heads, edged closer to their mothers to escape the worsening conditions. And still the wail rose and fell, carried on the wind, and the closer they came the more certain Vespasian became as to the cause of such agony; so it was with the grim look of a man who has just had his fears confirmed that, as they crested a small hillock, he beheld the cross, some few hundred paces away.

On that cross a figure writhed. A quarter of a mile beyond it two horsemen sat and watched their approach.

'Bastards!' Vespasian spat, kicking his mount forward, despite knowing that there was no chance of catching the two men; sure enough, as he approached the cross the men turned and galloped off to disappear over the next hill. 'Let them go, we won't catch them.' Vespasian hauled up his horse and walked it round the cross.

The crucified man sagged forward, the weight of his body taken by the nails hammered through each of his wrists, just below the base of the thumb; watered-down blood streamed down his arms and onto his chest, wracking in a futile attempt to draw breath. Lack of oxygen triggered the instinct to breathe and he convulsed up, pressing down on the nail transfixing his feet to the upright and pulling up on his wrists; his face twisted with pain as he sucked in air with shuddering gulps and then exhaled with the wail that by now had become forlorn and almost mournful.

With prodigious effort he remained in the upright position for another series of jerked breaths; as he emitted the wail he opened his eyes and became aware of Vespasian. 'Finish me, master; for the sake of all the gods.'

Vespasian nodded and drew his sword. 'Who did this?'

The man grimaced, every muscle in his face seemed to spasm at once. 'He said to tell you he was The Cripple.'

'What did he look like?'

The man shook his head; diluted blood flecked into Vespasian's face. With a final burst he managed: 'He was carried in a chair.'

Vespasian knew that he could not expect him to go on. 'You will be given a good burial.'

The man's eyes flickered open in time to see a sword flash forward and punch into his heaving chest; rigid, he looked straight at Vespasian as blood bubbled from his mouth. With the faintest of nods the life faded from his eyes and his head lolled forward.

'Who was he?' Vespasian asked, yanking his blade from the cadaver.

'Manius, master,' one of the freedmen replied. 'He was an overseer.'

'And it looks as if his charges are long gone,' Magnus said, jumping from his mount and picking up a couple of discarded leg-irons.

'They always worked in pairs,' the freedman pointed out. 'Where's Manius' mate?'

The question was barely out of the man's mouth before the answer shrieked in the air.

Vespasian turned his horse. 'They must have been waiting for us to get here before they crucified him; we may have a chance to stop them before they raise the cross.'

And now the chase was on for the nails were being hammered home, each strike producing a howl of rising anguish. Through the now steady rain they beat their mounts in the desperate hope that they could rescue the overseer before the cross was raised and the jolting ripped all the ligaments in the feet and wrists; if that was avoided, there would be a small chance that he would be able to walk and have reasonable use of his hands again, provided that infection did not carry him off.

Vespasian slapped his horse's rump with the flat of his blade, cursing the outlaw who called himself The Cripple for freeing his slaves and killing his people in retaliation for Vespasian disposing of, as was his prerogative, poachers found on his estate over five years previously. It did not seem right, a massive overreaction on The Cripple's behalf, and yet it had happened. Now there could be no end to the affair until The Cripple was dead and his men either captured or, likewise, slain.

They reached the hill over which the two horsemen had disappeared and a new expanse of rain-soaked country was revealed. In the distance, partially obscured by sheets of rain, was a small group of people from whose midst the screaming emanated. With what seemed like reckless casualness they carried on with their grim task as Vespasian and his comrades thundered towards them. Five hundred paces, four hundred paces, three hundred and fifty, and then, with less than three hundred paces between them, the cross was raised and the victim shrieked to his gods as the nails ripped his joints and the upright thudded down into the ready-dug hole. With no time to stabilise the cross with wedges the outlaws jumped onto their horses and galloped away, leaving the man hanging forward with the upright slanting at an angle.

'See if you can catch them,' Vespasian shouted to the freedmen, knowing in his heart that it was most unlikely. He pulled up his mount next to the overseer hanging from the nails in catatonic terror, his eyes transfixed by the sight of the nail-head protruding from his feet. Vespasian and Magnus leapt from their horses; stretching up, Vespasian was just able to reach the crossbar as Magnus bent down to take a grip on the upright as close to the ground as he could.

'Ready,' Magnus shouted.

Vespasian nodded.

'Three, two, one, now.' Magnus heaved on the upright, extracting it from the hole as Vespasian took the ever increasing weight on the crossbar. Slowly the cross came out of the ground but each small, jarring movement sent shock waves of agony through the victim's body and he howled his pain in a manner Vespasian had seldom heard before. As gently as possible they laid the cross down so that he lay on his belly; with the ground supporting his weight the pressure eased and the pain subsided a fraction. Vespasian took his belt and, with care, passed it under the man's stomach and then fastened it tight around the upright, binding him to it. Now came the difficult part: to turn the cross over so that the overseer lay on his back and the nails could be removed. 'You turn it, Magnus, and I'll hold him.'

Magnus sucked the air through his teeth and took hold of one end of the crossbar as Vespasian held an arm with both hands in an attempt to prevent gravity exerting too much pressure on the wounds. Slowly the cross was lifted; the victim choked back his screams as his body once again was subjected to the agony of the nails. Vespasian held him firm, taking as much of the weight as possible as the crossbar passed the perpendicular and then was eased back down so that finally he lay on his back, his chest heaving erratically. But one look at the wounds told all that was needed to know: the erecting and the lowering of the cross had worked the nails hard and the wrists were now punctured by huge holes three times the size of the originals when first they had been hammered home. The wounds to the feet were no different; the overseer would never walk unaided again and he would be unable to care for himself for the remainder of his life. He looked up at Vespasian and his eyes showed that he too knew; with a glimmer of a smile he accepted his fate: better to die cleanly than live as a useless wreck.

'Is there anything you can tell me about who did this to you?' Vespasian asked as he prepared his blade for the killing blow.

The overseer shook his head. 'Only that they're cunts,' he croaked. 'Kill them.'

'We will.' With a punch, Vespasian sent the tip of his sword up, under the ribcage to explode the heart; a soft breath escaped from the already dead man.

'Here come the others, sir,' Magnus said. 'And it looks as if they brought someone for a nice cosy chat.'

'Just answer the senator's question or that could be you very soon,' Magnus said, pointing down to the dead overseer still nailed to the cross. 'Except not quite so dead, if you take my meaning?'

The captured outlaw glanced down at the man he had so recently crucified; his expression showed that he took Magnus' meaning only too well.

Magnus pressed his advantage. 'The only question is: will you make more noise than he did bearing in mind that you had to hurry whilst nailing him up because we were fast approaching, whereas we won't be under such pressure and will be able to do it nice and leisurely like? No rush, we'll take our time and try not to break into a sweat.'

The outlaw looked around the group surrounding him, his eyes flicking back and forth to try to detect any sympathy in one of the ten men; he found none. 'And if I co-operate?'

'Then,' Vespasian said, 'you can be as dead as he is without having to be nailed to the cross.'

'A quick death?'

'You have my word.'

One more glance at the hideous wounds to the overseer's wrists was enough for the outlaw to come to a decision; he sank to his knees in preparation for the killing blow. 'If you go two miles due east, across two valleys,' he said, pointing to the scrag-strewn hills on the far side of the gully, 'you'll come to a stream.

Turn south along it and after a mile or so it passes through a small coppice of pine trees. The camp is in there.'

'How many men does he have?'

'It's always changing but at the moment there are about twenty to twenty-two.'

'Good; you can lead us there tomorrow.'

The outlaw looked up in surprise. 'Tomorrow! But I thought you gave your word.'

'For a quick death, yes, but I didn't specify when. How do I know that you're telling the truth? If what you said is correct then you can expect a swift death when we find this Cripple.' Vespasian frowned in confusion as the outlaw looked terrified at the prospect of having an extra day of life.

'But you gave your word!'

'Why are you so anxious to die?'

The man's eyes flicked involuntarily to the west.

Vespasian felt a sense of foreboding creep over him. 'What do you know?' He grabbed the outlaw by the hair and yanked him to his feet. 'What is it that you would rather die now? What?' He kneed the man in the groin and let him go to double over on the ground, hyperventilating. 'What have you done?'

The outlaw clutched his groin, his face screwed up in stomach-piercing agony.

'He should count them not rub them,' Magnus observed as they waited for the outlaw to be able to reply.

'Now tell me what you've done,' Vespasian repeated as the man's breathing grew less laboured, 'or you'll have nothing to count.'

The outlaw looked up at Vespasian, saliva trickling from the corner of his mouth. 'We were a diversion.'

Vespasian's foreboding turned into a bitter chill. 'For what?'

'For The Cripple's revenge.'

'Revenge? Revenge for killing a few poachers five years ago?'

'Poachers? Not poachers. Revenge upon you.'

'Me? What have I done to him?'

'You made him the way he is. We were supposed to lure you away, which we did, so I can only assume that when you get back he would have had his revenge.'

Vespasian looked at Magnus and indicated to the outlaw. 'Bring him with you; I'm going back fast.'

Through the driving rain, Vespasian rode with six of the freedmen, flogging their mounts so that their rumps bled, so anxious was he to get home; and yet a part of him did not want to make haste as it feared what he might find. What had The Cripple done and what had he, Vespasian, done to deserve it? How had he made The Cripple as he is? Was he some legionary he had punished? An enemy warrior that he had severely wounded? A criminal whom he had sent for justice?' It could be any one of those or something else that he had overlooked or forgotten. All he knew was that he had felt unease in the back of his mind ever since they had found the crucified mule. He had warned Flavia against going outside by herself because of that unease, not because … Flavia! Flavia had gone out that morning just to prove how stubborn she could be. Vespasian swallowed and beat his horse some more but failed to get any extra speed out of it; it was already at the limit of its endurance and he cursed himself for the fit of pique that had caused him to make the beast suffer even further. But his remorse was short-lived as the image of Flavia in the hands of The Cripple or one of his minions burned in his head; he sent up a prayer to Mars that the boy Philon had sent after Flavia and Domitian that morning had found them and they had returned swiftly.

Realising that his son had been with his wife and he had not felt any concern for his safety came as a jolt to Vespasian; surely he should have more concern for his son's wellbeing? Perhaps he was still finding it hard to forgive the boy for his betrayal of the whereabouts of the pearls, something he had still not yet confronted Domitian with. He was coming to the conclusion that it would probably be best if his son were unaware that his parents knew of his treachery on the basis that if he were to do something similar again he would be a lot more secretive if he knew that he was under suspicion, whereas if he felt safe he might be less careful. The boy would need careful watching; if he was still alive, that was.

Fear gnawed at Vespasian's vitals as his horse hurtled through the rain; fear alternating with guilt: why had he not seen that what had happened this morning was but a diversion? The mule's head had made him suspect that they were going to be attacked but then, when he had heard the first crucified overseer's cries, he had been drawn out to investigate with all the available freedmen, leaving the farm complex defended by old men and women and children. What had he been thinking? He had been outmanoeuvred very simply and then he had compounded it when he had chased after the sound of the howls of the second overseer; the outlaws had obviously waited to crucify him until Vespasian and his companions had found the first man and given him the mercy stroke. Chasing after the second man had gained The Cripple at least another half an hour for whatever he had planned. An hour and a half in all, Vespasian reckoned he would have been away by the time he got home. An hour and a half; much destruction and death could be meted out in an hour and a half.

Fear and guilt played with him as the soaked miles went past and he was in such a deep introspection that, with over a mile still to go to the house, he hardly recognised the cross, at first, for what it was: the third he had seen that day.

The third.

And as he focused on it he felt his stomach heave and vomit spewed up his gullet and then sprayed over the horse's mane. He tried to avert his eyes but he could not; for the cross was occupied and although he was approaching it from behind it was obvious who was on it for they wore a stola and, also, standing before the cross was an upright rack to which had been strapped a youth. Unharmed in any other way, he had been tied to the rack and his mouth gagged so that he could make no sound. But his eyes showed the horror as Domitian stared up at the crucified body of his mother, Flavia.

CHAPTER XIIII

'FLAVIA!' VESPASIAN SHOUTED as he leapt from his horse. 'Flavia!' He ran around the cross and looked up; with one glance he fell to his knees, heaving dry, strangled sobs.

Flavia stared down at him; her eyes frenzied with pain. She too had been gagged so that her shrieks of agony would not draw people to her in time for her to be saved. Nailed she was; nailed to the cross, the wounds deep and washed by rain so that white bone was visible within. Blood stained her stola and her head had been shaved. She writhed up in an attempt to draw breath through mucus-laden nostrils, her throat gurgling with fluid before she coughed and choked through the gag, her chest juddering and her pain made even more unendurable.

'Get her down!' Vespasian shrieked at the freedmen who stared at the mistress of the estate in evident revulsion. They jumped to his command as Vespasian rushed to Domitian and eased the gag over his head. The boy spat the wadding from his mouth; to Vespasian's disgust he saw that it was a ball of Flavia's hair. As it flew towards him the scream that followed was like nothing that he had ever thought possible for a human; the shrillest of harpies could not have produced a more fearsome sound. It continued as Vespasian loosened the knots that bound Domitian, who could not tear his eyes from his mother as the freedmen lowered her cross. Vespasian gathered his son in his arms and attempted to give him some paternal comfort as tears streamed down his own face. Tight he held him, muttering platitudes in his ear although he knew full well that it was not going to be all right. Finally Domitian began to calm and Vespasian held his face in both hands. His son gazed back at him, eyes still wide with fear. 'I thought they would do that to me too, Father. I thought they would crucify me too. Me!'

For a moment Vespasian struggled to comprehend the true significance of what Domitian was saying as he screeched on about his near scrape with a hideous death. And then he understood and it was with his full strength that he slapped his son across the face. 'What about your mother?' His voice was low and threatened further violence; he pointed to Flavia, writhing with every jolt of the cross as it was lowered. 'What about *her*? Not you; you're fine. What about your mother? She's the one that's suffering.' He backhanded another sharp slap across Domitian's face, unable to control himself as the boy looked at him with puzzled eyes.

Another slap.

Domitian yelped and jumped up. 'You'll pay for that, Father. No one hits me.'

Vespasian lunged at his son, attempting a full-blooded punch, but Domitian was too agile; he slipped under the blow and, without a glance at his crucified mother, ran off in the direction of the house. Vespasian spat after him and then turned back to where his wife was now being laid down.

Kneeling next to Flavia, Vespasian slipped his hands around her head and undid the knot that bound her gag. With care he removed it as each minute movement was amplified a hundredfold by the nails skewering her joints. Flavia's eyes never left his as he peeled away the gag and then pulled the wad of her own hair from her mouth.

'I'm so sorry, husband,' Flavia whispered, her voice halting and strained. 'I'm so sorry.'

Vespasian took the water-skin offered by one of the freedmen and poured a few drops into her mouth. 'It's my fault, Flavia; I shouldn't have left the complex.'

'Nor should I. I did it to annoy you.'

'It's no matter.' Vespasian touched the head of one of the nails transfixing her right wrist. 'We'll pull these clear, Flavia.'

'No, Vespasian; I'm finished.' She took a ragged breath. 'I don't want to suffer any more and I've no wish to live like him.'

'Who?'

'The Cripple, of course; he showed me his wounds as I lay on this cross, gagged and screaming on the inside as they approached with the mallet and nails. He showed me what you had done and how he could never walk or use his hands properly again.'

'What *I* had done?'

'Yes, Vespasian. You and Sabinus.'

'When and where?'

'Here on the estate, forty years ago.'

'Forty years ag—' And then the realisation hit him; forty years. 'That runaway slave boy! The one we crucified the day after Sabinus returned from his time as a military tribune. We crucified him over by the gully on the far eastern border of the estate.'

'I know, he told me everything before he ordered the nails to be struck home. How he had been nailed up without mercy and left to die.'

'But I pleaded with Sabinus for his life.'

Flavia shook her head and grimaced in agony. 'I don't think he remembers that. He remembers only the nails being hammered home and the jolting as the cross was raised upright and then he remembers his father cutting him down and keeping him alive so that one day he could have his vengeance. Finish me, Vespasian; I cannot live any longer.'

Vespasian touched his wife's cheek; tears trickled down his. 'If that is your wish, Flavia.'

'Give my love to our children; especially to Domitian because I think of all three he's the one who's going to need it most. I heard you just now.'

Vespasian stopped himself from saying anything derogatory about his youngest son.

'The Cripple said that he didn't crucify Domitian because he's about the same age as he had been when he suffered that fate. He wanted to show you that he was better than you. He also said that he thought he could do a good deal of harm to him by just tying him up so that he had to watch me struggle on the cross.'

Vespasian doubted it but did not say as much. All he could do was stroke his wife's cheek. 'I could have been a better husband to you, Flavia.'

'No, you couldn't; I had all that I wanted and you provided the money for me to do so. Caenis will fill the gap that I leave; give her my blessing and tell her to act like a mother to our children. Now do it, husband; there's no more to say.'

Vespasian bent and kissed Flavia on the lips; she responded and closed her eyes. He understood that she did not wish to see his face as he dealt the final stroke. He pulled his sword free and for the third time that day poised it by the heart, holding the back of her head with the other hand. 'I'll avenge you, Flavia, and I'll mourn you, wife.'

'Do so, Vespasian.'

Likewise closing his eyes, he tensed and then sent his wife to the Ferryman; she made no sound to mark her passing, or if she did it was masked by Vespasian's raw howl of misery and rage as he exploded the heart of the woman who had borne his children. When it was done he collapsed forward onto Flavia's corpse and lay there shaking with grief for he knew not how long.

'We'd better get her home, sir,' Magnus said, putting his hand on Vespasian's shoulder. 'And you need to get out of the rain.'

Vespasian opened his eyes and found himself lying on Flavia's unmoving breast. He lifted his head and realised that he was very cold and wet; he had forgotten about the rain from the moment that he had realised that it was Flavia on the cross. He raised himself up and saw that in his anguish he had left his sword embedded in his wife's chest.

'I'll do that, sir,' Magnus offered, grasping the handle.

'No, Magnus; thank you.' He moved Magnus' hand away and gripped his sword. 'It's my job.' He gritted his teeth and then twisted his wrist so that the suction lessened and he could ease the blade loose. Flavia's blood coated it; he wiped it clean on the grass. Still in a daze he got to his feet, with Magnus' help, and looked around. 'Take her body off that and bear her home.' The freedmen were afraid to meet his eye having witnessed his grief over the death of his wife. His gaze alighted on the captured outlaw; he pointed his sword at the man. 'And then nail him up in her place.'

The outlaw fell to his knees. 'But you promised; you promised me a quick death.'

'You knew that this is what The Cripple was going to do when you acted as a diversion for him, didn't you?'

'I didn't; I swear I didn't know what he was going to do. I swear it!'

Magnus pushed down Vespasian's sword arm. 'We need him alive, sir. More than ever now seeing as only he can lead us to The Cripple; and I assume that is what you want above anything else at the moment.'

Vespasian nodded; his eyes were dull. He sheathed his sword. 'You're right, Magnus; finding that bastard and finishing him is the most important thing right now.' He looked back to the prisoner. 'My word still stands: you will get the quick death I promised if you lead us to The Cripple.'

The morn dawned bright; the rain clouds of the previous day had dispersed in the night and the fresh smell of drying land filled the air as the sun gained in warmth, cresting the tips of the Apennine Mountains.

Vespasian stood with Gaius next to Flavia's corpse, lying in state in the atrium with her feet pointing towards the front door. He took her hand and looked down at her; her face was calm, now, in death. The women had washed her and bound her wounds and then dressed her in her finest clothes. A wig had been arranged on her head and make-up applied so that she looked to have colour in her cheeks and lips and seemed to be but sleeping. There was much he felt he should have said to her but now that chance was gone. He regretted the way he had treated her: she had always come second to Caenis but she had accepted that from the outset; he had been honest with her about his mistress but that still did not stop him from wishing he had been more loving towards his wife. Once the initial desire for her had worn off with the arrival of the third of their children he had concentrated his passions on Caenis and had rarely ventured into Flavia's bedroom. He apologised to her shade and felt as if he was being told that there was no need to do so.

It was with a wan smile that he squeezed her cold hand and let go as Philon came into the atrium. 'Are the men ready, Philon?'

'They are, master; every able-bodied freedman on the estate and four trusted slaves. Seventeen in total, including Magnus and me; all of us have provisions for three days.'

'Good; we shall need each and every one.' With a final glance down to Flavia he strode from the atrium, heading towards the stable yard, leaving Gaius to watch over Flavia.

'It's a nice day for it,' Magnus said in an attempt to be cheerful, sitting astride his horse, with Castor and Pollux waiting by his side, as the rest of the freedmen and the four slaves mounted up behind him; the prisoner was secured between two of the riders.

'It'll be even nicer when that bastard's dead,' Vespasian replied, taking his mount's reins from a stable-lad. 'Or, better still, when he's nailed up for the second time.'

'He should be getting the hang of it by now, if you take my meaning?'

Vespasian could not help a smile as he vaulted up into the saddle. 'I do indeed, Magnus; and believe me, once he's up I intend to keep him hanging around for a good long time.' With that he kicked his horse forward and trotted out of the gates with revenge in his heart and seventeen men, and the prisoner who would lead them to The Cripple, at his back.

Vespasian watched as two of the slaves made their way up the rocky slope on the further side of the gully. The slaves, both Getic and therefore natural horsemen, had been promised their freedom whatever the outcome of the expedition and so could be trusted not to make a run for it or to side with the enemy against their master.

With the natural ease of men born to the saddle, the two Getae rode their horses up the steep incline with about four hundred paces dividing them; each held a bow in his right hand, with an arrow nocked ready should they spring an ambush. But none came and as they reached the summit and were able to look over into the next valley; they both raised their weapons in the air to signal that all was clear and the main body could follow them up the hill.

And so they passed out of Flavian territory and into the wild upper Apennines, peopled by runaway slaves and outlaws of all kinds. Up they climbed, their horses struggling on the loose scree as none of the riders had the natural touch of the two Getae.

As he rode, Vespasian's mind filled with images of his dead wife in happy times and those less so: the first time he had met her when in Cyrenaica she had come to solicit his help as the quaestor in the province in rescuing her then man, Statilius Capella; she had caused a stirring in his loins at first sight. However, she was no longer in the province by the time Vespasian had returned from his mission, which had left Capella dead, killed by a lion. They had met again by chance, four years later in Alexandria, where he had been sent by Caligula to obtain the breastplate of Alexander the Great from his mausoleum so that the brash young Emperor could wear it as he crossed the pontoon bridge that he had had constructed across the Bay of Neapolis. She had been the sometime mistress of the then prefect of Egypt, Flaccus; that arrangement had been discarded the very same evening when Flavia had joined him in his bed. He had married her soon after returning to Rome with the stolen breastplate; she had been in the full knowledge that Caenis could never supplant her position as wife because of the Augustan law that prohibited senators from marrying freedwomen. It was not until they had been married that Vespasian had discovered the extravagant nature of Flavia's financial outlook, which had been in direct divergence from his own attitude to money. This had been the main source of conflict between them and his regular annoyance at her profligate ways had slowly quelled the stirring in his loins each time he looked at her. But, for all that, she had given him three children and had remained a loyal, if not entirely faithful, wife. But those bad memories of her he tried to cast right to the back of his mind and he focused on the happier times: the births of their children; their young desire in the early days of their relationship; and, of course, their real friendship – when they were not arguing about money, that was.

Thus Vespasian crested the hill and followed in the path of the two scouts across the valley floor and then up the other side, rising even higher as the foothills of the Apennines neared the main body of the mountain range. Again the scouts indicated that the further side was free from danger and again they led the group down into the valley at whose base, just as the prisoner had said, ran a swift-flowing stream.

'Let him go forward, Philon,' Vespasian said, referring to the prisoner. 'If he tries to make a run for it bring down his horse; we wouldn't want him thinking that he can avoid taking us to his master and escape a lingering death at the same time. Would we?'

Philon grinned and turned to the prisoner. 'We would not, master. You heard that, you piece of shit?'

The prisoner nodded and was led away without protest.

'What do you plan to do once he's led us to their camp?' Magnus asked.

Vespasian looked up at the sun that was now well into its eighth hour. 'Wait until nightfall and then take them as they sleep; that should lessen the odds against us.'

The sun had long since slipped behind the western slope, casting the valley into shadow, which deepened gently as Vespasian looked down at the copse, straddling the stream, in which the prisoner had assured him The Cripple had his camp on this, the eastern bank.

They had approached on foot having left their horses tethered further back up the valley with one of the freedmen attending to them as well as to the prisoner, who had also been well secured and gagged. With no fear of an equine cry to alert the prey of their approach they had worked their way up the slope overlooking the copse and now lay hidden amongst the rocks, waiting for night. It was hard to tell in the failing light but it seemed that the camp was still inhabited, in that there was a very faint smell of wood smoke in the air; however, there had been no sign of it wafting up through the trees so it could have been the result of fires left to burn low. Vespasian could see no movement around the copse nor came there any sound of voices from within it.

'Do you really think that they would have left so quickly?' Magnus asked, keeping his voice low as he squinted with his one good eye down the hill; he stroked the flanks of his dogs, calming them into silence.

'I was afraid that they might; after all, they would have expected me to come after them for revenge. I'm hoping our prisoner will have some idea where The Cripple might have headed if he proves not to be here.'

Magnus gave up trying to see something helpful and sat down with his back to the boulder. 'So we go in anyway?'

'If there's someone there then hopefully we'll catch them napping. If it's deserted then we'll just have to encourage our friend to suggest some other hiding places.'

'I imagine that if someone who seems to have as much power as this Cripple does wants to get lost, they can do so very easily.'

'We'll see, Magnus. The thing is that something tells me that this is not over yet. He may have crucified Flavia but do you think that has satisfied him? I don't.'

A slow smile of understanding crept over Magnus' face. 'You mean that he's expecting you to come after him.'

Vespasian nodded, not taking his eyes off the copse. 'I think so. I've kept on asking myself, why Flavia? And the only answer I can come up with is because he knows that a man will always avenge his wife.'

'A fair point. So if he's expecting us then what do you think he has waiting for us?'

'A trap, naturally.'

'And we're just going to walk into it?'

'No, we're going to spring it and then turn it in on itself.'

'We are?'

Vespasian grinned. 'Yes, we are.' He turned to Philon. 'How long?'

'They should be here any moment, master. I sent them back half an hour ago and told them to arrive as the light finally went so there would be no chance of them being seen.'

'Just heard.'

'Let us pray not.'

Night fell quickly in the valley and that event heralded the arrival of the slaves with the horses tethered in four trains.

Vespasian went up to the older of the two Getae. 'You're clear what you have to do?'

'Yes, master,' the slave replied in a whisper. 'Just give the word.'

Vespasian looked at the other three slaves, each leading three or four horses. 'Take no unnecessary risks; let the horses do the work.'

The slaves assured him they would.

'Go then.'

As the slaves led the horses down the hill Vespasian followed, along with Magnus and the freedmen. Picking up speed as they made their descent, the stealth with which they had first approached now evaporated as the horses' hoofs struggled on the darkening ground and they vented their growing unease with equine calls. But this was of no concern to Vespasian as he knew it to be unavoidable; he drew his sword and followed as fast as he could in the dimming light, his heart racing as he contemplated potentially outsmarting his opponent.

On went the horses, gathering even more pace until they reached the eves of the copse and the slaves released them, jabbing their rumps with the tips of their swords, drawing small points of blood and sending the beasts whinnying into the trees as if a unit of cavalry had just charged in.

And then it came, just as Vespasian had expected: a shrill, bestial screech of agony; and then came another. Vespasian accelerated forward, aiming towards the source of the noise, with his freedmen and Magnus and his dogs surging after him. With his sword low, ready for a belly-thrust, he charged under the first boughs, swerved around a shadowed trunk and glimpsed a figure jumping down from his hiding place above and moving ahead of him in pursuit of the horses. Vespasian threw himself at the man, thrusting his blade forward to feel it strike flesh that resisted for an instant before the stroke carried home into the kidneys. The shriek was piercing as the outlaw was punched forward to fall to the ground with his arms flailing above his head; the element of surprise now gone, the freedmen roared their war cries and hurtled towards the outlaws as they sprung their ambush on the riderless horses. So complete was the surprise that many of the outlaws assumed the scream and the war cries had come from one of the non-existent cavalry and continued in their chase of the decoy horses, as Vespasian and his companions crashed into their rear reaping many a life before the real situation became apparent to them.

With the hunters becoming the hunted, they turned from the horses to face their real foe but, in many a case, were too late; blades swiped and punched out of the night, slashing open throats and torsos. Vespasian hurdled the man he had downed, kicking a foot out to smash into another man's kneecap as he turned to face him, catching it at an angle, cracking it sideways. Howling as his leg buckled under him, sinews tearing and liga-ments snapping, the outlaw collapsed forward; Vespasian brought his sword slicing up so that his momentum drove the blade deep into the man's chest to burst out the other side with an obscene gurgle of escaping air bubbling through blood. Dead almost instantaneously, the outlaw flopped to the floor, pulling Vespasian's wedged-in sword down with him. Letting go of the handle, Vespasian kicked the corpse so that it rolled onto its side; he knelt and pulled at his weapon, twisting it as he did in order to break the suction. With a jerk, it came free and Vespasian raised himself back up, seeking another victim in the gloom as a flash of white light streaked through his head and his ears rang. And then all became dark.

'At last you awake.'

The voice seemed distant to Vespasian as it cut through the pain in his head. He stirred again, feeling his wrists bound behind his back.

'Freshen him up.'

A shock of cold water splashed over his face and chest, causing him to splutter and choke as he breathed in more than a few drops. Coughing and shaking his head he opened his eyes; dawn glowed golden through the trees.

'What a pleasure to see you again, Titus Flavius Vespasianus.'

Vespasian turned his head to see a man of similar age to himself, seated on a chair just a few paces away to his left, totally bald with a thin, sunburned face; he recognised him almost immediately despite the many intervening years since he had last seen him.

'And looking so healthy and well, too.' The man smiled but there was no warmth in his eyes; he held his hands folded on his lap; the fingers were twisted and still. 'You're looking at my hands, I see.' He lifted his right arm; the shape of his hand stayed the same, the fingers locked rigid. 'If I really put my mind to it I can sometimes move my little finger; although, I will admit, I haven't tried it for a few years as there's very little point, don't you see.' He held up his hand, palm towards Vespasian, and made a show of deep concentration.

On his wrist, just below the base of the thumb, was a large, puckered scar, livid in the growing light. The wound made by a nail pounded through skin and bone as he was transfixed to a cross as a youth, all those years before. Vespasian recalled the image of his face staring in catatonic horror at the sky only too well, even though it was forty years since it had been etched into his mind.

'There, you see; I can still do it.' The little finger twitched a couple of times and then became still again. 'I'm not nearly so mobile in my feet, however.' He extended a foot towards Vespasian; it too was scarred horrifically where the nail worked a huge hole as he had pushed down on it in the effort to free his chest to take a breath. 'Or foot, I should say.' He extended the other leg; it finished just above where the ankle would have been. 'They had to take it off because it was becoming infected. Do you know how it was done?'

Vespasian did not answer.

'My father hacked it off with his sharpest sword. It wasn't very sharp. It took four blows, although I only remember two of them; passed out, don't you see. He was determined to keep me alive even though he knew that I would spend the rest of my life depending on others. I even have to have someone sponge my arse for me, although I have got over the indignity of that now; I can take a good sponging and barely feel any shame. You can see now why they call me The Cripple.'

Vespasian cast his eyes around to see that he was surrounded by over a dozen men and about the same number of women, some of whom held babes.

'Are you looking for your friends?'

Again, Vespasian did not answer.

'They're quite safe; those that survived, that is; your slaves rode off as soon as the second ambush was sprung; your dogs ran as well, but that's slaves and dogs for you and we should know because most of us were slaves once. The freedmen tried to resist but women raining rocks down from above are quite hard to fight.'

Vespasian could not control his expression.

'Of course there was a second ambush; does it really surprise you? I know you're clever and I assumed that you might try some sort of a ruse so I thought that if I hid the women up in the trees with a bag of rocks each, that would cover that eventuality. And it did so splendidly; we captured twelve of you alive. Just think of the noise you'll all make when we crucify you all together. I say "we" but I mean my men as, unfortunately, I won't be able to join in the fun. But I'll enjoy watching; oh yes, I'll enjoy that. It's what my father kept me alive for: revenge. He was the overall leader of the many gangs of outlaws and runaways throughout the Apennines; he was a proud man, a citizen, who had been dispossessed by Augustus when he came to power so that he could pay off and settle his veterans. He was not going to let me die without revenge and although my life has not been easy, I thank him for that now that I have you. I'll have your brother someday too and then I can go to join my father's shade.'

Vespasian shivered at the thought that such a righteous act of justice meted out so long ago could have such repercussions decades later.

'All these years I've been waiting for you to spend a prolonged period on your estate so that I could have the time to get down here and then set a trap for you. Having you killed with an arrow from a distance, or stabbed in the forum in Rome, wouldn't do, don't you see; the only way you can possibly understand what I went through is by going through it yourself. How did your wife enjoy it, by the way? How rude of me not to ask earlier. She didn't seem to be liking it all that much when we left her. Still, no one was asking her to enjoy it, only suffer it.' The Cripple gave another cold smile. 'But that's enough talking about it; I think we should think about doing it. The crosses are very nearly ready.'

'So they've got you too, sir,' Magnus said as Vespasian was pushed by an outlaw into the little circle of prisoners squatting, their hands tied behind their backs, on stony ground not far from the stream; four outlaws watched over them. 'I was beginning to hope that you had got away and were attempting to organise a rescue.'

The outlaw cracked a javelin haft onto the top of Magnus' head. 'No talking!'

As the outlaw moved away, Vespasian squatted down next to his friend, close so that they would not be heard if they whispered. 'I'm sorry to disappoint you; only the slaves got clear and I doubt very much if they'll be coming back to help.' He looked over to the edge of the copse where twelve rough crosses were being constructed and holes dug to sink them in. 'I think we have to get out of this by ourselves.'

Magnus grunted and indicated with his head to the four guards surrounding them; each had four or five javelins stuck in the ground next to them. 'I imagine they've got other ideas.'

Vespasian could but agree. The guards were too far away to be able to rush at, even if they did manage to untie their wrists. 'Still, I'd rather get brought down by one of their javelins than wait around to get nailed to a cross.'

'There's a lot of merit in that argument, sir.' He leant closer to Philon on his other side. 'We're thinking of rushing them; pass it on.'

Vespasian did the same to the freedman on his other side.

Within a few moments there were surreptitious nods of agreement. Vespasian prepared himself for a desperate course of action that would more than likely result in the deaths of many of them including himself – but they were all dead anyway if they did nothing.

With very little to lose he gave the nod and leapt to his feet, his eleven companions a moment behind him each making for the guard nearest them. The first javelin whistled between his legs, scraping the inside of his left knee but doing no real damage. It was Philon who stopped the next with a direct hit on his right thigh sending him tumbling back and Vespasian realised that the guards were aiming low, having had orders to incapacitate, not kill; it was futile. Cursing, he lowered his head and sprinted, his bound wrists chafing, as Magnus roared and tumbled over with a javelin in his calf. Praying for a misaimed shot to give him a fatal wound, he pounded on, straight at the guard who now only had him to deal with and one javelin with which to do it. But the outlaw was no mere inexperienced youth prone to panic; he side-stepped Vespasian as he attempted to head-butt him and brought the haft of his javelin cracking down across his back, flooring him so that his face scraped against loose stones, tearing skin from his chin.

Vespasian cried out as the point of the javelin was rammed into his right buttock.

'Try running with a javelin in your arse, *senator*,' the guard sneered, grinding the tip so that pain shot through all parts of Vespasian's body and he had to force himself not to howl and lose what little remaining dignity there was left to him.

Rough hands hauled him up by his wrists, almost dislocating his shoulders; the javelin remained embedded, causing excruciating pain with every slightest movement. Magnus and Philon were still down, along with five of the freedmen; only three stood, unwounded. Vespasian could not see the missing one.

'I was *so* looking forward to you all trying that,' The Cripple said, behind him. 'Although I didn't expect one of you to get clean away; he was lucky.'

Pleased to hear that one of his men had escaped, Vespasian turned. The Cripple sat in his chair, carried on two poles by four of his men.

'Not that I really needed an excuse to hurt you more; it's just much more satisfying when I take away any last hope of avoiding such an unpleasant death, don't you see? Much more satisfying.' Again the smile was cold, the eyes remaining dead. 'Still, enough of fooling around; it's time to watch your friends get nailed up and when they're all comfortable it will be your turn.' He nodded to one of the guards. 'Bring them all over.'

The first mallet blow caused Philon to scream as if his innards were being cut out. Vespasian closed his eyes but could not block out the sound. Other blows began to rain down and two more of the freedmen began their piercing cacophony, much to the amusement of the outlaws who mocked their cries as they hammered away.

'Open your eyes and watch,' The Cripple said, 'or I'll have you crucified upside down.'

Vespasian did as he had been told just as Magnus was being hauled, struggling, towards a cross by two outlaws. As he was pushed down to his knees one of the outlaws manhandling him suddenly let go of an arm. It took Vespasian a few moments to realise that the shaft freshly protruding from the man's neck was an arrow. His mate stared at it, confused; it was the last thing he saw as his head was punched back with an arrow's bloody tip bursting out the back of his skull.

Vespasian whipped around to see the four slaves and one more rider charging towards them, their horses in full flight with Castor and Pollux bounding along before them; the two Getic slaves sent shaft after well-aimed shaft into the outlaws at prodigious speed. Down the outlaws went, either from hits or to take cover. Vespasian threw himself to the ground as the shots hissed in; the skill of the former horse-warriors showed in their accuracy from a galloping steed. Within twenty heartbeats the riders and dogs were amongst them, the archers picking off easy targets whilst the two other slaves jumped from their mounts and slashed and hacked with soon-bloodied swords at fleeing outlaws, releasing the freedmen whilst the dogs savaged the wounded.

Vespasian felt his bonds being cut.

'There you go, Father.'

He turned around to look into the grim eyes of his eldest son, Titus.

Titus held out a hand to help his father up. 'I'd say we got here just in time.'

Vespasian hauled himself to his feet. 'A little too late for Philon and a couple of the lads. By the gods above and below, I'm pleased to see you.' He embraced Titus whilst all about the freedmen wreaked vengeance on their erstwhile tormentors. The Cripple could do nought but sit and watch.

'Is that the man who killed Mother?' Titus asked.

'It is.'

Titus walked up to The Cripple whose eyes were no longer dead but showed, instead, fear. 'One of us is going to enjoy this and one of us won't.'

It was an hour past midday when they had finished; the babes and young children they had spared and kept for slaves; but the rest who had survived the rescue attack, even the women in return for their part in the ambush, they made suffer.

Philon and the other two freedmen who had received nail wounds had been taken back to the farm complex, by the newly freed slaves, for treatment but the rest of the freedmen had stayed and worked with enthusiasm and the air was filled with the sound of wretched misery.

Seventeen crosses in all were lined up on the rolling pasture in the same place that Vespasian and Sabinus had first crucified The Cripple and now they were about to erect the eighteenth and last.

'There'll be no one to cut you down this time,' Vespasian said as he hauled the terrified man from his chair. 'A few of the lads will stay here and see to that. And when you are dead they'll take your body down and leave it for wild animals to consume; there'll be no peace for your shade.'

Vespasian, Titus and Magnus stretched Flavia's murderer out on the cross; his pleas and screams attracted no pity, just grim satisfaction. And it was with the same satisfaction that Vespasian transfixed the first wrist, through the original scar, before handing the mallet over to Titus for him to have the pleasure of the second; Magnus did the foot, slowly.

And so the man was crucified for the second time, his shrieks and howls no less penetrating than when Vespasian had first heard them forty years previously. But this time, as he rode unhurriedly away, Vespasian knew that he would die on the cross and wished that he had done so the first time. It was with this wish going around his head that the tears began to fall as he mourned the wife who had not deserved to die the way she did. Tomorrow he would bury Flavia and then soon he would return to Rome to forget.

PART IIII

❧ ❧

ROME, APRIL AD 65

CHAPTER XV

R OME WAS AGAIN obscured; hardly any detail beyond the city walls could be made out as Vespasian and his family stared down at her from where he had last seen her as but a shrivelled carcass writhing on her seven hills covered by a funeral shroud of thick fumes. This time, however, it was dust and not smoke that rose in the air and shrouded her features; the dust of a thousand building sites.

'You can almost hear the money pouring in,' Vespasian said to Titus, sitting on his horse next to him.

Titus rubbed the back of his neck, which had thickened remarkably in the eighteen months that he had been away serving on the Governor of Asia's staff. 'In my final few months in Asia we practically tripled our tax revenues to send cash back to Rome. Temples were stripped and local businesses were made to pay far more than they could afford. It was the same all over the eastern provinces and if it carries on then the consequences could be very severe indeed, Father; there's a lot of resentment already in Syria and Judaea especially.'

Vespasian looked at his eldest son, proud of how he was progressing up the Cursus Honorum and reflecting that when he had been his son's age he had first met Flavia; he shifted his position on his horse so that the wound in his buttock was rested. 'That, I expect, is of little concern to Nero, provided as much coin as possible has already been extracted.'

'Well, all I can say,' Magnus said, sitting to Vespasian's other side, 'is that I'm very glad that I'm far too small a person to be noticed and therefore have a reasonable chance of hanging on to the little wealth that I might have set aside for my old age.'

'Indeed, my friend,' Gaius agreed from the comfort of his carriage that he shared with Domitian, 'you are most fortunate. I intend to remain as inconspicuous as possible and keep a tight grip of my purse-strings until the last brick has been mortared into place and the final piece of scaffolding has been dismantled.'

Vespasian did not look so sure of the possibility of his uncle's strategy. 'I'm afraid that may be rather difficult, Uncle; I imagine that the Emperor is going to want the Senate to vote him all sorts of new taxes. I think that hiding in your tablinum is not going to be an option unless you want to become even more conspicuous because of your absence.'

Gaius' jowls juddered at the thought. 'Oh dear, dear boy; oh dear.'

And it was in a city of wooden scaffolding, piles of building materials and countless workmen, slave, freed and free, that Vespasian, Titus, Magnus and Gaius found themselves as they passed through the Porta Collina a couple of hours later. Immediately their pace slowed as the streets, narrow at the best of times, were obstructed continually by the accoutrements of reconstruction and a procession of builders' carts delivering endless materials, their daytime ban being rescinded for the reconstruction.

They had left their horses and Gaius' carriage outside the gates with a few of their slaves to make the arrangements whilst the rest had been sent on ahead, with Domitian, to warn the small staff remaining in Vespasian's and Gaius' houses that the masters were approaching.

Pushing along the Alta Semita it was apparent that the fire had caused far more damage on the southern side of the street; indeed, this close to the gate the street seemed to be the demarcation line between those houses that had remained untouched and those that had suffered.

'I'll leave you here, Father,' Titus said as they approached the acute junction of the Alta Semita and the Vicus Longus, at whose apex stood the tavern that acted as the headquarters of the South Quirinal Crossroads Brotherhood. 'I'll organise a meeting with Quintus Marcius Barea Sura tomorrow so that we can discuss the financial details of the marriage contract. He's keen to have it done as soon as possible, as you know.'

'Tell him that I'll be at the Senate House in the morning, we'll do it there.'

'I will, Father. I'll see you then.' With a sad smile, as he took his father's forearm, Titus conveyed the depth of his sorrow that Flavia would not be a witness to the wedding and then, with a nod to Gaius and Magnus, walked away downhill, into the centre of the city.

'Looks like the lads have got a bit of work to do,' Magnus commented, his eyes on the tavern that was in the process of almost complete reconstruction. 'The second time in twelve years.' He shook his head and drew the wind through his teeth in disbelief.

'Have they been doing what I requested?' Vespasian asked, looking up at the hod of roof tiles being winched up the none-too-reassuring scaffolding that covered the front of the building.

'I expect so; I'll go and find out. Tigran was outraged when I told him and he said that he was going to call a meeting of all the brotherhoods who had suffered in the fire, which was most of them, and get them to join in the campaign.'

'No need to ask.' Vespasian pointed to a recently finished building; fresh red paint had been daubed on both sides of the doors. '"Nero me rebuilt caused to be" and "Fire are the colour from Nero's beards". I think that makes it quite clear.'

Magnus looked surprised and impressed. 'I'm amazed the lads could write so well.'

'Well, obviously it's not fantastic grammar, but the sense is there.'

'You should tell them to write something on your tavern,' Titus pointed out, 'as it will look a bit strange if it's the only building without.'

'Fair point; I'll do that.' Magnus turned to Vespasian. 'Are you sure you don't want me to accompany you home, sir?'

'We'll be fine, Magnus. I'll see you tomorrow.'

'I'll have Tigran have some lads waiting at Senator Pollo's house at dawn.'

'Thank you, Magnus,' Gaius said, as he and Vespasian moved off along the Alta Semita towards its junction with Pomegranate Street.

'I'm so sorry for your loss, my love, she was a good woman.' Caenis held Vespasian's hands, as they stood in the atrium of his house; she looked up into his face as she expressed her genuine sympathy at the news of her rival's death. 'Flavia was very good to me and I shall miss her.'

Vespasian stroked her cheek and then looked around the room, seeing signs of his late wife everywhere. 'She wanted you to fill the gap that she leaves and act as a mother to the children with her blessing.'

Caenis kissed the back of Vespasian's hand as it passed her lips. 'Of course I will, my love, of course. Would you want me to move in here?'

'You don't mind living with the memory of Flavia surrounding you? I doubt it.'

Caenis gave a sad smile and shook her head. 'You're right: I don't think that I could; I would want to change things but would feel that I was intruding if I did. Perhaps you should move into my house.'

'Along with Domitian?'

Caenis could not conceal a flicker of reluctance passing across her face. 'Naturally Domitian can come to live there; I'll try to provide him with the guidance that Flavia would have wanted.'

Vespasian checked himself from saying that Domitian was not at all susceptible to guidance, however good and well meaning. 'I suppose that I should sell this place.'

'That would be a foolish move.'

Vespasian paused for thought; he saw his error almost immediately. 'Ahh, any cash that I released would just end up being taken by Nero.'

'It's been terrible these last couple of months; Nero's Golden House has—'

'Sucked Rome dry?' Vespasian interrupted.

'And continues to do so. There is almost one suicide every three or four days as informers concoct false charges against the wealthy that Nero is only too pleased to believe; and with all the rumours going about that he caused the fire it's only too easy for him to imagine that there are conspiracies against him everywhere.'

'So the graffiti is working?'

'Very well; but it's not just the brotherhoods who have been doing it; the common people have started to question how the fire started. Now that they can see this huge palace rising in the centre of the city they are starting to wonder at the coincidence that so many of their homes were destroyed and then Nero builds himself one massive one on the ruins.'

'And builds it so quickly.'

'Indeed; the more intelligent of them have realised that the plans must have been drawn up before the fire for it to have progressed with such speed. Epaphroditus is looking for something to distract them from their muttering against his master.'

'A scapegoat?'

'Yes, someone else to blame for the fire.'

'The followers of Paulus of Tarsus,' Sabinus said in response to Vespasian's question as they and Gaius walked down the Quirinal Hill the following morning; their combined entourages of clients made a formidable escort now that Sabinus had made his uncle's house his temporary residence whilst awaiting the rebuilding of his house on the Aventine. 'Epaphroditus told me yesterday.'

Vespasian sighed. 'I'd prefer the blame to stick to Nero, but I can't say that I'm not pleased that the little shit and his followers are going to suffer.'

'It's well overdue, dear boys,' Gaius said with certainty. 'They've been allowed to spread their atheist filth for too long unchecked. Have you still got that scoundrel Paulus under arrest, Sabinus?'

'I have, Uncle; he's safely imprisoned in the Tullianum. I debate with him from time to time. He genuinely believes his lies; he is a spiritual man who would have found great solace in my Lord Mithras but I cannot persuade him. We've also got one of his rivals, Petrus; we finally ran him down a couple of days ago. He and Paulus have been arguing for years, apparently, over whether non-Jews should be allowed to join their sect; they seem to have come to some sort of compromise and were in the process of setting up a temple, or something like it, here in Rome. A nasty thought, and I should know after what I witnessed when I was Governor of Thracia and Macedonia.'

'Indeed, dear boy,' Gaius agreed, 'we were there, remember; we saw how many you had to nail up when they refused to sacrifice to the Emperor.'

'Quite; but it was easier to catch them there. The trouble with Rome is it's so big they can go unnoticed; my information is that their numbers are growing at quite a frightening rate now that there's a rapport between Paulus and Petrus, and so the thinking is that we use this chance to get rid of them before they get too established.'

Vespasian thought he saw a flaw in the plan. 'What evidence do you have that will make the accusation stick?'

'Other than in a time of crisis or doubt people enjoy picking on a minority and giving them a good bashing?'

'Yes, other than that.'

'Well, it's to do with an old prophecy.'

Vespasian was interested. 'Oh yes?'

'Yes; it's from Egypt and it says that Rome will burn as the Dog Star rises. Now it transpires that this prophecy was well known amongst Paulus' supporters because many see Rome as an oppressive place rather than the inclusive and tolerant society that is its reality.'

'So when did the Dog Star rise last year?'

Sabinus grinned. 'Very conveniently on the night the fire broke out.'

Vespasian tapped his forehead with his fingers. 'Of course it did, I remember Magnus mentioning it. So, was that coincidence or was it planned?'

'Well, that's a very interesting thing. If it really was Paulus' people, one could say that he had planned it thus and would claim the prophecy as his own to bolster this religion that he's conjured. However, if it was actually Nero's doing then it could either be a coincidence or—'

'Nero chose the date on purpose with an eye to putting the blame elsewhere should people begin to realise who really burned down the city.'

'Precisely. And if that is the case then Nero was planning this for at least a year.'

Vespasian frowned. 'What makes you say that?'

'The November before the fire, eight months before it, whilst you were in Africa, Nero finally got around to catching up on all the appeals to the Emperor that were outstanding due to his obsession with building a temple to his daughter. One of those appeals was Paulus'. Now, Nero didn't know exactly who Paulus was but he had heard of the worshippers of the Christus, who hadn't, since Claudius clamped down on them and expelled them from the city? Now, whether it was a spontaneous decision on Nero's part or whether he had already decided that this sect would be the perfect scapegoats, I don't know; but what is certain is that when Nero found out that Paulus was a follower of the Christus and when Paulus then claimed that the end of the world would be heralded by the rise of the Dog Star, he immediately delayed his execution and told me to keep Paulus safe as he thought that he'd found a use for his death.'

Vespasian's smile was slow in growing. 'Which he has; a perfect use for his death; doubly so because he's a citizen.'

'What difference does that make?' Gaius asked as they entered the partially rebuilt Forum of Caesar, still missing the equestrian bronze of the dictator destroyed in the fire.

'Because he will be the first citizen to be executed for being a member of this intolerant sect that denies the existence of the gods, refuses to sacrifice to the Emperor and is generally anti-social and keeps itself apart. It will show that Rome will not tolerate such beliefs in its citizens.'

Gaius was confused. 'But Sabinus told me that he was condemned for causing a riot in Caesarea, not being a member of a proscribed sect; even if there were a law against it, which, to my knowledge, there isn't.'

Sabinus slapped his uncle on the shoulder. 'Somehow, Uncle, I think that there soon will be. Although, in a way I feel some regret as I've found him to be a spiritual man and very knowledgeable about my Lord Mithras, which is unsurprising seeing as he comes from Tarsus, one of the great centres of my religion. In my view he could just have easily preached Mithraism, there are so many similar elements and he would have caused a lot less trouble.'

'But then he wouldn't have been the leader of the sect,' Vespasian reminded Sabinus as they stepped out into the Forum Romanum. 'He'd have been just another Mithraic preacher and that would never have suited Paulus.'

'Father Jupiter Optimus Maximus, or whatever name you wish to be addressed by, in offering this bull to you we make a good prayer that you may be propitious and of good will towards us the Senate, and our Emperor, Nero Claudius Germanicus Caesar, and to Rome, the city in which you dwell.' Aulus Licinius Nerva Silianus, the senior consul, stood, with his palms upraised and a fold of his toga covering his head, at the top of the steps of the rebuilt Senate House; smoke from the altar fire spiralled skywards behind him. Senators, over five hundred of them, stood before the building, bearing witness to the sacrifice of a pure white bull. Behind them, covering almost the entire forum, the people of Rome looked on in reverential silence as Vestinus Atticus, the junior consul, stunned the beast with a mallet blow to the head and Silianus slit its throat.

More prayers were intoned as the sacrificial blood streamed into a bronze basin that quickly filled and then overflowed, so that the steps of the Senate House were stained deep red and the iron tang of life's fluid filled the warming, post-dawn air. The bull crumpled to its knees and then keeled over and was soon being eviscerated by the two consuls. As Silianus held up the liver, announcing that it was perfect, an eagle passed high above the forum, it's wings beating with slow majesty as it steered a direct

273

course due east; many would swear later that the bird had a burning coal clasped in its talons – although how it did so without causing itself serious injury, none could quite say, unwilling as they were to let practicality get in the way of an otherwise impressive omen.

Silianus pointed to the sky as the eagle flew over the vast construction site of the Golden House and on to the Esquiline. 'Jupiter Optimus Maximus has accepted our sacrifice. What is more he has guided our thoughts with this omen. We shall now take our places and await the arrival of the Emperor, who will grace us by taking time out from overseeing the reconstruction of our city to make a plea for our aid. Conscript Fathers, until his arrival we shall hear from the prefect of Rome, Titus Flavius Sabinus, who will report on the progress of the reconstruction.'

Vespasian looked at his brother in surprise. 'You didn't say that you were due to speak this morning.'

'I didn't know; I haven't really got anything new to say that no one already knows.'

'Then it's a trap, dear boy,' Gaius asserted. 'Silianus wouldn't have put you on the spot like that unless there was some way that he could gain by it. My advice is to make a very short statement heaping praise upon the Emperor for the excellent job he is doing co-ordinating the resources; even though we all know that he's just concentrating on his new palace complex and letting unscrupulous contractors milk as much money as possible out of the rest of the reconstruction by employing shoddy building practices, if only half of the rumours are true.'

'You're right, Uncle; I'll be fulsome with imperial praise and brief with hard fact.'

And he was true to his word, Vespasian mused as his brother delivered a flowery paean of praise for the Emperor's selfless struggle to improve the situation of the deserving people of Rome and neglecting to say that in Nero's mind that amounted to one person: himself.

'And as to the progress of the public works,' Sabinus declaimed as he drew to a close in the high-vaulted chamber that smelt of fresh paint and sawdust with an undertone of sweat, 'we have recently imported another two thousand public slaves from the slave markets of Delos and work is underway in all the public buildings being reconstructed at the Treasury's expense. And that, Conscript Fathers, is all I have to report.'

'Our thanks to the prefect of Rome,' Silianus said as Sabinus made his way back to his folding stool between Vespasian and his uncle. 'But before you sit down, prefect, would you tell us who was responsible for the disaster, as I believe that you now have that information?'

Sabinus came to a sudden halt as if he had walked into an invisible barrier. Vespasian now understood just why Epaphroditus had furnished his brother with the information as to who was to be the scapegoat for the fire: Sabinus was to be the one to falsely accuse the sect and in doing so it would make it seem that Nero had been wronged by the people's suspicions, something that would not have been possible had the Emperor, or anyone closely associated with him, made the claim.

Vespasian watched the very same thoughts go through his brother's head as he too realised that he had been manoeuvred into being the one who would be responsible for protecting Nero's reputation with the people. To do it successfully would mean that he, Sabinus, would have to persecute the sect without mercy.

Sabinus turned and faced the senior consul. 'Without doubt it was a new sect of gods-denying atheists. They have in the past refused to make sacrifices to the Emperor or, even as with the compromise reached with the Jews, *for* the Emperor.'

Silianus took on a grave countenance as mutters of outrage circulated in the chamber. 'And what evidence have you uncovered that supports this claim?'

Vespasian could see that his brother was thinking fast.

'I have confessions from a number of slaves who are members of this sect, made under torture in accordance with the law, that the fire was organised by two people: Paulus of Tarsus and an accomplice of his, Petrus. Both of whom are in my custody in the Tullianum and—'

'In your custody!' The voice was immediately recognisable and Vespasian did not need to turn his head to know that Nero was standing, unannounced, in the open doors of the Senate House; it had been a well-planned move as was attested by the expression on the face of Epaphroditus, standing just behind the Emperor.

Sabinus spun round. 'Yes, Princeps.'

'For how long have they been *in your custody*?'

Sabinus swallowed. 'Paulus of Tarsus was originally under house arrest when he came here almost four years ago to exercise his right, as a Roman citizen, to appeal to you. You heard his appeal two Novembers ago and passed a sentence of death upon him but, in your wisdom, ordered that it should not be carried out immediately but instead that he should be kept in the Tullianum.'

Vespasian closed his eyes and was relieved when Sabinus was adroit enough at the farce being acted out not to add: until it suited Nero's purpose to have him executed.

Nero, resplendent in purple and gold, stepped into the chamber, his expression one of melodramatic shock, his arms raised and his mouth and eyes wide open. 'And so you took him back into custody and whilst he was under your jurisdiction he and his accomplice organised the destruction of our city!' Nero looked aghast and raised his hands to the heavens in appeal to the gods that this appalling fact may not be true.

Sabinus stood silent; Vespasian could see that there was very little point in him trying to defend himself against the charge that he was in some way responsible for the fire by his lack of watch-fulness. That it was improbable that Paulus could have organised anything from within the depths of the Tullianum was over-looked by all.

'And what about his accomplice?' Nero continued once he had received assurance from the heavens that the appalling fact was indeed true. 'Is he a citizen too?'

'No, Princeps; he comes from the province of Judaea.'

'Where is he?'

'He is also in my custody.'

'And for how long has that been the case?'

Sabinus swallowed again. 'A couple of days, Princeps.'

'Two days! Two days and he's still alive. He should have been brought to me so that I could order his crucifixion as soon as you apprehended him.'

'They will both be before you in the morning.'

'No, that's not quick enough; bring them to my gardens on the Vatican Hill this evening. I will judge them then before the people he caused to be homeless living in the refugee camp there. I want them to see their guilt. In the meantime make sure that notices go up around the city proclaiming the culprits so that all the people know who was responsible for the destruction of their city; and then get rid of that malicious graffiti accusing me! Me!' Nero shrieked the last word and had turned puce; his eyes flashed about the chamber as if he suspected everyone within of daubing new-built walls with accusations against him. It was a few moments before he collected himself and drew a few deep breaths. 'And send me as many of these miserable creatures as you have; it's time I started making an example of them. And have that Jewish delegation from Jerusalem that have been waiting to see me since before the fire come to witness it; I want to send them back to Judaea, with their plea dismissed, left in no doubt as to what I do with intolerant religions.'

As Nero strode from the chamber, Sabinus regained his seat, his forehead beaded with sweat. 'That bastard Epaphroditus! He's played me for a fool.'

Vespasian could but concur. 'But that was a hard one to see coming. What are your options?'

'Options? That would be a luxury. If I don't ensure that the people direct their hatred away from Nero then I might as well open my wrists now. I'll have the notices say that it's every citizen's civic duty to round up these atheists and bring them to the forum.'

'That went well for your brother.'

Vespasian looked around to see who had addressed him, as he filed out of the Senate House at the close of business, to see a tall, spindly-legged middle-aged senator, standing next to Titus, with

277

a beak of a nose and a wide forehead with thick brows all combining to give an avian impression. There was no indication that the remark had been facetious.

'This is Quintus Marcius Barea Sura, Father,' Titus informed him.

'Yes, we've seen each other in the Senate.' Vespasian gripped Sura's proffered arm. 'I'm pleased to make your acquaintance, Sura; and, no, I thought that it didn't go too well for my brother at all. But why is it a concern of yours?'

Sura's head jerked a couple of times in a creditable impression of a bird pecking seed. 'No concern of mine, my dear Vespasian; it was just an observation.' He came closer and lowered his voice. 'We all know that it was a farce but none of us would say so out loud. However, the fact that Nero chose Sabinus to act in the farce with him can only be good for your brother as Nero will see him as an accomplice and therefore very much on his side rather than against him; very handy in this climate, I think you'll agree. I only share this with you so that you can understand my thoughts and perhaps we shall find common ground considering that our families may well unite.'

'Indeed, they may, Sura; shall we walk?'

'But why so quick?' Vespasian asked Sura as they strolled past the newly completed House of the Vestals. 'The dowry of a million is more than acceptable but surely it will take you some time to raise that amount in cash? Do you really think that you can have that by the day after tomorrow?'

'I have it now, in gold, ready waiting at my house; the result of my year as Governor of Hispania Baetica. I'd press for the wedding to be tomorrow if it wasn't for the reopening of the Circus Maximus and the racing in honour of the festival of Ceres. Having such a sum in cash there is one of the reasons I wish the wedding to happen hastily, if you understand me?'

Vespasian could see the point. 'If you try to put such a sum in a bank then Nero would hear of it?'

'It's always best to keep news of one's good fortune from the ears of the Emperor when he is so enamoured of cash.'

'When is an emperor not enamoured of cash?'

'Precisely; my elder daughter's husband's family, the Ulpii, do more than their share of keeping Nero's attentions away from our family by regular interest-free contributions, shall we say, to the imperial purse.'

Vespasian turned to Titus. 'You're happy that this should happen so quickly?'

'Of course, Father. I want to get remarried as soon as possible; my future father-in-law is keen that his daughter should be a senator's wife.'

'Ahh.' Vespasian gave a questioning look to Sura.

'Titus is of the age to be eligible for a quaestorship but they come at a price at the moment and there are not many families who can afford them. However, my elder daughter's husband, my son-in-law Patruinus, is willing to request a quaestorship for Titus next time he makes over a loan to Nero, which will be in a couple of days' time.'

Vespasian was astounded. 'Why would he do that for my family?'

'Not for your family but for mine.'

'And why, therefore, have you chosen Titus to be the recipient of such good fortune?'

Sura's head jerked again in its pecking-like way. 'Well, I would have thought that was obvious, Vespasian; dark days are coming with Nero lacking an heir – granted, the Empress is pregnant again, but even if the issue survives it would firstly have to be a boy and then manage to live fourteen years to be of an age to succeed his father.' Again Sura's head came forward and he lowered his voice. 'That may be possible for the child, Vespasian, but do you think that it would be possible for, well, let's not stoop to treasonous thought, but you get my drift, don't you?'

'I do; and I share that analysis.'

'I knew we could find common ground. You see, Vespasian, in these dark days to come we will all be looking for allies and support and I've singled out you and your family as being one of potential; you, a hero of the invasion of Britannia and a crucial part of the suppression of Boudicca's revolt; brother to the prefect of Rome, at least for the time being. And also you have the pleasure of the lovely Caenis as your mistress and what she does not know of imperial politics is not worth the knowing. All in all when the dice are cast and the dark days begin, I, as a betting man, would say that you could have quite an impressive throw. I think that they are reasons enough. Now, shall we agree to the match and set the wedding for the day after tomorrow, the day Patruinus takes his money to the palace?'

Vespasian did not need to think too long. 'It's a deal, Sura; the day after tomorrow it is.'

Sura grasped Vespasian's forearm. 'Excellent, excellent. One piece of advice before I go: take advantage of Sabinus taking the prisoners to the Emperor this evening; if you go with him Nero will associate you in his mind with the deception that he's trying to create. That can only be good if he thinks of you as a part of his scheming; it would give him more reason to believe that you love him, and you know just how important that is for Nero.'

Vespasian smiled at Sura, impressed by his shrewdness. 'I do believe you might be right; thank you, Sura, for the good advice.'

'I'm sure you'll repay me one day.'

'I'm sure I will.'

The effect of the notices was swift and brutal in its violence and surprised Vespasian not one bit as he accompanied Sabinus, escorted by his lictors, across the forum to Rome's only public prison, the Tullianum.

'Hatred is a very easy thing to stir up,' he mused as he watched a gang of youths drag two screaming slave girls towards an almost full, temporary compound, guarded by troops from the Urban Cohorts, that had been set up in front of the rostra.

Sabinus was unmoved. 'That's the second time we've filled that compound this afternoon. I've already told Marcus Cocceius Nerva, the praetor who assists me with prisoners, to take more than two hundred of the miserable creatures over to the Vatican

Hill. The gods only know what Nero's going to do with them to keep the people amused.' He knocked on the heavy, iron-reinforced door of the Tullianum.

Vespasian watched the two girls get pushed through the gates of the compound. 'You can be sure that they won't be coming back across the river.'

The door was opened by a huge, bald man of insalubrious appearance and unwholesome smell, wearing a stained leather apron over a greasy tunic. 'Good afternoon, prefect.'

Sabinus stepped past the man into a low, damp room, lit only by a few oil lamps. 'Blaesus. I've come for the two prisoners.'

Blaesus gave a cracked-tooth grin. 'I'll send Beauty for them; he'll enjoy that. Beauty!'

Vespasian walked through the door and the atmosphere of close incarceration came back to him immediately from the days when he had been one of the three junior magistrates overseeing book-burning and executions; it had been in this very room that he had witnessed the strangulation of Sejanus and his elder son, Strabo. He shuddered at the memory of what had happened next when the two younger children had been condemned to the same fate as their father: as it was considered unlucky to execute a female virgin he had been forced to order the deflowering of Sejanus' seven-year-old daughter; he could still hear her screams as he walked out of the building, unwilling to bear witness to the deed that he had set in motion. It was not a recollection that he cherished.

A rumbling growl brought him out of his unpleasant introspection; from a dim corner appeared a hirsute man, dressed only in a loincloth, his flat face almost completely covered in hair.

'Fetch them, Beauty,' Blaesus said with a certain degree of affection for what Vespasian could only assume was a sort of pet. Evidently pleased by having been entrusted with such a responsible task, Beauty grabbed a ring of keys hanging on the wall and lumbered towards a small door in a partition at the far end of the room.

Vespasian looked at his brother in surprise. 'You're not keeping them down there?' He pointed to a trap door in the centre of the room that he knew gave access to the damp and dismal cell that was home for every prisoner he had ever known incarcerated in this place.

Sabinus shook his head. 'No, I didn't think that he deserved it.'

'You've had that partition built especially because you think he doesn't deserve it, after all the grief and death that he's caused. He's really got to you in your conversations.'

Sabinus shrugged. 'He's a spiritual man, like myself. He's just misled in his beliefs.'

'Are you telling me that you have so much sympathy with the bandy-legged little shit after all you've done to suppress him?'

'Your brother has begun to open his mind, Titus Flavius Vespasianus,' Paulus of Tarsus said as Beauty opened the door with a sharp growl to invite the prisoners to step out. Bow-legged, short and bald and with half an ear missing from when it had been cut off as he led the Temple Guards in the arrest of Yeshua bar Yosef, the man he now worshipped, all those years ago in a garden outside Jerusalem. 'I was surprised to find out just how much we had in common. It won't be long before I convert him to the true light and cleanse him with the blood of the Lamb.'

'The Light of my Lord Mithras is the only light I need and I have bathed in the blood of the Bull.'

'There is only one Light and that is the One True God whose light shines on us through his son, Yeshua the Christus, who died for our sins. I'll soon have you acknowledging that, since you are so close to seeing the truth.'

Vespasian could tell by the ease of their speech that it was a conversation that they had often had.

'There will be no time for that, Paulus.'

'Ahh.' Paulus smiled to himself as an older man with long, dishevelled grey hair and beard came through the partition door. 'It seems that we're not much longer for this world, Petrus.'

Petrus scratched at the thick hair under his chin. 'I'll bear no sorrow in leaving it; God's house is preferable to Caesar's no matter how golden he builds it.'

'Indeed, brother.'

'Where are you taking us?' Petrus asked Sabinus.

'To be judged by Nero in his gardens across the Tiber on the Vatican Hill.'

CHAPTER XVI

THE SUN WAS nearing the horizon, shining into their squinting eyes, as Vespasian, Sabinus and their prisoners, preceded by Sabinus' lictors, crossed Nero's recently constructed bridge across the Tiber, at the apex of the dog's-leg the river makes at the northwest corner of the Campus Martius. Before them was a town of tents and shacks swathed in the stench of raw sewage rising from the river. Their passing drew little interest from the thousands of refugees whose daily routine was to pester the aediles from their areas for the chance of accommodation in one of the new-built tenement blocks as they reached completion; every day a few more were successful in bribing or cajoling their way out of the squalid refugee town and moving into a small room in a hastily constructed building that had been designed for short-term profit rather than long-term safety.

Vespasian looked around in disbelief at the squalor; having left Rome on the final night of the fire and only returned just the previous day, he had no idea of the conditions that the dispossessed had had to endure for the last nine months. 'How have they tolerated this, Sabinus? Why hasn't there been some sort of uprising?'

'Pah!' Sabinus flicked his hand towards a group of miserable-looking older men. 'What could they do? They have to be patient and wait upon their betters making things work again for them. We had a major recruitment drive and got a lot of the men of fighting age into the legions and the rest are just dross and women. They have no spirit left, just dull patience.' He turned to Paulus. 'This would be ideal ground for your tales, Paulus.'

'Truths, not tales, Sabinus; and I can assure you that my followers are ministering to these poor people and they are finding it to be a fertile field in which to sow the seed of the Christus' passion.'

'As are mine,' Petrus added.

'Well, for their own sakes, they had better desist and leave Rome,' Sabinus said, 'because they caused the fire and now they will pay.'

Paulus looked astounded. 'But everyone knows who really caused it.'

'Do they? It might be made to look otherwise; like someone tried to make his prophecy come true.'

Paulus thought for a moment. 'The Dog Star prophecy: Rome will burn at the rising of the Dog Star.'

'Yes, and you told Nero that prophecy and made it sound as if it was your own; he had never heard it before. He looked into it and it gave him the perfect opportunity and cover-story. You, the leader of your new sect, said the End of Days will be ushered in by the rising of the Dog Star and, very suspiciously, Rome burns the very night that star rose last year; the night, coincidentally, of one of the blackest days in the calendar. Of course it must have been you and your people who did it. You were a fool to yourself, Paulus, and now you are going to be Nero's scapegoat.'

It was as if there was a feast in preparation, for the smell of roasting meat cut through the stench of the encampment as they neared Nero's gardens, next to his circus on the Vatican Hill. A couple of Praetorian Guards stood to attention and two more escorted them as they walked, with twilight deepening, through the gates into what seemed to be an oasis of calm after the crowded conditions of the camp.

'I thought Nero said that he would open his gardens to the people,' Vespasian observed, looking about and seeing no sign of the refugee tents that he had expected.

'No, that lasted a few days until Nero realised that they would be here for a couple of years,' Sabinus replied with a wry smile. 'He got rid of them very quickly after that, saying that they made too much noise and he needed peace in order to be able to work harder to complete the city faster.'

'In other words, he couldn't hear himself sing.'

Sabinus chuckled as the two Praetorians, walking ahead of the lictors, led them deeper into the gardens; the smell of roasting meat grew, as did the ambient light emanating from a dozen or so torches up ahead.

And it was a sight that neither Vespasian nor his brother had been prepared for that greeted them as they arrived at a large terrace surrounded by a balustrade in the midst of which reclined Nero and his Empress, Poppaea Sabina, now noticeably pregnant again, eating from a laden table. But it was not this reasonably normal scene that so shocked Vespasian; it was what made it visible. At intervals around the balustrade great torches had been erected, a dozen in all, and Vespasian now understood whence came the smell of roasting meat.

'Prefect Sabinus!' Nero rasped as he licked the juice of a pear from his fingers. 'So you have brought me the culprits.'

'As you have ordered, Princeps; here are Paulus of Tarsus and Petrus of Judaea, ready for your judgement.'

'What's he doing here?' Poppaea asked, pointing at Vespasian.

Nero frowned at Vespasian. 'Well? What *are* you doing here?'

Vespasian knew that it would do him no good to feel any shame. 'I came with my brother to have the pleasure of seeing you condemn the two men responsible for the burning of Rome, Princeps. I enjoy seeing justice done.'

'Yes, quite; justice must be done.' Nero peered at the two prisoners for a few moments in the ghastly, flickering light. 'But there's no need to hear the case, I can tell they are guilty; but we shall take them before the people now.' He gestured to a shadowed figure beyond the balustrade. 'Subrius, have the people in the camp gather in my circus, as quick as you can, so they can see the truth of it. And make sure the Jewish delegation has arrived.'

'They're waiting outside the gardens, Princeps.'

'Good. Tell them to join me as I make my way to the circus.'

The Praetorian tribune saluted and hurried off about his errand.

Nero looked back at the prisoners. 'I remember this Paulus; he said something about the End of Days starting here in Rome when the Dog Star rose. Well, it seemed for a while that the prophecy might have come true, but ...' He gestured around him. 'Life still goes on.' He looked up at one of the torches. 'Not for them, obviously, but for most others.' He then glanced at a small group of condemned waiting in the shadows for their turn to provide the lighting. 'Except, perhaps, them as well. The day turns to night now but tomorrow it will be day again. So, it was not the End of Days; it was just you and your people trying to make it so. Now the people of Rome shall know the truth.'

Paulus did not flinch. 'The whole of Rome knows that it was you.'

'Silence!' Poppaea shrilled. 'How dare you address your Emperor without leave?' She placed a soothing hand on Nero's arm. 'Ignore his lies, my treasure; don't allow them to furrow your brow. The people know how much you love them and how hard you work for them; they would never believe such vicious slander. Let's put this to rest for once and for all.'

'Will the Emperor finally hear our plea, prefect?' a long-bearded Jew in his late twenties asked Sabinus as the Jewish delegation of six men joined Nero's entourage processing to the circus.

Sabinus did not look at the man. 'I don't think he ever had any intention of hearing your case, Yosef. Jewish priests imprisoned by the procurator of Judaea for refusing to pay the new taxes and then causing a riot over them are very low on his list of priorities.'

'But they're innocent.'

'What Jew is ever innocent?'

Yosef's eyes narrowed. 'You push us too far, Roman: Procurator Florus is squeezing us to get money to pay for your Armenian war and, also now, the reconstruction of Rome, and at the same time we are denied justice from the Emperor. Nine months we have waited here; nine months and he won't hear us.'

'Are you a citizen?' Vespasian asked, recognising the man, having seen the Jewish delegation in the theatre at Antium. 'If not then you have no automatic right to be heard by the Emperor.'

Yosef flashed a look of disdain at Vespasian. 'And who are you?'

'My name is Titus Flavius Vespasianus, Jew, a proconsul of Rome, and I would advise you to treat me with courtesy or I predict that you will never see your homeland again.'

'And I am Yosef ben Matthias, of a House of priestly blood, and I will give you this prediction, proconsul: if Rome continues the rape of my homeland there will be a fire in the East greater than the one I witnessed here in Rome.'

Vespasian stopped and turned to confront Yosef. 'And if that does come to pass, Yosef ben Matthias, ask yourself this: just who will be burning, Jews or Romans?'

'What would we care so long as there is a fire?'

'It will be Jews, Yosef, Jews who will burn; and I can guarantee you that Rome will not hurry to extinguish the flames until you are all incinerated.' Vespasian turned on his heel and followed Nero to the circus.

The circus was full as Nero stepped out, with his Empress, onto the sand to address the crowd from within another semi-circle of the human torches; more of the torches were spaced along the *spina*, the central barrier in the circus. He waited for the last of their screams to die down as Vespasian watched from the side with Sabinus and the Jewish delegation; the prisoners were nowhere to be seen.

'This evening, my people,' Nero declaimed in a high but weak voice that barely reached the huge obelisk in the middle of the spina that Caligula had caused to be brought back from Egypt, 'we have found the guilty people who destroyed our beloved city; atheists led by two men: Paulus of Tarsus and Petrus of Judaea, both of whom deny the existence of the gods and instead worship a crucified Jew.' The two Jews were dragged, naked, out of a grille gate, by a couple of Praetorians commanded by Tribune Subrius, and thrown down upon the sand before Nero. 'It is their followers that burn in the flames, a fitting punishment for their crime; and I promise you that the fires will not go out until every one of these atheists has been purged. And what, you may well ask, is the proof of their guilt?' Nero paused as the crowd's interest began to grow volubly. He indulged it for a while and then signalled for silence. 'The Urban prefect will give you all the proof you need.' He signalled for Sabinus to come forward.

'The bastard,' Sabinus muttered under his breath as he stepped out of the shadows; but Vespasian realised the truth of Sura's words: Sabinus was, in Nero's mind, proving his love for him and Vespasian was very pleased to have taken Sura's advice to associate himself with it.

'What proof do you have for my people, prefect?'

Clearing his throat, Sabinus struck a classic orator's pose, right hand down by his side and the left one clasping his toga on his chest. 'People of Rome, it is true what our Emperor says. I have heard confessions from many in this sect to the effect that they started the fire in a bakery in the Circus Maximus and then they helped the flames to spread as well as hindered the fire-fighting efforts of our gallant Vigiles; and finally when the flames started to die down they rekindled them by setting fire to the Aemilian Basilica.' Sabinus held up his arms to quell the growing outrage for, so far, his narrative fitted the known facts. 'And as for absolute proof of guilt, I give you this: a year and a half ago this man ...' He pointed down to Paulus. 'This man, before many witnesses in the Forum Romanum, predicted the day that the fire would start; and how did he know? Because he knew he was going to start it and when. It was in his interests to start it for he hates Rome and all she stands for. And I can bring forth dozens who will swear to the guilt of him and his accomplice kneeling next to him.'

Nero burst into tears of relief at the revelation as the crowd shouted their outrage. Poppaea placed a protective arm around her emotional husband and Sabinus held his hands high, helping to swell the noise. For a hundred heartbeats he let it grow and then he signalled for silence.

'I know that there have been other rumours, unsavoury, vicious rumours that had no place to be circulated. But ask yourselves this: why did such rumours emerge? Who was responsible?' He pointed down to Paulus and Petrus still kneeling on the ground. 'What better way to deflect the guilt than to blame someone else, someone innocent? And so it was the very people that perpetrated this outrage that tried to blame the very man who is making it all well again: our Emperor. Our beloved Nero.' Sabinus turned and gestured to Nero, who fell to his knees and clasped his hands, extending them to the audience; tears fell, glittering in the torchlight, and the crowd moaned with remorse. Each onlooker felt the weight of guilt from falsely blaming their Emperor, the very man who was rebuilding the city with such alacrity. The scale of their misconception now exposed to them, they called upon Nero to forgive them, for they loved him still. Nero trembled and sobbed, feeding off the emotion of the crowd who in turn reacted to his growing state.

Vespasian stood in wonder that with half-truths and groundless implications the mob could have been so swayed; now Nero had found their love again he was once more secure. The people would protect him for they would allow no assassin to survive the death of their beloved Emperor. But then Vespasian realised that the followers of Paulus and Petrus were a far more tangible target for the people's hate than the relatively removed Emperor. Everyone in the lower classes, no doubt, knew of someone who adhered to this vile cult and they would enjoy taking righteous retribution on them. A smile crept across his face as he understood that once there was no one left to persecute it would be easy to refocus their attentions back onto Nero; this was far from over. In burning their city, Nero had burnt the people's love for him and it was just a matter of time before they realised it; and then his, Vespasian's, class would be free to act.

'And what shall we do with these two villains?' Sabinus roared over the crowd's repentance so that only those closest to him could hear. He moved further down the track and roared the question again and then again and again until he had made a complete circuit of the circus. And there was only one answer and that was unanimous and it was: 'Death!'

And it was with joy that Nero complied with the wishes of his people; he pointed to Petrus. 'This man shall be crucified here, in my circus on the Vatican; he can share the same fate as the cruci-fied Jew he worships.'

Poppaea leant over and whispered into her husband's ear.

Nero gave a malicious smile and turned back to the crowd. 'But let us not give him the pleasure of aping the dead man he considers to be god: tribune, let him be nailed upside down.'

This met with the wholehearted approval of the people.

Petrus, to Vespasian's surprise, remained calm at the news of his hideous fate as Subrius ordered one of his men to haul him up. The condemned man glanced back at Paulus. 'I would not have been worthy to share Yeshua's death.'

'Go in peace, brother,' Paulus replied, before being slapped around the head by the other guard as Tribune Subrius led Petrus to where a cross lay on the ground.

Nero turned to Yosef and the Jewish delegation and indicated to the human torches and then to the two condemned men. 'See what happens to those who want no part of Rome, Jews; those who refuse to accept her and become a part of her. Go now, back to Judaea; go and tell your countrymen that this is what awaits them, fire and nail, if they continue to resist me.' Nero slammed his fist to his chest. 'Me! For Rome is me and I am Rome.' He raised both arms in the air to emphasise the point to an adoring crowd.

'But our petition,' Yosef shouted over the cheer that this last assertion had brought.

'Your petition has been heard and rejected; why should I spare those who withhold their tax from Rome? From me!' A shriek cut through the air; Nero licked his lips, savouring the pain as the mallet blows drove the first nail through Petrus' wrist, and glared at Yosef. 'Now go, Jews, go before you join him.'

Yosef paused as Petrus' agony intensified and then, with head held high, turned and led his delegation towards the gates to the jeers of the crowd, who pelted them with whatever they had to hand.

Nero watched them go as the final nail was struck home and Petrus lost consciousness. 'Bring him back round,' Nero ordered Subrius. 'I want him to know he's dying; and when he's dead, bury the body somewhere here on the hill in secret in an unmarked grave. I don't want his tomb to become a focus for any of his followers that somehow manage to evade justice and survive.' Nero then fixed his attention on Paulus once again. 'This man, though, is a citizen. Despite his turning his back on Rome I will still treat him as such. Let all witness that, although he wished to destroy Rome, Rome has survived in the form of her law. Therefore he shall be decapitated in accordance with that law. Prefect Sabinus, take this man back to the city and publicly execute him tomorrow morning in front of the refugees on that side of the river so that all the people know that justice has been done. But do it outside the city walls as I do not want his blood staining Neropolis or the Campus Martius.' Nero turned and took his wife's hand as Petrus' cross was raised; his wail bestial as he hung head down, his weight tearing at the three nails transfixing him. Nero smiled at the sight. 'Now, my dear, let us return to our dinner. Vespasian and Sabinus, join us.'

'That, I hope, is the last time I have to play the fool for Nero,' Sabinus said as he and Vespasian approached the gates of Nero's gardens having endured sharing dinner with Nero and Poppaea. The Empress's glances at Vespasian had been as cold as her remarks but Nero's buoyant mood, now that he felt that he had the love of the people again, had smothered any frostiness in the atmosphere. Paulus had been sent back to the Tullianum under guard for his final night in a world full of sin, as he had put it.

'Why do you say that?' Vespasian asked, knowing full well the answer.

'Because—'

Vespasian put his hand on his brother's arm. 'You don't have to tell me, Sabinus; I know what you think but I see it in a different light. You have been forced into being Nero's ally; he trusts you, in as far as he can trust anyone, and that is going to help keep us safe.'

Sabinus looked doubtful. 'That would imply that Nero has a sense of gratitude.'

'Gratitude has nothing to do with it; it's more that if he dispenses with you then a whole part of his narrative that Paulus and his followers started the fire would disappear; you are his proof. Now, once every one of those atheists has been dealt with, the distraction in the people's mind will have been removed and they will go back to blaming Nero; you, and now me as well, as I made myself a part of it deliberately, will be responsible for trying to keep Nero's version of the truth current.'

'And will we try to do that?' Sabinus asked as the two Praetorians guarding the gate moved aside to let them through.

'Oh, yes, of course we will; but not very hard.'

'Prefect Sabinus!' A short man with unkempt hair and servile demeanour waited just beyond the gate.

Sabinus glanced down his nose at the man, who rubbed his palms together and looked up with an attempt at an ingratiating smile but was unable to meet his eyes. 'What is it?'

'My name is Milichus, sir; I have been trying to see the Emperor but these men won't let me in.'

'And quite right too; why the Emperor would want to have anything to do with the likes of you escapes me.'

'Because there is a plot to assassinate him and I have proof.'

'You? How could you—'

Vespasian dug his brother in the ribs. 'Come with us and tell your story.'

Milichus bobbed and cringed in the recognisable way of someone weighed down with years of servitude. 'Thank you, sirs.'

'Well?' Sabinus asked as they made their way back through the refugee camp.

'I am the freedman of Senator Scaevinus.'

Sabinus was immediately interested as it had been Scaevinus who, as a praetor the previous year, had made subtle representations to him of a treasonous nature. 'Go on.'

'Well, this evening he came home having spent a good part of the day at the house of Antonius Natalis.'

Sabinus nodded, immediately realising the significance of this; Natalis, the fabulously rich grain merchant, had also sounded him out at around the same time.

'When my master came back he sealed his will and took his old military knife out of its sheath, tested it, and, complaining that it had grown blunt over time, gave it to me to whet with a stone until its point was gleaming. He then ordered the most sumptuous supper, more lavish than I have ever seen him eat, and whilst he did so he freed three of his slaves and distributed money to the rest and to his freedmen.'

'Did you get a gift?' Sabinus asked.

'I did, sir; not very substantial but nonetheless a consideration.'

'Sounds like he was planning to commit suicide,' Vespasian observed.

Milichus nodded, his head bobbing furiously. 'That's what I thought; he was downcast and very obviously deep in thought and any show of cheerfulness seemed to be put on. But then, when he had finished his meal, he retired to his bed and not to the bath to open his veins. But, before he did so, he asked me to get bandages, tourniquets and dressings for wounds ready for tomorrow.' Milichus gave a look to imply that the last piece of information was completely damning. 'My wife said it was my duty to report this.' He reached behind him, under his cloak, and pulled out a knife. 'This is the proof; this is what he gave me to sharpen.'

'Proof of what?' Vespasian asked, disliking the man very much.

'Proof that he is planning to kill the Emperor.'

Vespasian failed to see the connection. 'Why should that mean that your master is planning an attempt on Nero's life? I suggest that you have been disappointed by the gift that Scaevinus gave you and are trying to get him into trouble for petty revenge.'

'No, brother,' Sabinus said as they began to traverse Nero's Bridge. 'Both Scaevinus and Natalis have been associated with Piso; remember I told you about them the night the fire broke out.'

Vespasian cast his mind back and remembered the conversation despite the horrors of that event. He signalled to Milichus to drop back so that he could talk in private with his brother. 'So what do you make of it, Sabinus?'

'I think there may be something to this; if there is, what should we do?'

Vespasian took a few moments to contemplate the issue. 'Well, we could kill this Milichus and see what happens. My guess is they will make the attempt at tomorrow afternoon's reopening of the Circus Maximus; Nero will be far more exposed there.'

'You're right; that's when I would do it. But then we would have to kill the man's wife as well and that could be tricky.'

'Not necessary; she doesn't know that her husband met with us. Alternatively, I'm inclined to enhance our new status as supporters of Nero by taking the man to him and exposing the conspiracy, if it exists that is, because from our point of view it is still too early for Nero to go. Neither of us would stand a chance of benefitting to the highest level just yet, if, as Magnus would say, you take my meaning?'

'I do, brother. But if we are seen by Nero to have saved his life then we should be well rewarded.'

'A province with legions would be very useful to have in the family.'

Sabinus nodded slow understanding. 'Indeed and then perhaps I might not expose the next conspiracy. I think we take this Milichus home and bring him to the Emperor tomorrow morning after Paulus' execution.'

'So do I.' Vespasian gestured to Milichus to catch up. 'You're coming with us.'

'You should be very careful, my love,' Caenis said the following morning as they shared a pre-dawn breakfast of bread, olive oil, garlic and well-watered wine before the hearth-fire in the atrium of Caenis' house; a soft rain, falling through the central hole in the roof, speckled the surface of the impluvium. 'You don't know how deep the conspiracy goes; assuming that there even is a conspiracy in the first place.'

'I'm almost certain that there is one; it's been brewing for a long time now and it centres around Calpurnius Piso.'

'Yes, I would agree; *if* there is a conspiracy, it could centre around Piso as the Calpurnii have got the lineage to be able to lay claim to the Purple. But what is his power-base? What's going to get him there and then keep him in position? Why now? Who else do you think is involved?'

'He and Scaevinus are close, I've seen them together along with Antonius Natalis and the poet, Annaeus Lucanus. Seneca is also involved because he tried to get me to persuade Sabinus to join them; when I refused he didn't seem too pleased.'

Caenis was silent, chewing on a piece of bread; Vespasian watched her, sipping his wine, knowing that she was running possibilities through her analytical mind and he was not about to interrupt her as he valued her advice above all others.

'One of the prefects of the Praetorian Guard is involved,' she said eventually.

'What makes you say that?'

'Well, if Seneca is involved, and there's no reason to think that he wouldn't still be, seeing as he's already approached you and he has nothing to lose by Nero's death but, rather, everything to gain, then he would not allow the thing to happen unless there was a chance of the Guard supporting Piso, or whoever they plan to make emperor – perhaps even Seneca himself. Don't forget that without your brother they cannot guarantee the Urban Cohorts' support. Now, that being the case I think we can rule out Tigellinus as he has always been Nero's creature and has absolutely nothing to gain by his demise; his friendship with Nymphidius Sabinus also means that the Vigiles would remain loyal to Nero, which is all the more reason to have the Guard on the conspirators' side. It therefore has to be Faenius Rufus, which I know seems unlikely as he is honest and unbribeable and has never had a treasonous thought in his life. Now, if Rufus is a part of the conspiracy then it is fair to assume that there are some Praetorian tribunes and centurions involved as well so that he can guarantee the majority of the cohorts' support when, and only when, Nero is dead.'

Vespasian set down his cup. 'Ahh, I see; but Nero won't make that assessment, will he?'

'I doubt it.'

'So if the plot is exposed before Nero is killed, the Guard will remain loyal to him and he will suspect nothing, thinking that it is just a conspiracy of disillusioned senators and equestrians ...'

'Which means?'

'It means he'll have one of the prefects of the Praetorian Guard, who are ultimately responsible for his safety, overseeing the investigation with the help of one of the praetors.'

'And which one would you choose if you were Nero?'

'Prefects or praetors?'

'Prefects, as the praetor will obviously be Nerva, who has responsibility for prisoners.'

Vespasian did not need to contemplate the question. 'I'd choose the one who has a reputation for being honest and unbribeable so that no one could accuse his findings of being tainted with malice as would be more than possible if Tigellinus were to be put in charge.'

Caenis smiled and broke off another hunk of the circular loaf. 'Exactly; so how deep do you think his investigation is going to probe?'

'As shallow as possible; he'll obstruct Nerva at every opportunity.'

'Indeed; but soon the truth will come out because he won't be able to neutralise Nerva completely. It will have to, as some of the people Nerva exposes will give out names of others and so on; but it will take a while, a day or so. However, we will know the reality of the situation from the very beginning: we will know that the seemingly honest and unbribeable Rufus is, in fact, trying to cover up most of the conspiracy and that will give us power over him.'

'Power to do what?'

'Power to use him to pay a few debts.'

'That's brilliant, my love.'

Caenis smiled and reached over to squeeze Vespasian's hand. 'Thank you. I can think of a few people who are just about to become conspirators whether they like it or not.'

'So can I.'

*

The rain had set in by the time Vespasian and Sabinus reached the Forum Romanum, at the beginning of the second hour, but that had not deterred the mob from intensifying their search for the people they believed to be responsible for the destruction of their city, and it was with great enthusiasm that the execution announcement of the leader of that cult was received. Thousands waited outside the Tullianum as Paulus, restrained by Blaesus and a cowering Beauty, who, at the sight of so many people, dashed straight back inside, was brought out by Marcus Cocceius Nerva and handed over to Sabinus' custody to be guarded by a contubernium of one of the Urban Cohorts under the command of an optio.

'So the people have really been taken in by this,' Paulus observed, indicating, with manacled hands, to the mob crowding into the forum and baying for his blood.

'Of course,' Sabinus replied, leading them off on their short journey to the city gates, 'and they'll continue to do so until every one of your followers is dead.'

'And then?'

'Then we'll see,' Vespasian replied as the crowd parted for them and then followed as they headed across the Forum Romanum and on towards the Forum Boarium.

Paulus smiled; it was grim and did not reach his eyes.

They walked on in silence for a while; the crowd behind them making too much noise for conversation to be possible.

'My death won't save Nero,' Paulus said eventually, as they passed through the Porta Radusculana and the bottleneck thinned out the crowd. 'And it certainly won't halt the growth of the true religion; there are churches all over the Empire.'

'What?' Vespasian had never heard the word.

'Churches: groups of believers who come together to pray. Killing me will only strengthen their belief in the imminent coming of the End of Days. Do you not see? This world will not last, cannot last, it being so full of sin; Yeshua will come again soon and we will all be judged and those worthy will live in peace in the world to come. The poor will triumph and the rich will fall.'

Vespasian was unimpressed as they carried on down the Via Ostiensis, the rain falling steadily. 'Believe what you like, Paulus; offer the poor hope of a better life in a mythical afterlife that only you seem to know about. Say what you like because this world is all there is and in a very short time you will be dead.'

'Will I? Will I really? No, Vespasian, I won't be dead; just my body but not me. I will rise again to be judged just as Petrus will from his unmarked grave on the Vatican Hill. You can't defeat us.'

'Did Yeshua actually say any of this? Did he?'

'Don't let him rile you, brother,' Sabinus interjected. 'In the letters that I've seen of his, written to his followers, he doesn't mention a single thing that this Yeshua said, not one of his teachings; do you, Paulus?'

'What he said is not as important as what his crucifixion and resurrection mean and what he will do when he comes again.'

'You've just made it all up,' Vespasian scoffed as they came to more open ground further down the Via Ostiensis.

'The Lord Mithras will forgive him,' Sabinus affirmed as he halted the column on soft wet ground just to the side of the road. 'Optio, have the prisoner get to his knees and be prepared to do your duty when I give the command.'

Paulus was manhandled down, his knees squelching into the earth; he voluntarily extended his neck forward so that the blow could be clean.

'People of Rome!' Sabinus shouted so that the gathering crowd could hear him over the downpour. 'You are here to witness the execution of the leader of the cult that was responsible for the Fire of Rome. As Urban prefect I have heard many confessions that it was at Paulus of Tarsus' instigation that the fire was started in order to make a prophecy come true. The Emperor has sentenced him and his associate, Petrus of Judaea, to death. Petrus was executed last night before the refugees in the Vatican Hill camp and this man will be executed now, before you, so that all of Rome can have seen justice to be done.' Sabinus looked down at Paulus and lowered his voice. 'You are a spiritual man; may the Light of Mithras guide you.' He nodded at the optio.

Paulus did not look up. 'I will be guided by the One True—' The sword cleaved into Paulus' neck, slicing through it with barely a tremor.

Paulus' head shot forward, projected by the fountain of blood exploding from the wound; it hit the ground and bounced, leaving an indentation that immediately filled with rain, stained red. It bounced again and then again before coming to rest as the second and third indentations also filled. The crowd stared in silence; the body crumpled to the sodden earth. Vespasian breathed with relief at the demise of the man who had renounced the modern world in the course of building a religion. It was with surprise that he noted moisture in his brother's eyes that was not caused by the rain, as he looked down at the corpse.

A woman came forward from the crowd and approached Sabinus as the optio collected the severed head. 'Prefect?' Her voice was questioning and soft; behind her stood a slave with a handcart.

Sabinus looked up; whether tears were flowing down his face or not was impossible to tell but Vespasian rather thought there were and wondered at the change that had gone through his brother in the nine months that he had been Paulus' gaoler.

'Prefect,' the woman said again.

Sabinus nodded his permission for her to address him. 'My name is Lucina; I would like to take the body and give it a decent burial on my estate.'

'Your estate?'

'Yes, my husband owns land a couple of miles down the road.'

'Why do you want the body; are you a follower of his?'

Lucina shook her head. 'No, prefect; it is dangerous to be so at this time.'

Vespasian was not convinced that she spoke the truth.

Sabinus ran his hand through his hair and then wiped the moisture from his eyes. 'Very well, you may take it. Optio, give the body over to this woman. Have your men load it into the handcart.'

'My thanks to you, prefect; you will be remembered for this.'

Sabinus muttered something unintelligible and walked away.

Vespasian followed him. 'Why did you do that? I'm sure she was lying; she is a follower of Paulus.'

'Yes; I'd say she was.'

'And yet you gave her his body?'

'What harm can it do?'

'She'll make a shrine of his tomb.'

'It'll be outside of Rome.'

'People can walk there.'

'There won't be any of his followers left in the city.'

'What about in a few years' time, once all of this has died down?'

'I don't care about that. All I care about is that he gets treated with respect. Nero gave me no instructions as to how I was to dispose of the body so I've done what I think is best. In the end I grew to respect him even though he was no friend of Rome; I think that in a way he was searching for the same thing as I am but was just looking in a different place. But come, brother; let's not worry about Paulus of Tarsus; he's gone and will soon be forgotten, buried by time. It's the Golden House for us; it's time to take advantage of our new status as Nero's supporters and do ourselves a power of good.'

CHAPTER XVII

Scaevinus was adamant as he stared at the exhibit in Nero's hand. 'That knife is a venerated, family heirloom, Princeps; I keep it in my bedroom, but this ungrateful wretch ...' He pointed, with contempt, at Milichus, cringing under the gaze of his patron and Nero in one of the few completed rooms in the Golden House; round, with a domed ceiling that revolved and was covered in stars that were said to light up at night to give the impression of a moving firmament. 'That wretch stole it in order to weave a web of lies around it to implicate me in a ridiculous plot to kill my Emperor. No doubt he thought that the donative I bestowed on him was not sufficient for him to remain loyal, as if giving him his freedom would not be enough to guarantee that loyalty in the first place. As to my will, I often update and sign it; who does not? And yes, perhaps yesterday's meal was a trifle extravagant but I enjoy my table and it is the festival of Ceres so I was celebrating the reopening of the Circus Maximus for the traditional races on the last day of the festival; what could be wrong with that? And to add to the celebrations I freed three of my slaves whom I've owned for at least fifteen years each and who were eligible for manumission being over the minimum age of thirty. How does any of this point to there being a plot to assassinate you, Princeps?'

Portly and with the flushed-cheeked countenance of a gourmand, Scaevinus did not look to Vespasian to be a convincing political assassin. Indeed, since his arrest and appearance before Nero, something that took less than an hour after Milichus' stumbling accusation of his master before the Emperor, Scaevinus had shown no signs of guilt and his explanations had, so far, been completely reasonable. But, more than this, it was his apparent bemusement at the whole affair that seemed to completely exonerate him from the accusations.

Nero contemplated Scaevinus' defence for a few moments. He was surrounded by bearded and betrousered Germanic Bodyguards; his terror at hearing about a possible threat to his life had manifested in doubling his guard, summoning both Praetorian prefects and then refusing to leave the room. Vespasian had kept a surreptitious eye on Faenius Rufus but he had given no hint that he knew of a conspiracy let alone was a part of one; in fact, he looked as bored by the proceedings as Tigellinus and Epaphroditus, the only two other people present.

It had been Epaphroditus to whom they had taken Milichus first, a shrewd move on their part, Vespasian thought, as it meant that if there was nothing to the allegations, the blame would be diluted, whereas if there was substance then sharing the credit with the powerful freedman would boost their standing with him. As it was, it looked like the former would be the case.

'And what about you asking your freedman to get bandages, dressings and tourniquets ready for the morning?' Nero asked, his eyes narrowing.

Scaevinus held out his hands and shrugged, evidently bewildered. 'What can I say, Princeps? I gave no such order; you may ask anyone in my household and they will confirm that they did not hear me make any such request. I can only assume it is just another malicious lie concocted to bolster an already rickety case, Princeps.'

'But he did!' Milichus all but screamed.

'Silence!' Nero barked without taking his eyes off Scaevinus, his weak voice cracking. 'Speak again out of turn and I'll have your tongue removed.' Nero scratched the beard clinging to his sagging throat. 'There doesn't seem to be anything to incriminate you, Scaevinus; I'm minded to let you go. Take this ungrateful brute with you and deal with him as you will.'

Scaevinus bowed his head. 'Thank you, Princeps; I'm sorry that a member of my household should have been the cause of such anxiety to you. I shall cast him and his bitch-wife off with no support whatever and enjoy watching them sink.'

'But he's friends with Natalis!' Milichus shrieked in desperation. 'They spent the day together yesterday. What did they discuss? Question them separately.'

'Tigellinus, take his tongue,' Nero ordered as if he had requested nothing more than a cup of water.

Tigellinus gave his rabid-dog snarl of a smile and drew his *pugio*; it was then that Vespasian noticed a twitch in Faenius Rufus' demeanour that could have been said to be a small sigh of relief at the thought that Milichus was to be silenced forever. He was sure that he had seen it. Milichus was not lying; there really was a plot.

'Wait!' Nero said, raising a forefinger. 'Maybe there is some sense in what that vermin says; if nothing comes of it then he loses his tongue. It would be interesting to hear what they discussed from each of them.' He turned to Faenius Rufus. 'Prefect, have Marcus Cocceius Nerva bring Natalis in for questioning. Don't let him speak to, or even see, Scaevinus; but make sure that he knows that Scaevinus has been questioned and that's the reason why he is now being interviewed. If there is anything to it, I want you to dig it out.'

Rufus swallowed and saluted. 'It shall be as you wish, Princeps.'

As the Praetorian prefect turned to do Nero's bidding, Vespasian had the distinct impression that the situation was not at all how Rufus would have wished; Caenis' prediction was looking to be very accurate.

'It was merely a social visit,' Natalis insisted, shrugging off Rufus' question in a manner that did not fail to betray his unease standing before Nero with Centurion Sulpicius Asprus' hand on his shoulder. He looked back to the Emperor who was still surrounded by his Germanic Bodyguards. 'We discussed nothing of importance; we just enjoyed spending a few hours together, gossiping and the like.'

Rufus nodded, seemingly satisfied. 'That seems to tie in with what Scaevinus claims, Princeps; he said that they just passed the time in each other's company. Nothing specific.'

Nero was losing patience. 'Then get them to say something specific, Rufus.'

'Yes, Princeps.' Rufus turned back to the detainee; for a moment the look of a man about to sign his own death warrant flickered in his eyes and Vespasian was finally convinced. 'Give me an example of the gossip that passed between you yesterday.'

Natalis made a show of trying to recollect. 'The reopening of the Circus Maximus this afternoon.'

Nero shook his head. 'That's not gossip; the whole of Rome will be talking about that. I want something that only you and Scaevinus would know, the subject that you discussed most.'

Natalis swallowed and made another show of recalling, which was, Vespasian suspected, nothing more than a cover for a desperate calculation. 'We talked about how quick and well the reconstruction of the granaries went and how it was good for my business.'

It was a good bet, Vespasian conceded, with a slight feeling of disappointment.

'Good,' said Nero. 'Take him out and bring Scaevinus back in.'

Scaevinus looked about as he was led, by Tribune Subrius, back into the room, obviously hoping to see Natalis for the chance of some clue as to what to say.

Nero nodded at Rufus to ask the question.

The prefect cleared his throat as if trying to delay the moment a while longer. 'Give us a specific example of what you discussed with Natalis yesterday; the subject that you discussed most.'

Scaevinus frowned as if in thought. 'The reopening of the Circus Maximus?'

'Apart from the reopening of the Circus Maximus!' Nero exploded, his complexion matching that of Scaevinus. 'Answer!'

The same look of recollection masking desperate calculation came over Scaevinus. He took a deep breath and ventured: 'Natalis' business?'

'Yes, but what about his business?' Nero snapped.

'That it was going well?'

'There you have it, Princeps,' Rufus put in with a touch too much haste. 'I think that they have confirmed each other's alibis.'

'Do you, prefect?' Nero questioned. 'Do you indeed? Then he should be able to answer this: Scaevinus, just why is Natalis' business going so well at the moment? What's the reason he gave you?'

Panic caused Scaevinus' whole face to twitch. He looked around desperately for an answer, but there was none.

'Come on, it was only yesterday.'

Scaevinus closed his eyes. 'Because there is a good crop this year in Africa and Egypt?'

'Wrong.'

'Because the price has risen?'

'Wrong and it hasn't; I've fixed the price. You're lying; you were planning my death yesterday, not discussing how the speedy rebuilding of the granaries was good for Natalis' business.'

'No, Princeps, no; it was the granaries.'

'Too late. So who else is involved?'

'No one, Princeps; there isn't a plot.'

'Really? We shall see. Prefect Sabinus, send for Blaesus at the Tullianum and tell him to bring his pet along with him and all his little toys; I think we should question these two gentlemen more closely.'

It was not the tip of Centurion Sulpicius' sword digging into his back but, rather, the sight of the hirsute Beauty and the instrument he clasped in a great fist that weakened Natalis' resolve; the beast was obviously going to enjoy their time together and he had heard the dark rumours from the Tullianum as to its preferred diet.

Beauty approached him, rumbling the contented growls of a beast happy in its work; Natalis fell to his knees and sobbed. 'Gaius Calpurnius Piso was to take your place, Princeps; he was to wait at the Temple of Ceres whilst the deed was done.'

'Good. And who else is involved?'

'Seneca; he was to take no actual part in the assassination. He's waiting at his villa just outside the city to come and give his support for Piso; it would have been vital.'

Nero's face was grim satisfaction. 'I see; Seneca? Well, that is very convenient. But just you four alone would not have been enough. What you say now may have a bearing on the severity of your punishment. So name names and tell me just how was it going to be achieved?'

'There were a few of us,' Scaevinus admitted, eyeing Beauty whose impatient rumbles indicated that he had not given up hope of playing with his toys; Tribune Subrius held him firm so that he could not retreat from the beast. 'It was to be done this afternoon upon your arrival at the circus. The consul designate, Plautius Lateranus, was to fall as a supplicant at your knees, begging for financial assistance, and, as if by mistake, fall onto you, pushing you over and pinning you down.' He hung his head. 'I was then to stab you first.'

'First?'

'Yes.'

'Then who?'

'All those around you with the courage to strike through your Germanic Bodyguards.'

Nero blinked rapidly as he took in the implication of this statement. 'The closest people to me, apart from my Germans, as I come to the circus are always Praetorian centurions and tribunes.'

Scaevinus did not answer but his silence was eloquent; Rufus' right hand clenched.

'What are the names of these officers?'

Scaevinus shook his head. 'We don't know, Princeps; it was organised by intermediaries.'

Rufus' hand unclenched.

Nero's voice rose in pitch. 'Who were they?'

'They were only known to Plautius Lateranus.'

Nero turned in panic to his two Praetorian prefects. 'Rufus, find out who was meant to be escorting me this afternoon and question them, thoroughly. Thoroughly! Do you understand?'

'Yes, Princeps.'

'And have Nerva bring Plautius Lateranus here.'

As Rufus turned to go Centurion Sulpicius touched the hilt of his sword and flicked his eyes towards Nero; Rufus shook his head and marched out.

Nero missed the exchange in his consternation. 'Tigellinus, tell Piso and Seneca that I expect them to be dead soon.'

'Don't you want to question them?'

'No, the longer they stay alive the more of a rallying point they will be for dissent. They must die now; Rufus will dig out all the other names.' Nero struck an exhausted pose, his head in his hands at an angle, the first bit of melodrama that he had allowed himself in the crisis. 'Honest Rufus; he will get them. Now go, speed them to their deaths.' His head came up and his eyes opened wide; his fingers touched his forehead as if a thought had occurred to him. 'No, wait; I want you here with me.' His gaze turned to the Flavian brothers. 'You two; you go and tell them, and if they refuse then they know what they can expect.'

Vespasian and Sabinus hurried down a half-painted corridor; Rufus' footsteps echoed up ahead.

'Why do you want to talk with him?' Sabinus asked.

'I've got a couple of scores to settle,' Vespasian replied as they turned a corner to see Rufus not too far distant. 'Prefect! Prefect, a word with you before you leave.'

Rufus turned to see who was addressing him. 'What do you want, Vespasian?'

'Just a quiet chat.'

'I'm in a hurry.'

'No you're not.'

That seemed to stun Rufus and he recoiled. 'What do you mean?'

'Just that: you are not in a hurry and we both know why.'

'I don't know what you're talking about.' Rufus turned and carried on walking.

Vespasian kept at his shoulder, his voice low. 'Who would be in a hurry to unmask fellow conspirators?'

Rufus remained silent.

'I know, Rufus; Caenis worked it out last night and I've been watching you this morning. She said that there had to be one of the

Praetorian prefects involved and it had to be you and, because of your reputation, Nero would put you in charge of the investigation. Now you've got to investigate the people with whom you conspired. That will be tricky but not impossible if you convince them that their lives are forfeit anyway, but if they don't expose you then the conspiracy can live on and Nero will die. Am I not right?'

Still Rufus said nothing.

'Now, it strikes me that I can either tell Nero what a fool he is to trust you, not using that term, naturally, or ...'

Vespasian waited; it was not for more than ten paces.

'What do you want from me?'

'Just two names.'

'Two names? To do what?'

'Two names to be a part of the conspiracy; implicate them and you buy my silence.'

Rufus glanced at Vespasian; his look was of contempt but he nodded his agreement nevertheless. 'Who?'

'Catus Decianus and Marcus Valerius Messalla Corvinus.'

Sabinus looked in astonishment at his brother as Rufus stalked off. 'He really is part of it.'

'Of course,' Vespasian replied with a grin. 'Caenis is very good at political analysis. I expect she'll be having her own private little chat with our *honest* prefect. Perhaps you would want to add a couple of names to the list?'

'No, I'm fine at the moment; Epaphroditus and Tigellinus would be the only people that I would add and neither of those would be believable.'

Vespasian shrugged and carried on walking. 'As you will. I think that once we've seen Piso and Seneca we should report to Nero and then see if we can't do our uncle's favourite trick of being inconspicuous for a while.'

'You can try, but as prefect of Rome I rather think that the next few days are going to be rather busy for me.'

Gaius Calpurnius Piso greeted Vespasian and Sabinus as they stepped into his atrium; it was as if he had been waiting for visitors. 'Prefect, senator, welcome to my house; although I can guess why you're here. The arrests of Scaevinus and Natalis have not gone unnoticed and I'm under no illusions that they have not been made to talk.'

'Nero knows,' Vespasian said, 'and he's about to turn Rome upside down to find all the conspirators.'

'Then why isn't he hauling me in for questioning?'

'He wants you to take your life immediately so you don't become a focus point. Faenius Rufus has been charged with exposing the rest of the conspiracy.'

'Rufus? Well, he's honest and people will believe his findings, I suppose.' Piso gave nothing away; Vespasian admired him for it. 'You know that when Scaevinus and Natalis were taken in, people urged me to go to the rostra and declare myself, but I refused.'

'Why?' Vespasian asked.

'Because with Nero still alive it would have meant a conflict and many lives would have been lost. It was only with him dead that I could have succeeded.'

'A noble thought.'

'Of course; this whole thing was about noble action against ignoble tyranny. Do you have any other … er, calls to make?'

'Just Seneca.'

'Ahh! So he has lost his battle with his former charge. So Nero adds tutor to the list of murdered brother, mother and wife; he's running out of people close to him to kill. Poppaea better watch her step; or, better still, his other spouse, the vile Doryphorus. Ah well, I leave a sad world. There's no need to wait for me, gentlemen; it will be done quickly as I have no wish to tarry.'

'You should have joined us, not exposed us, Sabinus.' Seneca's voice was calm but Vespasian could feel a rage boiling within him as they sat in his tablinum after the four-mile journey from Rome; they had not been offered refreshment. Seneca's will was on the table before him. 'With you, we would have had Rome and we could have acted much earlier, before the fire, even.'

Sabinus was unrepentant. 'I promised to act in conjunction with my brother; together as a family.'

'Along with that, er, cowardly, yes, cowardly is exactly the right word, that cowardly uncle of yours who has single-handedly pushed back the boundaries of timidity and raised the inability to have an opinion to an art form.'

'But he's still alive,' Vespasian pointed out.

Seneca scoffed, waving his hand. 'Alive with no honour.'

'And no opinions. You, on the other hand, had many opinions as to how we should live our lives; great opinions, worthy ones worth contemplating and acting upon. Which you didn't, did you? No, you wrote of one code but lived by a completely different one: a code ruled by money. It was you withdrawing your loans to the Britannic chieftains, when you thought that Nero was going to pull out from the province, who sparked Boudicca's revolt. You single-handedly caused the deaths of one hundred and sixty thousand people. You raised the calculation of compound interest to an art form. So don't give our family lessons on moral fibre, Seneca.' Vespasian got up from his seat. 'I wish you well in your final hour. I hope you face it with the same fortitude as Piso.'

'Piso!' Seneca's laugh was grim. 'Poor Piso. He would have been dead today whatever happened.'

'How so?' the brothers asked in unison.

'Could you really see Piso as emperor? Do you think the legions on the Rhenus or the Danuvius or out in the East would have accepted him and sworn the oath of allegiance to him? What had he to recommend himself to the people other than an impeccable ancestry? Well, so do many of the Governors of provinces with legions based in them; your friend Corbulo being a good case in point. He was just used to attract other people to the cause. Once Nero was dead, Piso was to be taken to the Praetorian camp but before he could be hailed as emperor a Praetorian centurion was to murder him. Tigellinus would also have perished.'

Vespasian's eyes opened in disbelief. 'You're not waiting here to support Piso; you're waiting here to supplant him.'

Seneca's countenance was full of regret. 'And so the Empire would have fallen into my hands. I could afford it; Piso couldn't and didn't even realise that he had to purchase it in the first place. I've all my personal fortune ready to buy the legions and the Governors. It was all organised. It would have cost me everything I own but what a rich prize it would have been.'

'So this was what it was all about: not saving Rome from a madman but, rather, you becoming emperor.'

'And what a good one I would have made. An … inspiration, yes, I think I may use that word; an inspiration to all my subjects.'

'An inspiration for extreme greed, more like.' In disgust, Vespasian turned on his heel and left the greatest thinker and greatest usurer of the age to die.

Rome was a city of fear as the two brothers returned in the late afternoon; not even the cheers of the quarter of a million spectators in the Circus Maximus, ringing out around the city, could mask the unease in the wealthier neighbourhoods, as in each street they passed along suspects from the senatorial and equestrian classes were being hauled away towards the Golden House.

'Rufus has been busy,' Vespasian observed as they saw Afranius Quintianus being escorted from his house on the Caelian Hill by four Urban Cohort soldiers commanded by the praetor, Nerva. 'No doubt suspects are giving up the names of others to Nerva in the hope that it will save their lives.'

Sabinus' face darkened as, in the distance, yet another conspirator was being led away. 'Do you really think that we've done the right thing? Shouldn't we have been a part of the conspiracy? Nero would be dead by now because, had we been in the plot, we wouldn't have taken Milichus to him.'

Vespasian shrugged. 'But remember that had we joined the conspiracy we would've negotiated our rewards with Piso; we didn't know that Seneca was going to hijack it. Seneca wouldn't have been obliged to us in any way so you may or may not have remained the prefect of Rome and I may or may not have got a province with legions. So, with hindsight, we definitely did the right thing because, had we not exposed it, Piso would now be dead, as would be Tigellinus, and Seneca would be emperor with the backing of the Praetorian Guard gained for him by Faenius Rufus. We would, at best if we had not been a part of the plot, be supplicants or, at worst had we joined the conspiracy, be emperor-killers whom the new Emperor would be wise to make an example of just so people don't get the idea that one can assassinate an emperor and live. Remember what happened to Caligula's assassins?'

'Apart from me, that is.'

'Yes, but that was because it was never publicly known that you took part and we only just managed to do that.'

'Just is good enough, brother.'

'Indeed. And don't feel guilty about all these people being rounded up; Seneca would have made it a priority to do the same as soon as he got into power. They were doomed whatever happened, which is another very good reason never to join a plot against the Emperor.'

The cavernous atrium of the Golden House echoed with the sound of military hobnailed sandals as Guardsmen marched suspects in and then on to a place of confinement. Vespasian and Sabinus waited, next to one of the towering, white-marble columns, for Epaphroditus to send one of his messengers to escort them to the Emperor. It was with surprise that Vespasian saw Caenis coming towards them, skirting around a roped-off area where craftsmen worked on the mosaic floor that was nearing completion.

'What are you doing here?' Vespasian asked as she drew close.

'I came for a little chat with Faenius Rufus,' Caenis said, keeping her voice low. 'I noticed that you had a similar conversation; Decianus and Corvinus were both brought in a little while ago, protesting their innocence to all who cared to listen, which was nobody.'

'That's gratifying.'

'Nero is interrogating Decianus as we speak.'

'No doubt he's saying anything that Nero wants to hear.'

'They all are. Lucanus the poet even denounced his own mother, Acilia, earlier when he was promised immunity; a promise that Nero went back on immediately after he had the name and promptly sentenced him to death. He's not in a stable state to say the least; Poppaea has joined him in an attempt to calm him down. He's refusing to leave the domed room until the conspiracy is completely quashed. Even then, he's nervous of another one emerging so, apparently, he's given orders to prepare a journey to Greece where he intends to compete in all the games and festivals so that everyone can see what an artist he is and all thoughts of wanting him dead will disappear.'

'I think he's rather missed the point,' Sabinus observed. 'Still, I wouldn't mind him going away for a few months; I expect that it will be welcomed by everyone who survives this.'

Caenis smiled. 'You'll be all right, Sabinus, provided you remain Urban prefect you'll have to stay here along with the other magistrates. But he plans to take the rest of the Senate with him so that you can watch him perform.'

Vespasian groaned.

'And he's expecting all the wives to come as well; so, my love, although I'm not official, I'll join you and try to keep you awake.'

'That's some consolation, I suppose.'

'You could sound a little more enthusiastic.'

'I'm sorry.'

'Well, it won't be for a while yet as Tiridates has only just set out from Armenia to receive his crown from Nero's hand here in Rome; he won't want to leave until—'

A polite cough interrupted them. A palace functionary stood nearby. 'The Emperor has sent for you.'

It was a broken Decianus who was dragged, by two Guardsmen, out of the domed room as Vespasian waited with Sabinus to go in.

As their eyes met, Decianus blurted: 'I'm to be executed! Not even given the chance of taking my own life because of those foul lies you told about the black pearls. And I wasn't even a part of Piso's plot.'

Vespasian feigned concern. 'I'm very sorry to hear that, Decianus.'

'You can vouch for me, Vespasian; you can tell the Emperor that I'm too venal, too self-serving, too cowardly, even, to contemplate being a part of the conspiracy. You could tell him that, couldn't you?'

'I could, Decianus, I really could because it would not be a lie; you are all of those things and more. But can you think of one reason why I should, after all that you have done to me? Turning my own son into a spy in my own house; blackmailing my wife, just to name two of them. Let's forget leaving me and my friends to die at the hands of Boudicca. No, Decianus, I won't do what you ask; I won't help you because if I did I would have wasted my time getting you where you are.'

Decianus exploded with fury as the two Guardsmen dragged him off. 'You!'

'Of course; and it was my pleasure.' Vespasian turned away as Tigellinus signalled from the doorway that they should enter. He walked into the Emperor's presence with the sound of Decianus' protests in his ears as he was hauled off to his death.

'Is he dead?' Nero almost screamed the question as Vespasian and Sabinus entered the room, passing four Germanic Bodyguards.

Poppaea, sitting next to her husband, winced at the volume.

'Who, Princeps?' Sabinus asked.

Nero jumped up from his chair and stamped his foot. 'Who! Seneca, of course! Piso's gone and he's left me much in his will; what of Seneca? Is he dead?'

'He was still alive when we left him, Princeps.'

'What!'

'Calm yourself, my dear,' Poppaea said, standing and placing a soothing hand on his arm whilst stroking the swell of her belly. 'You'll disturb our child.'

Nero slapped off the hand. 'Fuck the child! Keep out of this, woman.' He faced back up to the brothers; there was no melodramatic posturing, no acting out of emotion; just panic; sheer, terrified panic. 'Why did you leave him before he was dead? Did you tell him the sentence?'

'We did, Princeps,' Vespasian said.

'And?'

'And we left him to carry it out.'

'Left him! Did he show signs that he was about to open his veins?'

Vespasian swallowed and looked at Sabinus and then back at a panting, puce Nero. 'He was sitting in his tablinum reviewing his will.'

'Not sitting in his bath with his veins open?'

'No, Princeps.'

'No!'

'My dear, calm; the child.'

'Fuck the child, woman! It's my life that I'm concerned about. Seneca lives and who knows what he might plan.' He turned, terror in his eyes, to Tigellinus, standing next to the closed door. 'Send a tribune to see it done.'

With a vicious smile, Tigellinus nodded. 'Gavius Silvanus will do it, Princeps; you can rely on him, unlike these two bunglers.' He stalked from the room.

Nero turned his attention back to the brothers. 'Twenty-seven so far! Twenty-seven! Including two of my Praetorians, Sulpicius and Subrius! They were there this morning, in the same room with me when I was questioning Natalis and Scaevinus! They were armed, they could have killed me. Me! The greatest artist to have ever lived.'

'My dear—'

'Be quiet, woman! They could have killed me! Do you know what Subrius said when I asked him why he wanted me dead?'

Vespasian shook his head. 'What, Princeps?'

'He said that he hated me! *Hated* me! He said that I killed my wife and my mother; such lies! Everyone knows that they had to be executed because they were plotting against me; I didn't kill them! And then he called me an arsonist. Me! It was the followers of that crucified Jew; everyone knows that; you told them so, didn't you, Sabinus? No one hates me! How could anyone hate me? I'm too perfect!'

'My dear, please—'

In one move Nero swivelled and lashed out with his foot.

Poppaea screamed as the force of the blow crushed her belly, knocking her back to crash to the floor. Her head cracked on the marble and she lay still.

For a moment there was silence as all stared in shock at Poppaea, inert on the floor, her legs apart and one arm under her back; a small rivulet of blood seeped from under her head.

Nero screamed and tore at his hair.

Poppaea convulsed; her legs juddered and her belly spasmed.

Despite himself and what he felt for her, Vespasian ran forward and knelt at her side; she was breathing irregularly. Again there was a spasm in her belly; a small, red stain blossomed on her saffron stola between her spread legs.

Nero screamed again and doubled over, his head in his hands.

Sabinus jumped to Vespasian's aid and looked around, helpless, useless.

Tigellinus dashed back into the room.

Poppaea's eyes snapped open; pain twisted her face. She convulsed again and the blossoming stain flowered. With a piercing shriek, she sat up and stared at the bloodstain growing between her legs; her stola now clung to her form, such was the flow. 'My child! My chi—' A reflex scream cut the word short; pain adding shrill resonance to the sound. She clutched her groin with both hands.

'Get a doctor!' Vespasian shouted at Tigellinus. 'Or a midwife or just a woman! Someone who might know what to do.'

Tigellinus turned and ran.

Nero continued to howl and rage, his head going up and down, his arms scrambling in thin air as if he were trying to gain purchase and climb away from his crime.

The red stain spread and was now forming a puddle on the soaking linen.

Poppaea had paled; her screaming ceased and her chest heaved in distress and fear as she gasped in air in choked, erratic gulps.

Vespasian and Sabinus each put an arm around her shoulder, supporting her in an effort to calm her. But Poppaea was not to be calmed and, with bloodied hands, scratched at their faces as Nero continued to claw at the air, howling like a moonstruck hound.

'Get away from her!' The voice was authoritative.

Vespasian and Sabinus leapt back, relieved to be clear of the lashing nails as Caenis ran in with Tigellinus close behind her. She braved Poppaea's flaying arms and firmly put her down on her back. 'Hold her there.'

Vespasian and Sabinus did as they were asked as Caenis pulled up Poppaea's stola, blood dripped from the fabric. With deft fingers she undid the knots of the loincloth and pulled it open.

Vespasian choked back a gorge-full of vomit. A thing of gore moved within the cloth; a thing that could rest in the palm of his hand. A tiny limb clawed at the air as if in imitation of its father; then it was still. Caenis pulled at the loincloth so that it came free; the foetus flopped into the puddle of blood.

Poppaea's struggles diminished by gradual stages.

Wringing out the loincloth, Caenis screwed it into a tight ball and rammed it between Poppaea's legs as Epaphroditus came running in. 'The doctor is on his way, Princeps,' he said, putting a hand on Nero's shoulder. Nero showed no sign of noticing and continued to howl at the domed ceiling.

Poppaea's breaths became weaker and remained erratic as Caenis held the cloth in place but it was fast becoming saturated again. Vespasian let go of Poppaea's shoulder; it was now obvious that she did not need to be restrained.

Caenis looked up at Vespasian. 'What happened?'

He nodded towards the clearly demented Emperor who seemed to be calming as Epaphroditus whispered in his ear. 'He kicked her full in the stomach; I saw the sole of his foot crush it right in. The child never stood a chance.'

Caenis assessed the flow of blood as the doctor arrived. 'Nor does she.'

'Let me see her,' the doctor said, kneeling down, frowning and pushing Caenis' hands away.

Vespasian glanced across to Sabinus and whispered: 'I don't think that it would be a good idea if we're left holding the body.'

Sabinus understood immediately and rose to his feet.

'I'll stay,' Caenis said, 'I may be of help.'

Vespasian followed his brother and headed for the door as the doctor examined an empress already more than halfway to the Ferryman. Nero's howls had decreased; Epaphroditus had managed to bring him back to some sort of reality.

He stared down at the fading body of his wife. 'What will of the gods could have caused that?' His voice was weak and rasped in his throat. 'One moment, she was fine, and then ...' He sobbed. 'And then she was on the floor bleeding. My child; my beloved child is gone. I tried to save him; I tried, didn't I?'

'Yes, Princeps, you tried; we all saw you,' Epaphroditus said, his voice soothing as he and Tigellinus led Nero to a couch.

Vespasian walked through the door, leaving the Emperor to concoct his version of reality that would reflect well on himself and not be the cause of any personal anguish.

'He'll never admit that he did it,' Vespasian said once they were a good distance away from the domed room.

'Yes,' Sabinus agreed. 'He'll probably never even admit to himself that she's dead. And we'll never admit that we were present. With luck he'll drive all real memory of the event from his mind.'

'If he still has a mind,' Vespasian pointed out. 'At one point I thought he was completely gone.'

'What's going on, Bumpkin?'

Vespasian turned as they came back into the atrium, and saw Corvinus, seated, with a couple of Praetorian centurions watching over him.

'What was all the screaming about?'

'I've no idea, Corvinus. But it sounded like the Emperor.'

Corvinus looked concerned. 'I'm supposed to be pleading my case to him; prove my innocence of being a member of Piso's conspiracy. Antonius Natalis accused me and now he's being given full immunity because he named so many. Nerva hasn't stopped arresting people all day; he seems to be thoroughly enjoying it.' A wicked gleam came into his eyes. 'I think I'll accuse you, Vespasian, in return for immunity if I can't persuade Nero of my innocence.'

Vespasian curled his lip. 'You could try, Corvinus, in fact please do. But we were the ones who exposed it; I don't think you'll be believed. If I were you, I'd send a message home to make sure that one of your slaves is sharpening your knives and filling your bath. I don't think that you'll have any problem conducting yourself as a dead man in the future as you once swore to do.'

Corvinus sneered. 'Bumpkin!'

Vespasian smiled and walked away. 'Dead man!'

'Apparently Seneca took all night to bleed out, and he spent a lot of it writing letters,' Gaius informed Vespasian, Sabinus, Caenis and Magnus the following morning as they gathered at Sura's house for Titus' marriage to Marcia Furnilla. 'His blood hardly flowed and in the end his people had to take him into his steam-bath where he suffocated in the steam. His wife tried to kill herself too but they bandaged her wrists and she survived.' Gaius was evidently enjoying the details. 'Over forty people have been convicted, including your friends, Corvinus and Decianus.' Gaius looked quizzically at Vespasian. 'A lucky coincidence or one of the perks of uncovering the conspiracy?'

Vespasian strove to look innocent. 'I heard that Corvinus was allowed suicide and his family will retain much of his estate, unlike Decianus.'

'All the senators condemned to death were allowed suicide, the equestrians and Praetorians were executed. More than half of the guilty were lucky enough to only be exiled.'

'Lucky?' Magnus scoffed. 'Lucky to have your wealth taken away and then be forced to spend the rest of your life in some arsehole of the Empire with only a few goats for intelligent conversation? Bollocks. You show me one senator or equestrian who would take that option over suicide and saving his family's status.'

Gaius contemplated this as Titus' party arrived to cheers and the usual ribald remarks.

'Someone must have named Faenius Rufus last night too, I assume,' Sabinus said as they followed the groom into the house. 'I don't know the details but I heard this morning that Nerva has been awarded Triumphal Ornaments for exposing Rufus; Nymphidius Sabinus has been made Praetorian prefect and I'm going to have a new prefect of the Vigiles once Nero gets over his period of mourning and feels that he can put his mind to it.'

Vespasian was unsurprised. 'Nymphidius getting his reward for his part in the fire. And now I suppose there'll be a scramble by some seriously poisonous bitches to become the new Empress.'

'That position seems to have been filled already,' Caenis said, her voice shaky.

This time Vespasian was surprised. 'That was quick; who?'

Caenis shuddered at the thought. 'That pretty young slave boy who looks remarkably like Poppaea.'

'The one that stood in for her on her wedding night because of her advanced pregnancy,' Gaius said, scandalised.

'Sporus,' Vespasian said.

'"Spunk" in Greek,' Sabinus reminded them.

Caenis shuddered again. 'Well, he won't be producing any more of that, that's for sure. Once Poppaea was dead, Nero had Epaphroditus fetch the lad and made the doctor castrate him then and there; I had to assist. It was the full version, not just, you know … I've never heard such screams. Anyway, Nero has given Sporus all Poppaea's clothes, wigs and jewellery and said that if he survives his operation, he will marry him on his tour of Greece, at one of the festivals, and he, or she as I suppose Nero thinks of him now, will be empress.'

Vespasian shook his head in disbelief as the bride and groom had their hands joined together. 'So in his mind he hasn't killed Poppaea at all.'

'No, for him it is as if it had never happened; he was even calling Sporus "Poppaea" as his genitals were removed.'

Vespasian turned his attention back to the ceremony, wondering just what the Greeks would make of their Emperor marrying a freshly castrated slave boy at one of their religious festivals and then proclaiming him to be the Empress Poppaea. 'Is there no taboo he won't break?'

*

It was through a sombre city that the wedding party walked. Business was carrying on as usual but the traditional shouts of 'Talassio', wishing the happy couple luck, were far less exuberant than they could normally be expected to be; even the enthusiasm for walnut throwing was muted and the newly-weds were showered with fewer nuts that fell from a lesser height. The wedding party themselves attempted to make up for the public's indifference and Vespasian had shouted himself almost hoarse by the time they were approaching his old house in Pomegranate Street, which he had given to Titus as a wedding present.

'You and your brother made more than a few enemies exposing that plot,' Sura said, moving next to Vespasian. 'Some say that you have blood on your hands.'

Vespasian cast a sidelong glance at Sura. 'I notice that you didn't call the wedding off.'

'I don't know any man who hasn't got blood on his hands to some degree. Besides, I can appreciate your calculation: you had nothing to gain from Piso becoming emperor.'

'He wouldn't have; Seneca was to double-cross him and take the Purple for himself by paying massive donatives to the legions and bribing the Governors of militarised provinces.'

Sura could not conceal his surprise. 'Was he now? Well, that might have worked because the legions will have a big say in what happens after Nero; someone like Piso can't just expect to make himself emperor and assume that the legions will all swear allegiance to him. My brother, Soranus, will be doubly relieved that he refused Piso's offer of a consulship should he join him.'

'Only a fool would have joined that conspiracy.'

'True. But soon there will be a successful one; one involving the legions.' Sura gave Vespasian a shrewd look. 'I believe that was you and your brother's calculation. Neither of you were in a position to gain because neither of you controlled any legions; granted, Sabinus does have the three Urban Cohorts and the seven Vigiles Cohorts, but he would hardly have been able to take advantage of the upheaval with that force. Am I right?'

Vespasian kept his face neutral and said nothing.

'You'd be more interested in seeing Nero's assassination and the start of the struggle to succeed him from the point of view of being the Governor of a province with legions. And so, when things calm down and Nero thinks to reward you for saving his life, that's what you'll hope for. Syria or one of the Rhenus or Danuvius provinces; then we shall wait and see.'

Vespasian gave no indication of agreeing or disagreeing.

Sura slapped Vespasian on the back. 'I can see that my decision to marry my daughter into your family is a sensible one. Once we've got Titus his quaestorship, then ... well, then we shall see what else we can purchase with my family's money.'

'You're a generous man, Sura.'

'No. I'm an ambitious one. But sensible enough to realise that without a glowing military record I won't stand a chance of rising to the top in the chaotic aftermath of Nero's death, so I need the patronage of someone who does.'

'Gaius Vespasius Pollo,' a Praetorian tribune standing at the doorway to Pomegranate Street called out, as the wedding party arrived.

Gaius looked in alarm at the tribune as he made his way towards him, through the wedding party. 'What is it?'

He held out a scroll. 'An order from the Emperor.'

Gaius paled and took it with a shaking hand. 'Dear gods.'

Vespasian's stomach lurched.

Gaius unrolled the scroll, glanced at it, went even paler, and then handed it to Vespasian.

'The bastards!' Vespasian spat having read it.

Caenis moved towards him. 'What is it, my love?'

'Seneca wrote to the Emperor as he was dying last night to say that Gaius was the go-between between him and Piso.'

'But that's nonsense.'

'Of course it is and Nero says here that he would not have believed it, especially as it was me and Sabinus who exposed the plot. He thought it was just Seneca having his malicious revenge and was going to ignore it until one of the conspirators independently backed up the accusation.'

'Who?'

'Corvinus. Gods below; what have I done?'

Gaius trembled. 'You've cost me my life, dear boy; by nightfall I'm to be dead.'

Vespasian looked around the faces of his family as the remains of a sombre meal were cleared away by four of Gaius' exquisite, blond boys; it had not been the celebratory occasion that it should have been on a wedding day, far from it. The rituals of the marriage had gone ahead and it was duly consummated but none of the guests had the heart to feel any joy and all thought that Gaius' death sentence was the worst possible omen for the union.

Gaius, himself, had said his goodbyes to the couple and then left the wedding immediately, with Magnus, and returned home to put his affairs in order and to instruct his cook to prepare the finest meal he had ever made.

It was the remains of this that were now being taken away and, as each plate disappeared and the sun began its journey into the west, Vespasian knew that the time, the unavoidable time, was drawing ever nearer.

Vespasian turned to his uncle, reclining next to him. 'I'm sorry, Uncle, we should have asked you to join us when we went to expose the conspiracy to Nero. That would have kept you safe from false accusations. We just didn't think.'

Gaius roused himself out of the reverie he had gradually fallen into as the meal had progressed and drained his cup without giving the vintage the attention it deserved. 'Of course you thought; or, rather, you didn't need to think as it was obvious what I would have said had you asked me.'

Vespasian's smile was rueful. 'You would have said that it would make you far too conspicuous to be a part of the exposure and that staying at home and studiously avoiding being noticed by anyone for either your actions or opinions was a much safer course.'

Gaius' smile equalled that of Vespasian. 'Something like that, dear boy. Ironic, isn't it? I would have refused the chance of making myself immune to false accusations because I would have thought it too dangerous and wanted to keep myself safe.'

Magnus turned to Vespasian. 'Can't you appeal to Nero and say that you falsely implicated Corvinus and this was his way of getting his revenge?'

Caenis, to Vespasian's right, shook her head. 'We discussed that but who would believe it now that Corvinus is dead? Nero would just think that Vespasian was lying to save his uncle.'

'Exactly,' Sabinus agreed. 'Faenius Rufus could, perhaps, have convinced Nero but he was executed this morning. Nerva tried to put in a word as a favour to me but Nero asked him whether he wanted to undo all the good he had done himself by trying to save an obvious conspirator, so, quite naturally, he backed off.'

'Still, it was good of him to try,' Gaius said. 'And it shows his respect for our family, dear boys. You should cultivate Nerva as he seems to be a man of ambition.'

'We will; seeing as he's done so well out of the conspiracy, he's extremely grateful to us for exposing it in the first place.'

'Yes,' Vespasian agreed. 'If you look at it that way then he can be said to be in our debt.'

'Fucking politics,' Magnus muttered. 'It's a grim world in which your class lives.'

'No grimmer than yours, old friend,' Gaius said, putting down his cup and heaving himself to his feet. 'I'm well aware of a lot of the very insalubrious things that you get up to in your world.'

'That's because I did a lot of them for you.'

Gaius chuckled and rested a hand on Magnus' shoulder. 'Too true, Magnus; and you shall find that well reflected in my will.' He looked around the gathering. 'I've got no cause for complaint; I'm almost seventy-five, which is far older than many of my generation reached, and I have the chance to end my life peacefully in the bath with my family around me and in the knowledge that, provided I leave a substantial bequest to the Emperor, they will inherit the main part of my estate. I've lived my life as I wanted to and not many people can say that.' His eye roved over four slaves clearing up. 'Leave that, boys, it's time to say goodbye.'

He smiled at his guests and headed out of the triclinium followed by his beautiful property. 'I won't be long.'

Gaius handed Vespasian his will as he emerged from his bedroom into the atrium, where the family was gathered to wait for him, some while later; he was dressed solely in a loose, white linen robe. 'Save it until I'm gone, dear boy. I've left you my boys as they are too young to free; the three slaves over thirty I've manumitted, they will count you or Sabinus as their patron. You'll have to sort that out between you. But the young lads are yours; I know you won't have much personal use for them, but please keep them for my sake; they're dear to me and have given me a lot of pleasure. Your freedman, Hormus, might enjoy them.'

Vespasian tried to look pleased at the bequest. 'I shall offer him the ... er, opportunity when he gets back from Africa.'

'I'm sure he'll grab it with both hands,' Magnus said, 'if you take my meaning?'

Everyone did but no one was in the mood for levity.

Gaius looked around the room and sighed. 'It's strange, I was once told by a soothsayer that I would die in my own house; a prediction that I took a lot of comfort in. I didn't suspect that it would be at my own hand.' He shook his head with regret and led them from the atrium. 'I'm told that my bath is full and warm and my blade is sharp; so I see no further need for delay.'

Caenis held Vespasian's hand as they followed Gaius to his bath house at the far end of the courtyard garden; high clouds above Rome burned with the evening sun as it sank for the last time in Gaius' life.

The bath house was brightly lit with many lamps and candles so that the marble walls and domed roof radiated golden warmth. In the centre of the room was a sunken bath, lined with aquatic-themed mosaics, mainly fish of differing species that seemed to swim as the warm water filling the bath rippled. Around the bath were set chairs for Gaius' guests. A knife lay on a low table next to the bath.

With a bravery that Vespasian had not expected of his uncle, Gaius did not hesitate; he slipped off his robe and lowered himself into the bath; water, displaced by his huge bulk, slopped over the sides wetting his guests' feet as they took their seats. Openly weeping for their master, Gaius' boys lined the walls to complete a sombre scene.

Gaius picked up the knife and ran his finger along the blade and then nodded with satisfaction. 'That should do.' He looked up. 'Well, my friends, it's time I saw what the Ferryman is made of; he'll have to work hard to row me across. I have to say, it was not a journey I was expecting to make today when I got up this morning.'

'Master! Master! Wait!' Gaius' steward came running through the door; he held a sealed scroll. 'This has just arrived for you.'

All present felt a thrill of hope in their hearts.

Gaius looked at the scroll, but did not take it. 'You read it, Vespasian.'

Vespasian unrolled it and read aloud: '"I hope I timed this correctly. Hopefully, about now, just before sunset, Gaius Vespasius Pollo is opening his veins. This letter would have given everyone hopes of a last-moment reprieve. I'm sorry to disappoint you as it is no more than a message from beyond the grave. I am avenged, Bumpkin. Corvinus.'" Vespasian's hands shook with rage. 'The cunt! I thought it really was a rescindment of the sentence.' He screwed up the scroll and hurled it into a corner.

'I never did, dear boy,' Gaius said, contemplating the knife. 'I never did. Life is not like that.' With a jerk he slit his left wrist lengthways and, even as the blood spurted, swapped hands and opened the right in the same manner.

The bath turned red; Gaius lay the knife down, leant his head back on the edge and closed his eyes; he gave a sigh that could have been construed as being either of contentment or regret. 'So be it. Farewell, all of you. And, Vespasian, look after my dear boys.'

Vespasian gripped Caenis' hand and felt tears of grief and shame trickle down his face; he watched his uncle bleed out, knowing full well that it was his fault. In his pursuit of vengeance, Vespasian had brought about the death of his uncle, Gaius.

EPILOGUE

✳ ✳

Thracia, April AD 67

I T HAD BEEN a long six months and for three of them there had been snow on the ground and a bitter north wind that ripped across the plain. Vespasian put his arm around Caenis as they watched five riders approach, from the south, over the expanse of grassland that had been their home during their exile; an exile for which Vespasian blamed no one but himself.

It had been a foolish thing to do and it had displeased Nero even more than it would have done had Tiridates, the recently crowned King of Armenia, not been at the recital. Indeed, the recital had been to celebrate Nero crowning Tiridates in Rome, not just once, but twice as the Emperor had enjoyed the first time so much. He had used the occasion to present himself as the supreme monarch of the world, seating himself on a curule chair on the rostra in the Forum Romanum, wearing Triumphal Dress and surrounded by military insignia and standards; the very image of a martial emperor had his physique not belied the fact. Tiridates had been made to walk up a ramp and then prostrate himself at Nero's feet; Nero had then stretched out a hand to the younger brother of the Great King of Parthia, raised him up, kissed him and then placed a kingly diadem on his head to the roars of a crowd so huge that not one roof tile could be seen, such was the competition for a vantage point. It was with tears streaming down his face that Nero exchanged courtesies with the new king and then ordered the doors of the Temple of Janus to be closed and declared that there marked the end of war.

So much had Nero enjoyed being the bestower of kingdoms that he restaged the whole event in the Theatre of Pompey later, emphasising to the crowd just how magnanimous he had been, before performing an ode that he had composed especially for the occasion.

And that was where the problem had arisen: it had been long, very long, even for Nero's standards; and all knew that it was absolutely forbidden, on pain of death almost, to leave during the rendition, whatever the excuse. Indeed, a woman in the upper tiers of the theatre had given birth at around the halfway point, her screams muffled by her neighbours.

As Nero had ploughed on, verse after self-praising verse, the sun had reached its zenith and the combination of heat and boredom became a soporific cocktail too strong to resist. Vespasian's snores had disturbed the enjoyment of the newly crowned king, who had glanced in his direction; his splutters and snorts as Caenis hurriedly awoke him caused Nero to stumble on a line, in outrage. And then, to everyone's horror, he started the whole composition again from the very beginning announcing, with a vicious stare in Vespasian's direction, that it must be heard without pause for his genius to be truly appreciated. It had been at that point that one enterprising spectator had feigned death and been carried from the auditorium as it was considered unlucky to have a corpse in the audience.

It was with great haste that Vespasian and Caenis had departed the theatre upon the eventual completion of the ode, losing themselves in the crush of people anxious to be away before the Emperor decided that his talent had not been thoroughly enough displayed to the eastern potentate. And they had not stopped such was Vespasian's fear of Nero's wrath for spoiling his performance. Moreover, Vespasian was still nervous of the Emperor's feelings towards him in the wake of his much-mourned uncle's forced suicide for his supposed role in the Pisonian conspiracy. From Brundisium, where they had taken ship to Epirus, Vespasian had sent Sabinus a letter saying that he would remain in hiding until the Emperor either forgave the insult or forgot about it, neither outcome seeming likely at the time. As to where they were headed he said that if they needed to be found, Magnus would know where to look bearing in mind that he had Caenis with him.

And thus, forty years after he had first come to this place, he had brought Caenis back to the land of her ancestors, the land of the Caenii in Thracia; the land from which, as a babe in arms, Caenis had been taken, along with her mother, as a slave to Rome. The land that she did not know existed until Vespasian returned with the tale of how her amulet of Caeneus had saved his life when he, Magnus, Corbulo and Centurion Faustus, as prisoners of the Caenii, had been about to fight to the death. The tribe's chieftain, Coronus, had recognised the amulet and upon questioning Vespasian it had become apparent that he was Caenis' uncle. He had spared Vespasian and his companions' lives and Vespasian had promised to one day bring Caenis back to the land of her forebears. This promise he had now made good but not in the circumstances he would have wished.

Vespasian squinted and shook his head. 'Your eyes are better than mine; can you make them out?'

Caenis peered into the distance. 'I think they're wearing uniforms under their travel cloaks; they must be official.'

Vespasian's stomach lurched. 'Praetorians?'

'It's too distant to tell for sure; they're not wearing helmets, just hats.'

'How have they found us?'

'You don't know that they have; it might be just a chance visit.'

Vespasian gestured about the landscape; other than the distant mountains to the north and west there was nothing to be seen. It was featureless grassland apart from the huge bowl, on whose lip they stood, in which the Caenii had their main settlement making it invisible until a traveller was almost upon it. 'Who comes here by chance?'

Caenis shaded her eyes. 'A couple of the riders are civilian; one of them is a less than competent horseman. I imagine that the soldiers are their escort.' She strained even harder. 'I think they've got some dogs with them.'

'Hunters, perhaps? Well, I don't think that we should hang around to meet them; let's get back down and get out of sight.' Vespasian turned and jogged back down the slope.

Caenis waited a few moments, still trying to make out the new arrivals, before following him down.

Despite being in his late seventies, Coronus still held sway over the Caenii and, even though Thracia had been incorporated into the Empire twenty years previously, Roman rule was hardly noticed. The taxes the tribe paid now went to the Roman Governor rather than to the king and their young men now enlisted in Rome's auxiliary cohorts rather than in the royal army. Other than that, life had gone on as normal after the annexation and the Caenii had been left to themselves to breed their horses and fish their rivers, so it was with surprise that Coronus received the news of approaching Romans; he rubbed the end of his nose where the tip had been cut off in a skirmish long forgotten. 'I'll send one of my grandsons to meet them.' He turned to a young man with wild red hair, protruding from beneath a fox-fur cap, and a beard to match, lounging on a bench by the doorway of the chieftain's hall. 'Caeneus, go and find out what these strangers want.'

Caeneus acknowledged his grandfather's wishes and disappeared through the door.

'In the meantime you had better stay here; and I'll deny all knowledge of you if it's you that they're looking for.'

Caenis took Coronus' hand. 'You are very kind, Uncle.'

The old man smiled down at his newly discovered niece, twenty years his junior. 'I know many people in this world who would never accuse me of that vice.'

Judging by the fierceness of Coronus' features, enhanced by his mutilated nose, Vespasian could well believe that assertion and, indeed, had suffered the proof of it when he had been captured by the Caenii. 'Don't resist if they resort to force, Coronus; I wouldn't want you or your people to suffer on our account. You've sheltered us for six months now, that's plenty of time for news of people hiding with the Caenii to get out and reach the wrong ears.'

'It won't come to that; there are only five of them.'

'Five Praetorian centurions with a mandate from the Emperor are hard to resist; if they return empty-handed or not at all then your tribe will suffer. It's standard practice.'

'Then we'll just have to hope that it's not you that they're looking for.'

'When was the last time that Romans came here?'

Coronus scratched his grey beard. 'I'm afraid to say that was you.'

'And I'm telling you that I was here forty years ago!' The voice came from beyond the leather sheet covering the doorway and was instantly recognisable. 'And I know he's here with Caenis, which is why I've travelled fuck knows how far so that these gentlemen can give him some good news.'

Vespasian smiled with relief. 'It's all right, Coronus; they can come in. It's Magnus and he would never betray me.'

Coronus pulled back the leather sheet and ushered the visitors in.

Vespasian took a step back as Castor and Pollux bounded in followed by Magnus, Titus, Sura, Hormus and, intriguingly for Vespasian, Nerva.

'It started, in Caesarea, with a complaint about people sacrificing a couple of birds to Apollo in front of one of their synagogues, as the Jews call their temples,' Nerva explained as they sat round a table in Coronus' hall and were served roasted goat, bread and dark Thracian wine. 'And then it escalated into a protest about the heavy and rising taxation that Judaea is subject to and then this was exacerbated by Gessius Florus, the procurator of Judaea, removing seventeen talents of gold from their temple treasury and sending it to Nero to help finance his Golden House. Needless to say, not all the money made it to Rome.'

'There's a surprise,' Magnus muttered through a mouthful of persistent goat; Castor and Pollux lay on the ground next to him, gnawing on huge bones.

Nerva took a swig of his wine and almost choked. 'Strong stuff! Anyway, things quickly got out of hand when the Jews started passing around baskets to collect money, mocking Florus for being poor. Having absolutely no sense of humour he crucified a few of them and that led to open revolt. The king, the second Herod Agrippa, and his sister Berenice tried to calm things down but had their lives threatened by the rebels and so fled. Florus appealed to his direct superior, Cestius Gallus, the Governor of Syria, for aid.'

'When was this?' Vespasian asked.

'Autumn last year,' Titus replied. 'Did you hear nothing of this, Father?'

Vespasian shook his head and broke off a hunk of bread. 'The whole point of being here was to be insulated from the world.'

Magnus finally won his battle with the goat. 'Well, it worked. When Hormus got back from Africa with a decent amount of cash for you, which we deposited with the Cloelius Brothers, it took me ages to figure out what you meant by me knowing where you were because you had Caenis with you.'

Vespasian turned to his freedman. 'Really?'

'Yes, master; the business has been a great success; it's growing all the time. I'll tell you after the gentlemen have finished.'

Vespasian had to suppress his curiosity for a while and turned his attention back to Nerva. 'So why did you need to find me just to tell me of a minor revolt in Judaea?'

'That's just it,' Nerva said, 'it's not minor. Gallus led an army of thirty thousand into Judaea to crush the rebellion. He did well at first, captured a couple of towns, dealt with over eight thousand rebels in Caesarea and Jaffa and pretty much got the situation back under control.'

Vespasian could see it coming. 'Until?'

'Until he got ambushed at a place called Beth Horon; he just walked into it and six thousand of his men were massacred before he could extract himself, leaving the Twelfth Fulminata's Eagle behind.'

'He lost an Eagle? To rabble like that?'

'They may be rabble, but they're fanatical rabble. Anyway, Gallus shamed himself even more by abandoning his troops and fleeing back to his province, where, I'm pleased to say, he did the decent thing. Lucinius Mucianus is on his way out to replace him.'

'Mucianus?' Vespasian mused. 'I suppose he has sufficient experience to put down the rebellion; he served me well as a military tribune in the Second Augusta.'

'So why did you come all this way just to tell us that?' Caenis asked.

'Because Mucianus is not going to fight this war, although he doesn't know that yet; Vespasian is.'

Vespasian was astounded; he felt Caenis' hand squeeze his thigh. 'Me? But Nero ...'

Sura smiled. 'Nero's made the decision that you are the most qualified general to take on the revolt, and my family's money as well as your brother Sabinus' and Nerva's petitions for you to get the command helped him make up his mind, although I don't suppose Mucianus will ever forgive us when he finds out.'

'Thank you, Sura,' Vespasian said, genuinely touched by the generosity of spirit. 'And you, Nerva, thank you.'

Nerva shrugged. 'I consider it to be a debt paid. I've risen highly in the Emperor's esteem since you exposed the Pisonian plot; although I think that Sura's money was more important than my requesting a favour in return for my service last year.'

Sura waved away the thought. 'The Emperor is preoccupied with his tour of Greece and the cash was very welcome; especially as one of the first things he did there was marry Sporus, or Poppaea Sabina as we must all call her now, and spent fortunes on the wedding banquet. He landed in the province last month and brought most of the Senate with him, which is why we've been able to act so quickly.'

'So you bought me the position?'

'No; I bought my daughter's husband the position of being second in command of what could be the biggest military operation since the invasion of Britannia.'

'He's right, Father; this could be very good for us. I'm to go to Egypt from here to bring the Fifteenth Apollinaris north, by sea, to Ptolemais where the Fifth Macedonica and the Tenth Fretensis will also be.'

'I've got their orders to march south from Syria with me,' Nerva said. 'I'm taking them to Mucianus. All being well, if Mucianus accepts the decision graciously, you should have three legions and the equivalent in auxiliaries plus Herod Agrippa's army ready by the beginning of the campaigning season.'

Vespasian was struggling to take everything in. 'All this has been organised already, so fast?'

Nerva nodded. 'Of course; it was imperative. We were lucky in that Magnus and Hormus had letters from Sabinus to various people in Nero's entourage and so came via us in Corinth; that's helped us find you so quickly. The Jews have to be crushed as soon as possible. They invited the Great King of Parthia in, in return for Judaism being the only recognised religion in Judaea; it would have given him access to our sea. Luckily, because his younger brother was still in Rome at the time, he refused the offer, but now that Tiridates is travelling back to Armenia he might well change his mind.'

'But what about Corbulo? He's still out in the East and right on hand.'

Titus shook his head. 'We don't know, Father. But you will find out. Nero has summoned you to Greece so he can brief you personally and give you the benefit of his advice. Corbulo has also received a summons.'

The Sanctuary of Olympia, ten days later

It was with a great show of humility that Nero came out onto the track of the hippodrome in the southeast corner of the Sanctuary of Olympia; it was the second day of the Olympic Games, which had been brought forward by a couple of years to enable the Emperor to compete.

Having been on his tour of Greece now for almost a moon he had excelled himself in winning already over two hundred victors' crowns, all for recitals at the many competitions that had been arranged so that the inhabitants of this ancient and learned country could have the opportunity to appreciate the ineffable talent of their Emperor. And they had many such opportunities, for Nero performed in every town he progressed through and such was his talent that the judges could award the prizes to no one else. And in the evenings the local dignitaries would vie to entertain the Emperor and his Empress, politely taking care not to notice that she seemed to have mislaid her breasts.

But it was not to sing that Nero appeared today; no, today it was a far more dangerous event that Nero had in his sights, for he wished to be crowned an Olympic champion in the chariot event, and to make it absolutely sure that he would be, it was in a ten-horse chariot that he made his way. The cheering of the crowd, thick around the stadium, echoed throughout the ancient sanctuary that had held the quadrennial games for over eight hundred years.

Having been told by the Emperor, upon his arrival at Olympia that morning, that he would receive him after the race, Vespasian watched, along with Caenis, Magnus, Hormus, Sura and the three hundred or so members of Nero's entourage, as the Emperor mounted the vehicle. The other contestants drew their four-horse chariots up to the staggered starting line, held in position by gates that would be raised into the air to commence the race. Although each of Nero's ten horses was being restrained by a groom holding its halter, their skittishness was apparent for all to see, having never been harnessed in such a grouping before. Untroubled by the state of his beasts, Nero took up all ten sets of reins, grasping them in one hand whilst acknowledging the crowd's roars with the other, as the grooms guided their charges up to the starting line on the outside of the seven other chariots now waiting.

'This is not going to end well,' Vespasian observed as the grooms sprinted aside, leaving Nero tugging on the reins but failing to keep his team from moving forward and pressing against the specially enlarged gate.

The starter, a priest of Zeus, saw the danger and immediately signalled the off. Up went the gates beginning with the outermost, Nero's, and then working inward towards the central barrier. As if shot from a ballista, Nero's team pelted forward, more in fear than eagerness, with the Emperor struggling to remain on his feet as they hauled on their reins. One by one the remaining teams were released, each a moment after the other, thus staggering the start. The chariots were not the lightweight

Roman design, but, rather, traditional wooden constructions that were based on the war-machines of ancient times, cumbersome, unwieldy and heavy. Nero's team, sharing that weight between ten, powered ahead of the four-horse teams, to the rapture of the spectators and to Nero's obvious terror, as it raced east, down the track to the first hundred-and-eighty-degree turn, with no discipline being instilled upon it. It was with an inevitability, which left many in the crowd shaking their heads, that not all ten of the horses realised that they needed to make the turn at the same time; with no help from their driver, who was now screaming in panic, they pursued their own agendas to mutual catastrophe. With piercing equine shrieks and thrashing limbs and twisting necks they fouled one another and crashed to the ground, tumbling and rolling in sprays of dust, sending the chariot careering towards the hippodrome wall, spinning horizontally as it went, casting Nero aside to slide on his back across the sand that ripped at his tunic and scraped the skin from his shoulders, buttocks and calves.

The crowd gasped, horrified by the outcome. The Empress jumped up and screamed into her hands as the rest of the field raced past the wreckage intent on completing the twelve laps that was the time-honoured length of the Olympic chariot race. Down Sporus ran, to the edge of the seating, to jump the ten feet onto the track; Epaphroditus followed as the race carried on. Vespasian watched in disbelief as the castrated slave ran along the side of the track, with no regard for personal safety, to rush to the aid of the person who had done such cruelty to him – or her. As the race progressed, Sporus and Epaphroditus pulled Nero to the edge of the track and sat him up with his back against the wall as they checked him for broken limbs.

With the final lap completed the three remaining teams pulled up before the priest of Zeus, with the winner to the fore. But it was towards the Emperor that the priest pointed with the victor's olive crown and it was with great shows of modesty and relief that Nero hobbled back down the track to receive his prize from the priest, who offered no explanation for his decision for none was necessary.

The victor crowned, the spectators began to disperse in search of other entertainment around the huge complex and Vespasian made his way to Nero's tent, erected next to the hippodrome. Epaphroditus admitted him and Sura into the lofty and spacious inner compartment, furnished with the lavishness of one who thinks nothing of spending a good portion of the Empire's wealth to build himself a house.

'Ahhh, the sleeper!' Nero, lying flat on a couch, fixed Vespasian with a stare that he did not care for as the Empress rubbed salve into his grazed behind. 'You think that perhaps I have forgotten the insult?'

'I am truly sorry, Princeps,' Vespasian said in a small and humble voice. 'I don't know how it happened; I can only thank you for starting again at the beginning so I could hear the bit I'd missed.'

Nero grunted and winced as Sporus applied his attention to a particularly raw patch. 'I have never been so insulted; however, it was as well for me that you chose to run and hide as I would not now be able to use your talents since you would have followed your treacherous uncle on his last journey. I need you now and you know what you must do.'

'Yes, Princeps; I will not fail you.'

'See that you don't and I might think better of you when you return.' He gestured to a scroll-case that Epaphroditus was holding. 'Those are Corbulo's orders; he is waiting for you at Corinth to brief you on the officers of the Fifth Macedonica and the Tenth Fretensis seeing as he has the best knowledge of them. Once he has done so to your satisfaction, give him his orders; I'm sure he will be pleased to set down the burden of the East that he has shouldered for so long. You will find ships waiting for you as well as two auxiliary cohorts in Cenchreae, Corinth's east coast harbour. Now go.'

'Yes, Princeps; and congratulations on your splendid victory.'

'Yes, it was stunning,' Nero replied with no trace of irony whilst dismissing Vespasian with a wave of the hand; the Empress bent to kiss her husband's behind, gazing at it as if it was the most beautiful sight in the world.

Vespasian took the scroll-case from Epaphroditus and walked away; Nero moaned with pleasure as the castrated Sporus buried his face between his buttocks.

Corinth, two days later

'Well, Vespasian, to sum up, I don't mind admitting that my influence has vastly improved the abilities of both Sextus Vettulenus Cerialis and Marcus Ulpius Traianus as legates.' Corbulo paused for a self-satisfied snort as he looked down his long, patrician nose at Vespasian sitting, with Magnus, at the table opposite him, outside a tavern on the waterfront of Cenchreae, Corinth's port on the Aegean. Massed shipping bobbed at anchor, being loaded and off-loaded in a continuous cycle of trade. Just along the quay a party of surveyors that had accompanied Vespasian to Corinth were taking measurements on their *groma* for Nero's projected canal across the isthmus; beyond them, auxiliaries were being embarked onto transport ships. 'They now show good initiative and an ability to analyse military problems without emotion and act swiftly on their findings; they should be very good for you, especially as both have been out in the East long enough to have developed a great dislike for the Jews and their continual anti-social behaviour.'

'That's very gratifying to hear, Corbulo; thank you,' Vespasian said with sincerity.

Corbulo poured Vespasian another cup of wine, completely ignoring Magnus, as he had done for the whole meeting. 'Think nothing of it; it's the least that I could do seeing as our children are now engaged; it's a worthy match now that you have achieved the consulship and governed a province; even if you do come from a rural New family.'

Vespasian nodded his agreement, taking absolutely no offence at Corbulo's snobbishness; he had always been thus and Vespasian was used to it.

'Thank you, Corbulo, very kind of you,' Magnus said, snatching the jug as Corbulo set it down. 'I'll just pour my own then.'

Castor and Pollux looked up from their shaded corner at the sharp tone of their master's voice; satisfied that he was under no threat, they returned to their siesta.

Corbulo looked at Magnus and frowned, as if it was the first time he had noticed him. 'Are you taking your man, er … him, with you?'

'Magnus? Yes.'

'Do you think he's up to it?'

Magnus slammed his cup down onto the table. 'I'm the best judge of that, Corbulo, and yes, I am up to it; there's plenty of fight and fuck left in me, you'll see.'

Corbulo pointed at Magnus' glass eye. 'But you hardly do.'

The strained sound, akin to a ram in distress, issuing from Corbulo's gullet told Vespasian, who knew the signs, that Corbulo had made another of his rare forays into humour; albeit not very successfully. He put a restraining hand on Magnus' shoulder. 'I have your new orders from the Emperor, Corbulo.' He pulled the scroll-case from a satchel slung over the back of his chair and pushed it across the table.

Corbulo's mirth dried up and he looked at the thing in horror.

Vespasian recalled giving Corbulo a similar scroll twenty-four years previously in Germania Superior when he took over from him as legate of the II Augusta in the aftermath of the downfall of Corbulo's half-sister, Milonia Caesonia, and her husband, Caligula. 'No, I don't know what it says, Corbulo. Nero just said that he imagined that you would enjoy having the burden of command eased.'

Corbulo picked up the case and balanced it in his hand as if trying to guess the contents by its weight, just as he had done with the last one. 'Well, there's only one way to find out.' He broke the seal and removed the lid. The scroll was thin; he unrolled it; there was very little written on it. Corbulo paled, passed it to Vespasian and then stood up.

Vespasian read the three words and then looked up at Corbulo. 'I'm so sorry, Corbulo.'

Corbulo drew his sword. 'I've been too successful, Vespasian; I've been expecting this. I'm the obvious threat to him; remember that when you take command of my legions because Nero is right.' He fell to his knees and then, pressing the tip of his blade just below his left ribs, fell forward without hesitation. He made no sound.

Vespasian stared down at the most successful general of the age, as the little life left in him ebbed away, knowing, with a sickening realisation, that the same fate would await him if he was successful in Judaea and also, having displeased Nero, if he were not.

As Corbulo expired, Vespasian saw the trap and he grew in the certainty that the only way he could come home safely from the Judean revolt would be at the head of an army.

AUTHOR'S NOTE

This work of fiction is, once again, based mainly upon the writings of Tacitus, Suetonius and Cassius Dio.

Nero's daughter, Claudia Augusta, did die young and was deified; Nero's grief and the building of the temple did cause him to neglect the business of Rome in AD 63.

Tacitus tells us that Sabinus' son-in-law, Lucius Caesennius Paetus, did, humiliatingly, have two legions captured by the Parthians in Armenia and forced under the yoke that same year; the bitter rivalry between him and Corbulo in the prosecuting of the Armenian war made Corbulo less than eager to come to his aid. Nero did forgive him quickly upon his return to Rome on the basis that such a timid man would find the strain of waiting too long to hear his fate unbearable; to me that is the only glimpse of what may be Nero's sense of humour.

The Kingdom of the Garamantes must have been a wonder to behold up on a range of hills in the middle of the Sahara: we are told that Garama had fountains and running water in the streets and that an irrigation system, fed by an underground reservoir, kept the land fertile. It was self-sufficient except for olive oil, wine and, of course, the one commodity it really needed to do all the work, slaves. Garamantes skeletons do not suggest that they partook of strenuous activities, giving credence to their living a life of luxury whilst their needs were attended to by a multitude of slaves. The slave revolt is my fiction, although I would not consider it an unlikely event considering the situation.

It may seem surprising but camels did not start to spread from Egypt into the Roman province of Africa until around this time. However, Vespasian setting up a camel-importing business whilst he was Governor of Africa in AD 63 is my fiction; but someone must have done it.

Tigellinus' party on the lake is documented by Tacitus and was pretty much as described. Suetonius also tells us of brothels staffed with ladies of quality set up on the banks of the Tiber; I have combined the two things. As I always say about these things, you cannot make it up! However, Nero ravaging genitals, whilst dressed in wild beast pelts, did not necessarily happen at this particular party, although it was a hobby that he was immensely keen on, as Suetonius confirms.

Nero did marry his freedman and revelled in being a wife; however, Cassius Dio states that his name was Pythagoras and Suetonius says that it was Doryphorus, so I took my pick.

When the great fire started in a bakery in the Circus Maximus, Nero was, according to Tacitus, taking part in a competition in Antium. Whether he caused the fire to be set we shall, in all likelihood, never know, although Suetonius states that he did; however, much of the bad press that Nero gets is the result of later writers trying to damn the memory of the last Julio-Claudian to justify the new regime. I tend to the theory that he did and I find it telling that after it had died down once, it flared up again in the Aemilian Basilica, which was owned by Nero's henchman, Tigellinus.

There was a prophecy current that a great change would start on the rising of the Dog Star; Paulus telling this to Nero at his trial is my fiction.

Yosef ben Matthias, commonly known as the historian Josephus, was in Rome as part of a Jewish delegation to plead for the release of twelve priests around the time of the fire, and so it is not beyond the realms of possibility that Vespasian met him.

The Pisonian conspiracy must be rated as one of the most inept coup attempts ever made. It was uncovered by Scaevinus' freedman, Milichus, egged on by his wife. Rufus was put in charge of exposing all the conspirators even though he himself was one; he was eventually outed along with the Praetorian tribune, Subrius, and Sulpicius, the centurion. Seneca and Piso were also forced into suicide as was Seneca's nephew, Lucanus, better known to the English-speaking world as Lucan to prevent schoolboy sniggering every time his name is written on the blackboard. The future Emperor, Nerva, was awarded Triumphal Ornaments for his part in uncovering the plot. Whether Seneca was planning to hijack the plot and become emperor we shall never know for sure, but I like the idea.

Nero did kick Poppaea in the stomach whilst she was pregnant thus causing her death. However, it was not as a result of his state of mind during the unravelling of the Pisonian conspiracy; I just put the two things together for dramatic reasons.

Vespasian either fell asleep during one of Nero's performances or left early; either way he was in fear of his life and did go bravely into hiding, from which he was eventually recalled to put down the Jewish revolt. Corbulo was ordered by a jealous Nero to commit suicide but Vespasian giving him the note was my fiction.

Once again my thanks go to the people mentioned in the dedication at the front of the book. Thanks also go to Tamsin Shelton for her excellent copy-editing, winkling out the minutiae as well as spotting the mistakes so huge as to be invisible to most eyes! My thanks again to Tim Byrne for yet another fantastic cover. And finally, my love to my wife, Anja, for putting up with me disappearing into my study for six months.

Vespasian's story will continue in *Emperor of Rome* – well, what else could I call it?